A/Cross Sections

New Manitoba Writing

A/Cross Sections

New Manitoba Writing

edited by
Katherine Bitney and Andris Taskans

Manitoba Writers' Guild

Manitoba Writers' Guild
Artspace
206-100 Arthur Street
Winnipeg, Manitoba R3B 1H3
www.mbwriter.mb.ca

The Manitoba Writers' Guild gratefully acknowledges the financial assistance
of The Province of Manitoba, Minister of Culture, Heritage and Tourism,
Minister Eric Robinson, the Manitoba Arts Council, the Winnipeg Arts Council
(New Creations Fund) and Friesens Printing.

Cover and interior design: Tétro Design Incorporated
Typesetting and layout: Heidi Harms

Printed in Canada by Friesens Printing for the Manitoba Writers' Guild

Library and Archives Canada Cataloguing in Publication

Main entry under title:
A/cross sections : new Manitoba writing / edited by Katherine Bitney and
Andris Taskans.

ISBN: 978-0-9692525-6-6

1. Canadian literature (English)—Manitoba. 2. Canadian literature (English)—
21st century. I. Bitney, Kate II. Taskans, Andris III. Manitoba Writers' Guild

PS8255.M28A37 2007   C810.8'097127   C2007-904440-9

To all the Manitoba writers who have gone before us

/ CONTENTS

A/Cross Sections

New Manitoba Writing

/ INTRODUCTION

/ BY KATHERINE **BITNEY** AND ANDRIS **TASKANS**

When Robyn Maharaj, executive director of the Manitoba Writers' Guild, approached us with an offer to edit an anthology of Manitoba writing, to be published by the Guild in celebration of its 25th anniversary in 2006, we jumped at the chance. We had been participants in, and observers of, the Manitoba writing scene for decades; now we would have a chance to take its measure.

Robyn brought to the table ideas for a book that would feature essays on the founding of the Guild, along with a list of past presidents, a timeline of important literary dates, photographs from Guild conferences and testimonials from Guild members. As our conversations progressed, it became apparent that the best way to acknowledge the worthy achievements of the Guild would simply be to publish as much new Manitoba writing as possible. Guild members would be invited to submit, but the anthology would not be restricted to them. The flood of submissions that followed meant that the lists and testimonials soon had to be discarded. Only three Guild-specific contributions survive: Sandra Birdsell's factual memoir of the Guild's founding, Daria Salamon's touching recollection of Sheldon Oberman's mentorship skills and Smaro Kamboureli's mischievous revisiting of the Guild's (fictional) early days.

Choosing to publish Manitoba writing required us to define who is a Manitoba writer or, at least, which writers' work would be eligible for consideration. Some of the many contributors to *A/Cross Sections* have lived in Manitoba all their lives while others were born here but moved away. Still others had immigrated and settled. Then there are those who came to Manitoba, stayed a long or a little while, and subsequently decamped. In the end, for the purpose of this anthology, we defined an eligible writer as someone who lived and wrote in Manitoba for all or a portion of the period 1981–2006, regardless of the writer's place of origin or subsequent residence. These are the writers who influenced the Guild's development and/or were influenced by it, directly or indirectly.

From the start, we agreed that we wanted to publish work by our friends and colleagues who had passed away. In most cases, we were successful in obtaining previously unpublished work and offer our gratitude to the writers' estates for their assistance.

A/Cross Sections includes work by familiar names and by new voices. It features many of the individuals we editors associate with recent and contemporary Manitoba writing. Unfortunately, we were unable to solicit work from everyone. In the end, we read over 120 submissions and selected the work of ninety-one contributors, making *A/Cross Sections* the most inclusive anthology of its kind in this province to date.

Although our title hearkens back to two previous Manitoba anthologies, *Section Lines*, edited by Mark Duncan (Turnstone 1988), and *A/Long Prairie Lines*, edited by Daniel S. Lenoski (Turnstone 1989), there is at least one crucial difference between our anthology and theirs. Those earlier volumes collected their editors' choices of the best of previously published writing. Almost all of the work in these pages is being published for the first time.

One of our earliest decisions was that, whenever possible, we would publish new writing only. A second was that, while the selection process should be generous, acceptance would be based primarily on literary excellence. A third was that we wanted to feature as many Manitoba writers as the Guild's budget would permit, which meant we would consider work in any genre, of any type. *A/Cross Sections* tries to be like the Guild in its inclusiveness, the way the Guild cuts across "sections" of different forms and genres, of rural and urban, of emerging and established, and across the barriers of class, gender, race and socio-economic background.

A celebration of the short form, *A/Cross Sections* includes stories, poems, memoirs, essays, anecdotes and a speech, along with excerpts from novels, plays and journals. This variety requires the reader to undertake radical shifts in reading strategy but offers manifold pleasures in return.

Although most of its content is "literary," *A/Cross Sections* contains some genre fiction, including Gothic, horror and Young Adult fantasy. This handful of "alternate" texts can give only a glimpse of the burgeoning growth in Manitoba of writerly practice in a wide variety of popular forms and genres: children's picture and chapter books, science fiction & fantasy, historical novels, humour, home grown mystery, romance, travel, the thriller and much more.

The decades since the Guild was founded have seen an explosion of writing and publishing activity in Manitoba. The Guild started with approximately twenty members; it now has more than 600, barely 10 per cent of whom are represented in these pages. There is material aplenty for future anthologies.

Faced with scores of manuscripts in a variety of forms and genres, we struggled to come up with an organizing principle for *A/Cross Sections*. Bowing to the inspiration for this volume, we decided to open with Sandra Birdsell's fact-based recounting of the Guild's origins at Aubigny. It then seemed only natural to close with Smaro Kamboureli's fanciful take on Aubigny and the writing life.

But what were we to do with the other eighty-nine contributions? Because we were celebrating an anniversary, we decided first to gather the writers into rough groupings based on the decade in which each began to publish. Within those groupings, certain subjects/similarities/resonances began to emerge and so we clustered together works that appeared to us to speak to one another. A few pieces were paired because they contrasted! Many writers' submissions didn't suit any of the themes arising from their chronological groupings and were moved to areas where they seemed a better fit.

4

So there is a kind of non-rigorous chronological progression to this anthology, undergirded by a traditional reliance on theme (or imagery or style) to provide further unity. Nevertheless, out of the warp and weft of these and other commingling strands, occasional patterns or pictures emerge, which evoke developments in the recent history of writing in Manitoba. For example, many of the writers who first published during the seventies and eighties wrote of the Prairie and the Shield, and some of the pieces by them in this volume still share that fascination.

Having started with writers on the land, we end fittingly with writers on writing. In between, the reader will find many other thematic clusters and threads in *A/Cross Sections*, including meditations on mortality, identity, intergenerational relationships, poverty, inner city youth and so forth.

Another way of reading this anthology is to follow the emergence of writers from particular ethnocultural backgrounds. For example, the past three decades saw the rise in Manitoba of writers from a Mennonite background, the coming of age of a new generation of Jewish writers and the development of an Aboriginal writing community. All are represented here, although we wish more Aboriginal writers had chosen to participate.

A third way of reading this book is through the discernment of influences. Although Robert Kroetsch, who is credited with bringing postmodernism to the University of Manitoba in the mid-seventies, did not submit, his impact as writer and teacher is evident throughout. In fact, we've selected the recurring image of 'his' crow to be our guide through the first half of *A/Cross Sections*. The late Carol Shields was another writer of enormous influence, not only because of her books and teaching but because she popularized life writing for Canadian women by helping start the *Dropped Threads* anthology series. The longest "thread" in *A/Cross Sections* consists of writing by women on women's lives and concerns. Incidentally, when the Guild was established, there appeared to be slightly more male than female writers in Manitoba. If this anthology is representative, women writers now outnumber their male counterparts two to one.

In the end, we think *A/Cross Sections* achieves the goal we set ourselves: to celebrate the 25th Anniversary of the Manitoba Writers' Guild by presenting a dramatically varied compilation of work by many of the writers who have called Manitoba home during the period 1981–2006. We are confident that everyone will find something to enjoy, will discover a new writer or two, and will come away from this anthology with a deeper appreciation of the richness and diversity of contemporary Manitoba writing.

5

/ A LETTER TO MY FRIENDS WHO ARE THERE

On the occasion of the 25th anniversary of the Manitoba Writers' Guild

/ BY SANDRA **BIRDSELL**

You may recall that on August 22, 1981, the day was muggy and the fields beyond the tent had been harvested and were beginning to look a bit threadbare. All around us the earth sizzled with the sounds of insects giving off what might be their last call for the season, instinct telling them that in Manitoba a killing frost can dog the heels of late August. A fact we humans tend to forget from year to year as summer draws to a close and we continue to go about writing poems and stories and starting guilds for authors and being caught by surprise when frost nips our fingers.

Three years had passed since the idea to start an authors' guild was resolved at the First Annual Poetry Conference at St. John's College, an idea that originated with the Saskatchewan sisters Kate Bitney and Elizabeth Carriere, and with Andris Taskans. And now their idea had become a reality. As I recall we were a rather subdued group of people on that Saturday afternoon. As I recall there was a slightly worse-for-wear Volkswagen van parked in the field beyond the tent, and that lovely man, Sheldon Oberman, Obie, God rest his soul, was attached to it. Perhaps we were subdued by the

ROBERT KROETSCH AND DENNIS COOLEY ADDRESS THE GATHERING.

SANDRA BIRDSELL, DENNIS COOLEY, ARMIN WIEBE, MICHAEL RENNIE, ROBERT KROETSCH.

SMARO KAMBOURELI, BYRNA BARCLAY, PATRICK FRIESEN.

heat, and certainly by the mosquitoes. Mosquitoes can be a trial at any meeting, a contest in perseverance that you know you'll never win. But we had plenty of repellent to declare a short truce; we had coolers of cold drinks to combat the heat; there was plenty of goodwill.

Victor Enns had provided the tent in the same way he had gone about providing for us throughout those three years of planning meetings, the fundraising events, the Riverview Writers' Workshop that met monthly in his large and airy apartment overlooking the Assiniboine River. He had done so unobtrusively, efficiently; no task was too small. The white

BESS KAPLAN, SHELDON OBERMAN.

tent, what was a canopy, really, had appeared overnight, pitched in a field close to the amenities of his brother's house, near the town of Aubigny, which had grown up years ago on a floodplain. We could see the Red River from the tent and it was the colour of grey slate, narrow and running sluggish, its surface looking gelatinous.

The area had once been known as the Grande Pointe de la Saline, and now it was the parish of Aubigny. Unknown to me at the time of our Red River Writers' Weekend when we drove out from Winnipeg along Highway 75 to gather at the river and hold a poetry seminar, to host the inauguration of the Manitoba Writers' Guild, to throw a party, was that the land where we were meeting had first been settled by Métis squatters. My father's people, the Berthelettes, had been among them. An infant or two, a mother and son had been buried somewhere nearby. Their graves had been abandoned and ploughed over for wheat when the squatters were forced to give way to settlers arriving from New Hampshire. I wasn't aware of the history going on around us or I might have gone for a walk and paid attention. I was writing my first book and I might have named the town in those stories Aubigny. Nor was I aware that we, the founding members of the writers' guild, were making history and would be asked to recall the event twenty-five years later.

What I do remember most vividly is that in August 1981, my kitchen table was cobalt blue and my three children were seated around it at breakfast as I was about to head out the door. Both the table and the children were hard to miss. I had written several stories while seated at that glossy table, and although the marine paint proved to be as indestructible as the manufacturer had promised, it was soft, and when I pressed too hard the pen etched its surface. My children seemed quietly puzzled. I wasn't hurrying off to attend a church function or a Neighbourhood Watch coffee morning, but, rather, a writers' event, a field party being held twenty minutes down the highway.

9 ▪

First, I would make a brief stop at a roadside motel to pick up visitors from Saskatchewan. I'll be home before midnight, I told them.

Within three short years I had left the boardroom of Sunday School teachers and choir members at Elim Chapel for the boardroom of Elizabeth Carriere's apartment. Elizabeth, Patrick Friesen and I had taken on the task of drafting an executive structure, aims and objectives and points for a constitution. And while we worked at Elizabeth's teak dining room table and sipped at a seemingly endless supply of wine, I wondered where she had lived when she'd written her poem about irises. A mesmerizing chant-like poem that celebrated a clump of irises growing beyond a basement window, and whenever she read it, her voice brought to mind children in white ankle socks going past the window on their way through childhood. I was thinking of Patrick Friesen's poem . . . *why do I go into this secret room/ with my bowels churning?/ . . . to seize three words which I lack.* I was hearing Valerie Reed, *when the dogs bark at night . . . I feel my death/ standing in the street/ a stranger whom they chase away.* I was thinking about membership criteria, that I would need to ask my mother to bake a batch of zwieback for an upcoming authors' guild party that would feature Mennonite food. We were underlining the fact that because so many of us were of that ilk, we were sometimes referred to as the Mennonite mafia.

And then, with the directions unfolded on the dashboard in front of me, I became lost. *Hwy. 75 south to Ste. Agathe, left across the bridge, right at Hwy. 200 south, keep right on Hwy. 246 south, past Kiers to lot #480 on the Red River.* I'd been a townie most of my life and now I was a city dweller. Once we'd crossed the bridge at Ste. Agathe, the country roads looked all the same to me. Robert Kroetsch's *Seed Catalogue* poems unfurled beyond the windshield. *This road is the shortest distance/ between nowhere and nowhere./ This road is a poem.* Our Saskatchewan guests, Byrna Barclay and Nik Burton, politely remained silent until it was no longer possible. Nik snatched up the directions from the dashboard and we arrived at the tent meeting just as the poetry seminar came to an end. Robert Kroetsch was there to greet us, as were Smaro Kamboureli, Michael Rennie, Armin Wiebe, Dennis Cooley, Jacqui Smyth, Victor Enns, among many others, all of you already sweating with the heat and glancing nervously at threatening clouds.

And so the authors' guild began, and so it ended, just as the Red River Writers' Weekend began and ended in August 1981. Our idea had become The Manitoba Writers' Guild. We were no longer travelling that prairie road between nowhere and nowhere. We had arrived. I thought about the tall narrow window in Kate and Andris's house covered in Virginia creeper, the pale light shining through the balustrade of the stairs and into the room where we'd spent so much time during the past three years. The reams of paper spread about us on the carpet. A cabal of writers wrestling with an idea, and then as the evening went on, wrestling with the reality of a field hockey team in need of coaching, the ever-present need to earn a living, our sometimes breaking hearts.

I think I may have chaired part of the meeting and recall vividly the vote to bring an end to the idea. There were a few objections raised by people who had also become

10

lost and arrived about three years too late. They asked, was a provincial organization for authors really necessary? There were enough poets present to make the objections and the benches we sat on seem less uncomfortable than they were. The motion passed. The insects sizzled, and the clouds moved in lower, exciting the already voracious bugs. Music followed, provided by a Mennonite bluegrass band, Just Plumb Hollow, who, as the evening wore on and the mosquitoes won the contest, put down their instruments and flung their arms about one another and sang Handel's *Messiah* in four-part harmony. Then we fled back to the city.

And here we are twenty-five years later with too much history to remember and the space too small for me to name all of you who are there in a photograph beside me as I write. You are all across this country, writing stories and poems, and some of those writings owe their lives to the places where we began, and to the river that all too often rose high enough to cover the land where we met, and beyond. You are seated around tables beneath the canopy of the white tent expecting something to happen.

MEMBERS OF THE RIVERVIEW WRITERS' WORKSHOP AND FRIENDS.

/ VELA AQUAE
for Tracy Jager

/ BY GEORGE **AMABILE**

I tell myself, *don't make a sound.*
The river is asleep in its glistening skin
of lights, and all the sails of day are furled.

This is the hour of transparency,
a gift wrapped in veils of moonlight,
veils of air, a gift that cannot be returned,

or opened with vivid memories
of birdsong or desire. Only stillness
can unlock its *tai chi* auroras,

night scarves whispering the near
-ly inaudible music of butterfly wings,
the way light shifts in a backwater eddy,

the way the lift of a wave can change
the shape of the sky. Water has many voices.
They speak most clearly in the dark.

They are inside us, a rhythmic sentence
without end, that knowledge we have
sometimes, of being here and flowing away

through shadows into sunlit recognition:
that what we were and have lost
can return without warning—the way love

surprises an overcast afternoon—that everything
we have forgotten continues to dance
like deep sea ripples in deep sea light.

Nothing is only itself. Look at a leaf:
there are the branching veins
of tributaries, a river system, the tree

of blood in our hands that flows from a source
deeper than the languages that split and split
from the first word no one remembers.

We are veils of water, mist
rising from a morning lake, and as we speak
to each other with more and more intensity,

we begin to see: the river
and the sea: lights coming on
in the mind: sails crossing:

and what you think is what I thought,
or dreamed once, as a shadow
that shrugs off its dusty coat and stands, shining

now, where veils of air and veils of water clear
then fade into the cool dusk of summer,
into its fireflies and stars.

/ ORANGES

/ BY GEORGE **AMABILE**

Opened in fresh light, they look
like the fire that writhes
at the centre and feeds a swarm
of planets.
              Evenings, on the lake
a thin skin of orange flame
breaks into bull's-eye ripples
as the sunfish come up to feed.

/ WILDERNESS CAMP

/ BY GEORGE **AMABILE**

The moon breaks
                into flaked highlights
on the chipped obsidian plate
of the lake. This
is what we came for,
                this vacancy
this empty-hearted Night.

Watching shadows
                dance as the flames dance,
we drift into shallow sleep.

Suddenly,
        it's cold. Wind comes in off the water
digging through layers of ash
fanning the coals to an incandescent rubble
like the stones of a city
                that was not there
before and won't be again.

DIARY EXCERPT
August 13, 1980. The Lake.

/ BY MELINDA **MCCRACKEN**

The following is an excerpt from Melinda's journal in 1980 when she was a single mother living with her aging parents at the cottage. She captures the conflicts arising between herself and her ailing father.

Father and Mother decide to go into Kenora to look at rugs. It is raining. Molly and I decide to stay behind to play Monopoly. The big blue car trundles on up the road with Mother at the wheel. We wave goodbye and go back to our Monopoly table. Molly begins to set the money out on the table. We have forgotten how much money to give out as we don't have the instructions. We hear a couple of toots on the horn, which is a musical three-toned horn. Then I think I hear tires scudding. And then I hear more toots on the horn. I run out the back door with Molly in hot pursuit. There is the car stopped about three-quarters of the way up the hill, which is rather steep, that leads down to the cottage.

Father in his yellow Perry Como cardigan is standing in the bushes on the right side of the car, the door open beside him. The car slips down the hill backwards. A couple of turns of the wheel and the door of the car pushes Father further down the hill too. Mother has the window closed so she can't hear me say, "Why doesn't he get in the car?" She is wondering the same thing. I open the car door and ask if I can put my foot on the brake for her.

"I've got it in Park," she says.

"That should do it," I say, feeling in charge of the situation. Mother gets out of the car and I get in. The car stays parked on a 45-degree angle. Mother goes around to where Father is now kneeling in the bushes, knocked down by the car door.

"Why don't you get in the car?" we both say.

"I can't," he says, a seriously anxious look on his face. "My foot is stuck."

"His foot is stuck under the car," I say to Mother, then lean out the car door where Father is stuck. I see one of his white plastic loafers jammed on top of the other—nowhere near the car.

I pick up the top foot off the bottom foot so that he is stable, then heave, holding him under the arms, and pull him into the car. Mother straightens his feet out and puts them in. He holds his neck stiff and lets himself be moved like a helpless invalid. Mother gets out of the way and I back down the hill. For a moment I had thought the car might roll down and crush his feet.

Molly has disappeared back into the cottage. I am nervous and shaky underneath but my voice radiates calm.

I back the car down the hill. Mother stands in the way of backing up straight. I holler for her to get out of the way, and then back up easily down the hill.

Mother, it seems, had driven too far to the right and had hit a birch tree and THAT is why the car would not go up the hill.

After a moment, I ask if they would like me to come with them to Kenora, much as I hate it, and they say yes. So I run back down the hill in bare feet to get my shoes and purse. Molly has laid out all the Monopoly money neatly on two sides of the board ready to play. I tell her that Nana and Papa need us and that we have to go to Kenora to look at carpets too. Mother later tells us that that was the first time she has ever tried to drive up the hill.

The first night we arrive at the cottage, Father turns all the electric baseboard heaters on high as usual, closes all the windows and then sits down near the fireplace on a stool to light the fire. Molly and I have just gone in for a swim to cool off. The air is hot and oppressive outside. When we come up from our swim, I stand watching him build his fire. The temperature in the room is soaring up to 90 degrees.

"Why are you lighting a fire?" I ask, or something to that effect.

"If we're going to have this trouble every time we're here . . ." he begins.

"I'm not trying to make trouble," I say, my voice rising. "It's too HOT!" I go and open a window.

He says, "Close that window."

I say, "I won't."

He gets up and comes into the kitchen where I've gone.

"You're going to have to change your attitude towards me," he says.

"It's not my attitude, it's the fact that it's too HOT in here. I'll close the window if you turn off the heaters. I'm just trying to compromise. You don't want compromise. That's no way to get along. You want everything all one way."

Molly and I go into the other room and read a Little Lulu comic. I turn down the heat and open the patio door. Molly has just been swimming and says she is cold. I close the patio door, a nod to the other side, but I close it anyway.

Father then closes the door into the living room to keep all his heat in. When we emerge for dinner into the living room the room is relatively cool. Father is sitting innocently reading the paper.

Later on, Mother and I go out in the backyard to see if we can see any meteor showers. I tell Mother that it's amazing how one person can keep everybody all riled up all the time. "There must be a calm, serene, mature, intelligent way of dealing with this," I say. "I think the problem is that one gives him credit for being an intelligent human being and you let him go ahead, and he acts like a screwball."

She tells me that Father has turned up the heat and closed the windows in my room. I get riled up. I think, should I go and open his window? Or is that just stooping to his level? Shouldn't I try to be above those tactics? On the other hand, playing a few pranks might liven up his otherwise dull routine. Should I take the cord from his electric blanket and throw it off the deck into the dark forest? Should I tie his pyjama bottoms in knots? I sit there seething, thinking about opening his window to the fresh night air. Finally I decide to go into my room and make up the bed.

The room is boiling. I open all the windows and turn off the heat and make the bed. It cools off fast. On the way out, I mutter half to myself, "It sure was hot in there." He passes, hears me, says, "Bet you like that."

I retort, "I was thinking of opening your window because I thought you might be too warm." But I don't do it. I am so riled up I don't go to sleep until 5 a.m. and when I do I have a dream that Pop has vomited all over everything. They say that when you feel hostile to someone, you have dreams that make them appear ridiculous.

At dinner, that same night, Father says to Molly, "You have no right to express an opinion about the carpet. You don't know anything."

Molly says, "I do know something. I'm in Grade Two."

Mother says, "Telling a person they don't know anything is a real putdown."

"Yes," I say, thinking of the gracious Doug Gibson and how he might deal with a kid who expresses an opinion about a carpet. "There are much better ways of telling her." I'm thinking that he might have said, "That's a good opinion, Molly. It's nice that you have some good ideas on the subject."

Father goes on. "You don't know anything about money."

I say, "I'm surprised that you take her seriously."

Mother says, "You could say it in such a way that she learns something."

We are the picture of liberal tolerance, Mother and I. But Pop just wants to put down a six-year-old kid.

/ CAMPFIRE

/ BY JIM **TALLOSI**

Orion's dogs howl
the hunter joins us
visits our camp

we are
with as little game
as he

game is scarce
among the stars
he offers light
we offer him tea
or brandy

his dogs bark
at ours
at wolves
on the cliff
they are scared, uneasy

they sense the presence
of other animals

    beluga, polar bear
    hare, weasel
    ptarmigan, snowy owl
    bison
    horse
    turtle
    tern, pelican, gull
    snow goose

    all white or almost white

we exchange stories
of where we have been,
of wendigoes

who has heard
their ice hearts
throbbing?

/ TRACY AND CLAY

/ BY DAVE **WILLIAMSON**

Eleanor Mason, Barb Jenkins's mother, was now ninety-five, but she didn't want to miss the party they were having at Victoria Beach for her one and only granddaughter. Mrs. Mason couldn't stay overnight at the lake anymore, so Jenkins had to drive into Winnipeg on Sunday morning to pick her up from the home. She talked and talked for the whole hour and a half it took to drive back—"She's always been such a pretty girl, with a forehead you can see. I don't know why so many girls her age want to cover their foreheads, do you? Girls with their hair pulled back off their faces look so much happier and more confident, don't you think? . . . And Clay's a nice young man, isn't he, even though he wears an earring . . ." When they got to the cottage, Eleanor was ready for a pre-party nap. Jenkins left her in Barb's care and, around 12:15, he headed next door to help with preparations. He went the front way in order to get the full effect of the banner.

It stretched across the length of the deck that stood out from the front of the Sanderson summer home. In two-foot-high red letters, it read *Congratulations,* TRACY AND CLAY! It was actually two banners, side by side, one on which *Congratulations* was done in a breezy freehand script, the other bearing the names in Gothic capitals. Both were the handiwork of Jenkins. The *Congratulations* banner had been done years ago for a party celebrating the wedding of Louise Cassell to Jeff Daulby. The Cassells owned a cottage several lots north of the Jenkinses' (formerly the Masons') on Sunset Boulevard. A group of forty or fifty beach friends of the Cassells and the Jenkinses got together three or four times a summer for a major party. Almost any occasion was reason enough: a sixtieth birthday, an achievement, a forthcoming wedding. Or the reason might be that there was *no* occasion. When the group found out that Louise Cassell was getting married, four couples took on the responsibility of organizing, and the Featherstonehaughs offered their place as the venue. Hal Featherstonehaugh had a vague recollection of seeing a Jenkins cartoon somewhere (probably at university all those years ago) and he asked Jenkins if he'd do a banner for the party. Now, to the uninitiated, a talent for drawing is a talent for drawing any damned thing—from a thumbnail sketch to a billboard. Jenkins balked when Hal told him the size he wanted; he ended up agreeing to do it more as a favour for Barb. (Since he didn't swim, sail, play tennis or putter around in the yard, she liked to be able to point to *something* he could do.) He bought a roll of seamless white paper and spread it out on the cottage

21

floor. He'd been six years younger then and could kneel on the floor and bend over his work for the length of time necessary and still get back to his feet without stabbing pains. He was in a good mood (he *liked* Louise Cassell, one of the beach kids who always said "Hey, Mr. Jenkins!" to him and gave him a smile that would melt the knees of an army) and managed to execute a *Congratulations* that had a certain élan. It took him about five hours to sketch it and colour it with poster paint. He spent most of the next day printing LOUISE AND JEFF. When the group gave Jenkins and Barb effusive compliments on the banner (which, in this initial stage, was one continuous length of paper), Barb came up with the idea of cutting off the specific names and saving *Congratulations* for a future pre-wedding party. There had been at least one a year since then. (Jenkins's favourite was the one for Jo and Ed, because it took far less time; he even decided to use an ampersand—JO & ED rather than JO AND ED—since the three-letter AND tended to detract from the two-letter names.) And now the party was for his own daughter and her new fiancé. By now, *Congratulations* was wrinkled and tattered (much like Jenkins himself, he might've said), but, seen from a distance, it still had pizzaz, and, besides, it had become something of an institution at the group's special celebrations, so there was no question about its being used. And though Jenkins felt a little odd about doing the TRACY AND CLAY section because his own kid was involved, he was generally acknowledged as the sign-painter-supreme at Victoria Beach.

Most of the group didn't know Tracy that well—the beach parties were held by and for the old folks. Many had seen Tracy as she grew up—doing cartwheels and back handsprings on the beach. She could still do an aerial—a flip that always boggled Jenkins's mind because it was, in effect, a no-handed cartwheel. Some had engaged her as a babysitter when she was in her early teens. She hadn't been here at the beach for a few summers—kids tended to outgrow the beach and leave the all-night camp-fires at Scott Point to the teenyboppers. She'd brought her first serious boyfriend Bill down here only once or twice—he was the kind of guy who preferred urban shadows to beach sunlight (his legacy to her was a smoking habit that Clay was helping her to kick). Lately, she'd been down here the odd Saturday—she'd drive down with or without Clay—and she'd made a point of looking in on some of the neighbours so that she wouldn't seem so much of a stranger when the party rolled around. As was the case with these events, the party had been planned a good six months in advance, soon after Tracy became engaged.

Tracy engaged! Jenkins could hardly believe it. He'd seen her through so many stages, it sometimes felt as if he had several daughters, or as if she were a cat with nine lives. When you least expected it, she'd confess to a big bash she'd put on at the family house in the city when Jenkins and Barb were on vacation or at the lake, an event they'd known nothing about, one that attracted kids from all over, kids who brought booze and pot and cocaine, a party that required rearranging of the furniture, tough guys to act as bouncers, food and music brought in from God knew where, and featured all manner of little atrocities that had to be covered up or cleaned up, like vomit on the broadloom, blood on the wall, urine in the bathtub, semen in the sheets. Oh, she'd been a model child while she was a kid competing against the world, first in artistic gymnastics and then in rhythmic gymnastics—her life was so organized (so many hours for school, so many for gym, every day) and her diet was dictated by the sport and she had no sense of the luxury of spare time. When she quit gymnastics, it was as if she'd been released from solitary confinement. In no time, she had her own car and, keeping a change of clothing in the trunk, the back seat littered with fast-food wrappers, she bombed around town, flitting from place to place, never lighting for too long in one spot, rubbing it into her head that she was *free*, free of the cloistered exis-tence imposed by a difficult sport. Where her parents had regarded her regimented, list-making life as wonderful preparation for young adulthood, it became something to rebel against when her career ended. She was still fun to talk with, when Jenkins could keep her in one place for longer than five minutes. But there were the times that weren't fun, like the time he had to track her and a girlfriend to a hotel room where they were doing who knew what with two young men Jenkins had never seen before. All, Jenkins swore, in the spirit of trying out her wings. She'd taken jobs here and there, hung out with Bill for longer than anyone hoped, and at last went to college and learned how to be a computer analyst. And somewhere she'd met Clay Heller and, after going on a few trips with him, she made the unexpected announcement that he'd asked her to marry him. Good old Clay. Jenkins hadn't thought there were guys like him around anymore. Clay Heller, a young entrepreneur who already had his own clothing line—you were pretty cool if you wore a Clay Heller sweat shirt with the great c logo, a c almost as jauntily curved as the c in Jenkins's *Congratulations* sign.

Tracy and Clay had already held their wedding social and made about ten thousand dollars. The social was a Manitoba phenomenon—Jenkins knew this because he had once mentioned it at one of his national school-principals' meetings and a man from Alberta said, "A what?"

"A wedding social," Jenkins replied.

"You mean a wedding reception," suggested a woman from Ontario.

"No," Jenkins said. He went on to explain that socials had started, he believed, in the 1960s, when young people were rebelling against the old ways. Couples rejected the barbaric stag party (for men only) and the silly shower (for women only), believing that everything related to a wedding should be celebrated together. Instead of an all-male drunk where the groom had a ball and chain fastened to his leg and had to ward off an aggressive stripper (or perhaps a congenial prostitute), and instead of an all-female evening where the bride had to sit in a ribbon-festooned chair and be showered with batches of bathroom utensils, why not a *mixed* party, where all the friends of the bride and groom gathered together for a bash? This type of gathering was originally called a *stag and shower*, and organizers soon saw the potential for raising money by extending the number of invitees beyond the couple's immediate friends. To facilitate this, tickets were printed. It became common for people who didn't know the couple at all to buy tickets and go for the dancing and the inexpensive booze. At some point over the years, the event became known as a *social*. It soon featured money-making

23 ■

schemes like the silent auction. The organizers canvassed local businesses for the items to be bid on. At Tracy and Clay's social, there were more than seventy donated items displayed—from a hockey stick autographed by Teemu Selanne to a ghetto blaster—and Tracy's maid of honour, an ex-gymnast named Sylvie, introduced a more exciting variation on the silent auction: you bought an envelope for a dollar and it contained either the number of one of the prizes or a note that read, *Please try again*. This proved to be extremely popular and the dollars poured in, the only limitation being the number of envelopes you happened to have.

It was *de rigueur* that the parents of the couple attend the social and help out at it. Clay's father, Hank, a sporting goods salesman about ten years younger than Jenkins, carried cases of twenty-four bottles of beer (what the kids called *two-fours*) as if they were pillows, helping Clay and the best man haul them from somebody's van to the bar. He had arranged for the rental of the community club hall, located in an obscure part of Norwood, a Winnipeg suburb. The hall was typical of those used for socials— a cavernous wooden structure with fans that didn't clear the smoke and row on row of collapsible tables, and stacking chairs that didn't fit your bum. He also tended bar along with Clay's brother. Jenkins helped Sylvie with the prize table, pocketing the money when Sylvie got worried there was too much for her to handle. Clay's mother, Betty, and Barb looked after the food, a spread of cold meats, cheese, rye bread, potato chips, pretzels, pickles and lettuce. Betty was one of those tiny doll-like women with boundless energy, the kind that often married big ham-handed athletes like Hank. You could imagine him lifting her up and holding her overhead with one hand, the way Jenkins had held Tracy when she was about five years old. (Jenkins used to say, "If I lift her like this every day until she's twenty, think how strong my arms will be." No one could remember when he stopped lifting her, but folks said Tracy's gymnastics ability was helped along by her having to balance up there on the flat of her father's hand.) Barb said, "Betty's energy wears me out," but Barb could hold her own in breaking open packages and spreading plates around and cleaning up afterward. Jenkins kept an eye on Sylvie's cash drawer, sauntering over there when some galoot from the other side of town seemed to be harassing her, or when the crowd around her table got too big. Jenkins managed to fit in a few dances (he'd arranged for the music man, who brought all his own equipment and a selection of tapes the kids loved). He danced with Betty and Barb, but his feet hurt. The shoes he was wearing weren't the comfortable ones his foot doctor had recommended; they were the ones he called his *dancing shoes*—they looked good but they hurt like hell.

There were those in Jenkins's circle of friends who thought that socials were distasteful and selling tickets to them despicable. Nothing but a money grab. Some of those people were invited to the Sanderson party. Noreen Harrow was one—best not to mention a social around her or you might be harangued on how low-class such a practice was, and she'd tell you that she and her husband, Hamish, would never have condoned such an event for their daughter, Cindy, or their other daughter, Blythe. (What you wanted to tell Noreen was that there was likely no danger of Cindy getting married, never mind having a social, because she had a face that would stop a clock, and that Blythe had had a *secret* social—kept secret from Noreen, at any rate—before her wedding, though it hadn't done much for her marriage; she and her husband split up within the first year and Blythe now lived with a woman and was active in the fight for the right of same-sex couples to adopt.)

The fact was, though, that socials, popular as they were, had *not* replaced stags or showers. Jenkins would, when the time came, go to a golf course with Clay and Hank and other male members of the wedding party. If the outing was anything like others Tracy had told him about, there would be flasks in the golf bags, and one objective would be to get the groom drunk. If they gained the co-operation of the golf-course management, they'd arrange for a life-size nude doll to be lashed to the flag on the eighteenth green, likely sitting with her legs spread out in front of her and the hole . . . between her legs. There might be pranks played, like forcing the groom to wear a funny costume (mildly obscene) or requiring him to play the whole round with a putter and a shovel. From there, they'd go to a local nightclub (Tracy had wheedled a promise out of the best man that they wouldn't go to a strip joint or buy Clay an hour with a lady of the night) and see how many drinks they could pour down Clay's throat. Someone would make sure Clay got home okay (where, of course, he'd have to face Tracy, since the two of them had been living together for nearly a year). Meanwhile, there would be showers, the more the better as far as Tracy was concerned. Someone from Tracy's office would host one, a gymnast friend would host another, and she could count on at least two more. A couple of these would be the old-fashioned kind, where women like Barb and Betty and *their* friends and some of Tracy's friends dressed in their best clothes and brought gifts and expected Tracy to be surprised. Tracy would sit in a chair that was decked out like a throne and try to answer a list of prepared questions about Clay's favourite colour of lingerie or the like. One or more of these female get-togethers might be a stagette. For the stagette (oddly named when you considered that distaff terms like *stewardess* and *actress* were being dropped from vocabularies influenced by political correctness and feminism), the bride's female friends dressed her to look as terrible as they could. They took her out to a bar that way. She might have to wear a T-shirt that had Life Savers sewn onto it over a balloon bra inflated to crazy proportions. For a dollar, any man in the bar could bite off a Life Saver, and the candies on the pumped-up chest were bound to be chomped off first. On any given night, there might be three or four stagettes going in the same establishment; one bride might be drinking from a penis-shaped cup, while another could be wearing a penis corsage and a condom hat. The bartender would call a bride up to the bar to down a shooter, the object being to add drunkenness to her unsightliness. A variation on the shower was one at which the men from the wedding party waited on the assembled women with food and refreshments. A further variation was the Jack and Jill party, which came almost full circle back to the original social: it was a shower for bride and groom, attended by men and women, who brought gifts in the same way that women did at a regular shower. Tracy didn't want a Jack and Jill party or a shower where men

25 ■

served, but she was looking forward to her stagette and, even though she didn't want Clay messing with any babes at his stag, she was looking forward to having strange men bite candy off her boobs.

Alec Sanderson poured a beer for Jenkins. "Help yourself from now on," Alec said.

Jenkins toasted his host and took several mouthfuls in quick succession. The first beer was always the best. Jenkins had reached an age where achieving a tolerable reaction to booze was difficult. When much younger, he could have several drinks and become a scintillating conversationalist (in his own eyes, at least) and not have a hangover the next day. He'd never been one to drink himself senseless. He'd driven home when he shouldn't have, but he'd never fallen down drunk or thrown up because of too much alcohol. He believed he had a metabolism that sent him a *That's enough!* message long before he could become numb. Now, his limit seemed to be three. If he had more, he'd feel lousy the next day and it just wasn't worth it. But more and more he'd grown to look forward to that first one of the day. Most days, he had that first one after five o'clock. Today was an exception. This was a Sunday and the guests were arriving at the Sandersons' now, at one in the afternoon. Jenkins hated drinking too early (he'd get sleepy and that would piss off Barb), but, at this kind of do, you had to have a drink in your hand. "I have to have a drink to face these people," he'd say to Barb, pretending to make a joke of it though he knew that she knew he was only half kidding.

Jenkins saw big Alf Gorman and his wife Tilly coming up onto the Sandersons' deck from the back yard. Jenkins liked Alf and hoped he could talk him into telling his golf joke, the one Jenkins had him tell every time he saw him. It was about a man who meets this gorgeous young woman on the golf course and they play a round together and she starts him betting with her on every shot. Jenkins loved the way Alf spun out the story and it boiled down to her saying that if she sank the twelve-foot putt she was left with, the man could sleep with her. "And he looked at the ball and he looked at the hole, and he looked at the ball and he looked at the hole, and he said, 'It's a gimme.'" It sounded fresh and hilarious every time Alf told it. Some guys had the knack.

"Hello, Jenkins," Alf said, taking hold of Jenkins's hand and squeezing it. "What's the occasion?"

Jenkins looked at Tilly—surely *she* knew why they were here—but she had turned her attention to Maude Sanderson, who was offering her a cheek. "Tracy's getting married," Jenkins said. "My daughter, Tracy."

"Have I met her?"

"I'm sure you have, but, come on, I'll introduce you to her."

Jenkins looked out on the front lawn, where Tracy had been standing moments ago, under the clump of birch. She'd just done an aerial to prove she still could. Where had she gone?

"Daddy?"

Jenkins turned to the voice and there was Tracy, squeezing between Wendelin McPherson and Norbert Finnbogasson, coming his way.

"Oh, here she is, Alf," Jenkins said, "my daughter, Tracy. Tracy, this is Mr. Gorman."

"Congratulations," Alf said, "your dad says you're tying the knot." He bent to kiss her cheek. "When's the date and who's the lucky man?"

"September the tenth," said Tracy. "The lucky man is down there, talking to Mr.—?"

"Featherstonehaugh?" said Alf.

"Right, that's him. Dad, Mom sent word that Gram's ready to come over."

"Oh, good, okay," said Jenkins. "Alf, the bar's over there. Alec's pouring the first one. I have to go next door and help Barb, but dust off the golf joke, will you? I want to hear it when I get back."

As Jenkins made his way through the growing crowd, Alf said to Tracy, "What does your young man do?"

"Jenkins, it's been so *long!*" cried Jacqueline Mortimer. She seized Jenkins and hugged him. "Where have you *been* all summer? Why don't we ever *see* you anymore?"

Jenkins liked Jacqueline's perfume, but he found her powdered moustache rather disconcerting, especially with the orange lipstick bleeding into the vertical wrinkles along her upper lip. He hugged her back, wondering if she remembered the time they were both guests at Rudy Shore's ski place in Western Manitoba and she'd taken her top off in Rudy's sauna, right in front of Jenkins, who was the only other person in there at the time. Jacqueline's breasts weren't much more appealing than her mouth, but she seemed to think the gesture was some kind of *statement*. Jenkins was sure it wasn't meant as a pass but rather as some sort of declaration of independence (though she was still married to Ken). Or perhaps it was simply the way she thought you behaved in a sauna.

"We've been here every weekend," Jenkins said.

Jacqueline kept him in her clutches. "We *never* see you," she said. "You haven't seen the new addition Ken and I had built. You haven't been over to see my new *shower*. Outside. For getting the sand off before you come in."

"I seldom go on the beach anymore," said Jenkins, still in her embrace. "Jacqueline, I have to go and help Barb—"

"Where *is* Barb? Why doesn't she *ever* come to crafts?"

"She works most days now."

"Which of your kids is getting married?"

"Tracy."

"How's *Brian?* My favourite actor? I hope you haven't let me miss one of his shows. Has he been in anything lately?"

"Brian went to the National Theatre School in Montreal, and now he's trying his luck in Toronto. He's getting quite a few commercials, but it's a tough life."

"I know. All that auditioning. It's like applying for a new job every few weeks, isn't it. I'd go bonkers."

27

"Jacqueline, I'll see you later—I've got to help Barb."

"What's the matter with Barb?"

"It's her mother. Ninety-five and she insisted on coming out here for Tracy's party."

Jenkins pried himself away and bumped into Bea Branwell.

"Jenkins," said Bea, "what's this I hear about a book?" She was regarded as the most literate in the group.

"Oh, a little thing I wrote in my spare time. After a few of those articles in the paper, I was encouraged to do a book."

"Called—?"

"*Never Too Early.*"

"About sex?"

"No, no, it's about literacy—how to encourage kids to read."

"I thought it might be about sex in the morning."

Jenkins laughed and moved away from Bea, avoiding eye contact with anyone else in case he was detained further. He knew Barb would be fuming. She'd told him she needed help with her mother, because Eleanor wouldn't use a cane or a walker at an event like this. Eleanor liked to make a grand entrance on the arm of a man, preferably her son-in-law, and she liked to pretend that she could stand on her own if he let go of her. She'd shrunk in the last few years, but it took two people to deal with her, one supporting her and the other directing her. Once she was over at the Sandersons', everyone would make a fuss of her. She'd try to steal the spotlight from the bride. Though she was far from spry, her mind was sharp; she could still play bridge and go into club convention and that sort of thing. Where she had surprised Jenkins was in her attitude toward Tracy's less-than-perfect behaviour over the past few years. She said on a few occasions that Tracy's apparent waywardness could be blamed on strict parents. Barb used to argue with her, but, since she'd turned ninety, Barb let her talk. Everyone said how remarkable Eleanor was—why let something she said get you down? She *was* remarkable.

Jenkins jumped onto the back deck of their cottage. He could hear the din of the party behind him. He yanked open the door and was making his excuses before he could see anyone: "I'm so sorry—I ran into *Jacqueline* and you know how she likes to corner you—she would not let me—"

He could hear sobbing.

He wasn't sure where it was coming from. Counting the little room off the kitchen (where Jenkins had slept way back in his courting days), there were seven bedrooms. He could hear Dave, their dog, whimpering. He'd been closed off in the little room for a reason—Jenkins left him there. Jenkins looked in the room Eleanor had used ever since the cottage had been turned over to Barb and Jenkins—no one there.

"Barb?" he called, but not too loudly.

He ignored the room where Tracy slept and the one they'd put Clay into (more because Tracy preferred her old single bed at the lake than because they were prudish), and he looked into the master bedroom, which they'd renovated—made it twice as big—by extending it forward to give a better view of the lake through a new bay window.

Barb was sitting on the queen-sized bed beside her mother, who was dressed in her best light blue summer dress. Eleanor was lying flat on her back.

"Where the hell have you been?" Barb said in a mournful voice.

"I'm sorry—I—what's the matter?"

"She's . . . she's gone." Barb turned her face away and cried.

"What do you mean, *gone*?"

"I put her in here where she'd be more comfortable. When she went to sleep, I thought I might leave her while I slipped away for a while. But then . . . I thought, what if she tries to get up and she falls? And then . . . I thought . . . she doesn't want to miss any of it. . . . And I tried to wake her. Lydia came by to pick up the casserole and the peanut butter slice I did. Didn't she tell you I wanted you?"

"She must've told Tracy—and Tracy told me—but she said nothing about . . ."

"I wasn't going to tell Lydia I couldn't wake her!"

Jenkins sat down on the other side of the bed. He touched Eleanor's hand. It was still warm.

"Are you *sure* she's—"

"Of course I am. There's no pulse."

Jenkins looked at Eleanor's face. It was quite beautiful. And so peaceful. It struck him that she looked healthier in death than Jacqueline Mortimer did in life.

"She didn't cry out?" he said.

"Not a sound." Dave barked from his place of confinement. "Listen to him. He knows there's something wrong."

"What are we going to do?"

"The last thing I want to do is spoil Tracy's party."

"We can't leave her here."

"I don't know—I think we can. She's perfectly safe . . . now."

/ NIGHT POEM

/ BY PATRICK **FRIESEN**

across miles of evening
an iron bell

later a nighthawk drops
and you wait for the whirr
at the bottom of its parabola

something to wonder at

some thing

a ripple of dark
along your arms

a shape sifting along the foundation

and the smell of earthen cellars

such a strange
and attentive idleness

it may be her
leaning against the wall
her solitude soiled with shadows
and if it is
the sky reddening
you can break from
the world

/ GREEN DRESS

/ BY PATRICK **FRIESEN**

it will kill me
kill me

you in bare feet and a green summer dress

there's a long car
around the corner
perhaps a limousine
or a blue cadillac

you in the pale light of your summer dress
so light it flutters when the air moves

your eyes closed
your head
your head with the black hair
is tilted back to the sun

and I'm in the shade
as usual
wearing a panama
which I will lose
by summer's end

and it will kill me
whatever it is
this will kill me
what I've carried forever

I don't like long cars
they carry a human
like a little seed
while the driver never talks
there's just too much distance

but you across the yard
naked in your green dress
you

/ THAT WHEEL OF FISH AND LILIES

/ BY PATRICK **FRIESEN**

from open windows
they lean over the street
with their craving arms

from the red windows
a hundred tongues call
for blood and honey

everything passes through
your nerves those silver strings
tuning among the larkspur

barefoot in the fire
your words mangle
within earth's hallucination

and your throat burns
with coals of sound
lungs larynx and uvula

she hangs your skin on a nail
and *holy holy*
in the blasphemous river

she gathers ashes
and spreads them on water
that wheel of fish and lilies

a hundred tongues a thousand
clamour in the afternoon's heat
calling for death's incarnation

/ DEATH CAME CALLING

/ BY ED **KLEIMAN**

Only ten minutes had passed since Christine had hung up the phone—though to Michael it seemed more like an hour—before the red light from the ambulance on the street began flashing in the living-room window. It was now 2:30 in the morning, and Christine had asked that the driver not turn on the siren, but had neglected to say anything about the flashing red light. A few moments later Michael heard the gurney rolling along the front porch floor and the doorbell ringing.

He didn't know whether to be relieved or not. For the last hour and a half he'd had to labour for every breath. On second thought, he was relieved all right. He'd never have been able to keep breathing on his own till morning. The two men entered the house as if they were old family friends, gave him a reassuring smile, and helped him firmly from the recliner to an upright position, though his legs threatened at any moment to collapse beneath him. But the driver and his companion were not to be taken unawares. They let him collapse into their arms and a moment later he was lying on the gurney, which the two of them then raised waist-high before strapping him down securely.

Now he was being carried out the front door and down the front steps. He felt oddly embarrassed. Would any of the neighbours be witnessing the drama unfolding on the street before them? Probably not. But before Michael could turn his head to check for a light in the nearby houses, he was through the back doors of the ambulance and out of sight.

"I'll meet you at Grace Hospital," he heard Christine call. Moments later, the ambulance was climbing over the St. James Bridge and then picking up speed along Portage Avenue. As they raced by, the blinking red light flickered its message for mile after mile amidst the overhead lamps and sleeping Winnipeg streets: "Out of the way! Get out of the way!" Then Michael was being rolled along hospital corridors to a doctor's office and settled into a wheelchair. How did he get here so quickly? He couldn't even remember the ambulance arriving at the emergency door. Yet here he was suddenly having a stethoscope placed against his chest, then against his back. Blood was being taken from his arm. Christine materialized at his side. And a doctor was wheeling his chair around to address him directly.

"We have to take x-rays of your chest."

33

He had no recollection, either, of the journey down the hall to the x-ray room, but now the doctor was holding up two x-rays before him. "You've got a lung infection . . . How serious? Life threatening. As bad as the worst case of pneumonia I've ever seen. Just look at these . . . You'll notice that the left lung is clearly delineated, but the right lung is unrecognizable—a white blur. That's because it's totally filled with infection."

What followed were several injections; then a thick tube was inserted into the right side of his chest. At once, a dark thick liquid gushed from Michael's side and down into the container at his feet.

When Michael finally woke up, he was in a hospital room with three other patients, and Christine was promising she'd be back early the next morning. Intravenous tubes ran in a tangle from a metal stand into his left arm.

"So this is what happens," Michael thought, "when you have trouble swallowing and food goes down the wrong way." An offshoot of Parkinson's, he later learned. One of the punishments for growing old.

The next morning Michael awoke to the sound of other patients in the room discussing their illnesses. In the bed across from his was a giant of a Dutchman, Wilhelm, being addressed by a woman doctor. "The results of your biopsy are now in. No sign of any malignancy. You're lucky." Then she was gone and Wilhelm was fumbling with the phone to let his wife in on the good news. You would never have guessed—as Michael heard afterward—that the Dutchman was just recovering from an operation in which he'd lost part of his colon. Any food he ate still could not be digested and was periodically exiting, not into a colostomy bag, but through the same orifice through which it had entered his body.

Diagonally across from Michael was an Air Canada pilot who was also recovering from an operation. It was hard to tell who was worse off, the Dutchman or the pilot. The pilot's operation had involved two surgeons operating at the same time, each an expert in his field. The details reminded Michael of a Hieronymus Bosch painting. Ken's colon had fused with his bladder and both surgeons' skill had been pushed to the limit in separating the two without causing irreparable injury to either.

The fourth patient, across from Michael, to his right, was a street person, Lenny, who had, at one time (he let everyone in the room know) been one of the top real-estate agents in the city. Now his chart listed him as having "No Fixed Address."

"Could you let me borrow your shoes or slippers?" he asked when he saw that Michael was awake. "I'm expecting a government cheque to arrive at a friend's house a couple blocks from here. I'll be back before you know I've left." Apparently, he intended, if he was not able to borrow a raincoat, to tear through the streets dressed only in his hospital gown.

When Shirley, one of the nurses, entered the room to check Michael's IV, she was immediately besieged by Lenny with requests for a tin of Ensure.

"But you didn't touch your breakfast this morning."

"Won't stay down. You know that." Half an hour later, he was also bringing up the Ensure—all over the blankets. The care workers had clearly lost all patience with him.

"Yesterday you spat in your bureau drawers, and we had to clean that mess up!"

"The day before, you wet the bed!"

"And before that you dumped your food tray in the wastepaper basket."

Lenny smiled and was silent. But the smile said it all—that Lenny in the past, when he had been one of the top realtors in the city, had hired and fired, with scarcely a moment's thought, more important people than he was now surrounded by.

Michael never did see how the current confrontation was resolved because, just as voices were reaching a pitch of exasperation, two attendants arrived to wheel him downstairs to have still more x-rays taken of his lungs.

For the next few weeks Michael was scarcely able to focus—not even on a newspaper. Only disconnected and scattered impressions pierced the haze that so often enveloped him. But Christine was heroic, as were his friends, and their visits helped to establish a lifeline without which, he suspected, he would have been lost.

The doctors kept ordering more and more tests—a swallowing test at Deer Lodge Hospital, a nerve extension test at the Health Sciences Centre, with ambulance journeys for still other tests all about the city. And in the hospital room, Michael was aware that matters were going from bad to worse. Wilhelm could still not keep any food down; Ken was having hysterical fits in the night, pulling out IV lines, as well as the nasal tube that gave him nourishment; and Lenny had now taken to pooping in the bed after removing the adult diaper that near-hysterical care workers had swaddled him in the night before.

But Michael knew his own case was deteriorating when three different doctors visited him during the fourth week of his stay at the hospital. First came the thoracic surgeon, a slim woman who looked to be in her early twenties, but who must have been in her mid-thirties. "The antibiotics are not cleaning up the infection in your chest, though your lung is now clear. You need a minor surgical procedure, but a necessary one. Once I've opened you up, I'll have to clean the infection out manually."

In the afternoon, another doctor arrived—medium height, short beard, early forties and radiating confidence. "In case we run into difficulties, you'll be transferred to an emergency room and we'll be prepared there to sort out any problems on the spot. But believe me, it's highly unlikely there will be any problems. It's a routine procedure."

Later still, a blood doctor arrived and filled him in on all the blood tests that had been done. "The medication to thin your blood has been too effective, but by tomorrow morning everything should be more or less normal—though your hemoglobin is low. Still, the risk is minimal."

That night, Michael explained it all to Christine, who was not nearly as confident as he was. "Couldn't they give you the antibiotics for an extra week or two before deciding whether they'll operate?"

"They claim they already have."

"They all seem so young and impatient."

"At least they're not old and doddering."

"I don't think you should give them permission for a while yet."

"I've already signed the forms."

"Oh, Michael."

Late the next afternoon, when he was wheeled into the operating room, the doctors and nurses about him were all briskness and efficiency as they prepared to get down to business. Michael hadn't a fear in the world as he saw the anaesthetic being syringed into one of his IV tubes. For a moment, he was aware of the doctors and nurses crowding more closely about him—like soldiers at war swarming around a fallen combatant—and then there was nothing.

When he awoke it was to the sound of a doctor's voice saying, "I've already phoned the surgeon and she'll be here within the hour."

"Look at those blood clots forming along his back. I've never seen anything like it."

"Oh, my God!"

"Well, I'm not waiting. I'm going to intubate him now."

Then Michael was aware of the device in his mouth that made a whirling sound being removed and a tube being inserted down his throat. He tried to speak, but found himself gagging instead on the tube. His eyes swung wildly about, taking in the four doctors in the room—all of whom looked more terrified than even he felt at the moment. Sure enough, there was the emergency doctor who'd been so reassuring the day before. "Well, the worst that can happen," thought Michael, "is that I'll die. Things can't get any worse than that, though I do wish they'd get this damn tube out of my throat first." The last words Michael heard before he passed out was a nurse's voice reporting, "His blood pressure is still dropping!"

When Michael awoke again he was in a large cavernous room that he was sure must be in the basement of the hospital. A sign on the door nearby read "Intensive Care." There did not appear to be any windows and the overall effect was of being underground. Then Michael heard a newspaper rustling. He turned his head and there at a small desk beside him was a short heavyset care worker engrossed in a newspaper. Again Michael tried to speak. The tube was no longer in his throat; it had been replaced by a respirator whirring in his mouth. Attempts at speech only resulted in gurgling sounds before the saliva was sucked out by the tube leading out of his mouth.

"So you're awake now. Hold on to this cord and press the button if you need me. Your wife will be here in a half hour. I'll be keeping track of you for the rest of the night."

"What happened?" Michael wanted to demand, but the effect was again to create a gurgling sound in his throat. He'd have to be careful or he'd be drowning in his own saliva. Staring up at the ceiling, Michael waited for the hours to pass. In the dim light, time froze into stillness. And then Michael became aware of other beds in this cavernous room. Patient after patient lying helpless, with IV poles strung everywhere, respirators whirring, antibiotics, saline solution, blood transfusions all tying down the human consciousness. For how long? For days? Weeks? For the rest of their lives?

There must be other intensive-care wards throughout the city. Throughout the country. Everywhere. What about people who'd had strokes? People whose condition did not improve but who slowly grew worse, while medical workers prolonged the agony with whatever medical knowledge they could bring to bear?

Michael recalled a fellow student from his university days who, he'd heard, was now dying of AIDS. The student had been one of the lucky few to survive the holocaust, and then, in his adult years, after having fashioned a successful career in theatre, had blundered into another kind of holocaust that was afflicting millions. The symptoms were said to be horrendous. What could his experience from moment to moment be like? Did he ever think now of what he'd done to his own life since being welcomed into an adoptive home in North America after the war? To be kept alive—helpless as the pain increased from day to day, suffering all the ingenious afflictions that could torment the body—and not to be able to call it quits, but to be kept alive, painfully conscious, while the rest of the world went on in its own direction, for the most part oblivious of the silent suffering that ached everywhere within society. A burden that had the whole weight of the universe behind it.

Desperately, Michael looked about the room but could find no sign of a clock. Clutching blindly for the cord with the button, he pressed it again and again. He heard the attendant sigh, put down his paper and come to his side. Michael pointed to his wrist.

"The time? Is that what you're asking?"

Michael nodded.

"It's two thirty-five in the morning."

Michael closed his eyes. At least six hours must pass before he would have any company. Six hours to focus on all those silent forms in the cavernous area of the Intensive Care Unit. Time expanded, grew larger, became infinite. As his mind raced more and more quickly, it was able to explore in greater detail the pain that emanated from each of the silent forms in the beds about him. Hours passed; the silent pain in the room merged with his own and became irresistible; dawn must surely arrive soon, but when he pressed the call button again, the attendant told him it was now two forty-seven. Was that all? Had only twelve minutes passed? How could he ever survive the hours that still lay before him?

When morning finally arrived, Michael was a different person. Several lifetimes had passed in the night.

Now Christine was at his side. He hadn't seen her coming into the ward.

She had just appeared as if she had been there all along.

"Are you all okay?"

Michael looked up, tried to speak and started to gag on the saliva trapped in his mouth by the respirator. What he did next made Christine turn pale. With a jerk he lifted his left hand from beneath the covers and drew circles on his palm with the index finger of his right hand.

Puzzled, Christine shook her head.

37

Impatiently, he drew more circles in his left hand.

Then at last, miraculously, she understood—and the frightened look left her face. "Do you want a pencil and paper?"

He nodded, and a moment later, Michael scrawled out two words: "What happened?"

"Blood clots were forming around the tubes in your side. Then your blood pressure started to drop. Didn't you hear me when I told you all this a few hours ago?"

Michael shook his head. He had no recollection of Christine's coming to his side earlier.

"An ambulance will be taking you to St. Boniface Hospital for a CAT scan. It's the only CAT scan in operation on Sunday. The doctor wants to check if there were any other reasons for what happened after the operation."

When Michael awoke again, he was in a hallway at St. Boniface being attended by two ambulance drivers. The respirator had been removed and he was trying to cough up phlegm that had lodged in his throat.

"Do you want us to help you get that up?"

Michael nodded. From a kit at his side one of the drivers removed a long plastic tube which he proceeded to feed down Michael's throat. There was a wet, mechanical, gurgling sound as the mucous was sucked out of his body.

"Is that better?"

Michael nodded.

Then he was wheeled away to the room housing the CAT scan equipment. There he was lifted onto a wheeled platform that rolled him into the stainless steel apparatus that seemed a miniature cosmos of sounds and lights. A computerized voice told him when to hold his breath and when to breathe again. Outside the CAT scan, Michael heard the medical technicians conferring among themselves. Then it was back out and on to the gurney, out to the ambulance, and back to Grace Hospital.

When he was wheeled into his own room again, it was to a most extraordinary sight. At first, Michael did not know what to make of the scene, for one of the nurses, Megan, was astraddle Lenny, who lay helpless on his back. His body heaved and kicked beneath hers, but Megan was not to be deterred. At first glance, a visitor to the room might have thought they were making love. But then Michael realized that, while she held Lenny's head down with one hand, she was proceeding to shave off his beard with an electric razor gripped in her other hand. "This beard's coming off, do you hear? We're all sick of it getting dunked in your soup and collecting food from your dinner plate. Combing it clean every day has become a nightmare for us. But no more." And then the rhythmical movements of her body and Lenny's were finally still. Exhausted, she lifted herself from atop her helpless victim, struggled onto her feet, tugged her uniform back into shape, and turned towards the door.

But before she had taken more than a step or two, Ken, the Air Canada pilot, who had been watching the proceedings, called out to her: "Can I ask you a question?"

"What now?"

"Would you do the same for me if I were to grow a beard?"

"You won't be here long enough to grow a beard. You'll be well long before that."

"I'd be willing to hang around."

"You wouldn't be up to it."

"We could have a go. What do you say?"

"Why sure . . . if you're still here in a month's time."

"It would almost be worth it."

"What do you mean *almost*?" And with that, she was out the door.

The result of this encounter was that Ken's spirits were so uplifted that all the repair work done by the two surgeons finally kicked into gear and in the next few days he took to having a morning shower before breakfast. A week later, when Megan came by, he was dressed in his street clothes and, with his wife at his side, was strolling toward the elevator. Just then Michael was being taken for a walk through the hallway by Christine and heard their exchange.

"What? Leaving so soon?"

"I took a sudden turn for the better."

"Well, if you ever need a shave, don't be shy." And a moment later, she was gone.

"What was that all about?" his wife asked as they were getting into the elevator.

"A private joke."

But Michael's remaining weeks in the hospital were not so fun-filled. The character of the room changed with Lenny's departure to another ward. The patience of the caregivers had finally snapped one night when they discovered him using his bedsheets to do finger painting with his feces. An empty bed was quickly discovered further down the hall and, within minutes, Lenny was housed there and became the responsibility of a new group of unsuspecting caregivers. As for Wilhelm, he was discovered to be infected by a bacteria common to surgical recovery wards, and he was rushed into a private room that was quarantined.

Michael soon found himself with new roommates, all in better shape than he was. More weeks passed during which he was given one blood test after another. The infection clung on to him like a leech, but at last the sedimentation rate began to fall, and Michael, acquiring strength now, began to roam the halls on his own, pushing the iv stand before him. From time to time, he heard a voice from another patient who'd moved in next door call out in a rasping voice: "Help me. Help." Then the voice would be drowned out in a gurgling sound and there would be a rush of nurses into the room. "Bert's in trouble again. Lift him up higher in bed. Get him to cough up all that mucous and saliva. Keep pounding his back. Harder! There, Bert, now you're well again." And he was—till the next crisis.

As Michael continued to gain strength, Bert's situation got steadily worse. Michael tried to discover the cause of Bert's difficulties, but the nurses were all sworn to secrecy. Bert remained a mystery, never seen in the halls, a patient whose presence dwindled steadily to a series of coughs, hacks, cries for help and choking sounds of distress.

Finally, one day, Michael learned that his own infection was over and he fully expected to be discharged in a few days. Instead there was a visit from one of his doctors.

"There's been some debate about your case. The swallowing test has not proved satisfactory." Michael recalled the ambulance trip to the swallowing clinic at Deer Lodge Hospital. He'd been propped up at one side of an x-ray machine—a laryngograph—and asked to swallow a series of foods, starting with sauces, then cookies, then meats. To his astonishment, when he looked at the x-ray screen what he saw was the grinning head of a skeleton whose jaws clapped open and shut. His teeth with their dark fillings crunched savagely on food that laboriously made its way back in his throat, till suddenly, faster than the eye could capture, it vanished down his esophagus. What flickered and then imprinted itself on his mind was the image from a charcoal drawing done by Dürer during the plague of 1505. The drawing was of the triumphant figure of Death—a crowned skeleton with a scythe in its left hand—riding a horse that was nothing but skin and bones. And hurled from the drawing like a challenge to the world were the words *Memento Mei*. The words continued to echo in Michael's mind: *Remember Me*. Fat chance there was of forgetting. The crowned figure rode silently, blindly, within him.

The doctor's words continued: "If we were to discharge you now, you'd be back in a few weeks with another lung infection. We don't dare let you start swallowing food again in the normal way."

The alternative, Michael learned, was another operation—to insert a tube feed directly into his stomach. At first, Michael did not fully grasp the implications of what that meant, but when he did, he did not exactly feel like celebrating. True, he would live—Joy to the World!—but at a price. Rather than dwelling on the matter, he focused instead, in the next few weeks after the surgery, on recovering his strength. And then at last, on the day of his discharge, he was dressed in his street clothes once again. By then, however, he had determined not to let matters rest where they were, but to explore the possibility of attending the clinic at Deer Lodge with a view to recovering his ability to eat normally again. What was involved, he'd learned, was a series of swallowing exercises designed to strengthen his throat muscles. Surely not an impossible task.

As he and Christine turned into the hallway, they were brought up short by a figure in a wheelchair outside the adjacent room. "Tell me," the voice rasped, "tell me. How . . ." and then his voice collapsed into one long series of hacking coughs after another.

With a start, Michael realized that the twisted, crippled figure writhing in the wheelchair before him must be Bert. At last that rasping voice was attached to a visible presence. "Tell me," Bert began again, successfully this time, "how did you do it?"

"Do what?" Michael asked.

"How did you get them," the gravelly voice whispered, "how did you get them to let you out?"

Michael started to respond, but then thought better of it. Instead, he gestured vaguely in a movement that included the hospital halls, the care workers, the streets outside the hospital and the horizon beyond. Then he and Christine continued walking toward the elevator.

The drive along Portage Avenue left Michael speechless. Now they were part of a stream of cars and buses passing by at a great clip. As traffic lights changed and horns honked and jaywalkers dodged across their path, Michael felt as if he had been restored to the world. And then he heard the sound of an ambulance ahead. Traffic slowed as the siren grew louder, and the three lanes of traffic were funnelled into two. Ahead of them toward the centre of Portage Avenue, Michael made out the flashing lights—and then he caught sight of two cars, one on its side with the hood crunched up towards the shattered windshield and the other at right angles to the first, with a front door crunched inwards. But where were the drivers and their passengers? Everywhere showers of splintered glass glinted in the sunlight. And then further along the street, where the central boulevard widened, he caught sight of men, women and children lying on the grass, as if at a picnic, enjoying the warm sun. No sign of alarm or injury or argument. Instead there were smiles as they chatted to one another, all part of one large, close-knit family. They had survived and their mood was clearly one of elation, even of celebration. Michael waved to them as his car inched slowly by and several waved back. One would have thought they were old acquaintances, but although they were total strangers, Michael did feel a strong bond linking them together, all sharing a common secret—of grace or folly—mysteriously bestowed upon them from beyond.

/ THE DEVOURING

/ BY CAROL **MATAS**

Tammi gazed across the room at Greg and sighed. She couldn't believe her good for-
tune. Of course, *she* knew it wasn't just dumb luck that had caused her and Greg to be
together. No, it was her own perseverance. She thought back to when they had first met,
last year when they were both juniors at Fargo High. He had just moved to Fargo from
Chicago and everyone thought he was a geek. He was pale and skinny, slouched around
like a weird zombie. For some reason he'd taken one look at her, in biology class, as he
told it, and knew she was the girl for him. He started to hang around with her and she
discovered that he was smart and funny. He listened to every word she said as if she
were the wisest, most interesting person on the face of the earth. And when all her
friends told her she was an idiot to even give him the time of day, she didn't listen. The
whole school laughed at her, at their friendship, but she didn't care. And soon, he began
to change. He joined the track team, then the basketball team. He gained weight and
grew stronger. He grew even taller until he was six-foot-four, with huge shoulders and
the rest all muscle. His blue eyes sparkled. He let his black wavy hair grow. He trans-
formed in front of her eyes. His grades shot up until he was an A student and sud-
denly, as they went into their senior year, Greg was the most desirable boy at school.
And he was all hers. She couldn't help but gloat, just a little.

They were at a party, it was only midnight but suddenly she was very tired. That
had been happening a lot lately. Her marks had suffered this term too. With
Thanksgiving approaching they'd just finished their first round of tests and her marks
had been disappointing. All Bs. Not like her. Her mother wanted to take her to the doc-
tor because she said Tammi looked pale but Tammi figured it was just the stress of
senior year. The courses were tougher this year, especially since she was taking uni-
versity-level calculus, physics, geometry and the like. She was going to be a medical
researcher. Cure cancer maybe.

She signalled to Greg and caught his eye right away. They were so attuned to each
other, or he was so attuned to her, that she barely had to move or speak before he seemed
to know what she wanted. He said a few words to the group he was with and walked
across the room to her, the adoring eyes of the other girls following his every move.

"You tired?" he said, concern showing in his eyes.

"Yeah," she admitted. "I am."

"Well, come on then," he said, offering her his hand.

"You don't mind?"

"No way." He leaned over and whispered in her ear. "Same old group, same old stuff. We can do it all again next weekend."

She smiled. He was right. Nothing much changed in Fargo. Same people. Few surprises.

He was driving and they were at her house in minutes. She lived in the south end of Fargo, lots of new development, big houses, many of them on the river. Her dad was a psychiatrist at the Fargo hospital, her mom managed a store downtown—it was a gift shop, bookstore, coffee shop all in one, called Coretta's.

"Hey," she said to him, "Lauren and I are going to Mom's store tomorrow to get our cards read. Wanna come?"

Tammi's mom had begun to bring a tarot card reader in every Sunday to the store and it had attracted loads of customers. Tammi didn't believe in it at all—she was convinced there was a rational explanation for everything, but her best friend Lauren loved anything to do with the paranormal. She'd begged Tammi to go with her and finally Tammi had agreed. Lauren was hoping the psychic would tell her that Martin was going to notice her at some point this year.

Greg thought about it for a minute, then shook his head. "Can't," he said. "I have a track practice in the afternoon and tons of homework and tomorrow night I have to work." Greg worked at The Griddle, a coffee shop near his house downtown.

He and his mom had moved to Fargo after his mom got divorced. His dad had been rotten, beaten both him and his mom until his mom had spirited Greg away one night, not telling his dad where they'd gone. Now she worked as a nurse at the same hospital as Tammi's dad.

"Maybe I can drop by after work tomorrow night," he suggested. "And hear what our future will be."

When they kissed, it seemed to Tammi that she practically melted into him. It was an experience she was sure had to rate as a ten out of ten. She'd been kissed by lots of guys before Greg, of course. She'd always been one of the most popular girls at school. Tall, with blond hair and green eyes, Scandinavian blood in her veins, and brains too, boys had trailed after her. But not until Greg kissed her had she ever *really* been kissed.

They lingered outside for a while, just melting into each other, until suddenly a wave of dizziness over came her. Greg almost had to hold her up.

"Are you all right?"

"Yes. Of course. Just got light-headed for a minute."

"Here, let me help you." He practically carried her into the house.

"Don't say anything to my mom," Tammi warned him. "You know what she's like."

Greg smiled and nodded. Tammi's mom would have her at the hospital in a second if she even suspected anything like a dizzy spell.

"Sure you're okay?" He added, "Maybe you *should* see a doctor, Tammi. They don't bite, you know."

43

Tammi grinned. "I know! It's just that there's nothing wrong with me. Now go home. I'm tired."

Greg gave her a peck on the cheek and left. Tammi practically had to drag herself up the stairs to her room, pulling on the banister as she went. Actually, she *was* starting to feel slightly concerned. This fatigue wasn't normal for her and these dizzy spells had been happening more and more frequently. If things didn't improve she'd have to go see her doctor. But preferably without letting her mom know. She didn't want her mom hovering over her like she was about to die any second, just because she'd said she didn't feel well.

That night Tammi tossed and turned as strange dreams disturbed her sleep. A faceless figure chased her, then caught her. When she woke she could barely remember the dream. She paid little attention to her dreams although her father was always telling her how important they were. As far as she was concerned they were a bunch of neurons misfiring.

She still felt a bit tired in the morning but when Lauren came over her energy was contagious. She was just the opposite of Tammi. Short, with dark hair and brown eyes, she loved English, wrote poetry, and believed everything happened on a deeper spiritual plane than we all realized. The girls had been best friends since second grade though, so even as they grew up and changed, their friendship stayed intact.

Lauren forced Tammi to eat a big breakfast of waffles with lots of syrup and then they decided to drive to Coretta's, as it was getting too cold out to bike. There was a thin dusting of snow on the ground. The leaves were all off the trees. Everything looked forlorn, that horrible in-between time before thick snow transformed the city. Tammi's teeth chattered—the heat in Lauren's car never worked—but Lauren didn't seem to feel the cold at all.

They ran into the shop, Tammi chafing her hands to warm them. Tammi's mom gave them each a big smile and told them to go over to a booth—the card reader would be ready soon.

"What do you think she'll say?" Lauren grinned, very excited.

"Oh, that's easy," Tammi answered. "She'll see lots of money, fame, fortune, love. She'll tell us we're going to go on a trip somewhere, you know, all that. Come on, Lauren. They just look at you, size you up, then make some educated guesses. I could do it!"

Lauren was making funny faces at Tammi as she spoke.

"What?" Tammi said.

Lauren pointed.

The psychic was standing behind Tammi, no doubt having heard everything she'd said. She came around the table and sat apposite Tammi, who had turned a bright red.

"That's quite all right," the woman said, "I hear that all the time." She was a tall woman, with dark eyes, and long black hair, perhaps Native American. She wore lots of turquoise jewellery.

"Me first?" Lauren asked.

She smiled. "Of course," she said. "By the way, my name is Mara. Shuffle the deck, then cut it in three."

Lauren did.

"I see a young man, the name starts with an M."

Lauren looked at Tammi and raised her eyebrows.

"You like him very much. But he's not interested in a relationship right now. He's into some kind of sports. . . ."

"Football!" Lauren blurted out.

Mara smiled. "Football. And he has no time for girls. He won't treat you well. Find someone else." She paused. "I see a friend, a good friend, she's not well. She's sick. You'll have to be strong for her. You can help her get better. There's something wrong—something dangerous. . . . I can't see any more except I keep getting an image connected to dreams. . . . You're going on a trip this summer and you'll have a good time. Somewhere near water."

She talked on for a while longer and Tammi's reactions changed as she listened. One minute she'd say something *really* amazing like the remarks about Martin and football, the next she'd say just what Tammi predicted. You'll go on a vacation, near water? *Everyone* in Fargo, just about, went to Detroit Lakes, if only for a weekend at some point—it was only a couple of hours away. That was so obvious!

Then it was Tammi's turns. Lauren thanked Mara over and over. Lauren obviously thought Mara was the real thing.

Tammi cut the cards. Mara set them out. Then she looked up at Tammi, as if she'd seen something upsetting. Suddenly Tammi got very nervous.

"What is it?" Tammi said.

"*You* are Lauren's friend, the one who is sick. The one who is in danger."

"Hey!" said Tammi. "I thought this was supposed to be fun!"

"I'm sorry," Mara said, her eyes serious, looking right into Tammi's, "but I *must* warn you. It would be wrong not to. I do always try to make my readings positive. For instance, if I see someone will lose their job I might tell them that a good change is coming, because often something like that can be used for good by the person. And if I see death—I don't tell, because what would be the point? But I'm sorry, here I see danger, but you can do something. . . . It is someone close to you . . . you'll have to pay attention to your dreams . . . in fact the *key* is the dreams. . . . That's all I can see. But I feel that you are weak. If you want I can give you an appointment for a private session and we can work together," she suggested.

"Stop it!" Tammi pushed herself up and away from the table. "This is the stupidest thing I've ever heard. You think you can make lots of money off me this way, don't you? I'll be coming here every day until I'm 'cured' and you're rich. I'm telling my mother about you!" And she stalked away, furious. It was beyond belief!

"What's the matter, Tammi?" her mom said. "You're pale as a ghost."

"That 'psychic' is full of it, Mom," Tammi said. "She's just ripping people off."

"Well, people pay for entertainment, dear," her mom said. "And some really believe in her. She 'sees' things apparently."

On the way home Lauren was very quiet.

"Honestly, it's too stupid, Lauren," Tammi said. "She really upset me. I thought it was supposed to be fun."

"But she saw how you're always tired, and how you've been feeling awful."

Tammi stared at her friend. "You couldn't possibly believe any of this?" she said. "Not even you."

"Well," Lauren answered, "I know it sounds crazy but . . . all right. Go to a doctor. Make sure there's nothing wrong with you, at least."

"It'll be something stupid like low iron. Fine, I'll go tomorrow."

That night Greg came over after work. He circled his arms around Tammi and told her he was glad she'd finally decided to see a doctor. She told him that the psychic had just told her a lot of nonsense.

Later, in her dreams, she was chased again. Chased and then caught. And after the faceless man caught her he melted her into a pool of water and he swam and splashed and played in the pool and he laughed and laughed and laughed.

She awoke with a start. It was morning. She was so tired she could barely get out of bed. She forced herself up and called the doctor, asking to see her that day. She realized that she was too tired to go on her own. She broke down and told her mom.

"Why didn't you tell me you weren't feeling well?" her mom said. "I *knew* you weren't. You're so pigheaded, though, I figured if I said *anything*—all right, I'll pick you up at ten. You stay home and rest 'til then."

The doctor did the usual tests, checked her over, talked to her, sent her home. Probably low iron, she said. Or too many late nights. She wasn't worried.

Tammi dragged herself through the next two days as she waited for the tests. When they came back everything was normal except her white blood count, which was a bit low—something that can happen when a virus attacks the system. Her doctor said that the worst-case scenario was that she could be developing chronic fatigue syndrome but that there was no reason to panic. She prescribed rest, vitamins, good food and some relaxation. Her parents decided to take her to Sedona in Arizona for Thanksgiving.

"Mara says it's just beautiful there, she raved about it so much I just couldn't resist," said Tammi's mom. "Oh, and she told me to tell you that you'll dream there. And to pay attention to your dreams. They'll save you. Or they can save you. Or something. What did she mean by *that*?"

"She's a freak, Mom," Tammi replied with a grimace. "Still, Lauren's been to Sedona and she said it's wicked. When do we leave?"

"Thursday right after school and we'll come back Monday night. That gives us four whole days there. The sun, the heat, I'm sure it'll help."

"Can Bruce come?"

Bruce was Tammi's older brother, away at university in New York.

"No, honey. He's too busy, I already called."

As Tammi and Greg were driving home from school in Greg's old beater, Tammi told him of her family's plans. He turned pale and had to pull over, he was so upset.

"You can't leave me, Tammi. I'll die without you here."

Tammi laughed nervously. "Don't be silly. It's only for four days. I'll miss you too but, die without me? Come on, Greg."

"You're right." He laughed too and seemed to get control of himself. "It's just, well, we've seen each other every day since I got here, we've never been apart, and when you said that, I don't know what happened, I felt like if you went I'd, I'd, stop *being* or something."

"Well, you *will* survive," she smiled.

"I'll dream about you," he said looking deep into her eyes. "I'll dream about you and we'll be together every night."

"Greg," she said, "stop it!" And she swatted him on the arm. But she thought it was sweet, all the same.

Sedona was stunningly beautiful. It took Tammi's breath away. The sky was a deep, deep blue, the rocks a deep red and her first night there she dreamed. She dreamed that the faceless man caught her but this time she escaped. Only then, as she was walking through the desert, she noticed that she had two shadows. And in the heat of the desert sun the shadows began to fight. She needed water badly. The sun beat down on her. Ahead was a well. One of the shadows was pushing her toward the well but the other was pulling her away. She knew she'd die if she didn't get water. But somehow she also knew that if she got to the well she wasn't going to drink. The shadow pushing her was going to push her in and she'd drown. Death either way. By drowning, or by dehydration.

She woke up screaming. Her mother and father were by her bed. Her father insisted she tell him the dream. Unlike her others she remembered this one in every detail.

"I think it's just an anxiety dream," said her father. "It's natural to worry about dying when you aren't well." Almost as an afterthought, he added, "But if you have the dream again, try to see the face of the faceless man. That might give you a hint about where exactly these fears lie." He gave her a very mild tranquillizer, which he'd brought along in case she needed help resting, and she slept through the rest of the night.

She felt better the next day. Far better than she had in ages. A little energy returned, and some appetite too. She and her parents hiked in the morning, rested by the pool in the afternoon and had Mexican food for dinner.

That night her dream recurred. But in her dream she remembered what her father had told her and when the faceless man caught her she turned to him and demanded to see his face. He tried to resist but she grabbed him and pulled off a white mask. Underneath it was Greg's face. But it wasn't the Greg she knew now. It was the old Greg, pale, sick, thin, and his eyes were all need, need and more need. He reached for her and his grasp was so strong he pulled her to him, she couldn't get away and suddenly the sun was blazing down and the shadows were pulling her and pushing her and she kept thinking, either way I'm going to die, I don't want to die, it's so hot, I'm so thirsty, someone save me. And she woke up.

Well, she thought, of course it was Greg. She was always thinking about him. She was crazy about him. Naturally he'd turn up in her dream. It didn't mean anything!

Saturday her mother took her up the mountain where people meditated and she sat and stared at the landscape and she dozed off. And then a voice in her head, said very loud, "You have to save yourself." Her eyes flew open. She must have been dreaming again.

Or she was losing her mind?

When they returned to Fargo, Greg was at the house within minutes even though it was midnight.

"Go home, Gregory," her mother said. "It's late, we're tired. You can see Tamara is better." Her mother only used their entire names when she meant business, so Greg left without even giving Tammi a kiss. But suddenly Tammi was tired again and she went straight to bed. That night she had the same dream. Greg capturing her, the shadows fighting. She woke up in a sweat and called her mom. Her mother felt her forehead.

"You're burning up. Maybe the plane ride was too much for you."

Her dad saw her, said there was nothing to do until morning, so they gave her some Tylenol and she fell into a fitful sleep. She dreamed she was lying on a table on a big platter and Greg was sharpening a huge glittering carving knife, saying, "Mmmm, you are going to be delicious. I can't wait. Cooked by the sun, roasted to perfection, enough here to keep me going for years, for years."

Her mother drove her to the doctor, who said that perhaps it was the virus that had been percolating for a while, making her tired, and that once this was past, Tammi would probably start to get better. She did more blood tests.

Tammi went home feeling rotten, but she was afraid to have a nap. She didn't want to dream.

This thing with Greg in her dreams was getting very annoying. He should be saving her in the dream. Why was he the bad guy? It didn't make sense.

Later that day Lauren came over and actually brought Mara! Tammi couldn't believe it. But as Tammi lay on the couch Mara sat at the dining room table and laid out the cards.

"I see a boy. He's tall, he has black hair, blue eyes, he's close to you."

Lauren looked at Tammi and raised her eyebrows.

"Yes," Tammi said.

"He's hurting you," Mara said.

"No, that's my boyfriend you just described. He wouldn't hurt a fly. I'm sorry," Tammi said, "but you're wrong."

"I'm not wrong," Mara insisted. "He's with you always. By day, at night in your dreams. He's taking your life force. He's using you to nourish himself."

"Sounds like a vampire," Lauren said with a nervous laugh.

"Just like that," Mara said. "A sort of psychic vampire."

Tammi scoffed. "People can't do that. They can't take other people's energy!"

"You're tired all the time, aren't you?" Mara said.

Tammi nodded, reluctantly.

"And when you're with him, suddenly you'll feel dizzy because he takes whole chunks of you then. He comes to you in your dreams and drains you. I can see. Your aura is dull, lifeless. I can see him."

"What should she do?" Lauren said.

"She must stop seeing him at once, but that's not enough. She'll have to confront him in her dreams. That's the place she can defeat him. Remember that. I'll help you if you'd like my help," Mara offered.

Tammi was too weak to fight. She shook her head "no." Mara got up to leave. She and Lauren talked quietly by the front door, then Mara slipped out. Lauren came and sat beside Tammi.

"Tammi, what if Mara is right? Greg could be killing you. Think about it. When he first got here, he was so sickly and weak. And then you two got together and he got strong and you got weak. In fact the stronger he gets the weaker you're getting. It could be true, Tammi. I mean, it is definitely the weirdest thing I've ever heard, but why would Mara make it up? She's not mean or a troublemaker. And if it's true, you have to listen to her because only you can do something."

Tammi felt really confused. She knew Lauren had her best interests at heart. Maybe it was time to confide in her about the dreams. She told Lauren all about the dreams. Lauren was terrified.

"Don't you see," she said, "it *is* Greg. You can even see his face in your dreams."

"He's my boyfriend," Tammi objected. "That's why he's in my dreams."

"Why do you have *two* shadows?" Lauren asked. "We all have a shadow, but *one*, Tammi. And you know, the shadow is a symbol of our dark side and you don't have one dark side, you have two."

"So whose is the other one—Greg's?" If Tammi hadn't felt so sick she'd have laughed.

"Tammi, look," said Lauren, "I know you don't believe in any of this, but you're really sick and I'm really worried, so *please, please,* just consider for a minute, what if it's true? What if Greg *is* doing this to you? I mean it can't hurt to consider it. It won't make you *sicker*. And maybe you can figure a way out, if you'll only accept it."

Tammi grabbed Lauren's hand. She could see she was really upset. "Chill," she said. "I've just got the flu. I'll be better in a day or two. Chill out."

Greg came back and eventually Lauren left. Tammi began to drift in and out of sleep and at some point Greg must have left and she was dreaming again.

It was the same dream—almost. But this time she somehow knew that the well contained her salvation, water, and her death, but there was no way to avoid it. The shadows pushed and pulled her and she stood, paralyzed, unable to move. And then Greg was laughing, all healthy and strong. She noticed that he had a sparkling black stud in his ear.

When she awoke from the dream, she was so weak she couldn't move. She heard the doctor's voice.

". . . serious . . . we can't figure it out . . . hospital . . . rehydrate her . . ."

And then she was being lifted and put on something and carried somewhere and then she remembered nothing until she slowly awoke and found herself in a hospital room, her mother by her bed holding her hand.

"Honey! Hi! How are you?"

Tammi looked around, bewildered.

"It's okay," her mom said. "You're in the hospital. Your fever stayed up at 104, and we couldn't get it down, you wouldn't drink, you were completely dehydrated, so we brought you in and they've put you on a drip. Your fever is down a bit, 102, and at least you've got some liquid in you now."

Tammi looked up at the drip attached to her arm and tried to smile at her mom.

"Do the doctors know what it is?"

"They aren't sure, sweetheart," her mom said, trying to hide how worried she was. "They've run all sorts of tests but they can't really find anything wrong with you. Maybe it's some virus they just can't pin down, they don't know yet. Are you hungry?"

Tammi shook her head. She felt a little clearer now, but not at all hungry. She closed her eyes and drifted off. She awoke later to find Greg sitting beside her holding her hand. Her eyes flew open when she saw him.

He looked better than ever. And he had a black stud in his ear.

"When did you pierce your ear?" she croaked.

"Just before I came up here," he smiled. "To take my mind off worrying about you. I guess," he added.

Tammi felt so dizzy and weak she wasn't sure if she was awake or dreaming. Hadn't she just seen that stud—in her dreams? She tried to focus.

"Go to sleep," Greg urged. "You need to rest. Don't worry, I'll see you in your dreams."

Tammi was reeling. She had seen the stud in her dream *before* she'd seen Greg. What if everything Mara said was true? What if he *was* draining her? She was sick, really sick. And for the first time she realized that she could die.

"Greg. I need to rest," she managed to get out.

"I know, I'll stay right here, I won't move. You can sleep and I'll be here when you get up."

Tammi shook her head. If it was true, he had to leave. What had Mara said? "He takes chunks out of you when he's with you!" Something like that.

She gazed at him. He looked wonderful. Bursting with health. No, she was delirious. He loved her. She loved him. This other stuff was a lot of nonsense.

Lauren came into the room.

"Your mom said I could visit," Lauren said, "but the nurses said one at a time." She stared at Greg.

"I need to stay with her," Greg objected.

"Tough," said Lauren. "I'm her best friend. Now get out."

"Hey, take it easy," Greg said. "I'm going." He squeezed Tammi's hand. "I'll be back soon," and he kissed her on the cheek.

Tammi felt so weak she almost passed out.

"Stay awake, Tammi," Lauren said.

"Hey," Tammi whispered. "I'll be okay."

"Tammi," Lauren said. "I've been back to see Mara."

Tammi rolled her eyes.

"No, listen. She told me to tell you that you *can* stop him. In your dreams. That's where he gets you. It's real. If you stop him there you'll be free of him. I told her about the two shadows. She says you have to find a way to get him to take back his shadow. She says people with no shadows are evil. They haven't accepted their dark side and they'll do anything to believe they don't have one. They put it on others. They make others scapegoats for everything bad that happens."

Tammi held up her hand. Lauren was ranting. She tried to sort out what was fantasy, what was real, but she was so weak and she couldn't think straight. She just wanted the world to go back to being orderly, and scientific. She just wanted . . . She started to cry.

"I don't want to die," she said to Lauren. "I'm dying, aren't I?"

Lauren nodded. "You can save yourself, Tammi. I know you can."

Tammi remembered she had heard those words before. In Sedona.

She began to drift off again. She heard Lauren repeat herself, "You can save yourself, Tammi. You can," over and over.

She was in a desert. The heat beat down on her. She still had two shadows. She began to walk. She was nearing the well. Greg was there. He held out his arms to her. "Come to me," he said, his voice smooth like honey. "Come to me," and suddenly he was holding a long, sharp knife.

"Roasted to perfection," he grinned.

Tammi stopped. She stared at him. He was going to slice her up, take all of her. She began to tremble. She knew, somehow, that if he succeeded she would never wake up. She would die here, in her dream. She wanted to wake up. She wanted to live. She began to get angry.

And then she remembered how in one of her dreams she had unmasked him. This is *my* dream. I can have power here. If he can have a knife in my dream, so can I. And suddenly, there was a long knife in her hand.

Greg took a step backwards. He seemed shocked.

Tammi laughed. "Logical thinking," she said. "One of my best qualities."

"Put it away, Tammi," Greg smiled. "You don't need it. I don't need mine, either." He winked. "I'll kiss you to death." And he threw away his knife and began to walk toward her. He looked gorgeous. She wanted him to kiss her. He was getting closer, closer. And then she noticed he still didn't have a shadow.

She turned her head slightly. Both shadows were still there. But which was hers? Which was his? Suddenly she knew that the shadow was the key. Both had melded to her form, she couldn't tell them apart. He was getting closer. She had to act. She whirled around, long knife in hand and sliced at one of the shadows. It seemed to open up like a slit carcass and out of it poured all kinds of shapes and sizes, twisted bodies,

51

each seeming to radiate an emotion—hate, jealousy, pettiness. They cackled and shrieked and moaned and she saw that they were all her.

As soon as she recognized them they melded back into one dark form. She shuddered. They were all part of her, she knew that.

Without pausing, she sliced at the other shadow. Horrible forms flew out of that one, too, a terrified little boy sobbing and crying, "Don't hurt me, don't hurt me," a twisted figure full of rage and hate, running, screaming, "I'll kill you, I'll kill you," others pleading for help.

Greg stood still. A look of pure horror came over Tammi.

"That's you," she said to him. "Just like the others were me."

"It's not me," he screamed. "It's not. Stop it, stop it."

"It's you, Greg," she screamed back. "It's you and they're going to eat you up and kill you if you don't accept them. And kill me, too."

At that all the horrible forms started to come for them.

"Just admit they're you, Greg," Tammi screamed. "Just admit it."

"No," he raged. "I won't. They aren't."

Tammi held the knife in her hand. If he wouldn't admit it, she knew she'd have to kill him. It was so hot. She could hardly breathe. She could hardly move.

"Greg," she said, "I'll love you even after seeing all of this."

He stared at her and his eyes filled with tears.

"No, you won't."

"I will. I do."

Greg sank to the ground. "They're me," he cried. "They're me. I never meant to hurt you, Tammi."

"I know," she said.

And then, everything went black.

Later that night, Tammi's fever broke. That same night Greg had a breakdown and was put in the hospital himself. It took a while, but he got better, as did Tammi.

Was it all just delirium? Or had Tammi and Greg experienced something that no amount of logic or science could explain? Tammi never forgot it and when she read Hamlet's words in class that year, she knew what he said was true: "There are more things in heaven and earth, Horatio, than are dreamt of in your philosophy."

/ THE VISITATION

Death will be no more, neither will mourning nor outcry nor pain be
anymore. — Revelation 21:4

/ BY ARTHUR **ADAMSON**

I hear the black wings of mortality beating over my head
I hear hoofbeats in the night   I hear unearthly chords
sometimes it's hard to get up in the morning   especially in January
I'm lying in bed still in my pyjamas thinking
I should get out and do something   something to further history
someone's at the front door   a man and a woman
they are going to try to save me   of course anything is possible
the man tells me God has a message for the world
he reads a passage from Hosea   the two are standing
on my front steps   it's about thirty below
through the door ajar I look at them intently
as the man speaks his gloved finger in the Book
brushes the passage he quotes which is crudely underlined in ink
could these people possibly know something I don't know?
I study them for a clue   they look absolutely ordinary
now it's the woman's turn   she tells me about the garden
the tree of knowledge   the serpent   the calamitous fall
outside the sun reverberates in cascades of light
off the snow   it's brilliant enough for an apocalypse
the world is a place of horror   hunger and war
they say   but God is about to change all that
he is going to introduce plenty   joy and peace everlasting
and I am willing to admit that anything is possible
so I thank them   they go   and I wonder   could they have been angels?

/ TRAVEL DIARY

April in (and around) Paris, 1982

/ BY CAROL **SHIELDS**

Carol Shields travelled to France every year for the last thirty years of her life, staying for about a month each time. She and her husband Don would rent a car and travel the routes nationales *and back roads. She would spend the mornings in cafés writing.*

15 Avril 1982

We are in the Ardennes staying for a night or two in the village of Rocroi. It is a small grey village with the little streets running out like the spokes of a wheel from a circular court. In the centre are a few shops, a bar crowded with men, a brownish-yellow church (18th c) and the Hotel du Commerce where we are staying. The hotel is modest and welcoming, run, it seems, by fat smiling men and women. There is a restaurant, a bar, and a stairway leading to the bedrooms. On each floor is an immense old wardrobe and a little library by the window. Our room, which is large and airy, has a window looking over the back roofs.

We went for a walk before dinner on the earth ramparts which surround the village. The earthwork is enormously complex, a series of walls and ditches, tunnels and mounds, all in a star shaped form. One wonders what in this village warranted this kind of protection. It is all virtually intact, though of course grown over with grass.

In the restaurant we were all English speaking, a delightful French meal beginning with a delicious cheese tart. Lovely wine, wonderful bread, all cheerfully, benignly served.

The weather: chilly but sunny. The trees are just coming into leaf.

16 Avril

I spent the morning at the table in the bar of the Hotel du Commerce beginning my series of poems. There are chrome kitchen chairs, a lace tablecloth on each table, curtains at the window, a few plants. A few people come and go, ordering coffee or glasses of red wine. There is a constant chatter of French voices.

In the afternoon (after an abysmal picnic of hideous local sausage, all fat and gristle) we drove around the area, visiting the towns along the river Meuse. It's a wide pretty river. The towns are industrial but attractive. Slate mining seems widespread. The town of Charleville (Rembrandt's hometown) is a surprise. It has at the centre a graceful 16th-century square, the Place Ducal, the buildings around it are of a golden stone and have graceful mansard roofs. Very balanced, very French. The most French thing of all is the fact that this is a replica of the famous square Vosges in Paris.

We have eaten too much. Dinner was four courses, soup, pâté, jambon Ardennes (cru) and dessert. We ate too much bread too. Tomorrow we are resolved to be moderate (only Sara is sensible, ordering a salad alone).

18 Avril

We are in Picardie staying at the Hotel du Nord in the town of Saissons. Yesterday we drove through beautiful green countryside, mostly grazing country. Our picnic was by the side of a 12th-century church, overlooking a ruined castle. Then on to Laon, in the days of Charlemagne the capital of France. There is a celebrated Gothic cathedral here, 10th–12th century, with deep blue glowing windows and a surprisingly white stone interior. We then drove to Saissons where there is a famous ruined abbey, a magnificent lacy facade standing with sunlight pouring through its openings. Our hotel is above a billiard parlour, a touch sordid, so we drove a few miles to Coucy-le-Chateau, looked at the ruins and then treated ourselves to a formidable dinner at the Hotel Bellevue where we had Picardie specialties, lapin in mustard sauce and, for hors d'oeuvres, something called facile (a crepe with mushroom and cheese). The proprietor corrected our French and generally bossed us around.

[This evening, we are] all in a small hotel [in Paris] called Le Palma near St. Ferdinand Place within walking distance of Etoile and just around the corner from the Congress building. We did what the Michelin guide called a three-star walk, up and down the Champs between Etoile and Concorde. Everyone was out in their finery being a rather punk bright coloured affair, miniskirts on the younger women. Everyone wears scarves of all sorts, both men and women.

Dinner was in the neighbourhood brasserie where the waiter was friendly but brought us more expensive wine than we had ordered. Ah, France!

[19] Avril

One week today since we left home. Am still waiting for an attack of cultural shock, but for some reason Paris seems benign. We like the quiet street we're on, and Place St. Ferdinand is charming. Sara and I did les Grands Magasins today, stopping on the way to listen to the musicians in the metro. The strangest one was a harp and cello group playing Ave Maria. The harpist had a cigarette dangling from his lip.

Six of us went to a Chinese restaurant. Everyone talked fast, reminding us how much French we've forgotten.

20 Avril — another warm sunny Paris day.

I went with Sara as far as Les Invalides where she took the train to Versailles. Then I met Chantal (a funny meeting, she waiting at the gallery Figaro and I waiting for her at the journal *Figaro*, both of us realizing the error after half an hour—we met halfway between). We went to another outdoor Italian restaurant just off the Champs and sat in the sun (I had salade Italienne and she had pizza—then a huge profiterole for both of us). We stayed and talked, and then met later in their home for dinner. The three daughters Sophie, Geraldine and Natasha are charming. The youngest, Marie, is three, severely handicapped and has never been conscious. After midnight when Chantal drove us home.

21 Avril

I am writing in the mornings, but playing tourist in the afternoon. Sara and I went to the Louvre which was crowded with tourists, most of whom were doing as we were, dashing through and searching for the big three, the Mona Lisa, Venus de Milo and Winged Victory. There are almost no direction signs, as though the French were trying to keep us from seeing just these things. The Mona Lisa is behind several glass barriers, and the reflections make it difficult to see. It was fun to stand there and listen to what people said: "She looks so vulnerable." "Yes." "See how soft her hands are. Now that's vulnerable." "Yes." "She's just frozen in an instant of time. Not like she's static. It's just a frame of film." "I see what you mean," etc.

We walked over the Pont Neuf to Notre Dame, this is not my favourite cathedral. There's something chunky about those twin towers. Sara climbed to the top.

Dinner was with Willy Norup at the local restaurant. He looks prosperous and pleased with himself, as well he should.

22 Avril

Sara stayed overnight with the Blondeaus. Donald and I drove out to Port Marly where our old boat La Bienveillant still sits. We had a long talk with Du Aime, whose boat sank in 1971—it is now fully restored. He has become a novelist and told us he is the author of *Birdy* and *Dad* (which just missed a National Book Award). He has, needless to say, become quite rich, an extremely vigorous and entertaining man. Our grande soiree was spent at La Forestière, a four-star hotel, I think the nicest we've ever stayed in, a country atmosphere with tennis courts and masses of flowers. Our chambre was charming with fabric on the walls, a lovely soft blue—and there was antique furniture, a lovely bathroom and a one-star (plus rosettes) restaurant. It was a lovely dinner, the food very original (I began with artichokes topped with celery-remoulade, ham and pistachio nuts). It was an excellent atmosphere, and I felt bathed in comfort and cleanliness and French civility.

23 Avril

We spent most of the afternoon by autoroute and spent the night in a country hotel near Cluny. They were getting ready for a wedding, and didn't have time to cook us much. In fact it was a dreadful meal and pretty rough accommodations. Perhaps we're spoiled after La Forestière.

24 Avril

We drove through Burgundy, which had the most beautiful scenery we've seen in France, very green and rich and rolling. This gradually changed toward Orange with a dryer climate. At Orange we found a small hotel on a pretty little square and a gem of a restaurant run by a young couple. I had cold eggplant beautifully arranged, and trout cooked in cream and fresh tarragon. We felt the ambiance was perfect.

25 Avril

We are at Montpellier at the Litourd Hotel and we're happy the hosts are amicable because we have asked them to assist us in our rendezvous with Margaret. He is skinny with a toupée and she is strong with blond hair—both smile more than average. The hotel is large and mostly empty. We had dinner at an Italian restaurant, Sara's choice, and it was delightful. The mistral blows like mad and it's cruelly cold.

26 Avril

We are installed in a holiday flat at Palavas outside Montpellier. It belongs to the brother of François Baguelin. It's what is called a studio, but there are bunk beds in the hall, a bathroom and wc and livingroom with pullout bed, a little kitchen niche and, best of all, a balcony with table and chairs, and here is where the morning sun shines. We are feet from a sandy beach and the blue Mediterranean. All around are hideous concrete buildings being erected. But we are sunny—our suitcases unpacked, and sleeping on our newly purchased sheets.

27 Avril

We are falling into our new rhythm. Don went off this morning to the Port of Sète, a town where the poet Paul Valéry came from and which he described as "a place where he would have wished to come from." I stayed home on the balcony and wrote a poem called "sleep" and Sara sat on the beach. In the afternoons we visited the old cathedral at Maguelonne—partly built in the 6th century and partly in the 12th. Over the door is a rather fat and petulant Jesus and to one side St. Peter and the other a lovely and primitive St. Mark, half crouching with a spear. Inside are lovely old 15th-century tombs, the wonderful kind with the sculptured likeness lying on top with folded hands.

From this pine-scented haven we drove to La Grande Motte, which is a mass of ugly concrete pyramid shaped buildings—a monstrosity. I went into one in search of a *Sunday Times*. It was full of red-faced German businessmen. We still don't know how we'll like it here, but it is very cheap ($40 a week).

28 Avril

This morning there were fishermen on the beach, pulling in all sorts of fish in a huge net. There was an instant flare of tourists helping themselves and we had a lovely lunch of sardines fried in butter.

In the afternoon we drove around a tourist circuit, through the rather wild gorge country just north of us. Visited a remarkable village called Saint-Guilhem-le-Désert. This is one of those postcard villages with flowers seemingly popping out of the walls. The church (founded in the time of Charlemagne) is lovely, but all churches are beginning to blend into each other—rather sad.

April 29

We were up early to meet Margaret, and there she was, on the train we had guessed she'd be on. Not bad for 17, and she'd had a half day at Amsterdam and Paris, meeting people all along the way. We let her sleep the afternoon away while we drove to Aigues-Mortes, which is a town completely walled in in the 12th century and almost completely intact. We raced around the wall (over a mile) and then took a guided tour up the tower of Constance, an almost impregnable fort. It was here that the Protestants were imprisoned in the 16th century. One woman, kept here for 32 years, scratched the word "Résistez" into the stone with her fingernail.

Afterwards we sat on the sunny square and drank wine and thought what a remarkable place France was.

April 30

Margaret's 18th birthday. It was overcast so we walked the tourist circuit in Montpellier, poking into shops and ending with coffee on the egg—this is the centre of the city, named for the shape. A wonderful chocolate cake from the pâtisserie for dinner tonight.

May 1

We were off early for Carcasonne, which proved a disappointment. It is a walled town but all of it reconstructed in the 19th century. Like Mont St. Michel it is exclusively for tourists and seems to have no life of its own. We went to the town of Limoux south of Carcassonne and found a marvellous old hotel with the curious name of Moderne et Pigeon. It had an enormous foyer and majestic stairs, all of it run by three old sisters (at least they looked like sisters). We had a delicious dinner in a restaurant and then drove a few miles to the village of Ste. Hilaire where the annual fête was being held. Everyone was in costume and wearing masks. The costumes were all beautifully made. Many of them were white satin with tall black witch's hats. Everyone carried "wands," which they waved when the band played. Confetti was flying like mad and we carried quite a lot back to the Moderne et Pigeon with us.

/ CROW CREATES EARTH

/ BY DENNIS **COOLEY**

(i)

speaks to the ear
listens to the shelled & installed heart
at the dearth of dirt rages
its lack of colour
our funda mental
colour blindness
the ragged absence of life

crow irate complains to high heaven
half-besotted berates the stars
which she sticks in her hair
in barrettes & hair fasteners
stirs with her seething
almost depressed uncrates the frame
which grates when she pulls it into place

her nails loud on the mesh
across which she drags her gravel voice
& the splotty surface begins below
to prime

crow raises a terrible hue & cry
talks to herself in an off-colour way
presses on the milky & silken sky
jumps on the sun till she is red-faced

in a foul
temper squashes it to chalky tempera
onto the canvas below tweaks out the filaments
first red green blue then millions
squeezes it all at last through

(ii)

says we all are reds
cardinal, carmine, cherry, coral, crimson (blushing crow has
unstemmed the crimson tide), rose, ruby, scarlet (her sins were
scarlet, her heart the same—compressed with sin to a sesame seed,
swollen with desire to a dirigible). Rouge, Rubric, Ruby, Ruddy.
reddish, ruddy, blood-red, carmine, cherry-red, crimson, ruby,
ruby-red
Russet, Rust, rufous the redness of birds
oh redness of fruit, redness of sin

we are animals then—bay, chestnut, flaming, foxy, reddish, sandy, [and
gods, even—titian, rubicund)no going back when
we have crossed the rubicund

To be that swift bright red, the sound of closing your eyes in the dazzling
light, its rush of gold & red in neon letters it is surely for crow from alpha
to omega such a day red river red rover what's come over

(iii)

you crow, grinning, in mimic glee, debraid the sun into green
alkali green
berlin green
brunswick green
chrome green
emerald green
aldehyde green
acid green
malachite green
victoria green
paris green
gaignet's green
methyl green
mineral green
mountain green
schweinfurth green
imperial green
vienna green
mitis green
scheele's green
swedish green
parrot green

■ 60

                    pickle green
                          pickerel green
                                nereid green
                                      green green

the world a smear of green arsenic

crow's buddy ezra says ·
a snotty green & is almost afraid
we will ask or speak to

                              (iv)
                              the world is then /was then
too also in addition in the end
        downcast, cast down, chapfallen, crestfallen, dejected, depressed,
disconsolate, dispirited, doleful, down, downhearted, down-in-the-mouth,
downthrown, droopy, dull, heartsick, heartsore, low, low-spirited, mopey,
soul-sick, spiritless, sunk, woebegone, dark, depressing, disconsolate,
dismal, in sin & error pining
                        (see also) sad
 (not to mention) discouraged, disheartened, oppressed, weighed down,
distressed, troubled, despondent, forlorn, listless, broody, moody, gloomy,
glum, morose

is crow knows and approves:
            verging on impropriety or indecency
risqué, broad, off-colour, purple, racy, risky, salty, sexy, shady, spicy,
suggestive, wicked: gamy, gamey, juicy, naughty. naughty naughty.
crow in her jet-black negligée
                          (is also) obscene
(related) naughty, warm, coarse, crude, gross, raunchy, raw, ribald,
vulgar, dirty, foul, indecent, indecorous, indelicate, inelegant,
unrefined, crow is a dodgy one, bawdy, off-colour, offensive, risqué,
suggestive, earthy, lewd, crow almost addled oohed & awed
  I.   (adj) using sexual language or images that may offend

is of a hue or tincture that is
Pale, without redness or glare, — said of a flame; hence,
    of the colour of burning brimstone, betokening the presence
    of ghosts or devils; as, the candle burns blue; the air
    was blue with oaths. Includes bluestockings, blue crab, blue devils,
blue laws, blue light as a night signal at sea, blue mould, blue monday,

which occurs more often than a blue moon, blue ribbon, blue water, blue
blood, blue on blue lewd crow damn near blue her opportunity

it's been a blue blue day &
             crow is given to

disguise, distort, embroider, falsify, garble, gloss over, misrepresent,
pervert, prejudice, slant, taint

                    (v)
             into a cold & impassive world
a cheeky crow steps across a sky that hangs
from a parachute, someone falling through
                    what crow leans to draw out of
crow shinnies her skinny knees up & down treads
out the grapes of wrath brings it into ferment packs it into
oceans plains plateaus moraines ravines mountains
stains into trucks into rail lines compresses
to concert halls pool halls tenement halls long hauls
through the sun's plummet combs out the spectrum
its colours pulse & shake crow trembles as she pulls them off
      the turning wheel that is earth

crow hunches beneath a gibbous moon
pisses until the seas turn green
pisses until the oceans thunder & hiss
pisses among the smoke & smash
pisses until the world is about to dissolve
the stars to go out in quick hot sizzles

             from the first decimals of time
             decides from that moment hence
             knows it is this she chooses
             it will be known as water

                    (vi)
crow laughs & chews the granular rocks
      she's found have caught her
             eye is an earth that rolls
      moon stares as crow is thinking
what she is making what becoming chews & chews
scowls & scolds until she heaves & hacks
spews a hot vomit   a spray of yellow & red

crow sniffs & spits on the brown & revolving dirt
crow wheezes & shifts squats & breathes
shits in the heavy & swaying pea-green seas

scans the magenta carmine cardinal mud
        says she's agonna call it earth
        as god is her witness
        so help her god

             (vii)
                crow grows infatuated
    with her work begins
to grow her toenails long & spiralling
to wear red & green & blue rings
in her ear around her ankle hears
planets in hoops swing her hair gets long & unkempt
crow chokes & her mouth opens
        opens wider & wider crow gags
                until it seems she will die until
                         at last   she

      re :leases   the bubble
  a blue & white sack once she swallowed
where now birds & fish wallow
      sounds & air & water
crow has summoned & unwound from inside her

          (viii)
      & when crow lifts off pow pow
      in a roaring rage half in love
         with what she's done
      the page she has registered
      with her stomping drags a lava of pigment
      the thick & glistening saliva she has left
      in globs & bubbles & pockmarks

      obsidian in its dark volcanic glass
         molten in Ethiopia
      darkly flowing glass in windows falls
         to the bottom & thickens

crow brings colour to our cheeks
      colours our perceptions
that the sun may set in topaz & aztec gold

cabo blue for morning, saguaro green for hills
creates the rivers from taupes the hills slip on
night moves suavely in mauves & hibiscus crow winces
minces when she thinks now
she may be beautiful /must be
purple whales rising to the surface
watches the carribean turn into electric blue
crow tints our days cerise vermilion
smears them in chartreuse in cyan in rust
fills in cobalt & ochre indigo & goldenrod
woad & madder slate & ruby
in cadmium & manganese blue in burnt umber
crow spills oil smears gobs of acrylic
until we all are people of colour
carmine cerise intaglio impasto
adds adobe and moonstone sapphire and bronze

(ix)
crow wrung from what she's done
a hunk of anthracite alone in the coal-blue cold
compresses with anger
more & more with pride
until her heart is a clear & sparkling thing
that cannot be marked & will not break
where it sits on top of her skinny legs
looking good in sun and moon
circling earth & water circling her
flight quick as a ruby-throated humming
bird that sips on the raw new light

crow has flung the stars in a necklace
over her shoulder & because she is
a ferocious highlander pinned
them there with the moon

(x)
cries out when she turns back
hears the round spinning
gasps when she sees the green
& blue world for the first time
so bright & wetly shining

/ THE PICTURE WINDOW VIEW OF HISTORY

/ BY PAMELA **BANTING**

On any given Sunday morning in July, around eleven o'clock, 1959, my dad, mom, baby brother and I would be in the car heading up the winding and seemingly interminable road into the Porcupine Mountains to Bell Lake, about twenty-two miles northwest of Birch River, Manitoba.

Dad glances over his right shoulder and reminds me to keep my eyes open, I might see something. Dad and I keep a lookout for bears, moose, jumpers, coyotes, beavers, rabbits, tiger lilies, Indian paintbrush. One time when we topped one of the steepest rises and came around the bend there were about thirty rabbits sitting together in the middle of the gravel road. I'd never seen so many rabbits together in one place. Why they were congregated there was a mystery. A beam of morning sunshine was shining down upon them like an illustration in a Sunday School book. They looked like sacred rabbits. It does pay to keep your eyes open.

I love going to the lake. Whenever we go up to Bell Lake or Steeprock Lake, the whole family watches for the short stretch along the road where you can turn around and see out over the trees all the way to Swan Lake. Once he is older and promoted to the back seat like me, my brother and I swivel around or kneel on the back seat and gaze out through the rear window, risking car sickness for a momentary glimpse of the valley in which we live.

Sometimes our father stops and we pause in our ascent to the lake, pull over, get out of the car, and look out at our valley. This is even riskier. The contrails of dust drawn up by passing cars full of picnickers also eager to get to the lake render us temporarily invisible and vulnerable to being struck by a vehicle, as Mom reminds us. We are daredevils, risking our lives for that glimpse! From that vantage point along the winding, dust-plumed, nauseating road on the steep slope up into the Porcupine Mountains we can see all the way to Swan Lake, a distance of about eighteen miles.

We stand and stare out over the valley, knees locked against the slope, and try to translate geography into history, to convert those spatial coordinates into the unknown temporal coordinates of the place into which we have been born. I think that if only I look hard enough, or if next time we remember to bring the binoculars, I will be able to discover traces of our history. Or if I concentrate, I will get a vision or an impression at least—like a heat mirage—of the people who lived here before us and the events of their lives. Staring into the beyond, concentrating, paying attention, keeping my eyes open, waiting for sudden insight, trying to intuit that unknown history amount to an almost mystical practice. Just as the area's early explorers David Thompson, Simon J. Dawson and John Macoun had each at different times lifted their dripping paddles up out of the Swan River or Dawson Bay, let the canoe drift and looked up to admire the blue Porcupine Mountains in the distance and imagine the valley's future, when it is our turn to live we look down from those same mountains and out toward Swan Lake, unknowingly returning their gaze from a vantage point made possible by an old logging road swathed through the dense bush thirty years before by my grandfather and other sawmill operators, and try to imagine or guess at that lost past.

Geologist and explorer J.B. Tyrrell recorded in his report on his 1889 expedition into the valley, the history of exploration, the fur trade and early Indian and Métis agriculture of the area, and yet I, growing up there between the mid-1950s and the early 1970s, knew and was taught nothing of that history or of his having been there either. I remember in grade five tracing in pencil crayon on maps of Canada the exploration routes of Cartier, Champlain, Radisson and Groseilliers, La Vérendrye, and other Canadian explorers, but I don't recall ever being taught that any explorers, fur traders or surveyors went through the Swan Valley or even passed nearby. The European history of our area was never alluded to in school nor did we study the Native history of any region of Canada, let alone of our apparently obscure valley. Until very recently I didn't know that Emily Murphy, a writer and the woman who became the first female magistrate in the British Empire, had lived in Swan River for four years during the early days of its settlement and had published an entire book, *Janey Canuck in the West*, about her observations and experiences there. The impression I gained at school and carried with me until a couple of years ago was that nobody had lived in or come to our valley prior to our grandparents' arrival, nothing had ever taken place there, and nothing ever would. The stories we non-Native kids of the village inherited were of the first white settlers there, our grandparents. Judging by the complete lack of stories about the time predating our grandparents' appearance, the impression I got was that when they had arrived they had discovered nothing and talked to no Native people, which was far from the truth. So convinced was I that, just as the No. 10 Highway, the Trail, bypassed our village, so too history had bypassed the entire Swan River Valley, I never even looked it up once I left there and went to live in Winnipeg, a city full of libraries and archives. History was what happened elsewhere.

But to be fair to those pioneers our grandparents, the very earliest of them began arriving in the Birch River area only about 1903, and to be sure they didn't arrive in the area as academic historians, with their moving expenses reimbursed by their university and with a grant for a new computer and the libraries and archives of the world at their disposal. Many of them arrived there hungry, often with several hungry children in tow and in immediate need of food and shelter in a place with none to offer other than through the kindness of strangers. Moreover, even by the time of Tyrrell's visit fourteen years earlier, as he himself says, the remains of the old wooden fur trade forts in the area were already so deteriorated as to be almost indiscernible. When he visited there, the site of Old Fort, HBC, consisted of nothing more than "six hollows or depressions, some of which were doubtless cellars, and two heaps of stones where chimneys formerly stood."[1]

By the time I was of an age to start asking questions about the valley, both of my grandfathers had died of cancer, one grandmother had had a series of strokes and been placed in a nursing home way down in southern Manitoba, and the other, for whom settlement had been an un-settling experience, was not always psychologically stable and her information not wholly reliable. There were no books in our community, and there was no one I could ask about the history of the valley prior to the arrival of the pioneers. It seemed to me as if history had halted at the perimeters of our valley. As if the Duck and the Porcupine Mountains had proven formidable obstacles to history, though my school books had taught me that even the Alps had not deterred Hannibal. Maybe the very forces of history were shunned or repelled by Unorganized Territory. Or was it history itself that organized territory? It was a chicken-or-egg question I could not resolve.

In fact, our history as inhabitants of the Swan River Valley was neither absent nor truly invisible. It just didn't look like a history: it looked like farmland. It was not recorded in any books we knew of, but it *was* written on the land itself. Farmland was land that must at some point have been taken from the Indians. I knew that much. When we stared out over the valley through the rear window of the car we knew the Indians lived out there on the reserve at the edge of Swan Lake. We surmised that they were located there on the lake on stony, swampy, unproductive reserve land because of us. But when or how that happened we didn't know. I wanted to know more, more about their lives prior to and during the time of our grandparents' arrival, and I wanted to know where I fit into the picture.

Of course we asked our parents about the Indians, and they would tell us what they knew, but we were not in a position to ask the Indians themselves. Because we lived in the town and most of the year they lived out at Swan Lake. Because it was none of our business to question them about their lives nor could we expect them to offer us a spontaneous description or a history lesson. The reserve was about twenty miles away northeast of town on gravel roads. You couldn't just jump on your bicycle and pedal out to the reserve and ask your burning and embarrassing questions—did the Indians of this area use bows and arrows, did you have horses, did you ever camp on the land along the river that is now our yard? Though Indian kids would occasionally break into our store in the middle of the night, steal some guns and ammunition and bicycles and pedal back toward the reserve, the police would usually find the bikes wrecked and abandoned somewhere along the route to the reserve, so I knew it was quite a long pedal, especially as the gravel was very deep in some places. Even as a very small child I knew perfectly well that such questions were romantic, drawn largely from the black-and-white western movies I loved to watch on TV. And though I very much wanted to know whether there was any local truth in those television portrayals, just as I would not have gone to the locker plant and quizzed Mr. Sadler on how he butchered a cow or a moose and made hamburger out of them, neither would I have stopped Mr. Moore on the railroad tracks during his daily constitutional walk and asked him about the tools and techniques upon which his and his ancestors' economy was based. Economics was a touchy subject for everyone in Unorganized Territory.

In the summers, when some of the Indian families moved off the reserve and camped in tipis along the Birch River directly across the road and the railroad tracks from our house, my brother and I were told not to go wandering over there. And not to stand on the tracks peering through the trees and gawking at them either (which we had already done). Nobody needed us staring at them, our parents told us. Everybody had a right to their privacy. How would we like it if the Indians came and stared through our dining room window at us while we ate our dinner? Chastened, we would stand in front of the picture window in our living room and watch the smoke from their cookfires snake up through the giant poplars a couple of hundred yards away. We stood there and silently compared that image with the black and white ones flickering on the television set beside us, and wondered and wondered as the theme music galloped off into the sunset.

One night while she was watching TV an Indian man who had had too much to drink looked in my aunt Lily's living room window. Seeing a man's face suddenly appear in her picture window nearly gave her a heart attack, and whatever it was he saw in the living room caused him to lose consciousness and pass out backwards onto the lawn. Meeting one another's gaze through the picture window almost finished them both off.

All I knew about Indians that I could not absorb with my own two eyes on days when Indian families came into town to pick up their mail, cash their cheques, shop at our store and others, and socialize, from questions I asked our mother and father or from staring out the picture window, I learned from the Hollywood westerns on television and tried, with my brother and my friends in our play, to copy. We were loyal adherents to both the gun and the bow and arrow. When we weren't Apache Indians we were Arizona cowboys, approximately equal time. In combining the look, the work and the stories of local men like ranchers and cowboys Ernie Brandt, Cliff Claggett, Carl Leslie and Edwin Lamb with those we saw played out on programs like *Roy Rogers, The Lone Ranger, Bonanza* and *Gunsmoke*, our version of history was an unreliable mixture of local stories and American frontier television shows.

Together this lack of local history and these cowboy programs gave me a sad case of gender malaise. We were nobody, living in the middle of nowhere, and to top it all off I was a girl. It seemed as if life as a girl was not worth living, or at least life as a girl without the compensatory prosthesis of a horse wasn't. Though, to my amazement, my brother largely rejected the cowboy mythology and didn't like or trust horses, I tried, arguing like television lawyer Perry Mason, to make a convincing case as to why our parents ought to buy me a pony. At times I almost made myself physically sick from the combination of longing for one and repeating both my request and my rationale ad nauseam. For me, horses were a powerful symbol of history, independence and destiny; the horse was a strong propeller of narrative. I would lie in my twin bed at night trying through false prayer, will power and force of thought to stave off a future as female. Lacking any knowledge of the past and fearing an extremely limited, embarrassing future as a breasted creature, I craved an alternate destiny. Or rather I craved a destiny, not just a default position. My fantasy of being independently mobile, able to ride off into the fields, the bush or up into the Porcupine Mountains, a fantasy I nurtured to counter the incredible bad luck of having been born a girl in a semi-remote and book-less world, lasted all through my early childhood until puberty, when I knowingly, and with great sadness tinged with revenge, acknowledged my defeat, halted my incessant demands for a pony and turned my attention to boys. If I couldn't have a horse of my own, then I would at least have a boyfriend. Or maybe a small herd.

As children, we did not play Crees and fur traders, or Crees and colonists. We knew nothing about the history of the Cree, Ojibway and Assiniboine who had lived in the valley for generations. We didn't even know they were Cree, Ojibway or Assiniboine. We didn't understand the métissage of the Métis kids at school. And we knew even less about the lives of our own ancestors in Europe. I was fascinated by and brimming with questions about Indian technologies, but had I been asked in turn if I knew any of the skills of my grandparents or parents—how to care for cattle, horses, pigs or chickens, how to grow a good crop of wheat or oats, how to separate milk from cream and churn butter, how to knit a pair of socks—even had I been asked if I could identify the uses of many of the items we sold in our own hardware store, I would have had to say no. I didn't know who the Indians were, I didn't know who I was either, and I didn't know how to do anything except school work.

Nevertheless, just as ontogeny recapitulates phylogeny, individual lives recapitulate the history of their locale both at conscious and unconscious levels. The history of the Swan River Valley is a history of abandonments by Europeans (abandonment of the fur trade, the telegraph, the planned route for the transnational railroad, the headquarters of the capital of the Territorial Government), abandonments that had already shaped my life and those of my generation even before we or our parents were born. We grew up knowing that most likely we too would have to abandon the community our parents and grandparents had slaved to build for themselves and for us. Abandonment was our theme, our subterfuge. In our family it was what our father worked so hard all the time to prevent by being so deeply involved in town committees and by supporting his fellow storekeepers and the farmers of the district, and it was what we children knew deep down we would have to do when we reached eighteen. We were traitors lurking within our own families, waiting like a band of masked outlaws to make a break for it between bouts of gunfire during a holdup.

I wanted to be in that history and I wanted to belong to that place. I wanted to carry the insignia of place and history on my skin. My strongest desire was to absorb Birch River into my very tissues. In those days before sunscreen and holes in the ozone, I tanned easily and deeply and never burned. One summer when I must have had a really good tan, my aunt Kay remarked that I was "as brown as a little Indian." To me, that

69

was the highest of compliments, maybe to her, too, as I had inherited her colouration. To me, being brown didn't mean that I was pretending to be an Indian, other than in our play and games, though I was flattered enough by the comparison to remember her words. Children have a much more fluid self-concept—Indians one minute, cowboys the next, boys, girls, human, animal, vegetable, mineral. What my tan meant to me was that the place had marked me. I had been imprinted by the weather, and I looked as if I belonged there.

We non-Aboriginal, non-Métis, non-boys obviously carried the insignia of history in our European-derived names and on our white, breast-destined bodies, too, whatever shade of tan, but the tremendous gap in the history pertaining to our own locale, together with the extreme differences between our climate, geography, flora, fauna and cultural resources, and those of Britain, rendered European history unimaginable. It was a failed narrative, largely irrelevant to our lives. I was only one child who needed those gaps in our history filled, needed a way to be or become indigenous to that place aside from suntanning and repudiating my gender in order to become someone who might have a story behind them. An intimately known and shared landscape carries an ethical force capable of regulating people's behaviour toward one another. Had the narratives of the Swan River Valley been available—the Aboriginal history, fur trade history, the treaties, surveyors' reports, women's history, government land policies— had even one book pertaining to local history, say Daniel Harmon's journal, been provided to us as school children—we could have made sense of our world. As it was, the lack of local history reduced the Magna Carta, the kings and queens of England, even their spectacular beheadings, feudalism, mercantilism, the Enclosure Movement and the Potato Famine to no more than a drab series of dates and a map unconnected with any story, and left us bereft, unable to place ourselves in history or geography. Anthropologist Keith Basso, whose many years of work with the Apache people taught him about sense of place, observes that

> [l]ong before the advent of literacy, to say nothing of "history" as an academic discipline, places served humankind as durable symbols of distant events and as indispensable aids for remembering and imagining them—and this convenient arrangement, ancient but not outmoded, is with us still today. . . . [W]hat people make of their places is closely connected to what they make of themselves as members of society and inhabitants of the earth, and while the two activities may be separable in principle, they are deeply joined in practice.[2]

Children need to have a sense of their own roles in the unfolding narratives into which they are born. Even in their merry-making and their make-believe, children are serious creatures on important ontological, epistemological, ethical, historical and other forms of quest. Children are natural historians. They need and deserve more than a television screen, computer monitor, rear window or picture window view of history. They need to be able to look out over their valley and knowingly return the gaze of all of their ancestors and predecessors in a given place, not just those of one or two generations of their own nuclear family.

NOTES

1 Joseph Burr Tyrrell, *Report on North-Western Manitoba and Portions of the Adjacent Districts of Assiniboia and Saskatchewan* (Ottawa: Geological Survey of Canada, 1892), 115.

2 Keith H. Basso, *Wisdom Sits in Places: Landscape and Language Among the Western Apache* (Albuquerque: University of New Mexico Press, 1996), 7.

/ BY UMA **PARAMESWARAN**

I
(1975)

Let us pledge to stand together
As the Inuit igloo
      of packed snow
      tight smooth edgeless
Withstands the Arctic's wintry wind.

Come, let us build our temple
Where the Assiniboine flows into the Red.

III

(2005)

I am come to a place past a fading collage
>of nostalgia for another land where mangoes yellow and red
>peeped with wonder at the purposeful spruce spare and tall
>against blinding snow;

>of protests proclaiming alienation, marginalization,
>discrimination, racialization
>of women, races, classes, ages, shapes and colours
>in language deemed meet
>for poetry
>and for the corporate ladder we call academe;

>of thankless service to various causes
>social, political, altruistic, educational;

>of secret trysts with the muses moving to music
>beyond measurable decibels,
>dancing with their shadows as they teased me
with poems and stories to magical dells
that have ever been and never reached.

I am come to a place where the land I stand on
Calls me
To know it as I had never known before.

I had searched and sieved through history texts
for resonating names to suit my prairie rhymes—
>Giovanni Caboto, Jean Baptiste La Vérendrye,
>   de Champlain, Vilhjalmur Stefansson,
oh how the syllables echoed like an honour roll of drums,
and names that are etched in the honour rolls of war—
>Allan Edy, 25; James Johnston, 26; Harry Edwards, 24;
>James Smith, 27; Normand Edmond, 21; Frederick Watson, 26;
>Mark Brown, 30; all pilots in the Battle of Britain.
And met too that nameless woman who from Orkney Islands
>came across the seas in search of the man who had sired
>the child within her, first white woman to stand on the patch
>I call my own, this prairie gold once bush,
>through which in travel and travail she sought for help.
>Nameless she remains, woman-mother-pioneer.

73

I did not know then
> when the mangoes red and yellow
> peeped with wonder at the purposeful spruce,
that history texts had redefined, obliterated or consigned
to nothingness the unwritten, deeply etched memories
of peoples who had walked this land longer than anyone
can rightly ascertain.

Now I walk the land whereon I stand
to meet the past beyond my past
that has been forever, never known.

Aditi, goddess of the seven dimensions of the cosmos,
celestial light that flows through the universe,
permeates the consciousness of sentient beings,
mother of humankind,
I see you here,
Aataentsic, who, seeking for healing herbs,
tripped and fell through a hole in the sky,
and was caught in the wing-arms of the Great Geese,
who set her up on the back of Turtle,
which became the earth we know,
where she gave birth to humankind.

Aditi, mother of us all,
Did the birds walk kiiqturtut around you
as you lay birthing?
And when the babies came,
Did they swaddle your babies in qulittaq,
spear fish with their kakivak to feed you,
and dance the qilaujaniq?

Aditi, mother of us all,
Did you send one of your sons,
a sage with knowledge drawn
from the fount of Vedas
to our Arctic snows?
and did he teach the Harvaqturmiut
about reincarnation? that the souls of the good
return to earth again as human beings
and the souls of the evil as beasts?

74

and to give the name of the noble dead
to the next newborn so they will be here again?
Nowhere else do we find this thought,
not even among those nearest them,
the Quernermiut, Haunektormiut, Hailignayokmiut,
Inuits with other sagas than ours.

Aataentsic, mother of us all,
I stand enthralled in the presence of your children,
with their stories and myths so like our own,
with names more liquid gold than any I've known:
Tsimshian, Kwakiutl, Nootka,
Mohawk, Mi'kmaq, Salish, Haida,
sounds that danced to caribou drums
ere the Kabloona came
and stilted their steps,
and changed their names,
and penned them in the rez.
And fed them booze,
and no, let me not go there,
for we dance to the future,
red, white, black, yellow and brown
we dance together around the totem
Maple, so white and red,
and the purposeful spruce
straight and tall
against blue-tinged snow.

Aditi Aataentsic, mother of us all,
Bless us now.

Note: All the following are Inuit words:

kiiqturtut: walking in a circle around a woman in travail
qulittaq: caribou-skin parka
kakivak : instrument used to spear fish
qilaujaniq: drum dance
kabloona: Inuit name for non-Inuit, i.e., white people

/ NOW AND THEN

/BY DAVID **ARNASON**

It's a bright March day, colder than it should be but still not very cold. The sun is bright on the snow that fell all day yesterday and then through the night. My grandmother was born here 126 years ago, but I have no idea what the weather was like. Probably something like today.

Everybody had come down with smallpox. Well, not everyone, but pretty close. Her two older sisters had it and came out marked, but my grandmother was somehow immune through all that tragic winter. It was mostly infants and old people who actually died, and because the ground was frozen and there was no way of burying them, their bodies were piled on the roofs of the makeshift huts they lived in. That was so the wolves wouldn't eat them before spring came and they could be planted in the earth.

That's the story my mother told me, and I believe it. Looking out over the lake from where I sit it is easy to believe that you are at the North Pole and nobody else exists in the whole world. My mother knew a verse in Cree that one of the children from the reserve near where she lived had taught her on the way to school. She said she thought it was a dirty verse, because he laughed when she recited it aloud. She never forgot it and after she taught it to me, I never forgot it either. I know some Cree speakers but I don't dare recite the verse for them, because it might just be nonsense, or so corrupted by my mother's memory and then my own that it might make no sense.

My grandmother died in 1964. She was eighty-eight years old. The night she died I went to the beer parlour in Libau with many of the mourners, including my uncle who lived with her and took care of her. Everybody left, and then there were only the two of us. He didn't want to go back to the house where his mother had died, so I took him home with me to Transcona where I lived at the time. The next day we went to the zoo, and the following day to the planetarium. When I finally took him home to Libau, everybody was upset because no one knew what had happened to him. Now he's dead too.

Last year I lived for several months in Kiel, Germany. The weather wasn't much better than it is here in Gimli, but I was happy because nothing in Kiel triggered memories. Everything was brand new and none of it tied to a past that meant anything to me. We travelled all around Europe in the wonderful trains, and we visited cathedrals laden with history, but it was somebody else's history and so it did not weigh on me.

My grandmother's house had a parlour, a room reserved for special visitors, and it had an old piano that was hopelessly out of tune and one of those strange desks with hundreds of tiny drawers and a curved slatted front cover that went up and down. There was a small chesterfield with an antimacassar and my grandfather's books, untouched since the day he put a shotgun in his mouth and pulled the trigger some fathomless time ago. I used to go to his grave on a summer's day and marvel at the granite slab that marked it. It was only years later that I learned that the granite slab marked his father, and my grandfather was in a grave nearby marked only by a row of white stones.

My mother grew sweet peas in her garden. My father planted wooden stakes and wove a web of string for the sweet peas to climb. On the south side of the house Mother grew hollyhocks, red and yellow and white. There was a plum tree in the bush near the house, and my mother picked it to make jam every September. She planted two small spruce trees that she found in the ditch in the curved flower garden near the road, one for me and one for my brother. They are still there, though many other families have grown up in that same place.

We had a ghost. Her name was Ricka, and she had come from Iceland around the turn of the century. My mother had nursed her in the nursing home, and she came to live with us when I was only about three. I remember her sitting in a rocking chair, with her long grey hair braided, and singing to herself. She had a picture of the baby she had given birth to in Iceland and who had died before he was a year old. I didn't know at that time that death came to children, and it was a frightening revelation. She ate oatmeal porridge and she broke up pieces of toast into her cereal. Then one day she was simply gone. No one explained to us what had happened, and we didn't ask in case she had died. I still don't know.

We used to shop at the Lakeside Trading Company on the corner of Centre and Main in Gimli. You could buy anything there from food to hardware, and the building smelled strongly of leather from the horse harnesses that hung from the walls. I remember barrels of flour and of raisins and of oatmeal. You made a note and gave it to the clerk. Then he walked around the store gathering up your merchandise, and he wrote down the numbers in a book. I never saw any money change hands, though it was wartime and my mother tore out pages from my ration book to give to the clerk. I loved my ration coupons, those brightly coloured scraps of paper, and I hated to watch them disappear.

I fell hopelessly in love in the first grade with a bossy little girl named Irene. She always made me carry her books home, though she lived only a couple of blocks north of the school and I lived a mile and a half away in the country south of town. I was always half a-dreams those days, and though my parents knew my penchant for getting lost in daydreams they became worried when I didn't get home till well after dark. Then one day, I was told that I could go home with Irene and play with her until nine o'clock when my parents would pick me up. We played all sorts of games, all of them of her invention and all of which involved her dominating me in subtle ways. The next day at school she did not appear. She was missing for a whole week. Finally I asked a classmate about her, and he told me that she had moved away to Winnipegosis. I still fall in love with bossy girls.

And I suppose that is why I am telling you all this. The amplitude of these anecdotes is proportional to their distance from me in time. I think I am growing old, and I don't want to. I have been blindsided by life. Just moments ago everything was expectation. I had plans. I lived in many different futures in my imagination, and I slept well at night and dreamed dreams of power and success. Now, I want to live in the past. I would be willing to live my life over exactly as it happened, taking the good with the bad, as if it were a movie that I could replay whenever I wanted.

But of course life doesn't do you that sort of favour. I remember riding an Icelandic pony high in the mountains of Iceland. The trip was seventeen kilometres, and the highest eight were in deep snow. We followed an ancient trail marked by cairns and the horses took us through a landscape so rough and jagged I would never have set out on it if I had known in advance what to expect. Still, every moment of that ride is as fresh in my mind as if it had just happened.

I look forward to spring, though it will take me to my birthday and to the knowledge that I cannot recover all those things I have lost. My unplanned future is hurtling towards me and I am helpless to resist it. Lately I have begun to dream of houses with secret rooms that contain artifacts from the nineteenth century, gas lamps and old irons and lockets with pictures of beautiful women carved in ivory. I am unreasonably happy in these dreams, and when I waken from one of them I am desperate to recover it.

Sometimes my children arrive in my dreams in the guises of their former selves, but never as they are now that they have moved on and made their own lives. Sometimes I am a child myself, and those are the most troubling dreams. Once, my brother and I found eight puppies in a brush pile in the spruce bush across the road from where we lived. The mother was a yellow dog of indeterminate breed and she let us approach and pet the puppies. In memory, this is one of the happiest moments of my life, but in dreams I am full of trepidation. I sense how powerless I am to save those pups, though in real life we did save them, bringing them home to Mother and finding new homes for them all.

Rabbits. I remember rabbits in the bush near home. I set snares for them and skinned them for their fur, and Mother cooked them and we ate rabbit stew. They seemed distant and other then, deserving of their fates, but now I have rabbits living in the back yard of my house in Winnipeg, and I am concerned about them, fearful of dogs on the loose and feral cats. I have given them names and learned to identify one from the other. I bring them food, sunflower seeds and rye bread. They have become so tame that I can walk close to them and they will not move. It bothers me that they are so trusting.

Since I was young, I have wanted to buy a convertible and drive through our too short summers with the top down. I always thought that I would get one some time in the near future. I rented one in California and drove through the starry desert night in February and I was happy. But I have not yet bought one, and it looks as if I probably never will. It was a small dream and easily realizable and yet it failed and continues to fail me.

I should make lists, try to figure out what I want and what I need and put my life in order. But I know that I would lose the lists, that the priorities I set would never arrive in the correct order. I know because I have tried. I have bought electronic organizers and failed even to learn how to use them.

I miss important meetings and forget about important dates. Yet if I do remember, I am always precisely on time.

And meanwhile important events occur. Countries go to war, and thousands are slaughtered in the most inhumane ways. Innocent people are tortured together with the guilty without anyone much noticing the difference. Whole galaxies are whirling out of control. Black holes in space are swallowing stars and spinning them into some unimaginable other place. And I am living in the past, living in memories that need careful examination and I don't have much time to get it right. So, a beginning.

/ SOME JOURNAL ENTRIES

/ BY MARTHA **BROOKS**

27 July 99

When I'm feeling frustrated with editors, I have to refer to my own claim: What some writers may think of as tedious rewrites, I think of as perpetual promise.

26 October 99

I am called a playwright. In actual fact I no longer write plays. But my journey into playwrighting gave me power—an understanding of voice stripped to its barest bones—and like all travellers who have been away and then return to give illumination back to the community, I was able to give something back to my fiction writing.

3 June 01

Sunday in the neighbourhood. Screen door letting in Sunday sounds, smells—somebody's bacon frying—another yard where stones with a sharp clomp clap are being reordered and piled. Miss Walker strolls slowly by beyond the grape leaves, with her cat on its blue leash. I am reading while robins call to each other (building nests for this year's crop of fledglings) about jazz voices from the past, Sylvia Syms, Maxine Sullivan, Bobby Tucker—life and music on 52nd Street in times where second-line musicians made number two scale at $66 a week.

13 May 2003

Fiction, then, can be a tool for breaking down barriers, a tool to chip away at bigotry. At least for the time it takes to read, a book becomes a persuasive vision of the (often) unimagined life.

23 November 03

Back from Iceland—the land of sagas and giants, volcanoes, geysers and trout steams. A journey back to the land of my ancestors. My own profound connection with the prairie landscape now seems like historical displacement.

16 October 04

It's only good when it's working. Which is about five percent of the time. Anybody who thinks that writing for a living might be a good idea had better know that and get over it. Truth is, days go by. The screen glows. You have applied your ass to that chair for hours at a time. Nothing is happening. Phones ring. Emails bother you. You go for a walk. You go to Berlin, where people who've read your last book ask: Did you know somebody like this? Because of course when it's working it's real to the reader. Now they can't believe you made it up! They want to know: Did someone close to you commit suicide? Was your father a bastard? Did your mother die when you were a child?

You meet a man in Berlin, a famous writer, much more famous than you, and he says that writing for him is a joy—pure joy. You think that he is lying. You bet he has bad days. He just doesn't want to share that information.

But you're glad of the five percent when for you the world cracks open and you fall inside and the walls inside your words are illuminated and shimmering with life. Life so real, so visceral and palpable that your readers believe it. And see themselves. Or find a piece of themselves again—a piece they thought had been lost forever. That's why you're a writer.

15 March 06

So writing, the creation of fiction *is* a kind of madness. But you're also quite mad without it—without the act of creation. If you are an artist, if you've taken up the call, so to speak, once you've opened that door it can't be shut again. Not without the knock on the other side that must be answered. To refuse it invites pathology. The only thing is to recognize the need to do it and make good and straight and clean with it. Then the beast is satisfied. Will lick its paws and let you rest for a while.

18 March 06

Went to see the Neil Young film *Prairie Wind* last night and listening this morning to his 1992 release, *Harvest Moon*. Am reminded that a song is such a pure thing. And Neil is a purist—no matter how many people he has onstage playing and singing with him, it's all about the song, the lyrics, the integrity of the piece and its intention to connect with the listener in some way, the tough and tender message not lost in fancy delivery.

/ BONES, FOR JOHN BERGER

/ BY MEEKA **WALSH**

"I'm looking for peace. Maybe I'm being morbid but I'm feeling restless and I know I'm looking for peace. Listen to this. *What reconciles me to my own death more than anything else is the image of a place . . .*" She lifted her pretty eyes from the page and looked at him.

"What are you telling me?" he looked back at her. "Are you saying that being well-placed is adequate payback for dying? That you'd go, so long as you're content with where? Get away."

"Not now," she returned. "I mean, not now but when it's time. I'll tell you—to hold off the evil eye, an untimely angel, a rabid fruit bat—that what I'm saying is—when I'm old, three score and ten and another score that would make me ninety and add a bonus of five because I've never smoked. In other words, a long life. But give me this—I have to know where, need to know, and then have it known so that there will be no mistake. Know that it's here that I'm put, placed, located."

Two fine, sensual, healthy people. It's summer and they're sitting on the hard sand at the edge of a lake and their legs, like the stalks of cut willows, drink the clean, grey water that washes the shore without haste or wasted movement on a sunny and balanced afternoon.

She holds a thin book. It's called *And our faces my heart, brief as photos.* She's read it through before. Reads it often. It lends itself to reading aloud in sections which she also often does, and he listens because he's learned that she picks carefully. He's learned to pay note. These readings aren't idle. "*. . . a place where your bones and mine are buried, thrown, uncovered, together.*" She's picked up where he'd stopped her, put in a word for life, indicated his preference for the warm present.

It's the middle of summer and they've spent enough time at this lake, near a small fishing town, a place where she's always come, all her life, all her life's summers, all of memory's summers back to the beginning even before memory called up words or words coloured memory—they've spent enough time in the sun exposing skin on either side of the searing hours to have turned the colour of honey. (She remembers being a reed of a girl and thinking summer, and the time she lived each year by the lake, was as long as the time she didn't, so profound was the presence of this place that two months near the water occupied the same time as all the months in the city.)

She looks over at him, this man she loves, and she thinks of spooning buckwheat honey from a jar, dark and thick and lustrous, slow and viscous. She thinks of its heavy smell, how the smell rises when she heats it to add to a cake in which the key ingredients are the dark honey and strong tea. She looks at the skin on his upper arms where the surface is uninterrupted by the dark hairs she's come to think of as elegant, which cover his forearms, his chest, his belly, his legs. Threads for weaving in a rug that would be as weightless and fine and costly as the hairs combed from an alpaca. His skin is buckwheat honey. "Mine too," she thinks. "Mine is also smooth and lustrous and aromatic. Bears, with their strong abrasive tongues, would love us to death if they found us here by the water and they were hungry.

In Greece, she was told by friends, the honey is dark. And there are other parallels too, with this place she loves.

"Did you know," they'd said, one day when these friends from Greece were visiting and they'd all gone out walking, she wanting to show them this very special place, "did you know that you have chamomile growing everywhere here, just like in Greece?"

"No," she'd answered. "Show me. I didn't know. What I know about chamomile I learned from the Beatrix Potter books; when the Flopsy Bunnies were naughty and ate the wrong things they had to drink chamomile tea for the stomach which I also do and always feel better because I would have wanted nothing more than to live in a cozy small cave at the base of a tree in a set of rooms furnished with tables and chairs and little beds of the absolutely right proportions, which real furniture in a house never is, for children. With cupboards and dishes and white aprons and friendly small animals, all of whom could speak and never had anything really unkind to say."

They pointed out the chamomile, which was everywhere, once she knew what to look for. There it was, growing flat and soft with its flowers like very small daisy heads and the buds, soft round green balls like unopened mimosa blossoms. By the road in the clay and grit and sandy soil, in the cracks of the odd sidewalks laid down inexplicably on one part only of the main street—thick, old, intermittent slabs mixed from the same recipe as the coffered ceiling of the Pantheon in Rome—used in these two places only, two thousand years intervening and then the knowledge lost. And also in the grounds around the old school. Oh, the school. Here I go, memory. The limestone and brick three-storey school with the big doors right in the middle of the building's flat front and the tall windows that drank in the light and the wide front stone steps with the metal shoe scraper lodged in that same concrete of the lost technique, but all of that aside, it was the fire escape. On one side of the school, from the ground rising up to a door without a handle that opened from the third storey stood the fire escape. Let me be clearer. The fire escape was central to that town's every child as an absolute and true measure. You confirmed your verity in relation to that structure. No question. In the summer the school was empty, sealed. There were no entrances and no exits. Rectangular, solid and mute. Flat all around. No columns or arches or cornices, no ledges. A practical, rational stone and brick box, but appended to it was opportunity, chance.

A galvanized tin chute hooked to the wall of the school from the third floor to the ground, straight down finishing in a short stiff lip that guaranteed your stagger at the end. The fire escape must be challenged. Upended, mounted bottom to top. No one child passing by could deny it. And if you had the stuff to make it to the top and then loosen your grip on the tin curls that formed the upper edges of the chute on either side, make yourself let go and land at the bottom (which was the inevitable part) and make yourself do it again, then you knew there was nothing coming in the rest of your life you couldn't make your way through. Because, for sure, you did it alone—up and down—alone with your queasy gut, alone with whatever incantatory thing you told yourself.

The chute was like half of a big tin tube, so climbing wasn't just a matter of getting up. You took off your shoes and your socks or you unbuckled your sandals; you needed your feet to work the round sides, using them like monkey hands. Then you set them apart wider than your shoulders to make a tight cork of your body, remembering gravity and the polish on the surface from weather and bum shines. You counted on the grip of damp kid feet pliable as Plasticine and you planted them there on the curve, your both hands on the curled edges, and you started out. The first of it was easy; you were bigger this year and up wasn't so far. I can do this. The tin was warm and smelled like splashed water sizzling off a heated stove element. You made yourself look back—couldn't leave it alone—to see how far up your braggadocio had hauled you—and you were up. Far enough up that a backward fall onto the dirt and cinders and spare grass and chamomile would hurt the breath out of you. Too high to shrug, push yourself off and do a backward jump down. Too high now. There you were, alone with nobody, so you had to be the kid you were and the kid's adult too and the adult looked at the wrists supporting the hands that held you not up and not down and not safe yet either, and you noticed that these wrists were thin kid's wrists and that a lot was riding on them and this same grown-up looked tenderly down at the brown feet wedged against the sides of the chute so that the toes were going white at the ends and that made the dirt under some of the nails seem worse than would ordinarily have been evident and also that the little pink hump on the instep from where a mosquito had bitten yesterday was quite pink and maybe infected and then you were the kid again and only you were going to get to the top or stay partway up forever until you fainted and slid to the bottom and cracked your head and your brains fell out and you would never be right again. So you monkeyed your way up, almost there and so high up, this third storey high, that a wind whistled and the chute rattled and you looked only straight in front of you with your head low so all you could see was the polished grey tin. Your eyes were full of it, brain colour, and maybe you'd gone blind from the height and the strain and what you were seeing was the inside of your head and now how would you get down. You let one hand ease off the rail and clutched at the flat of the platform at the top and on your stomach pulled all yourself onto it and lay there. And now was the worst part because nothing in the world was higher up than you were except the shingle roof and you didn't want to be there either. Something inside you bleated out a series of n's, a living-thing whimper that wasn't any part of a word. Only in nightmares did you fly and then never fast enough or high enough to get safe but part of you wanted to belly-balance on the platform rail and see if maybe this time flight would work and you didn't care what happened so long as all this ended. This was something bad and awful and how did you come to be here? Something terrible and bad was happening and like the strange and unformed things that frightened you when you were alone, whatever it was was always going to be in your life and you knew this was true and you were as alone as you feared to be.

Then you were hurtling down the fire escape and there was nothing in the world outside the sound and the grey metal and it was never going to be otherwise, and then you were on the ground and brushing off your knees and sick and dizzy and happy and proud. Also—you'd learned some things.

"Did you ever do anything like that?" she asked. "You know, dare yourself silly?"

"Well," he said, "I did the winter thing, tongue on frozen metal. It was at school in grade three and I put my tongue on the railing outside the door. A grade sixer told me—do it, twerp, or I'll cream you—and he pushed my face down. So, I didn't exactly volunteer but I guess I didn't have to do it. The bell rang and all the kids filed inside. Some Christian soul must have mentioned it to a teacher because mine came out with a kettle of warm water and poured it over the rail, and my tongue and I were free, but I remember that it seemed to me I was stuck at least an hour. It was horrible, truly horrible, because you couldn't scream or move or anything. Pretty effective torture, actually. Once I was freed, the worst part, and what's stayed with me, was a sense of bewilderment and injustice because the teacher, for some reason, was mad at me. Without being able to articulate it then, I recognized that everyone hates the victim and that the best thing not to be or not get caught out being, was weak. Which, when you think of it, limits your options pretty profoundly. I mean—don't show fear or compassion or weakness or concern. Don't be vulnerable or irresolute. Don't waver or question your actions or anything. That's a lot to learn that's pretty sour from one small frozen wet tongue on a rail."

"You see how what shapes you forever is what happened when you were a kid?" she told him. "And you see how it's not just big things, it's anything that ends up being something that matters to you that can do it?" She went on. "And also, when you're a kid you don't understand a whole bunch of things. I mean the things in the world that other people are doing or why. But actually, as a kid you do know a huge amount of other stuff. You really are more in touch—like Wordsworth's idea of children trailing knowledge or something."

The day was warm and perfect and here they sat, at the water's edge, two honey-brown people smooth with accomplishment, easy with the success they'd earned as adults and far far from the children they'd been who'd been curdled by fear at different times in their young lives.

"Listen to this," she says, picking up her book again. "Listen to what John Berger has to say about his bones, after he's dead. *They are strewn there pell-mell. One of your ribs leans against my skull. A metacarpal of my left hand lies inside your pelvis. (Against my broken ribs your breast like a flower.*) You see, he must believe that some essence remains with the bones, that it matters where and with whom your bones end up. So, I have a plan for mine, and yours, if you agree."

But he interrupted her because he was still thinking about the past and not about a distant, sunless future. "What, about your confrontation with the fire escape, beyond the mastery of it and the confidence it must have given you, do you think was so shaping? That was one of the shaping events you were talking about, wasn't it? But was that what you drew from it—confidence and pride?" He wanted to know.

"Wouldn't it be easy," she answered, "to select the tools and qualities you needed from single events? Picture it, like shopping or even a challenge to wrest a golden vessel from a dragon in order to hold courage or nobility for all your life? There, you could say, got that one. Then checking your attribute list you'd want courage, nobility, grace, generosity, peace, tolerance, and out you'd go to pluck them from opportunity and by the time you'd finished you'd be this dazzlingly whole human being. I don't mean to sound arch. I'm just musing here. But you're right, there was more at the time and my remembering that day, which to most everyone else would seem to be without incident, picks it out as one of those significant kid things we're talking about.

"I've said this before—about memory and how it slides things around sometimes, to accommodate need or to make sense of events. So I can't be sure that my presentiment up there at the top of the fire escape that something awful was going to happen (I mean beyond my trying to fly from the ledge or faint and fall and crack my head open), something real and central that confirmed basic, entrenched, core fears, like being abandoned or finding my parents dead in their bed and being an orphan and all alone was, in fact, pre-knowledge or whether I put it together later. That's what I mean about memory.

"So what happened that day was this, and I know I'm remembering this part right. Once I'd pulled myself together, after the slide, and kind of strutted stiff-legged and proud around the playground and tried out some of the swings and stood again on the ground at the bottom of the fire escape to measure its height once more and check it out narrow-eyed with knowledge, I headed back to our cottage. And almost home I remembered that my parents had told me, don't be gone long, when I'd headed out earlier. Have you noticed even now as an adult, that instructions that come to you from the other side of a screen door never seem really important? It's like the mesh filters out the weightiness and only the sounds—individual, light and fragmented sift through and kind of drift off? Well, anyway, I hadn't paid attention and while time means something different for kids, it now occurred to me that I had been gone long, and now what?

"Don't be gone long because why? What was going to happen? Why be not be gone long? And if gone long, then what? I ran the rest of the way home. The car was gone. Okay, I told myself. Both parents drive, one's gone off in the car and the other one is in the cottage, waiting—mad, but waiting. I'm going to get it but I've come down the fire escape and I can handle this.

"I opened the screen door to the kitchen and called out, 'I'm home.' There was no answer. 'Hello,' I called and moved into the living room. No one there, no one calling back. 'Hello,' I continued to call and checked the bedrooms. All empty. I went back out the screen door because whoever had stayed behind waiting for me must be sitting out front, in the yard. 'Hello, I'm back.' The lawn chairs were empty. Down at the beach, they're on a towel, reading. I remember walking slowly now, to the sand path that led from the front yard to the beach, real panic rising to my mouth and moving down from my belly to my legs, walking slowly because if there was no one on the sand then the thing I feared most in my life and knew would happen one day was happening. I was alone. I'd been left behind. I'd been abandoned like I always knew I would be so I was in no hurry to confirm this worst ugly thing in my whole life, the heavy dark thing so big I could never move it aside or see beyond it to anything else. It was, by itself, the end. I guess if someone had asked me, as a kid, what do you think death is like, actually been mean enough to ask a kid that, to make them really think about it, I would have described what I just did—this huge dark, heavy thing.

"I kicked off my sandals to take up more time and I stood on the path with the warm sand under my bare feet. Then I walked from the path with its small banks of sand and grass and chokecherry stems to the beach. No one there belonged to me. The beach might as well have been empty although it wasn't, because no one there was for me. Other mothers and children and couples and people lying on beach blankets alone in the sun not knowing that a heavy black thing was going to fall on top of all of them and me, soon. I couldn't believe that the lake (this same one we've got our feet in today on this perfect afternoon) which in the morning had been blue and grey and quiet with only goosebumps of sun on its surface raised by the light wind and warmed through midsummer to the perfect swimming temperature, this lake with its tiny quick fish in schools briefly at the shore, this lake with sailboats and motorboats and kids on animal floaters and gulls, that it was now all wrong. I couldn't believe the sun would stop and the sand would grow cold. That all the sounds would cease—the birds and the wind and the children and the small waves at the shore and that plane overhead and our ears would be stuffed with silence. I turned and walked back to the sheltered path and there my legs stopped and I sat huddled in incredulous terror that everything I'd feared worst was happening. At my back was one of the banks of the path that had been pushed to a low rise through years of feet scuffling sand on the way to castles or a swim. The sand was warm and I pushed my little shoulder blades into it. At least it's warm, I remember thinking. I leaned my head back. What did it matter if I got sand in my hair and down the neck of my jersey? In misery I lifted my eyes and there were the pines my father had planted when he'd built the cottage. Tall now, and thick, set in a row but each tree with its own character. So, some were stout and some narrower and each reached out to the water or the sky or toward the town, as it chose and they continued to stand and their branches balanced the wind and dipped in a sure and measured manner, moving with the rhythmic breath of a creature at rest and, without willing it, my breathing, which had been rapid and erratic, slowed, and we breathed together, me and the line of trees in my yard.

"So long as this row of trees stands guarding me, so long as the black thing doesn't crush them, I could be okay, I maybe could make it. Understand, I wasn't planning ahead, thinking of my life as an abandoned child, I wasn't planning meals or my education or where I'd go when winter came. I was a kid and signs and bargains drawn meant a lot. Let the pine trees stand and I'll be fine, at the count of seven. After seven, if the trees are still there I'll be okay. Deal? Who was I talking to, who was I bargaining with? And then I remembered my huge accomplishment from earlier in the day, conquering the fire escape. I counted to seven, slowly and in a quiet voice, but a voice that came from the throat of a person who'd gone up the tin chute and hurtled down and had come through it fine—six, seven. The trees stood. I let my body fall into the shape of the warm sand nest that cradled me and the pines soughed and I had a sense, whatever flicker of such things a kid can grasp, that things would go on beyond me, that I would be here, all right. Here for a long enough time and the pine trees would go on beyond me, and the lake and sand beach and the wind and other birds than the ones I could hear and other kids. I guess, as I think of it, I had a glimmer of the idea of eternity. But I also know it had to do with that row of trees still behind us today in my yard. Anyway, I hold to that same conviction now." She examined the indefinite outline of her feet in the water at the shore.

"Then what happened?" he asked. "What did you do then? Did your parents come back soon?" he wanted to know, concerned for this child left by her young self.

"Oh, yes. They probably weren't gone more than a couple of hours. We'd been invited to someone's house for lunch or something and I guess, exasperated, which my mother was a lot, they just left without me. You wouldn't do it today and they probably shouldn't have done it then either, not because it wasn't safe but because it was kind of mean. They were big into teaching lessons by demonstration and here I am now, this entirely responsible human being but actually little more secure than I was then. I'm not sure what the lesson was that I learned. I guess punctuality or not to take instructions through a screen door. But they came back. Obviously, I survived. I wasn't one of those kids who would do anything stupid like turn on the stove or play with matches. They actually knew me, from the outside anyway, better than I knew myself. They figured I'd eventually come home and sit and wait. Which, from their perspective, was exactly what happened. About the terror and panic—evidently they had no idea. As a kid all you would have been able to articulate was 'I was scared,' but I was learning to save these things for the row of pines. After all, wasn't I the kid who'd mastered the fire escape?

"It's interesting, this notion of learning from experience. I'd been schooled, as this skinny, dreamy, gritty kid to learn from experience. I was this kid who always came awake partway through explanations so that everything was always indistinct (I think of my entire childhood as a kind of swampy jumble of directions and instructions only half understood). *Let this be a lesson to you* was something my parents said often so I'd take something in, in whatever way I did and tuck it away with my growing stock of knowledge gained and I'd move on, or up, since I was adding years, growing, an ascension to

wisdom and maturity. And I was learning things, learning to make my way and extract-
ing stuff, sustenance from my didactic little life. I was always a serious kid.

"I can't think of a thing I would have valued that wasn't learned here, in the sum-
mer, at the lake. I know I resisted learning at school; nothing there ever made real
sense to me. Like the phases of the moon. In grade five, I think, we were learning the
phases of the moon, which was not a poetic exercise and actually—what are the phas-
es of the moon? It doesn't click into place in segments; it's a continuous process: full,
to gone, to sliver, to crescent, to wobbly half, full half and then miraculously and to me,
suddenly, whole, and the going again and gone and so on. But here we were in school,
using a compass, which in itself was a challenge for me because I never had the right
length of pencil to put in the metal grip at the opposite end of that ice pick of a device.
They should never have allowed children to handle those things. Anyway, we were to
use the compass to draw a series, however many, of little circles and then fill them in
in the various stages of waxing and waning but I don't remember those terms being
applied because they would have caught me, I would have seized on those words,
plucked them from the lesson, held them to my thin chest and run with them out the
door, down the hall with the waxed and polished brown linoleum and out of the build-
ing that constrained me in a state of confusion from grade one through to the time
when I moved to the next school for junior high. We were supposed to draw a series
of small circles and fill in first a sliver, then a crescent and so on to a whole complete
dime-sized disk and then back down. I did it, more or less, and even while I was doing
it, and still today, the question is this—which part was the moon and which part was
moon gone? Did the dark part you sideways-leaded in with your pencil represent the
moon or its absence? Think of it. Was the black the missing part or the present part?
I never raised my hand and asked, Miss McGregor, is the dark part the moon or where
the moon is missing? I was smart enough to say nothing.

"So everything of value was learned here. How to swim underwater, make yourself
go down and drag along the bottom—sand and stone and little fish. I don't remember
ever running out of air. If I think of it now, I stayed under a half-day at a time. Honest.
And how to thread a fish hook through a salted minnow sideways so it swam alive at
the end of your line and seduced every hair-bone-filled, sweet-fleshed perch in the lake.
How to sharpen one end of a willow wand, stripping away the grey brown skin, then
the inner bitter green ribbon to get to the white wood. To make it a sharp enough point
to puncture and hold a raw wiener to char it over a driftwood fire on the beach when
it got dark and the sand was cold and sliding under your feet and a few gritty grains
got into the bun and still it was the best you ever ate and no one could cook them bet-
ter. Knowing how to open a pocket knife—and the fact of owning one—and use it to
slim a branch so you could cook meat on it meant you could survive in the wilderness
if your plane crashed. Where else other than here could you learn that? And to identi-
fy a quartz crystal and take it and another one into a dark place and smash them
against each other and see and smell a spark and now you had the magic of fire. What,
in school, could match that? Those were the things I grew on. Things learned here."

He watched her telling him about this place. She'd told him, right from the start of their being together, that nowhere was more loved than here, no place was she happier, more at home than here. He'd found it comfortable, a nice place, an honest, spare landscape and that about it appealed to him too and he loved her and that was another reason to favour it.

"When we're lucky," he told her, "we invest a landscape with meaning, we attach ourselves to it and are the fortunate ones who can say—we are rooted here."

"That's right," she said, "Except it wasn't me who invested meaning here; it was here which gave me meaning. Remember the row of pines, the wind, the lake that's always speaking. No, this is here. Before me, for me while I'm here alive, and then after. Of all of the things in my life that have changed, have slipped or washed away, this is always just as it is now. This is my fixed point. I start out from here. I site myself with all of this at my shoulder and when I look back, I'm located. Wherever it is I have to go I can find my way home. So, are you in?" she probed. "Are you with me, like this?" and she read again from the small book: "*The hundred bones of our feet are scattered like gravel. It is strange that this image of our proximity, concerning as it does mere phosphate of calcium, should bestow a sense of peace. Yet it does.*"

"I'm not going to dwell on this final resting place stuff indefinitely. In fact, once it's all settled I'll have no need to speak about it again. Think of it," she leaned toward him and rubbed her warm shoulder against his warm shoulder, "With you I can imagine a place where to be phosphate of calcium is enough. That's the end of that section in the book. Wonderful, isn't it? He loves her so much." She looked out over the lake.

"And I love you that much," he told her, "and I don't terribly care for discussions of this sort but the last part you read sounded as much like a marriage proposal as anything else and I promise you we'll be together now and for the fourscore and ten, et cetera, that you've already added up and then forever after in whatever form that is. Now, enough of that while the sun is shining," and he bumped her warm shoulder hard with his to call it to an end.

"Deal," she said. "It's a deal. You and me, pared, when the time comes, down to clean phosphate of calcium, under my susurrant pines and with lake as cello or piccolo we'll be rock happy forever. I won't speak about this again. I'm content." And when he turned his head to take her in fully he could see that she truly was.

It was a fine summer and the mild weather lasted into the fall. They continued to drive out to the lake for weekends until finally the nights grew too cold and they closed the cottage and made it secure and began to plan their earliest return. By November the water would begin to freeze at the shore and the late fall storms on the lake would be over. But this year was different.

In the city one weekend there were high winds. A few branches lost brittle ends but there was no other damage. Settling into a late dinner in front of their fireplace, a ritual they said carried them over the winter, they were interrupted by a phone call from a friend whose newer cottage was built to allow year-round use.

"Did you hear about the storm?" he asked.

"I think so," she answered. "At least I heard a report on the radio that said there were high winds, very high winds at the southern end of the lake. Was that the storm?"

"It was," he said, "and there's been a fair bit of damage. I've been down to your place and I think you should come out."

"Were you all right?" she asked.

"We've had some damage, nothing that can't be fixed, but if I were you I'd drive out." They talked briefly about other things and then hung up.

"There's been a problem at the lake. Apparently a storm. But we're high. I can't think what could have happened at our place. Still, Michael said I should drive out so I'm going to, tomorrow. Can you come with me?" What she wanted to do was pull on her parka, open a second-floor window, launch herself from a sill and fly to her lake in the instant. Instead, she said, "We'll get up early, eat breakfast in the car and come right back. I'm sure it's nothing."

Something about the qualities or properties of lead had always drawn her. Probably that it was potentially deadly. It had been removed as an ingredient in paint when it was discovered that babies gnawing on crib bars painted with it in nursery colours suffered serious and permanent damage. How many, she wondered. And why were they left awake in their cribs long enough to absorb sufficient quantities of paint to harm themselves and what inarticulate grief impelled them to gnaw in the first place? Then there was the metal's surprising weight and poreless density. She associated it with death and sealed containers. Also there was the smell she tied to first attempts at learning to print in school. Those were lead pencils, weren't they? She'd had difficulty making her pages tidy and couldn't master the mimicry necessary to form the alphabet and always had to erase and rework her papers and still the letters didn't stand straight as soldiers.

The lake, open long past its usual time, moved heavy and dark, like rumbling sheets of lead pushed into reluctant movement from under the surface. She'd never seen it like that. Not wild and dangerous and quick as it was in a summer storm, now it was sullen and intractable, aggrieved and foreign. She could see it there, at the end of the road as they drove toward the cottage.

When they pulled into the driveway everything seemed the same. From the back of the cottage nothing appeared changed.

"It looks like we're okay," she said too soon. Then they walked toward the lake and the row of pines. They were still there, in a row. But now, instead of the solid pallisade guarding the cottage, protecting her through all her life, the sentries of her being, the staunch guarantors of a safe forever, they all leaned, all of them, to the cottage and could crush it and her and her summered past and her secured future if an unkind wind or the obdurate strange lake moved toward them again.

The path was there where it ought to have been but its high, warm sandy banks had been flattened and filled in by a sludge, a mass frozen where it had washed up from the lake into a taffy of sand and pine cones and wood chips and whatever else the lake had carried with it as it pushed forward and congealed in its unfamiliar tracks.

Their boots cracked this hard mix as they moved over it and down to the lake, which had pulled back to its habitual bed, gloomy and restive and dark as sheet metal.

The high water had gnawed and sucked the sand and earth from the high ground in which the row of pines had been rooted. Uneven caves were hollowed along the length of this row and the roots hung down like the limp and fleshy strings of pumpkin innards scooped for Halloween.

It occurred to her that before everything fell and cracked, now, while the frozen air held things fixed, she'd slide herself—maybe just briefly to try it—through this curtain of roots and under the mangled quilt of earth and grass and sand and lie quietly there at the core, in the heart and arteries of the trees she so closely loved.

Seeking the peace she'd felt necessary in order to carry on, she'd recognized this place. Its authority, its certainty had given comfort since she'd been a scrawny girl. John Berger had confirmed, and she herself had read to her lover, *What reconciles me to my own death more than anything is the image of a place,* and they'd made a pact just this past summer and agreed that from this she'd move on with the surety she required.

"And now what?" she asked. "What now?"

/ HANGING ON LION'S GATE BRIDGE, A WESTERN

/ BY BIRK **SPROXTON**

The bridge (*the lion, the gate*) shook deep
girders hooked into slush and slime
(under the watery heave and tide).

From the traffic roar a voice called,
"Hang on cowboy" so I leaned
into the rail, ready to slap leather.

He arrived quickly, a lone stranger,
hooked fingers into my jacket & held on,
his bike in one arm, me in the other.

We stood a moment trembling, a two-
wheeled four-legged ménage à trois,
men and bike, a grim tableau
hanging on the (shaking) sidewalk.

Then he was gone. Lean in the saddle
my partner faded, the sunset sank, the cars
galloped along. I stood alone, empty
arms hanging glad heart drumming
to the horsepower beat & the shim
shim shimmy of the bridge
                    a lion   a gate

/ JOHNNY CASH

/ BY VICTOR **ENNS**

True to form
I only leave
the car when
I get hungry.

We were somewhere
in Peace River country.
Only my parents knew
how to get to that farmyard.

I wear my
red & blue Carnaby St
jeans with white stars
running up my legs.

My T-shirt is red mesh and sleeveless
full of little round
holes, my nipples
jauntily say, hello Alberta!

I say a reluctant hello
to the boy who has gotta be
younger than me, and look
his head is shaved. Ha. Ha.

What does he know? His parents
are gone for two days.
They have left him in charge of
all that they have to keep them
for the winter.

He serves us buns and coffee,
the butter he churned
this morning. He is ahead
of me.

In the living
room he swings the record needle
over the spinning vinyl.
It's not the Beatles, hell no
It's Johnny Cash.

I don't know nothing
I don't know shit
I've been listening to a.m.
twisting the dial.

There is none of that up here.
Johnny is walking out
of Folsom, with the country
blues again. I can barely hear
this story.

My cousin sits back
and says *let's thank*
God for shotguns
and Johnny Cash.

Yesterday I shot this bear
coming toward the calf
on a rope, unknowingly
I had set bait.

I blew out the bear's heart
once or twice, he was
as surprised as I was.
I have what's left
hanging from a rope.

It was Johnny who was here
for me, who had a song to sing
when I had blessed blue nothing
but a dead bear to string.

Let us pray.
Say Amen!

/ JIMMY BANG'S SIREN BLUES

/ BY VICTOR **ENNS**

Been tryin to sleep, all I hear is sirens fillin up my head
been tryin to sleep, all I hear is sirens fillin up my head
spend each late night hour wonderin who's gonna end up dead.

Sirens in the morning, sirens in the afternoon
live close to the police station, firehall's 'round the bend
But the ambulance comes wailin every night around ten.

Been tryin to sleep, all I hear is sirens fillin up my head
been tryin to sleep, all I hear is sirens fillin up my head
spend each late night hour wonderin who's gonna end up dead.

Sirens in the daytime, more sirens late at night
I hear them through my window, no matter how tight
closed against the darkness, the wailin comes through the night.

Been tryin to sleep, all I hear is sirens fillin up my head
been tryin to sleep, all I hear is sirens fillin up my head
a bottle of booze on the nightstand, bottle of pills in my hand.

I'm listenin to the sirens, gettin closer tonight
I'm listenin to the sirens, gettin closer tonight
Maybe this one's for me, I've finally got it right.

/ MOONLIGHT REHEARSAL

An excerpt from a novel

/ BY ARMIN **WIEBE**

Gretna, Manitoba, Die Mennonitische Schule, October 31

Abend vor Allerheiligen. The Kanadier say Halloween. The Mennonitische Schule tries to for-bid the students from making celebration of such a pagan Katholisch fest. Prinzipal Schapansky in morning chapel speaks about October 31, 1517 and how Martin Luther nailed the 95 Theses on the church door at Wittenberg. Of course Funk finds much to schpott at in the hallway and the toilet. In Literatür class we read Hamlet *and the Prinz has back come to Denmark from Wittenberg, and so Funk, pious as a deacon's wife, asks Schapansky if that is the same Wittenberg as Luther's Wittenberg, and Herr Schapansky, who is hoch gelehrt in the United States, says, "Ja, Hamlet would be familiar with Luther's teachings," and he shows us in the Shakespeare text where the Dichter is making wordplay with Diet of Worms. Schapansky seems always pleased when Funk asks such a question and I wonder if Schapansky has awareness of Funk's behaviour when out of the sight of the elders. Our friend Kehler loves a Witzenkrieg also, and sometimes plays along with what Funk has started in class by asking one question that twists things so Funk will be the one with the red face.*

But Kehler stays no more in our room. To help him pay his Schulgeld, Kehler is working for Lutheran Baumeister, a German who offered Kehler room and board and work. So Kehler has no time for Funk and his Dummheit. He spends each minute in school working on his studien because in the evening he is working busy with the Baumeister.

I try to be diligent with my Studien also, but to be in this cramped room with Funk or alone with my thoughts for hour after hour leads me to schrecklich dreams. I fear this night, for this Abend vor Allerheiligen has awakened what I have so long tried to forget. Oh Funk, why did I let you lead me from my desk to partake in this Halloween custom? To go about in the darkness and push over toilet kiosks and smash face-carved pumpkins that people had set out with candles burning inside gave me too much remembering.

And then to hear Klavierenspiel through the frostich air. Prost simple Musik but Klavierenspiel it was, and then Funk says to me, this is the house where stays the Mexikaner Kehler. And so we nearer by went until through a window we could see a woman wearing marriage dress playing piano beside our Freund Kehler. Before I could still my heart, Funk was knocking on the door and then the woman with the white gown opens the door and Funk says to her that his friend is famous Klavierspieler von Russland and the woman us invites inside. Kehler is sitting still by the piano and his face doesn't look happy to see us there. But

Maria, the Jungfrau in the marriage dress, is so peppich and allürisch that Kehler matters little to me and I let her lead me to the piano bench. I think only to play some simple Volkslied like "Hänschen klein, geht allein" but when my stiff fingers reach for the keys there is only one place to begin and as soon as Beethoven's chord murmurs through the room I forget where I am and . . .

Beethoven Blatz rolled the practice grand piano to the centre of the rehearsal studio, positioning the instrument so the keys caught the pale moonlight sifting through the dusty Gothic windows. Waxed spots on the floorboards and the slightly raised piano lid gleamed; the glass lamp set near the music rest glinted. He felt for a match in his pocket, then decided there was no need.

Blatz tiptoed toward the orchestra chairs to grab the piano bench, but his eye caught the rotating stool in the corner, so on a whim he carried it to the piano and centred it in front of the keyboard. He sat down, reached for the pedals with his foot, then rose and spun the seat to raise it, then sat again, pulled the stool in closer, and adjusted the sleeves of his dress coat. His fingers touched the opening chord, then arpeggios trickled from his fingertips so softly even Blatz could barely discern whether his ears were hearing the piano or if his brain were merely echoing the melody his heart murmured day and night.

The adagio sostenuto, a hymn to Christ walking on moonlit waters—the argument he had used to justify the playing of music beyond the Bach hymns in the Gesangbuch —and the argument was not completely false: Beethoven Blatz felt the sustained slowness of the opening movement as a barely perceptible breathing, a bridge from the mildly stifling peace of the village to the footloose minuet of the allegretto with which he danced into the liberating thunderstorm of the presto agitato. Even that first time when his fingers had furtively fumbled over the racing arpeggios and fortissimo chords he had felt such a surge of longing and hope, and yes, confidence and belief that one day he too would break free from the smothering cloud he felt himself moving inside most of his days. Even that first time he stumbled through Beethoven's Sonata 14 in C sharp minor he had a dream that one day he would play the sonata through the way Beethoven had written it to be, free and unrestrained, played in a great open space with no fear of incurring the censure of dull slumbering souls, and he had wished he could move the piano out from the chalk dust school house into the open air, to the top of a mountain or perhaps a fishing boat moored twenty yards from the shore of the Black Sea.

Yet even now, when his heart and his fingers knew Beethoven's score from memory—for Blatz had copied the sonata from the library sheet music collection five times, each time noting more and more, and still he wished he could see the work in Beethoven's own hand, dreamed of travelling to Vienna to study Ludwig's manuscripts—even now he felt there was still a restraint to his playing, a failure to achieve a complete letting go, as if he were still furtively playing Beethoven's music in the school house, fearful that villagers whispered he had strayed from God.

Sonata quasi una Fantasia—a sonata, but almost a fantasy. Beethoven's subtitle suggested a discomfort with the confinement of the classical sonata form, a hesitant desire to break free: a state of mind Blatz felt matched his own. As his fingers rippled over and hammered the notes of the presto agitato through to the crashing end chords he felt as near to flight as he thought a man could get. But when the last chord faded he was always ready to return to the hymnal arpeggios of the opening movement. As he did so again this night in the rehearsal studio with the moonlight sifting through the dusty windows, he recalled the apocryphal story of how Beethoven had composed the Moonlight Sonata while playing for a shoemaker's blind sister on her poor harpsichord by moonlight after the wind snuffed out the candle. Blatz had read enough of Beethoven's history to know that Ludwig van had not given Sonata 14 the name Moonlight, that it had been named thus by the poet Ludwig Rellstab. Ludwig van Beethoven had named this music Sonata in c sharp minor op. 27 no. 2 and had dedicated the sonata to Giulietta Guicciardi. Blatz knew all this, but still a part of him believed the story of how Beethoven and a friend while walking down a dark street one night heard one of Beethoven's compositions being played inside a humble cottage. Stirred by this, Beethoven knocked on the door and discovered a blind girl who played by ear music she had learned while lurking outside the house of a lady practising on a piano. The thought of the great composer in a tiny room composing on a poor instrument this music that so obsessed him seemed to offer Blatz some hope that he too perhaps someday could create beauty.

Blatz's fingers entered the final third of the opening movement. Behind him, a skirt rustled. He hammered the right little finger melody, maintaining the arpeggios with his remaining fingers as a barely audible violin joined in, another note for the chords that punctuated the climbing and falling melody, blending in, not breaking out, but adding an amused tone to the adagio sostenuto, confusing Blatz with fear and desire that barely allowed him to play the movement through to the two-handed whole-note chord of the closing bar. Blatz smiled in the darkness now, and he paused a mere second before starting into the tripping minuet of the allegretto.

The violin bow rapped his right knuckles lightly. Blatz stopped, held his breath. Sonia's scent settled over him, tickled his nostrils.

"Always Blatz with that hundred-year-old German music," Sonia said in Ukrainian. "When will you open your ears to the twentieth century? Play some Rachmaninoff, Prokofiev, Shostakovich, yes, Shostakovich!"

Blatz turned on the stool. "But aber der Beethoven is a genius," he stammered in a mixture of German and Ukrainian. "The Sonata 14 is a bridge from das Klassische to das Romantische. Two traditions in one composition. Sonata quasi una Fantasia!"

"Ah yes, my dear Beethoven Blatz . . ." Sonia deftly flipped Blatz's hair off his forehead with her bow. ". . . the German genius moved forward with his times. He was no slave to Mozart or Hayden. He embraced the spirit of Napoleon and broke free of stifling tradition."

"Aber meine liebe Sonia, you cannot mean that Mozart or Haydn could ever be stifling!"

"Oh yes, my lovely man who would be Beethoven, oh yes, even Mozart stifles when turned into a god—an everlasting, unchanging god." Sonia pushed against Blatz's shoulder with her bow hand. He raised his heels to allow the stool to spin him around until he faced the keys. He reached out to play the opening chord, but Sonia pushed him into a further spin, which rolled the stool away from the piano. She pirouetted between Blatz and the piano, raising her violin to her chin and poising her bow on the strings in a single legato slur.

"Bitte wait!" Blatz cried. "Played right, Sonata 14 is as revolutionary and modern as any young Russian, yet Beethoven never forgets the sonorous nature of love."

"But Blatz, mein lieber Herr, the adagio sostenuto is not a love song, it is a funeral hymn by a genius who desired love but feared it more." Sonia's bow repeated the legato slur. Blatz, wide-eyed at her silhouette in the moonlight, breathed in her presence, a scent of toilet water mingled with the smell of his sisters. For a moment he feared the desire stirring in his trousers, became aware of his own smells, his seldombathed body, his rarely cleaned suit. Then the legato slur of Sonia's bow drew off into the opening chord of the adagio sostenuto and Sonia pirouetted out from between Blatz and the piano. Blatz, ignoring but not fighting the squirming in his trousers, rolled back to the keyboard and reached out for the opening chord. His eyes followed Sonia as she danced out of sight behind the raised piano lid for a bar of the repeating legato slur, emerging on the other side as her wrist raised to slide the bow over to the G string. Blatz started into the opening arpeggios, his fingers finding the keys effortlessly even as he gazed on Sonia's dancing feet, her dancing bow, her dancing shoulders draped with a fluttering shawl. Despite Sonia's pirouettes, despite her improvised harmony, Blatz played the adagio precisely with perhaps even more restraint than he would have used had he played it inside the village church, had there been a piano in the church. At the same time his eyes never wavered from Sonia's pirouetting figure and her bow flitting and floating from string to string, never playing Beethoven's melody, but always resonant, always sonorous, never a hint of discord. Even their breathing aligned, their unison gasp breaking the silence before Blatz's fingers trickled into the allegretto. Sonia's bow droned in contrast to the carefree trippling, then danced when the movement slowed, the violin building in tempo so that when Blatz reached the end of the allegretto he plunged into the presto agitato with nary a pause and for the first time in their playing Sonia's violin joined his piano in the melody and for the first time Beethoven Blatz felt that he had come close to the passion of Ludwig van. His heart hammered so ferociously he was awed for a moment that his body might splinter in the way of Beethoven's pianos when the composer had forced divine thunder from this mortal instrument. And all the while he felt hitched to Sonia's violin, led so fast he almost missed slowing down for the final hammering notes.

Panting, Blatz turned on the stool to gaze into Sonia's eyes. Her shoulders heaved as she gulped for air, but her violin never left her chin as she returned his gaze, her eyes gleaming darkly in the moonlight. Her bow moved back to the strings, caressed high notes so lightly the sound barely breathed in Blatz's ear.

At first Blatz thought Sonia was playing a Shostakovich violin concerto and for the first time he regretted not exploring beyond Beethoven, for he could hear how the piano might go well with the violin. Blatz had never allowed himself to improvise, never allowed himself to play by ear. A flash of horror called up the blind girl who had learned to play Beethoven's music simply from eavesdropping outside a window. Doubt shivered down Blatz's spine even as Sonia's violin rose to a pitch that called out to be tempered by bass chords and Blatz felt that as a man he must respond, that he must reach out. His mind counted down the scale to resonant chords, but before he could reach out for the keys Sonia started into a raucous scraping of the bow and sat down on his lap, continuing the zigzagging melody that cried out for crashing piano chords but her foot kicked out sending the stool swirling across the floor, leaving Blatz no choice but to reach out and clasp Sonia's squirming body to keep them from spilling onto the moonlit floor.

And still she played, her hips writhing in Blatz's lap as she drew the horsehair over the strings, writhing even when she paused as if she were listening to a piano bridge setting up the next violin solo. Her foot kept the stool in motion, kept Blatz away from the keys, kept him squirming with the ache to reach out to complete the music.

By now Blatz realized that Sonia was not playing Shostakovich or Prokofiev; she was composing, creating as she played, having used Shostakovich's notes as a stairway to a song of her own, a spilling of her own passion, raw music not yet shaped, not yet tamed, and the whispered rumour flashed through his head, the rumour that Sonia was a gypsy, that her dark eyes contained a history of roaming and sleeping on grass beneath wagons, hearing fiddlers dancing around campfires.

A flash of sheet lightning lit up his mind and he glimpsed a basket on the back step of a village house, saw a dark-eyed infant blinking from a smothering blanket.

Blatz gasped, turning sideways to gulp air, even as he pressed his cheek hard against the crocheted shawl covering Sonia's back and his long splayed fingers clutched her ribs as if sustaining a ten-note chord over endless bars.

. . . the presto agitato I just had entered when my ear began to detect mistonisch sounds as I played the high notes over the treble staff. I further played but when the mistonisch high notes appeared again I felt such a disharmonisch scratching through my bones I understood those Hamlet words from Shapansky's class about "sweet bells jangled, out of tune and harsh" and I could not play more. I could not stay. I feared what I might do. Yet I feared to venture out alone into the dark night where toilet kiosks were being overset and face-carved pumpkins smashed in the street. I feared where this dark night will take me. Back in the dormitory room, having left Funk behind with Kehler and the woman, having stumbled along the dark shadows hearing the Shovahnacha in the distance doing mischief, I now hear ängstlich Aufruhr in my head that mixes Sonia's himmlische Musik and the Götterdämmerung of the Anarchists. But I feel too, and I fear it, a winzig kleine flame of something, an itch of music, not hope, no there can be no more hope, just Glut, an ember that hardly glows but will not die, and tonight the Klavierenspiel and the woman Maria in her marriage dress breathe on

that Glut, threaten to grow it into a flame, and I fear what a flame in my soul will have me do. Already the jangled notes of Maria's piano have me casting my eye on my piano-tuning tools. I have read in biography that Beethoven in the fury of his composing would test limitation of his pianos so that strings snapped and hammers broke. Can such a Klavier be found as I would need to play the horror music of my heart? Could such horror be even music?

Blatz stumbled back to his dormitory room as the moonlight gave way to the pale rays of dawn. His nostrils still breathed Sonia's scent, his fingers still clasped her skin, the action of his heart still hammered with desire untempered by the guilt of its fumbled release. Sonia had insisted that he let her return to her room before a master or a servant discovered their disarray. Blatz, swimming in emotion and lust never before experienced or even dreamed of, would have preferred drowning in the moment rather than venture into the chill air of reality, but Sonia, having led him into the salty sea, pushed him back out. "I must go at once," she had whispered. "I must take care of your mischief." Despite her tousling of his hair as she spoke, her voice had been stern, almost German. Blatz had been confused, startled by the abrupt shift from reckless passion to matter-of-fact practical urgency. But when his door clicked behind him he was relieved, until he felt village eyes burning his back. He did not turn to look, but sank to his student cot and cupped his face in his hands. In the stillness before dormitory doors began to open to begin the day, faint music stirred his inner ear that would not leave him in the full light of day.

/ from THE DISTANCE BETWEEN TREES

/ BY HARRY **RINTOUL**

(A single spotlight on Almira.)

ALMIRA: Trees. Nothing but trees. Bush so thick you couldn't walk through it. Trees, trees and more trees. Nothing but trees. Miles of trees. A rich brilliant green wall between land and sky in the summer and this bleak grey oppressive wall closing in around us all fall and winter. Full of darkness and fear. Trees as thick as people on city streets. Or so I've heard.

(Spotlight fades to black.)

(Moonlight. Silence.)

ALMIRA: The presence of the past.

ANDREA: The past present.

KATIE: The future of tomorrow is yesterday.

ALL IN UNISON: To begin.

KATIE: It is night. Stars twinkle and squint. A million billion eyes peering down out of the darkness.

ANDREA: The souls of dead children, old women used to say. And a few still believe though they never speak this belief, afraid they will be laughed at and spoken of behind their backs. Thought old. And old-fashioned.

ALMIRA: The souls of our dead children, looking down on us from their velvet blue heaven. Watching over us.

ANDREA: Old women turn fitfully in their beds. Dreaming of the lost and the forgotten, the disappeared and the begotten.

KATIE: The gravel roads lie still. A serpentine brown, dusty carpet twisting and turning and sliding through the fields and hummocks like a fingertip aimlessly moving down a lover's back.

ALMIRA: Because no one here travels at this hour save for matters of life.

ANDREA: And death.

KATIE: Land and sky is.

ALL IN UNISON: Still.

(Silence)

ALMIRA: A small brown bat swoops quietly across the road and drops slowly over the ditch to feast on a banquet of moths. Rabbits huddle on the edges of hay pastures quietly chewing timothy sandwiches and tender young shoots of brome salad with a sansousse of dandelion. Delighting in a gourmet feast of wild chamomile and black-eyed susan.

ANDREA: The houses, spread miles apart, are dark. The barns silent. Only the solitary yard lights reaching to the sky. A coyote walks through a yard, offering the chicken shed a cursory glance. There are easier meals. Rabbits in the hay meadows, ducks asleep on the riverbank. A large dog, though ignorant of the coyote's presence now, would awaken alert when one little Rhode Island Red squawks. So, the coyote pads along on silent feet.

KATIE: A whip-poor-will whippoorwills.

ANDREA: A dog barks.

ALMIRA: The earth holds its breath.

KATIE: Husbands lie beside wives. Wives wrap arms around husbands.

ALMIRA: Flatulent men, drunken men, boring men, snoring men sleep on couches. In the spare room. In the cabs of their trucks. On the front deck.

ANDREA: Brides,

KATIE: young happy brides,

ANDREA: brides of a day, a week, a month and some of years,

ALMIRA: those of years are very, very few, if you listen to their men,

KATIE: stroke and caress and straddle rousing husbands.

ANDREA: Or lie there.

ALMIRA: Close their eyes. Remember what Mother told them.

ANDREA: Praying to God it won't take any longer than it did last night.

KATIE: Hoping, really, really hoping it lasts longer than it did last night.

ANDREA: Panting and grunting like a slobbering bull—

KATIE: That's it, that's it, honey, just like that, just like, just like that—

ALMIRA: Slamming up and down, punching the air from her lungs till her rib cage hurts.

KATIE: Too deep— Too deep—

ANDREA: Grinding and grinding away.

KATIE: Honey, stop, slow down, you're hurting me.

ALMIRA: Why is it taking so long?

ANDREA: He isn't drunk.

ALMIRA: Until he's hurting her. And—

KATIE: She makes him come. And he's done.

ANDREA: He drops, a spent weight upon her . . . 'scuse me? She makes him—

KATIE: She makes him—

ALMIRA: Enough. *(glares at them)*

ANDREA: Old women open their eyes. Listen. For husband's breath. The slow shallow rattle of life.

KATIE: The exhale of youth.

ANDREA: He is still alive.

ALMIRA: Still ALIVE.

KATIE: She closes her eyes to return to dreams

ALMIRA: of youth and wealth and the good, good life she gave up to marry the man, the farmer in bed beside her.

(Andrea and Katie look at her.)

ANDREA: Clocks tick. Water pumps whir. Fridges refrigerate. Taps drip.

KATIE: Boots stand by doors.

ANDREA: Jackets hang on hooks.

ALMIRA: Clock radios wait in anticipation of the alarm hour.

KATIE: Babas and tantes, uncles and omas, guidos and mommas dads and moms and poppas

ANDREA: share the wall and the mantle and the desk top with the oldest son, the architect in Vancouver, the oldest daughter, a lawyer in Toronto.

105

ALMIRA: With the child that died.

KATIE: Clean houses. Clean kitchens. Tidy living rooms with every pillow in place on the couch. Every book lined up on the shelf. Coffee mugs full of pens and pencils. Fridge magnets. Every knick-knack, souvenir and memento is placed carefully to provide, when needed, immediate nostalgia.

ANDREA: Save in those households with babies and small children where toy soldiers stand guard on the ramparts of Lego castles. Pencil and crayon scrawls on the living room walls represent trees and birds and babies and monsters. Where "babies" and teddies sleep, eyes wide open on the shelf under the television. On the couch. In a corner of the room.

KATIE: In bed, a baby rolls to its mother, finds the breast. Latches on. Sucks. Sleep and contentment are not interrupted by the sleepy muttered, Don't bite Mommy heard only by Daddy and the damned cat lounging in the bay window that Daddy wishes would live outside. He listens to their breathing and, secure they are content, he is appreciative, indebted, pleased, Thank you God, glad neither of them has woken up, pads on to the bathroom in bare feet, steps on a toy car, curses and lifts his foot to his hand, turns, loses his balance, slams his elbow against the wall. Stifles a scream so he won't wake anyone up.

ALMIRA: A man lost in dreams awakens suddenly. He looks into the glare of the moon shining in his window. A full moon lighting the night like day and he shifts his body to escape its glare, his foot pokes his wife in the back of the calf of her right leg.

ANDREA: She mumbles, go to sleep. Thinks: inconsiderate bastard. And he turns away from the light of.

ALMIRA: The lonely man lies awake. Waiting. Thinking. Dreaming of . . . Turns to look at.

KATIE: The full moon. A full moon on midsummer night's eve. The summer solstice.

ANDREA: Spring is dying before our eyes. Summer tears herself from Spring's womb.

KATIE: Spring belongs to the moon.

ANDREA: Summer is the sun.

ALL IN UNISON: Summer is the sun.

/ THE WIDOWERS AT MIDNIGHT

/ BY MARGARET **SWEATMAN**

In the beginning, was George's devotion to Doris. He often told himself (and he never told anyone else) that "he loved Doris more than life itself," the phrase coming to him with all the mystery we find nightly when the dreamed ones speak; it drifted like a melody when he was brushing his teeth or gazing out the window at the elderly neighbour woman who always wore mauve. He loved her more than life itself.

When Doris died, he didn't stop loving her. His love for his wife sustained him for another three years. He died on a Thursday, in love with Doris, secure in his knowledge that his life had been fostered, nourished by a stream of gratitude for the miracle of married love and its consequence, that he had needed never to look further: he'd found his obsession, the lodestone for his forbearance and his grief. Even his teeth were intact. Everybody loved him back.

Richard was another story; something of a rogue, elegant and cruel. Cautious men and wise women chose to live beyond his touch, out of range. Those few who saw a lot of Richard over the years were diverse in their professions but shared a particular element, a base metal, like zinc; beautiful people, their style a sheet metal protecting them from Richard's charm. Belinda, his wife, was a fly caught in his ointment. She lost her powers. Even her famous complexion was ruined at the end.

Yet when Belinda died, Richard removed himself from the world. He bought the house on the hill, the one with a driveway made of broken limestone, winding its way whitely through an avenue of tall, narrow ash trees. He lived alone on the hill for so long, people forgot to be wary.

Even George who, it might be argued, had good reason not only to fear Richard, but to hate him, even George fell into the delusion that the man on the hill was not the man who had come like a phantom into the bliss of George's married life and made a mockery of every surface thing, every smile Doris had given him, every satiate sigh.

Jack was a red herring and never knew it. Our contempt for him made us uncomfortable and it was a relief when he offered us a chance to divert it, by running for mayor. He won in a landslide and remained *His Worship* until we were convinced that he was long dead, for no one wished to bring him out from his gilded cage, subjecting us once again to his terrible loneliness. There he would be, worse for wear, taking long walks on the dike on cloudy days, and we'd cringe from the sight of him, his misalliance with the hours, his deafness to the overtures of dawn or starlight when loneliness is seemly, a particle of grace.

Jack's impenetrable yet transparent self-assurance and his undifferentiated longing combined to make him lecherous, and he sought the company of women randomly, in an almost innocent condition of surprise. When his wife Rachael was first diagnosed, it was Jack who assumed the glory. That he found love a burden became his calling card.

He pursued young women without their fully knowing it, presenting his desires with such a lopsided, hapless grin that they could deceive themselves into thinking he really did just want to run his spatula fingers over the heated rubber of his car window and gaze at them with avuncular interest, his Chrysler smelling of dust and rose pollen, for he always wore a yellow rose in his lapel, a signal of his wife's disaster and his appalling state of abandonment.

Like many hopeful womanizers, Jack was a connoisseur of depression. Long, tearful dialogues over coffee, he alluding to a dark well of suffering, she (mysteriously, Jack found countless she's) succumbing to the secret worm, to that favourite vice of the hope-less—to confession—and its aesthetic of choice—infinite detail. The time, date, place, correspondent, the *mise en scène* of slights, disappointments and betrayals, Jack soaked it up. She would feel post-coital when she left him at the café, walking dizzily outside to find the day long gone, the legitimate world on its way home from real jobs.

Maybe Richard's wife Belinda was already in decline when Jack laid his big fleshy palm on her arm to say, This is confidential. Belinda dove into divulgence as if onto clean sheets, pouring her anguish and her tears down the funnel of his droopy, mushroom-coloured ear. When Richard walked in and discovered them tête-à-tête over cold coffee, his body (like a jockey's) tightened, he smiled a cruel smile, he put his finger to his lips, and he said not a word. His silence drove Belinda mad. She was dead within the year.

It wouldn't be right to exclude Alexander, though his history dilutes the satisfaction of cool indignation. He kept to himself, on the mirrored elevator to the twenty-fifth floor, walking the course, remembering the sea, his mind a ship scudding before the wind. Alexander was a restless man, a mimic with a tendency to lose weight, and he was filled with unusual courage, even at the lip of the grave.

Alexander loved his wife, Louise. He loved her in the uncommon way; he didn't forget. He followed through. If he found his admiration on the wane, he invented ways for her to rediscover the self she could keep from him, the self he would love again. He knew it saved neither of them. He didn't expect to be saved, though he wished for it: who among us could have resisted what might have saved us?

When she died he was angry and humiliated. He held the soil in his fingers and let it rain down on her coffin, and he never said a cordial word to anyone, ever again. He had met his midnight. He'd placed the cold moon under his tongue, like a lozenge, and let it devour him, dream by dream, atom by atom. Though the same fate would greet cruel Richard, deluded George and spurious Jack, Alexander was the watchtow-er, and the watchtower will crumble. As the story ends, it's crumbling now.

/ from ALL RESTAURANT FIRES ARE ARSON

/ BY BRUCE **MCMANUS**

(The outside of a funeral home. Tom stands alone. Ron, wearing his clerical collar, comes down the stairs and joins him. All the while:)

RON: Well. It was an open casket. Geoff looked twenty. Give me a cigarette. There's some kind of killer on the loose.

TOM: I don't smoke.

RON: Pay attention. Something has to be done. *(Ron pats his pockets looking for a cigarette.)*

TOM: You don't smoke.

RON: You think I'm kidding. Death is on a rampage.

TOM: You just never noticed before.

RON: *(patiently)* We have a right to peace, it was promised to us if we were observant and loved God. The dead may find peace but it brings turmoil . . . fear and chaos to the living. That's not peace. There's a killer loose. I got to have a smoke. *(He looks around wildly.)*

TOM: When you lose it, you really are a model.

(Ron takes a big breath. He reaches in his pocket for a pill case and takes a pill.)

TOM: Are you going to shoot up here?

RON: I've got a road ahead of me. There were five ex-wives or lovers in there. Weeping and crying. Where were you?

TOM: I only knew him well enough for the steps outside.

RON: Okay. I am a pastor and a shepherd and I will mind my sheep.

(Ron exits as Tanya hurries down the stairs and joins Tom. Tanya looks shaken.)

TANYA: I can't believe it.

TOM: What?

TANYA: How does someone die of carbon monoxide poisoning?

TOM: Happens all the time.

TANYA: Does it?

TOM: Four or five times a year.

TANYA: We bought the furniture. Five hours later he's dead. You're alive then you're dead. I can't get my mind around this.

TOM: Death . . . quite the phenomenon.

TANYA: Are you trying to be cute?

TOM: No. Respectful. I'm trying to respect death so it doesn't mark me.

(Tom smiles and Tanya smiles uncertainly.)

TANYA: That sounds . . . pre-civilized.

TOM: *(laughs)* It's animal. Lie still in the bushes when the wolf goes by.

TANYA: I don't know what to make of you.

TOM: *(confused)* It's simple. I'm frightened of death.

TANYA: I never thought about it. I never think about it.

TOM: I really wish I could stop thinking about it.

TANYA: That sounds horrible.

TOM: It is. It really is.

(A woman in her fifties comes down the stairs using a cane.)

TANYA: I suppose it was your job. Being a police officer.

TOM: No. I had a gun then. I never drew it even once, let alone used it. But I had a gun. I was an agent of death. He employed me. Now . . . I'm game.

(Tom smiles, sharing a joke maybe. Caron approaches the two and embraces Tanya.)

CARON: Tanya. Tanya . . . how are you?

TANYA: I'm just dandy. And how are you?

CARON: I am just great, considering.

TANYA: You've hurt your leg.

CARON: A hip replacement. I'll be fine in a year, they say. Then we'll do the other one. I've had to give up running. And walking on ice. Hi, Tom.

TOM: Hi, Caron.

TANYA: You remember Tom?

CARON: We dated.

TANYA: Like cool . . . tell me, have you talked to the family?

CARON: They're stunned.

TANYA: No wonder. I was with him that night. I mean before it . . . I saw him. I should speak to them. God knows what I'll say. What can you say? *(Tanya hurries up the stairs calling after her.)* Don't go away. Tom? Wait for me.

TOM: I'll be right here.

(Tanya exits. Caron and Tom look at each other.)

CARON: All the time we were going out I was seeing Jim. The whole time.

TOM: Someone told me.

CARON: I regret that. I didn't mean to hurt. I did hurt you, didn't I?

TOM: I cried a few times.

CARON: I always meant to tell you how sorry I was. To call you or something. Time flies, doesn't it?

TOM: It hurries along.

CARON: I married Jim.

TOM: I know.

CARON: About five years ago I got a postcard with a phone number on it. There was lettering . . . Call this number. I did call one evening. A woman answered. I asked for Jim. He was there. Life is funny, isn't it.

TOM: Time flies. Life is funny.

CARON: He'd been seeing her about ten years. Before the kids left home.

TOM: What goes around comes around.

CARON: I know how I hurt you. I'm sorry. But you were too slow to move, too quiet, too polite, too generous. Jim and I screwed the first time we met.

TOM: He told me that. I ran into him one day.

CARON: You'd drop me off at my place and Jim would come in through my bedroom window and we'd fuck all night. *(pause)* I wonder who sent me that number?

111 ∎

TOM: Life is full of mysteries.

CARON: I took him for everything he's worth. The kids hate him. The bimbo
         dumped him. He's miserable.

TOM: That's great for you, Caron.

CARON: No it's not. I'm alone. I still miss him. I love him.

TOM: So sorry.

CARON: I hope you've been happy?

TOM: Sometimes.

CARON: The bastard told me he used to let his friends watch us through the window.

TOM: We were just kids, Caron. Just kids. We didn't know anything.

CARON: You're not going to tell me, are you? Oh well.

TOM: Jim told me about the bedroom window. He didn't want me hoping, he said.

CARON: Tell me. Did you ever forgive me?

TOM: No.

CARON: *(hesitates for a second, evaluating the intention of Tom's remark)* Will you?

TOM: Jim and you deserve each other. I believe that.

CARON: Okay.

*(Caron turns and walks quickly offstage as Tanya comes down the funeral home steps.
Tanya calls out, "Caron?")*

CARON: *(turns and screams at Tom)* Life is shit and you're shit. All of you are shit.
         (exits)

TANYA: Caron . . . Caron! *(to Tom)* What's up with her?

TOM: We talked about old times.

TANYA: What is happening to everybody? I go away for a few years and everyone is
         going crazy and getting old and dying. What the fuck is going on?

TOM: Life.

TANYA: You're a cop, do something.

TOM: I can buy you a drink.

TANYA: I'd like that.

TOM: I'll buy you one.

TANYA: Thanks.

TOM: Mind you, the last guy to buy you a drink is dead.

(Tom smiles at Tanya, who is stunned. Then Tanya sobs.)

TOM: Hey . . . sorry.

TANYA: That's all right. (She sobs again. Tom puts his arm around her.)

TOM: Hey hey.

TANYA: It's okay, I'm all right, really.

END OF SCENE.

(Tom enters his darkened apartment and switches on a light. Tanya follows behind. She is tipsy.)

TANYA: There wasn't anyone in the bar over forty. What's going on? In New York you can find all kinds of places . . . my god, a student apartment! (She surveys the disordered, under-furnished apartment with amused dismay. Her shopping bags cover the floor.)

TOM: I've got beer.

TANYA: Of course you have. Beer. All right.

(Tom goes to the fridge and opens two beers. After a second's hesitation, he pours one of the beers into a glass. Meanwhile, Tanya walks briefly around the room looking at it all and speaking.)

TANYA: Three chairs, one table. A TV chair and a TV and a hide-a-bed . . . Well!

TOM: Say whatever you want.

TANYA: Do you want some stuff? I got two marriages' worth of furniture.

TOM: I don't need anything.

TANYA: You do . . . you really do.

TOM: I can sit. I can stand.

TANYA: You can wallow in dissolution and despair.

TOM: Glad you like it. I've got your bags.

TANYA: They're the nicest things in the room.

(Tanya looks at the shopping bags. She walks to one and takes out a pair of shoes. She slips off a shoe and tries one on. She takes a few steps, then turns to Tom.)

TANYA: Well??

TOM: Ummm. Looks new.

(Tanya snorts, steps out of both shoes, and sits. Tom sits.)

TANYA: You notice I didn't check the chair for mustard spills before I sat?

TOM: You have great manners.

TANYA: I've been back two weeks and I've been to two funerals.

TOM: It's like the rainy season, only for death.

TANYA: It's creepy.

TOM: I'm getting used to it.

TANYA: You're not really thinking something happened to Cindy, are you?

TOM: Ron seems to need this right now.

TANYA: It wasn't like . . . murder or something.

TOM: Unlikely. The husband's dead. *(pause)* It's a cop joke.

TANYA: All restaurant fires are arson. The husband always did it.

TOM: You dated a cop.

TANYA: I never drank so much in my life. Do you miss it?

TOM: Nope.

TANYA: Everybody misses something they did every day for years.

TOM: It's with me every day. But I don't miss it. Everybody is a liar. No one cares about anyone else. Evil cannot be stopped. I am not always a good person.

TANYA: A hostile and untrusting world.

TOM: You learn to live without trust. Like losing your appendix.

TANYA: What now? You're still young.

TOM: I'm waiting.

TANYA: For what?

TOM: I became a cop because of injustices done to me. I would bring justice to all who deserved it. It was a big feeling. I'm waiting for something like that.

TANYA: I was a big boss. I made money. I spent it. I wanted love and I married instead. Twice.

TOM: I married for love. Twice.

TANYA: And now you're waiting.

TOM: Yes.

TANYA: What to do while you're waiting? Decorate? Every single time I was alone
          with a man in an apartment like this I ended up having sex. I was a lot
          younger then.

TOM: Don't worry about it.

(There's a knock at the door. Another knock. Ron calls from behind the door, in the hallway.)

RON: Tom . . . are you there? I lost my key. Tom?

*(Another knock. Tom and Tanya sit quietly, saying nothing. After Ron has left, Tanya rises
and turns off the ceiling light. Illumination from the window dimly lights the room.)*

TANYA: I had my breasts done two years ago. Do you remember my breasts?

TOM: I do.

TANYA: They were bigger than all of us.

TOM: They were . . . extraordinary.

TANYA: Right after I sent away this young man I was seeing, I got my breasts done.
          I can wear ordinary clothes now. I don't even need a bra really. I put it on
          out of habit now.

TOM: I haven't slept with a woman in two years.

TANYA: No man has seen my new breasts. They're very comfortable but they're
          not what they were. Men used to stare at my old breasts. Men in cars
          would honk their horns. Boys would stare. Once I saw a man walk into
          a telephone pole as he turned to watch me walk by.

TOM: Tanya. Can I see your breasts?

TANYA: What kind of girl do you think I am?

(Tom stands and begins taking off his shirt.)

TOM: I tore a muscle in my chest. I was working out and took too much weight. I
          was trying to do what I always did. My body didn't like it. See? *(His shirt is
          off and we can see a severe scar across his pecs. He cradles his stomach.)* The big
          fat gut is beer and sloth. I've got to do something about it. All women
          remind me of other women when I'm having sex. It's confusing.

(Tanya removes her blouse.)

115

TANYA: They didn't do a great job. They had to get rid of a lot of stuff, and some skin and you can't do that and have everything perfect. *(Tanya is in her bra.)* See. I'm wearing an ordinary cheap 34B with no underwire. The Bay. I used to have to go to Toronto for bras. I can sleep on my stomach now. Ready?

(Tom nods. Tanya takes off her bra.)

TANYA: Well?

TOM: They're beautiful.

TANYA: That's what I think. They're so cute. *(She walks to Tom and feels his chest, running her hand over his scar.)* Ouch. *(She smells between Tom's breasts.)* You smell like a man.

(Tom touches Tanya's breasts.)

TANYA: I can feel that.

(Tanya takes Tom's hand and leads him to the bed. She stops to remove her skirt. Tom takes off his pants.)

TOM: I've had operations on both my knees.

TANYA: My ass is gigantic.

TOM: It looks great.

TANYA: I don't care if you call me by your ex-wife's name.

TOM: You can call me honey. It's the safest.

TANYA: Well. Kiss me.

(They kiss. They get into the bed.)

TANYA: Which is your side?

TOM: I sleep alone. Both sides are mine.

(There is a moment of rustling silence as they settle into bed. Ron enters the apartment talking.)

RON: Tom . . . you home?

(Ron turns on the light and sees Tanya and Tom in bed.)

TANYA: Hi, Ron.

RON: Lost my key. But I found it. And now . . . I have a meeting. For about an hour? An hour. And I better rush. It might be an hour and a half. *(He turns off the light.)* About an hour and a half. But no longer than that.

(Ron exits, shutting the door behind him. There is silence from the bed for a few moments.)

TANYA: Well.

TOM: Yeah.

TANYA: My place next time.

TOM: Next time?

TANYA: We'll see.

TOM: Okay.

END OF SCENE

/ TREASURE

/ BY WAYNE **TEFS**

Relieved to have escaped the insistent rasping drone of his Bloomsbury landlady's voice, and nursing a headache of unknown origin, Arnold relaxes on a bench in St. James Park. Around him unfolds a Sunday, warm but damp in the way of English afternoons in April. Arnold sits on the bench with his thin legs extended before him. On the grass around the duck pond water fowl grub for food. Mallards, teals. Arnold spots a black swan strutting among them, neck crooked, one beady eye cocked at him, and this ordinary bird with its ridiculous walk plunges him into a funk.

Pencils. In his high school days, Arnold filled out his father's income tax return. A fastidious carpenter, but unschooled, his father struggled with the tax man's jargon and intricate forms. He added sums poorly. He refused to use a calculator. So Arnold did calculations for him. He went through the old man's return, punching the InstaCalc, scratching figures with a pencil his father provided. The lead was always blunted, and Arnold waited as his father produced a pocket knife and whittled the end sharp. Waited and sighed. One day as he scribbled figures, his father, checking the work, pointed to a sum with one gnarled finger. There was dirt under the nail hovering over the numbers and a purple bruise at the knuckle from a glancing hammer blow.

"Personal deduction," Arnold said in answer to the implicit question. He felt a lump form in his throat and he tapped the pencil on the table top. "Total of the above columns." He pointed with his finger and added in a voice he intended to be calm, "I'm doing Mother separately."

"Separately. That's new."

"Yes. It's better." As if that explained the change, as if that was the reason.

"How's that?" his mother called from the kitchen where she was fixing sandwiches. She kept her ears tuned to their conversation, not wanting to be left out of the family business. Arnold's father studied him through the bottom half of his bifocal lenses. Steel-grey eyes, the eyes of someone who hurts without thinking about it. When he'd filled in the forms in previous years, Arnold had always included his mother in the return he'd prepared for his father, listing her under "dependants." That's what she was, his father had insisted in earlier years, and Arnold had acquiesced, even though filing a separate return for her would have saved them hundreds of dollars. Thousands.

That year he refused to tick off the box reading "wife" and scratch in the correct amount under "dependant." In April his father had laughed when his wife suggested they drive to the world's fair in Montreal, and in May he'd sent back the colour television she'd ordered from the Eaton's catalogue to make up for the lost trip. She had sniffed into a tissue as she told Arnold these things.

"So," his father said.

Arnold held the pencil above the columns for a moment and glared back at his father. He was filling in the forms, he was in charge. And he wanted his father to know it.

"Say again?" his mother repeated, but neither man answered. For years they'd maintained a conspiracy of silence around their quarrels. Pretending it protected her.

Arnold busied himself with a calculation.

In the moment before Arnold returned to the forms, his father smiled, a wicked lip-smile Arnold had seen once when his father was cheated by a contractor. Before the contractor could stop him, Arnold's father had walked over to the man's pickup and smashed his bare fist through the windshield. Arnold could recall nothing about the contractor, what he looked like, the colour of his pickup, only glass showering through the air like raindrops.

But he would never forget the look on his father's face. The look of defeat.

The answer Arnold called back to his mother, the events of the rest of that day had faded forever, as had his mother's frail voice chirping from the kitchen, but his father's face, ugly with the anger that comes with defeat, exaggerated by the refraction of bifocal lenses, had filled Arnold with a shame he could never undo, a sharp pang that came back to him whenever he came across a blunt lead pencil.

Stolen kisses. Did he feel so guilty because he'd usurped his father's place with his mother? Or did he feel rotten because he'd hurt a family member? He was always delivering pain to those he loved. His sister was another thing. She was two years older than him and had suffered the brunt of his boyish stupidity. He'd struck her between the eyes with a baseball in a game of pepper he'd coaxed her into playing when she preferred talking on the phone. She had a scar there all her life. He lied to their parents about a broken basement window, blaming it on her pet cat. She never found out about that. Most painful was the night of Sandy Murphy.

Summers in Red Rock the kids on their street stayed up late, playing teenage games past the twilight hours. Hide and seek, capture the flag. In the murky scrambles for the flag, to make it home free, girls feeling the first rush of desire brushed hips and breasts against startled boys, and boys suddenly aroused from playing-field innocence, coltishly lunged back, planting rough kisses on flushed cheeks. This had happened to Arnold only once. He hardly slept that night.

Because she was older, he should have known it was a common thing for his sister. The blond bombshell, the kids on the block called her. Marilyn Monroe was in the news in those days. Otherwise, Arnold thought, there was no connection between the

119

sex kitten of Hollywood and his fifteen-year-old bowlegged sister, who washed the dishes while he dried, who had saved his life by grabbing him by the hair when he was drowning one summer day. But during capture the flag he'd come upon her standing with Sandy Murphy in the shadows of a low building. He couldn't see very clearly what was happening, but Arnold was about to speak when something stopped him. What stopped him was the way his sister stood on her toes and reached her upturned face to Sandy's. Something about the angle of her neck. Arnold fled in panic. He crawled under the porch and sat trembling until he heard someone call an end to the game.

He couldn't figure it out. Touching someone, kissing, felt exciting when it happened to him. But for his own sister he knew that it was wrong. And Sandy Murphy. That was the worst part. Sandy had stolen Arnold's hockey puck one time—and he cheated at the ball game they played in the sandlot and called cricket.

On the steps at home he said, "I saw what you did."

Savagery flared his voice, and defiance hers when she answered, "Piss off."

He grabbed her by the shoulder. In his grasp her collarbone felt like a chicken wing. That small and frail. "Bitch," he said, his voice barely croaking above a whisper. She laughed at him, teeth bared. Under the bright porch light her hair shone luridly. Glossy magazine platinum. "Slut." He muttered it under his breath.

Her hand moved so fast he saw only a shadow. Then he felt the sting on one cheek. Tears burning his eyes. He was on both knees retrieving his glasses when she wheeled and leapt off the porch and bolted into the shadows. The word she said back to him hung in the still air. Suck. It was an hour later before he found her sitting on the front steps, face buried in her hands.

They sat in silence watching the moon rise over the house tops. After a while she touched his hand with hers. "I didn't mean it," she said.

He said, "Me neither." And he knew they were both lying, and that made it hurt all the more. The start of lies. They had lied before but never to each other. They had never lied about lying.

Even then he realized it wasn't the blow to the face that stung. It was the words. He had always thought too much of himself. He still did. The thing was, she shouldn't have been able to spot it that easily, it meant everyone did, and that they despised him whatever they said. Lately his landlady seemed to be smirking whenever he caught her eye. She probably thought he was a snob. Arnold said it aloud to the mallards round his feet. Snob. Snob, snob, snob. It had the ring of truth to it, didn't it?

Number one. The thing about guilt, Arnold realizes, is not the injustice of what you feel, but the disproportion. He knows these jewels of pain, which he turns over on his tongue like treasures from the past, mean nothing to anyone else. Perhaps they never had. His father wouldn't recall peering at Arnold through his bifocals. A pensioner living alone in a one-room apartment with other pensioners who play bingo and eat meals from trays, the old man forgets things he's done the day before, and sometimes when he picks up the telephone he confuses Arnold with his own younger brother, dead now more than a decade. Arnold's sister never dated Sandy Murphy, had married a real estate agent and moved to Toronto. She has three children of her own and had a mastectomy last year. What could suck mean to her now? Once a friend said to him over drinks, "There's nothing wrong with going for number one." Arnold had felt sick. When the tab came he insisted on paying. Number one. The idea of it sickened him. He treasured it against himself because his friend had meant to make him feel better—him, betrayer of home, of family, of friends, the egotist who had left everyone for St. James Park and the Tate Gallery.

Brass coffin. Arnold was packing for London the summer his aunt died. Shaken, confused, his white-haired father stopped by Arnold's place every day on his return from the hospital. At the bay window Arnold watched the man who'd taught him to drive turn his Dodge Dart into the parking lot, his thin birdlike head barely visible above the wheel, glasses flashing splotches of sun as he craned his neck to look for other cars. Arnold wanted to rush down to the lot and wave him into the parking space, make sure he did not crash the Dodge and injure himself, hold the frail old man in his arms. But instead he watched and waited until his father made his protracted journey up the stairs to Arnold's apartment.

"About Katie," his father said when they were seated with steaming mugs of tea. "I know you're busy." The old man was perplexed about what kind of coffin to buy. The brass, he said, were ridiculously expensive, but the wooden ones shoddy. He was a carpenter, he knew about wood. He wouldn't have brought it up but he knew Arnold was leaving for London any day. He placed the mug on one arm of his chair and drummed the other chair arm with his mottled fingers. Arnold felt the same way he'd felt at the kitchen table years earlier. He could hurt his father too easily. All he had to do was say nonsense, or some other cavalier but callous word, and the old man would crumple.

"I'll change my ticket," he said. "Stay for the funeral."

"No. You've got your work. Your studies."

"They'll keep. I'll sleep on your sofa. You could use some company right now."

His father had folded his hands together and was studying them. He was seventy-two but those looked the same as when he was fifty. He had worked with his hands all his life. Life was etched on each of his fingers. The old man said sharply, "I don't need a babysitter. Just some advice."

"At least let me go down there with you." Arnold meant the funeral home.

"You're busy with all this." One arm took in the half-packed boxes piled around the rooms. "Besides, I should do this thing alone. She's my sister."

They sipped their tea and thought their private thoughts. Sometimes Arnold wished they were Italian. He pictured things being thrown about the room, faces crimson with rage, heated words followed by tearful embraces. They were not Italian. They were German, and Protestants.

Arnold stood by the car door and his father rolled down the window. His eyes looking up at Arnold's face seemed coated in film. He held the wheel in both hands, fingernails long, yellow and broken. "Forget the cost," Arnold repeated, knowing this is what his father wanted to hear. He leaned into the window and breathed in the mixed odour of dust, stale air and fear.

"I want the brass," his father said. His lower lip trembled but there was an edge to his voice, the voice of a man about to do something important, close a big deal, make a profit. Arnold remembered his father had worn a three-piece suit when he went to meet his lawyer and sign papers. Hair slicked back.

On the phone the next day his father said, "I got the brass and I like it." He spoke with the confidence of the man-about-town who used to open conversations by saying to whomever was on the other end of the line, "Herman Buechler here . . . " Arnold pictured him at the kitchen table, pencil in one hand, telephone receiver in the other, concluding the arrangement with the funeral home, what the old man called "closing the deal." His father added, "I'm not completely hopeless, yet." And they laughed. But Arnold heard the silence ticking in the room at the other end of the line, a silence his aunt had bridged for his father, and Arnold felt a sharp pain around his heart, not for his dead aunt but for the father he had to abandon.

Black swan. And this picture he cannot shake from his sight. His mother on her knees in the garden pushing at the soil with her fingers the way she did when planting geraniums. Tears streamed down her cheeks. She was making a grave to bury the black swan. They were living temporarily on a plot of land, in a farmhouse, while Arnold's father was overseeing the building of a house in the city.

This is what had happened: Arnold's mother was furious with the black swan she kept around the farm yard.

"But you bought it as your pet," her husband argued.

"As Arnold's pet." She stood with one hand on her hips in the middle of the kitchen. She'd been peeling potatoes.

"He hates the thing. If you haven't noticed."

"Oh," she said. "I knew you would take it like that." She dropped the paring knife on the counter and kicked her shoes off.

"You're telling me you did it for him?"

"I thought it would be good for a boy to have something around besides empty space and sow thistles. I didn't expect the damn thing would eat the peas. Or chew up the power cords."

"So you hate it too."

"What I hate is having to do the chores by hand. In case you haven't noticed."

Arnold was on the porch with the newspaper. He looked at the words on the sports page but he wasn't reading anything. Wrangle, wrangle. Their voices swam through the screens. His hands shook. At one end of the porch he kept his athletic equipment, skates, tennis racket, baseballs. He took his bat and headed for the pond behind the barn. He hated the thing. It smelled in moulting season and pecked at his pockets when he was working in the yard and dropped green shit in the grass, which he

122

stepped in with his bare feet. Since his mother had brought it home, his parents had done nothing but wrangle.

He couldn't remember much about what he did behind the barn that afternoon. Blood, a sickening squawk, fluttering wings. Or what occurred between the time he stopped swinging the bat and his mother's silent devotions at the far end of the garden. Gracie the gravedigger. In his memory he stood cold and unmoved off to one side. There were no tears in his eyes. The tough guy. His father had the steel-grey eyes, but that day Arnold was the killer. He saw himself as a mass murderer, hair on end, a gaunt face, a rictus smile. But he knew that guilt liked to play these tricks with memory.

Coin of a secret realm. He doesn't really feel awful when he remembers these things—the black swan, his father's steely eyes, Sandy Murphy. Turning them over in his memory on the park bench, London's wan spring sun warming him, Arnold realizes they constitute a treasure, the rich coin of his life. They've purchased his membership in the club of human frailty, the only club where Arnold will ever truly belong. Belong. That was the key. He was always a coward, doing homework for teachers out of timidity and shame, pressing the bell on Mrs. Valencourt's door and running with the other boys, the gang. He feared being left out. And he avenged himself on a school chum who hadn't included him in a game by punching him in the face and making his nose bleed. He stole ten dollars from his mother's purse so he could brag to the gang. Shameful. At a family reunion he'd stooped to telling stories at his father's expense to get a laugh, to be loved by cousins unworthy to lick his father's boots. Yes, it was shameful, his behaviour. But the guilt was precious. There was always despair about his work, his ridiculous studies, his pathetic character. Yet whenever he needed proof that he mattered, Arnold had only to dig out one of these coins, turn it over in the palm of memory, and there he was, etched clear as the rate of exchange, plain as the pain he delivered so often and so casually—that elusive thing Arnold thought of as Arnold, vile and wretched, yes, pathetic even, but solid with life, authentic, indisputable, real.

/ TRUTH OR CONSEQUENCES

/ BY JACQUI **SMYTH**

It's the hour after school and she's in her mother's bedroom, watching game shows on the portable TV. She's half lying on the double bed, with her back against the head board. Winter, and although the days are getting longer, at this hour the light outside her mother's upstairs window is already as blue as the light of the television set. Outside the snow absorbs the dying light and glows purple in this dappled dusk. She's hoping that her mom won't come home after work, that instead she'll be tempted and go for drinks to the downtown legion, because the house is a mess and he won't have time to clean up. She knows that downstairs the ashtrays overflow with Du Maurier and Players butts and that glasses sit half empty on every crowded surface. They're playing Black Sabbath on the stereo; that's right, the first album with the black cover and purple lettering. They must be crazed on bennies, their card game keeps getting louder and someone is chasing someone else through the kitchen and back into the livingroom; although only in retrospect will she come to know this. She doesn't know that it's dope they're smoking; she thinks the slightly dank smoke is from the Drum tobacco of Gordie's rollies.

The toilet flushes in the bathroom, right next to her mom's bedroom, and then he is in the bedroom. Just like that. He's her brother's friend and her sister's boyfriend or he was, or he will be. At this point in their shared lives her brother no longer takes her out to the bush to set traps, instead he parties with her older sister. She's somewhere between traps and parties: that moment of endless sitcoms, hockey games at the Roland Michener Arena, and playing unsophisticated card games with her best friend: Crazy Eights, Gin Rummy, War and 21. He stands there in wide-flared Levis and a black Joe Cocker shirt, and then he dives onto the bed like he might be diving into the deep end of the Kinsmen Pool. He's laughing and she's laughing too as he screeches, "Let's make a deal, Jac." He's tickling her and she's laughing still, but then his hand reaches for the waist of her purple cords. He starts whispering faster, "C'mon, let's make a deal, little sister."

She can only tell him to get out of here, then yell for her brother, who won't hear over the sounds of Black Sabbath, and keep kicking, but then he's got her spoon style and she's kicking backwards without any effect. He doesn't undo the snap or zipper, instead he mushes his hand down her pants and somehow down her underwear. Her laughter has turned to crying but he doesn't seem to notice and his words speed up,

124

A/CROSS SECTIONS: NEW MANITOBA WRITING

"Let's make a deal, let's make a deal," and his finger rubs at the lips of her vagina and then makes a single hook. Just as quickly, he leaps off the bed like he's diving backwards and he's back in the hallway and down the stairs.

Monty Hall is asking a contestant if she wants door number one, door number two, or door number three. She'd give anything to be a contestant on that show, even if it meant losing.

/ DOMESTIC CONFUSION

/ BY JACQUI **SMYTH**

The wind still howls through the cracks
and the bare branches still tremble.
It's late January and that cannot change
but it will, in time, rushing in yet running
out and there's only reflection here, now.

Today, my son stands solid before me
blocks the wind, the branches
framed in the winter white window.
I am not Eve, but he, he is Jacob
his cup half-filled with 2% milk.

Yesterday my daughter crawled along
the trembling branches of lilac
gulping wind as she sang her ditty.
She challenged my nerves, dared
me to forget her snug in this moment.

Tomorrow my husband will rise
amidst grey dawn, an alarm beeping
to conceive how light he has become
like an hallucination rounding the corner
I'll catch his earlier self in the gold glaze.

Next week the cold snap will break
and the wind will no longer howl
and the branches will not shudder
and the grey light of dawn will shine
    rosy hue across our beds
    each and every single one
and teach us to forget to remember.

/ THE MUTTER ROOM OR LOUTS WITHIN THE UM

/ BY VALERIE **REED**

it's not that i like clutter

it's just that half the time
i didn't know WHO was in the kitchen
sons dirt dishes
pets papers books
eggs apples
leftovers all kinds

the girlfriends were the worst
they came to me unmothered
and expected to stay forever

is she not running a B and B for
the bashed and battered

now they send me emails
warning they are on their way again
to 'visit winnipeg'   left luggage of their youth
and can they see me

no i am invisible
not the beacon of oddballness now
but the wreck they don't want to become

they come
their great escapes to proclaim
and their current successes and always jobs
and trips from/ to/ through/ on

127

their eyes track me in the kitchen
like watchful fruit
now in their thirties they say
their 'biological clocks are ticking'

i say that ticking is just the timer
on the bomb of childbirth
the original IED to blow up your life
like no other event you have ever not quite been in

they think i am 'kidding'
yes and kidding means just that
KIDS and you the mother forever
cornrowed into care

these gen-x girls of constant sorrows
they were raised by other feminist/mothers
experiencing so-called LIB
unlike me who had no daughters
and fought sons daily and said
lib is a myth/ a miss/
equal pay for equal work is what i want/
keep the trappings
they are just that

those sons heard
do not get married
do not have kids
do not get outnumbered by pairs
of eyes in the dark

but what did this so-called lib do

free a whole generation of young women
optimistic to work and play
and have kids if necessary on their own
free them from being in the kitchen
with no other options
and put them right back there again
when the fathers ran away
to play another day
with women half their age
and forgot to pay / forgot!

kids are not visitors in a female life
they come to stay

so at midnight in the clutter of exhaustion
from kids and lives and motions and
money making work   women still can
put their heads against the wall
and cry the fridge a bib

well if i hadn't kidded, i would not have had the kids
and maybe i would have had something else
instead of babies' bibs
and their reply?
you were BEFORE the pill

remember katherine anne porter
who took 25 years to write the ship of fools
from within the ship i might add
raising three kids 'on her own'

that crazy fifties phrase
on her own meaning the parenting buck
stops here and the buck just left forever
ten minutes ago and won't send any back

so now i have a standard email reply:

Val is not at home
she is having a — hip/ knee/ breast/ heart
replacement   on — (fill in dates)

but what i really want to say is
if you must kid
kid once

then you won't be outnumbered in the kitchen
by ravening teenagers who'd as soon look at you as spit
and sometimes do both
their friends think you are 'cool'
the sons know you are a curse

their ex-girlfriends roam the world on birth control
in packs of fading beauty
uncertain exactly what to do next
after the first big trips that kind of show
liberation is maybe just a north american/ industrialized
first world nation issue

and what else

these thirties think
in the kitchens of their minds
oh i'll visit wpg
see what i left behind
think how lucky i got out

and maybe meet again one
of those sons in her kitchen
someone's always hanging out there

she's usually home
and i know the porch has a spare
key

after all the clock is ticking
and it isn't telling time

/ GET DOWN TONIGHT

/ BY LINDA **HOLEMAN**

Nash's parting gift was the new roof. We'd needed one for years, but you know how it is. The shoemaker's children go barefoot and all that.

Two weeks after he left he arranged for a crew to start. Guess he was thinking about the fall rains coming on.

For those first two weeks without him I watched television. Actually I didn't watch; I just turned them all on. There were five of them—a portable on top of the big one in the living room, another portable on a Lazy Susan on the fridge in the kitchen, a slick white set in the bedroom, and an ancient black-and-white on an upended crate in the second bedroom. It—that second bedroom—used to be our boy Arlen's room, although Nash had been sleeping there since Arlen hightailed it away from home three summers ago, right after he turned seventeen. But we still called it Arlen's room. You just do that. And it was the worst affected by the leaking roof. It was painted a deep purple; Arlen had chosen it from a paint chip called Claret. I learned, from the Emeril Live cooking show, that claret is a clear Bordeaux. But on the lumpy walls it turned the colour of a bruised eggplant, and it had bubbled and chipped down one corner. Some days the furry black mould that edged the baseboards gave off the mushroomy odour of rotting leaves. I was faithful about getting out the bleach and scrubbing at it, but after a heavy rain it would be there again.

With all the televisions tuned to different channels, I could breathe more easily.

When I was growing up, my father had run a one-man television repair service out of our house. He started out fixing radios, but when he knew televisions were on their way in, he learned all he could about them by the time they made it up here to Canada. Our family was the first in the neighbourhood to own a television, a huge mock oak cabinet that took up half of our tiny living room and was never turned off.

Sometimes neighbours would drop in to marvel at the grainy black-and-white Indian Head test pattern. It annoyed my mother, who didn't like unnecessary social visits during the day. She didn't mind when the neighbours came in for the six o'clock news, which was the only actual program for a while, because by then dinner was over and she was ready to sit down with a rye and cola, an ashtray in her lap, and put up her feet. Later, when *Duffy's Tavern* and *The Honeymooners* aired, she even invited her friends over, and I remember the noise of that hot, cramped, smoke-filled room as it filled with the combined laughter of the studio audience and the women from the street.

My father's workshop was in the basement, and he often left a television or two on all night, testing them, he said. The sound hummed up through the floorboards, lulling me to sleep. Sometimes my father brought a portable upstairs and worked at it on the kitchen table, his box of fuses at his elbow. He'd move it to the top of the fridge or onto the already cluttered counter when my mother set the table for lunch or dinner. He kept it turned on, even if the picture was snowy or the horizontal hold was shot. We'd all stare at the screen as we ate; a lot of the time the volume was just fine, and we could still get the drift of the program.

Ever since, the sound of televisions has brought me a real, deep feeling of comfort. So when Nash left and I turned all of them on at a good volume, I was finally able to get to sleep. It had been a long time since I'd been able to sleep properly, not only because of the troubles, but because of the enforced heavy hush of my bedroom. Nash needed complete silence to sleep. He complained that he could hear the television in my room from Arlen's room across the hall, even with both bedroom doors shut and the volume turned low. I bought a pair of headphones from Radio Shack, but it wasn't the same. It made me jumpy, those voices speaking so intimately into my ears, like a direct line to my brain. I wanted the sound to swirl around my whole body, lifting me, filling the still air. Filling me.

To keep the peace I gave up the headphones, turned off the television, and lay awake, staring into the blackness of the silent room.

Nash hadn't always needed such quiet, at least not when Arlen still lived with us. Arlen was a normal, noisy boy, a cute kid when he was small. But he grew into a sulky adolescent, given to long silences and an unexplained hostility that I found hard to take. It had to have been hard on him, what with his daddy and me always at each other's throats.

Arlen and his father agreed on one thing for sure. They both hated the televisions. Oh, they didn't mind the one, the big one in the living room, and they spent a lot of afternoons and evenings together watching football and hockey. Sometimes when Arlen was alone I'd catch him watching the Discovery Channel or one of the British shows on PBS, but at the sight of me he'd pretend he was only channel surfing. He'd move on to MTV or the sports channel as soon as I settled down on the couch beside him.

Yeah, both Nash and Arlen liked watching their own television shows, but hated me having the other TVs going. They'd holler at me to turn them off, that they couldn't hear with so much noise. One awful night, after Nash and I had another of our blow-ups, Arlen threatened to smash in the portable on the fridge with a ball-peen he waved over his head. I don't even know where he found that hammer, although I daresay it was from his daddy's truck.

Arlen hasn't missed sending me a birthday card and another at Christmas since he left. No return address, but I always checked out whatever province he might be in, stamped there in the postal mark. Those cards mean a lot.

I do miss my boy. Especially now, with Nash gone as well. Nash wasn't much for talking, but at least he was a body. Someone to make it worthwhile to open a can of soup.

The roofers started yesterday, but had to stop by noon. A light rain came up, accompanied by low, heavy clouds that looked as if they were set to stay. The noise stopped—the thumping footsteps overhead, the wrenching cry of old shingles being torn off, the dull thud as they were thrown to the hard-packed mud around the house. There was the metal screech and slide of extension ladders being pulled down and loaded up, and the roar of exhaust as the truck pulled away.

Nash said it would take them three days, if the weather stayed clear. I knew it could be anywhere from a week to two. They didn't come back that day, even though the clouds blew away by mid-afternoon. They didn't come the next day, either. I'd lived with a roofer long enough to know you never had one job per crew going—always two to three. It was an unspoken law, and of course I had inside knowledge. After all, I'd been the bookkeeper for Nash's business for all of ten years, although with things going more and more sour between us this last year, he'd taken the black binders and lined ledgers elsewhere just after Christmas.

Actually that hurt a lot, him making it clear he didn't want me handling the business end of things. Sometimes, thinking on it too much, I'm sure that was a worse slap in the face than Nash leaving.

The third day—a clear and hot end-of-summer day when the wasps were at their worst—the roofers were back. I smelled a hot stink through the open kitchen window, and turned Regis and Kathie Lee to mute, listening. There it was, the on and off whoosh of flames from the tank. I didn't know any tarring was necessary, but Nash makes sure his crew does a thorough job. I'll say that much for him.

They had a boom box up there with them, and someone was dancing on the flat roof over the back porch; the shuffle matched the beat of the music. I had a sudden memory of Nash with Arlen in his arms—when Arlen was still a bald-headed little rug-rat in a smelly diaper—dancing to KC and the Sunshine Band's "Get Down Tonight." Nash and I had never lost our fondness for the disco rhythms; I always suspected that Arlen had been conceived to an endless playing of Donna Summer's "Love to Love You" one unseasonably steamy September night in '75.

That old memory made me go to the hall storage closet and pull out the photo albums. It was well after noon when I realized I'd spent too long with the past, and I had a sad, empty feeling that I knew had nothing to do with missing lunch. The sound of the nail gun was fast and furious now, but still, the music kept going.

I knew the heat would be bad on the roof, what with the tar and all those black shingles. It would be good for me to get away from the albums for a few minutes, so I made up a jug of Nestea, squeezing in half a lemon for quality. I found some Styrofoam cups still in their plastic sleeve and carried it all out to the front yard, carefully high-stepping over the rolls of tar paper and stacks of wrapped shingles, the long metal strips of flashing.

133

I looked up, shading my eyes with the roll of cups. I never knew any of Nash's crews except his partner, Dennis Lafarge, who had been with him for six years or more. The younger men on the various crews came and went.

Dennis was here today; even with the sun in my eyes I recognized his familiar bowed legs in their grey sweat pants, the heavy steel-toed boots.

"Dennis!" I called up. "Dennis. I made some ice tea."

He gave a wave and then whistled around two fingers. The explosive shot of the nail gun stopped, then the music, and Dennis and another man clambered down the ladder.

You could have knocked me over with a whiff of garlic when I saw it was my own boy.

"Hey, Mom," he said, casual as you please, as if we'd seen each other over the Corn Pops that morning.

"Arlen?" I said, almost like a question, although I don't know what I was asking. "Since when you worked for Daddy?"

"Just started in June, when I got back here," he told me, taking the Styrofoam cup I held out to him. His hands weren't the slender boy's hands I remembered; they were a man's hands now, veined and scarred, his left thumbnail a hard purple-red square. Claret.

My own hands were shaking as I poured the ice tea into his cup, sorry to see he got a considerable number of floating lemon seeds. I filled another and handed it to Dennis, who moved away, inspecting something in the bed of his pickup.

"You look good, Mom," Arlen said. "I like your hair like that."

I touched my bangs with my knuckle. "I stopped smoking."

"Yeah. Dad told me." He drank the contents of the cup—seeds and all—in one long gulp. I watched his Adam's apple move as he swallowed, and I longed to reach out and cup my hand around it.

"You want some more?"

He shook his head, crumpling the cup in his palm. It folded in on itself until it looked like a giant sleeping cabbage moth, or origami gone wrong. "No thanks." He squinted up at the roof. "Finally, eh Mom?"

I nodded. "Never actually thought I'd see the day." I held tight to the jug so I wouldn't throw my arms around that big boy, wouldn't start asking too many questions— where you been, what've you been doing? How are you, really? And why are you here? Why are you here, Arlen?

"I can't believe Dad didn't get around to the roof all these years. But when he sent me on the job I realized it was just like him. Too little, too late, you know?"

I nodded, and we both looked up at the roof as if it echoed those last words.

"Did you mean to come by the door, Arlen, say hello, before the job was done?" *Did you mean to call me, to tell me you were back? Are you still so angry, then?*

Arlen squeezed the ruined cup tighter. "I did, Mom. I was working up to it. I been working up to it since I moved back to town. You know."

I nodded as if I knew. "Daddy living with you?"

"Nah. He asked, but I told him I figured working for him was enough. Don't want to overdo it." He smiled suddenly, and I remembered how he'd chipped that tooth, going head-first down a waterslide and into the bony skull of the boy ahead of him. The boy had needed six stitches.

"You have plans for supper?" I asked.

"Told my girlfriend—Amber—I'd take her out someplace."

The pitcher was wetting my tank top. "I bet she's pretty, name like Amber. You could bring her here. There's a little rump roast in the freezer. And I've still got some jars of pickled beets from last year. You always liked those pickled beets."

Dennis walked past, the tools on his belt clanking. "Ready to go back up, Arlen? Thanks for the drink, Terry. You doin' all right?"

"I'm all right," I told him. "Thinking of getting a telemarketing job for the winter."

"Sounds good," Dennis said, then started up the ladder.

Arlen handed me the folded Styrofoam. "Seven o'clock, Mom?"

"Seven is fine."

"And maybe we could watch TV, or something, later."

What was left of the cup was warm and dry in my hand. "We could, Arlen. We could watch television."

Arlen's Adam's apple moved once more. "You and Amber'll gang up on me for sure. Don't suppose I'll get to watch what I want."

Then he turned and followed Dennis up the ladder.

I went back into the house and took the roast out of the freezer. Then I checked the *TV Guide*, but the small print skittered like black aphids.

It didn't matter. I know the programs by heart, anyway.

/ PLANTING TREES IN EAR FALLS

for Sean

/ BY JAN **HORNER**

You tell yourself he went off to make his freedom
sowing seedlings in a desert
his blisters bound in duct tape
steel-toed, hard-hatted, bug bitten.
A life dictated by light, the six-week season
stoked with big proteins, pain killers
smoking weed, sucking beer, getting bushed.
Working the earth,
a rough northern nursery
unseen by ecotourists.

Here, this June's moonless night
transfixed by northern lights above
the avenue of leafy elms
you imagine him sleeping deeply
where no street lights glow
only the stars and this cosmic fire
its silent dance above him.

Tomorrow, bent with his burden of baby trees
his body harnessed and mind free
he'll quietly solve economic conundrums or
his idea of the world's problems, he thinks
he knows the city world of finance and markets,
where smart money says productivity
cannot stand still, must always rise
and the motto is more and cheaper.

■ 136

Tomorrow, filing among the deskbound
you will open a fresh ream of paper, feed the printer
stoke the market for armies of cheap migrant labour
their shelf life uncertain, their fortunes
subject to wet weather, poor terrain and
how well their backs and legs stand up
and you in your ergonomic space
warm, dry, you feed the printer
feed all those sons and daughters
to the voracious god of paper.

When did this start, the deforest then replant cycle?
Who cut this contract and who is speaking?
Some detached consumer of paper mired in the rubble of history
comfortable with her blue box and unread photocopies
diverted by books, typeface, scented ads.
Like a blind addict with insatiable needs
you toss and turn in a diminished bed
history's angel resplendent above you
disturbing your dreams with fierce whisperings
awake, awake from your anaesthesia
you must clean your house, you must change your gods.

/ LOOT

/ BY CATHERINE **HUNTER**

"I did this because I was hungry." — Michelle Debarras, "Bread"

After my mother died, I stole from her mailbox
the letter from the Christian Charity that contained
a pack of carrot seeds for Africa.
In black letters, on the white
shiny paper of the envelope, someone
had printed: *Que Dieu*
vous donne une récolte abondante,
and when I shook the envelope, I heard the rain.

I planted the seeds in the sunny suburban garden,
and they grew fat until this afternoon
when I unearthed them and washed them and chopped
them into rough rounds
for the soup and served it to you
here at the table we share, *la vision mondiale*
widening between us, and my grief
diminishing with every spoonful, as I ate
and ate and ate because, *mon Dieu,*
you wanted me to.

/ SPRING CLEANING

/ BY CATHERINE **HUNTER**

Suddenly, everything became too easy,
too June-day transparent, Gordon Lightfoot
gleaming on the stereo, molecules
of snow levitating through air, released
from gravity, the fruit let loose
from the bowl, oranges floating
one two three above the cherrywood table
polished sleek as a citrus leaf, salt
shaker of crystal, bright prism of wine
goblets and sun flying in
through the open window, the crisp
pleat of curtain, the glass rubbed sheer
with paper and vinegar, a silver dish of seashells on the sill,
and inches below the ceiling a cloud of ferns suspended
over the vase of Gerbera daisies and baby's breath, oh
and the baby sister, trying on noises,
juggling vowels while mama unties
the kerchief from her hair, shakes
out the dust on the back stoop, says
seashells, baby, say seashells
and baby says it, her lisp a mere
slipknot of a freckled thing,
a hummingbird's wing, slim hover
of syllables over the moment
when words go tumble, drift to sky.

/ HAPPY ANNIVERSARY

/ BY CATHERINE **HUNTER**

I can't imagine what you want to tell me
after all these years, but if I can find my glasses,
I'll read the note you wrote upon the calendar
before you turned the page and the thermometer
outside the kitchen window and this recipe
for pie and the way the light unravels
summer after summer and unknots the sky until
the mind falls open, spilling alphabets and fuses,
light bulbs, cat food, washers
for the bathroom tap and where I put that thing
I used to know the noun for and just when
and why I turned the oven on and yet
I don't regret that we can't start again.

There's still so much I have to tell you,
but I'm in the kitchen, making lists
of words I can't use any more
and all the things we'll never
grasp the purpose for, these cherries
in their clear glass dish and the reason
for these cats. Fold the towels carefully,
misplace them on a shelf. Let the papers slide
onto the floor. Gather up the knives
and organize them by their size and then forget
what they are for. Forget, forget. You've been
released.

■ 140

/ LEARNING TO FLY

/ BY JAKE **MACDONALD**

When Lisa left it was late spring. Ed walked aimlessly around the back yard of their St. Norbert home. A dirty-dog smell rose from the open yard. And in the river, filthy ice gnawed at the mud banks. Ed thought about wading in.

On the first of the month some strangers moved in next door. They looked like rednecks, the sort of people he sometimes had to turn down for bank loans. One night they had a party. Ed fetched his binoculars and doused the lights. They were old people but they made enough noise. The man of the house had tattoos on his arms and a scrub-brush of white hair. He was waving his arms in the air and dancing the hula.

One day the neighbour walked over to Ed's yard and introduced himself. His name was Buzz. Guys who danced the hula always had names like Buzz. "Now I sent away for these," Buzz announced, pulling a little envelope out of his pocket. "So you have to water them regularly."

He gave Ed some seeds, large and flat, pale as polished wood. He walked Ed around to the south-facing side of the house and showed him where to plant the seeds. "Honeydew melons," he said. "The best in the world. I sent away for them."

"I'll water them," said Ed diplomatically.

Buzz slapped Ed on the back. "I'm relying on you."

He was a retired merchant seaman. He had a beat-up old Piper Cub airplane that he kept tethered in a field across the road, and one day, to Ed's horror, he insisted they go for a ride. The plane had no doors and was held together with tape. They always say things are held together with tape but in this case, the airplane was actually held together with tape, shiny black electrical tape on the pipes inside the cockpit and wide swaths of grey duct tape on the underside of the fabric-covered yellow wings. At one point, as they swooped sideways over the river, Buzz seized his chest and theatrically screamed, "I'm having a heart attack!"

Ed planted the melon seeds. Before he drove to work in the heat of the early morning he would kneel on a piece of cardboard and check for some sign of emerging fruit. But by mid-July his efforts had produced only a limp stem that looked like a hank of fish line. What a waste of time, he thought. I'm a bank manager.

"Keep at it," Buzz instructed. "One morning you'll go out and you'll have the world's finest melons."

141

Late in the summer Ed had to go to Toronto on a training seminar and, while he was away, Buzz was killed in an accident. Buzz dive-bombed a barbecue party in his airplane and, while the onlookers cheered, flew straight into his friend's barn.

By the time Ed got home it was all over, even the funeral. There was a photograph on page three of the *Winnipeg Sun*. The plane was folded up like a cheap umbrella, sticking out of the wall of the barn. It was not a dignified image. But Buzz would have been proud of the five melons that had magically appeared in the mud of Ed's little garden. It was like a miracle. Ed knelt staring at the melons, touching them. They were a final gift from his friend.

Ed detached the melons from their vines. That night, he conducted a memorial service. He sat on the back deck and ate the melons, and drank Scotch, and spat the seeds across the lawn. While slicing open the last melon he noticed a tiny scrap of label sticking to the melon, and a little hole where Buzz had attached the dead vine.

/ AUTUMN TRILOGY

/ BY DI **BRANDT**

GRAND HOTEL

I am picking up the fallen petals
of the flaming crimson giant mums
on the Persian carpet in the Grand Hotel
of your heart: is the temperature right,
was the crystal sparkling, the Chopin
scintillating, the guests inspired, have
they fallen too soon, was it a short
season, have the botanists traded
longevity for splendour, are they
the renewing kind or the easily wilted,
these mums, the wild sorrow in your
dark eyes, your hurricane heart, touch
of October in the air, black geese high
above the trees, escaping winter

SILKE

I wrote Silke instead of Rilke trying to write
a poem for you, aspiring to his luminosity,
and the error of the first letter morphed
instead into smooth slithery sounds which
are me remembering your silke skin and sexy
sigh and steamy thigh and skilleful tongue
and sforzando hands and secret silv'ry song
and searing eye, and lucky me to have strayed
so shyly into your starry sparkle, and you so
slyly into mine

LONG LIVE THE QUEEN

for Gladys Irene Clarke Luke
Brooklyn, December 2005

The stars hang particularly low,
particularly bright, on this crisp
early December evening, sparkling
up the thin frosted bare armed
shadowy ash trees, everyone
scurrying home to electric lamps
and gas fires, heading into the
long night, when you have restored
to us the meaning of the season,
bells ringing along the lit busy
streets of Brooklyn, skin remembering
the glisten of hot sun, to celebrate
the passing of a grand old queen,
immaculate mother of Africa,
Barbados, Canada, New York,
and her formidable children, dread
locked, jazz bejewelled, honorary
gowned, that was a gorgeous
lived life, of heroic engagements
and delicious digressions, Gladys
Irene, and these are tears of
happiness from the flower bearing
avenue lined multitudes, bon voyage,
good job, mum, long live the queen

/ DANCING WITH HIPPOS

/ BY LARRY **KROTZ**

On Sunday morning Allan came over to the table where I was having breakfast to announce that if he could get enough people together, he'd line up a boat along with one of Kenya's leading ornithologists for a bird-watching excursion out on Lake Victoria. Right away I told him to count me in. Lake Victoria, shimmering beyond the bougainvillea, was the first thing I saw every morning when I stepped out onto the porch of the room where I was staying at the edge of this town of Kisumu. But so far I'd only observed it from the land. Which was the case for all the rest of the people in the little enclave of travelling scientists (all of them scientists except me, who was there to write about them). Everybody, from London, from America, and from Winnipeg, Manitoba, was a long way from home; Allan, retired from his post at St. Boniface General Hospital, now donated his time to AIDS research in east Africa. But being perpetually off somewhere in their lab coats fighting AIDS or studying malarial mosquitoes left them all little time to be tourists. This was their chance.

We took off in one of the project vans: Allan and his wife Myrna; Ian, a microbiologist, also from Winnipeg; Carolyn, a National Institutes of Health officer from Washington; Sam, a Nigerian headquartered in Maryland; and me. We passed a herd of cows, the requisite fleet of bicycles that were a common conveyance in Kisumu, some women coming from church, and soon were at the end of a sandy road making the acquaintance of our guides.

The leading ornithologist of the region turned out to be a lean, sad-eyed thirty-five-year-old in a ripped T-shirt bearing a logo for Nescafé. Tom Adere had a crew of three younger Luo fellows, with bare torsos, whippet-thin, eagerly personable, each with his hand-carved paddle and a dugout-style canoe about thirty feet long, made of teak planks and painted blue. When you go out onto the lake to look for birds, the canoe is the conveyance of choice because what you want is not only to see the birds, but to hear them. And when you paddle, you travel in silence.

Ten of us, including the Kenyans, scrambled into the teetering boat. Tom took one of the paddles, "to help steer," but, I noted, he never dipped it in the water. He was too busy expounding. Which was fine, for he expounded exceedingly well. He was one of those encyclopaedics for whom knowledge, trivia and perspective intertwine in such quantities to make you wonder, where does it all come from, where is it stored? He

146

A/CROSS SECTIONS: NEW MANITOBA WRITING

knew his birds (when the semi-annual count was held it wasn't difficult to accept his claim that he came up with 400 sightings), he knew the flora, he knew the geological and the human history.

We explored a couple of small creeks, then coasted along the shore, cutting through papyrus and elephant grass. Tom identified three varieties of kingfishers (this region possesses more subspecies of this fishing bird than any place else in the world) and then pointed to the further distance: Italian-built grain silos looming over the harbour, empty except for rats, a boondoggle of foreign aid. Overhead a cormorant flew low and, across the bay, the Uganda Railways ferry pulled slowly out on its way to Port Bell and Kampala.

Whatever we might declare as our reasons for travel, to see the world, expand our horizons, grow as human beings, one probably trumps all the rest. To get a story. Even more important, if we are lucky, to be part of a story. We are driven by a belief that through the very act of our travelling we'll somehow grasp hold of a narrative that is not only different, but decidedly better than what was available had we remained at home. It's part of a secret, or maybe not so secret, compact with the act of travelling itself. And you don't have to be in Africa for this; it's exactly the same if you're kayaking on the Pacific coast or taking in a festival in Quebec City. The important thing is that we're not at home and something had better happen. In our hearts we are at odds with anything happening as accident, otherwise we wouldn't make such elaborate preparations. But likewise we know that interesting things cannot occur in any way that is designed: John Steinbeck telling us that we don't take a trip, "the trip takes us." We plan for safety, comfort, predictability, then willingly hand ourselves over. A Russian proverb posits that "an opportunity to travel is an invitation to a dance issued by no less an entity than God," and such mantras resonate because of our hope that, as perhaps in a love affair, we may be taken into circumstances and the arms and care and hospitality of those we could barely have imagined to exist. As a result of having given ourselves over in ways we would not do at home, we hope to enter into exciting, perhaps even dangerous territory.

We were about forty metres from shore. On the lakeside a motorized boat went by, loaded with a dozen cheering party people on a Sunday outing. They were fifty metres off but making such a racket Tom frowned. "Such noise drowns out the sounds of the birds," he complained. And that it did; for a few minutes there was nothing but the whine of the other boat's engine and the whoops of the revellers. Then, as if an afterthought, he continued: "And it has the danger of alarming the hippos." This made us perk up our ears. Henry Morton Stanley, who circled this lake in 1875, all 1,600 kilometres on the Lady Alice, his boat that had been carried in pieces all the way from Mombasa on the heads of bearers, had noted that "hippos abound."

Tom's announcement received an immediate response; out of the hitherto calm waters something hit our bow, causing the canoe to lurch violently, a metre into the air. Then, like the breaching of a gigantic water main, a tidal wave cascaded over us. Chaos ensued. Ian tumbled backwards, his feet in the air, head clunking against the

147

bench I was clinging to. George, one of the paddlers who'd been leaning on the gun-wale, lost hold of his paddle and grabbed frantically at whatever was within reach. Carolyn, behind me, tumbled left; Sam fell right. The boy in the bow lurched forward, flailing madly, then came back down on his feet. At the back, Allan, Myrna and Tom were a blur. For a tumultuous moment everything was held in suspension, like a cartoon of Wile E. Coyote going over Niagara Falls. Finally we landed. Off starboard, the water boiled. Overhead the sky remained calm and a solitary egret arced out from shore.

By some miracle we'd landed flat, though we might as easily have capsized either to the right or to the left. We checked ourselves over like people who have just been sent sprawling by an out-of-control bus roaring through a huge puddle. The damage was slight. One paddle had gone overboard along with a set of binoculars, but a quick count satisfied that we'd lost no humans. A wet camera and a drenched bird book; Ian's knee with a nasty bruise; Carolyn's floppy hat now floppier than ever. Me completely wet but intact.

The people in the stern were not only okay, but for some reason had been spared the brunt. What's more, their vantage point had given them a perspective as to what had transpired.

"A hippo," somebody in the front exclaimed, "it had to be."

"Not one hippo," corrected Allan, "two of them."

He'd seen them, but couldn't tell exactly what had happened. They'd either come up under us after being frightened into some kind of underwater stampede by the other boat and its noise, or they'd been there all along and it was we who'd disturbed whatever they were doing at three o'clock on a Sunday afternoon and they'd risen in protest. Either way we were now just past them. It took us these few moments to discern the level and the nature of what danger we'd been in and might still be in, depending on how angry our hosts were. But Tom and his young helpers knew the score. "We need to get out of here," he commanded as paddles dug in, even his this time. As we moved speedily off I ventured a look, over my shoulder: two broad black backs and then a pink primordial snout. And following, like bubbles in the retreating eddies, four ancient eyes.

We paddled away decidedly chastened. For the next long minutes everyone was quiet in the way you are when you've been hit by a trauma. A couple of gestures at jokes were attempted weakly, like running ragged flags up a pole. Nobody laughed very hard. The skirmish had lasted for about seven seconds and appeared to have ended well. Had anyone fallen overboard there's no doubt it would have been bad.

Hippos, not stampeding elephants, lions, or wily crocodiles, are the largest killers in east Africa, the sworn enemy of fishermen, the bane of women scrubbing laundry at the mouths of rivers and children wanting to go for a swim. People in shoreline villages keep one eye peeled at all times. A hippo in shallow water or on shore will chase you down at great speed. The young men with the paddles argued about whether it was thirty-five or sixty kilometres per hour, but in either case the reckoning was remarkable. And then it will either trample you or rip you with its razor-sharp tusks. But in deeper water like that we were occupying, a human flailing about and trying to swim would be doomed by the simple dynamics of physics. It would be like getting caught between two suvs.

In the late afternoon we resumed looking for birds, trying to recapture a semblance of what not long minutes before had been normal. And we were rewarded with appearances by weavers, coots, white-throated cormorants and open-bill storks. At the top of a tree perched an unconcerned fish eagle and, in some bushes, a prehistoric-looking hammerkopf. Tom picked up his seminar—there was lots more zoological and ornithological information in his files and he was determined to give us our money's worth. But in the backs of our minds it was no longer about birds. Every time movement was detected in the water, another tentative joke came out. Behind it all, each of us was reflecting in his or her own way on the milliseconds that comprised "the moment." What had happened there? How close was I to actually being killed? Did I behave acceptably? Then, most importantly: how can this be configured into the story I'm going to tell once safely back on land? Each of us, perhaps even the paddlers who must have seen it all before, commenced privately weaving the narrative to be used to relay the afternoon's events: to our colleagues back at the hotel, to friends and families when we got home. Even to one another, as if in careful check to see whether what had happened was experienced similarly all round. What level of danger had we actually been in? Was that sufficient for a good story?

For dinner a few hours later we trooped to an outdoor barbecue restaurant where we found colleagues who hadn't been on the excursion. They were decidedly unhappy at having missed out on the action. A bit grumpily, they searched for tales they could dredge from their own memories to compete with this story of the moment. A tray of beer and plates of salad, tomato and onion floating in oil, along with a bowl of stiff, porridge-like ugali arrived carted in by two curly-headed little boys. Sam got on his elaborate satellite phone to make the evening call (in Maryland it would be morning) to his wife. As he walked around under the trees we could overhear his explanation amid laughing assurances that yes, he was alright. Ian shook his head and smiled into his beer. Behind us we listened to the surprised squawks, the swift chop, and then silence as the chickens that were going to be our supper were prepared in the small bamboo-enclosed cookhouse. Through each person's head ran a simple calculation. First, how in near-death experiences, "near" is the operative word. And then, is it better to be almost demolished by two hippos in Lake Victoria than by a bus in Winnipeg or Toronto? For story value there seems to be no comparison.

/ BIRD TO BIRD

/ BY JOHN **WEIER**

a couple of larks in the sand and brush along the addis to
nairobi highway and we've pulled our toyota onto the
shoulder to observe them   hope to identify them   but like
other larks these resist our efforts at classification   their
delicate lineation and dust colour   grey brown   brown grey
with streak   with stripe   with fleck of white of black   or
trace of rust without   their phantom habits   here   vanishing
there   one dozen lark species possible in the south of
ethiopia and we stand with binoculars raised and resolute
naming   degodi lark   no   foxy lark   no   look at the cheek
and cap   bird to field guide to bird   short-tailed lark   no
foxy lark   and talking back and forth   are these two even
the same species   yes   no   and rob with his digital poised to
send lark photos off to the world's lark experts for
confirmation   and then I get a burning on my left side and
spin   and there she stands beside me   almost touching   a
woman stranger   with a shepherd's crook   and a drove of
goats grazing on the far side of the road   she mumbles a
few words that I don't understand   but I say hello anyway
and smile   what else should I say   is there to say   black of
course   this woman   no   dark dark brown actually   and I
glance down shamed by my pale forearm   african woman
with beaded braided hair   dressed like she's about to head
off for dinner with friends in winnipeg though a tad dusty
a sheer print fabric wrapped round and round her waist
hanging to her ankles   red and green design on black
second fabric angled over one shoulder to shelter her back
and breast and belly   this one black and golden fringed but
leaving her sides exposed   and as she shifts her weight from
one foot to another I catch a glimpse of one full chocolate
breast shimmering   she flashes a broad and white-toothed
smile   I raise my bins again but a drop of sweat finds the

eyepiece   pull a cloth from my pocket to wipe and turn
back to the larks   silly larks   three quarter hour we stop
there on the nairobi to addis ababa highway to study these
larks   quarrelling   degodi   no   foxy   as if our lives depended
on it   as if anything depended on it   and this woman
standing next to me smiles   watches   watches   watches
holds firm her shepherd's staff   watches   and I wonder
what in this big round green earth must she think of us

/ UNDRESSES ME

/ BY JOHN **WEIER**

stop at a mobil station here on the brink of awassa and I've
stepped out of the land cruiser to stretch   five long hours
scrunched in the short back seat between traveLling
companions   my bunched and burning limbs   extend

unfold   as jean-clad attendants converge to top up our gas
tanks   yes   two gas tanks   and another strapped to the roof
rack   click click   and clunk   chirr   a rush of fuel   the
scalding african sun on my skin blistering sun   I glance

around   asphalt   picket fence   marabou stork   and
understand they're all women   have I seen this anywhere
before   gas station manned by all women   three women
attendants   and then I notice the fourth standing with

notepad and ballpoint pen next to the bumper of a nissan at
the other pump   short   slim   young   pretty   maybe twenty
years' gap between us   and she squints at me   meets my
eyes   smiles   ogles from eyes to my mouth   my throat

sliding   slowing   sliding   down   down my shirt   down past
my belt   thighs   knees   to stop at my sandalled toes   and just
as slow then riding back up   along calves   my belly   stares
at me   you know   the way they say men look at women in

the west   belly skin tingling   collarbone and up to my eyes
again   black white eyes gather mine   holds me with her
eyes   lips smile   I smile back   and every inch of me that
didn't before smoulders now   bones   blood   chirr   clunk

and I wink at her   her smile grows   she winks back   blinks
back   both eyes   smiles   smiles   what else I wonder   what
else can there be after this this moment already full
consummate   and I slouch back into the van   snug   smug in

the back seat   she likes the look of your wallet jo says   your
passport rob says   but I don't listen   turn to stare out the
window as we drive off to see   will this african love wave
at me   will she wave to me as the pied crow calls above

/ FOLLOWING YOU

/ BY MELANIE **CAMERON**

Two crows on a stripped, bleached log
that fuses to the ruddy
shoulder blade of the river.

This wood bone, this naked
sun-baked wing of silt, and still

there is something here for the crows—

if not something
to feed on, or something to weave into
a nest, then at least

the taut beauty of this

slowly unfolding

river. The crows

lift, pass

me, you, on the bank, one

by one. What mathematics
cannot foretell—that only
death will divide

two, when one chooses to follow
one, whether fleeing

from beauty, or tracing

paths deeper
into the open
surface
of love.

/ RECOGNIZING YOU

/ BY MELANIE **CAMERON**

How a pair of crows will always land
among others. How they will all
look alike. But how I will always
recognize

you, lift when you lift, bend
my open arms
like wings through air, toward and around
your bending. Then

how we will land again,

inside
one
another.

/ THE SUPERBEE

An excerpt from a novel-in-progress entitled "Exhaust"

/ BY WARREN **CARIOU**

I can trace my fortunes back through the avenues of disaster and choice and dumb-ass luck to a quiet Saturday in June, less than three weeks before my seventh birthday, when I was left alone at the ranch house for the first time. That was when I became who I am. Before that day I didn't quite exist, or at least I don't recognize my earlier self, can't draw the lines of causation back to that little creature who stares out of the family photographs, who occupies my earlier memories. But that particular day, things began to happen, things that led me to where I am now. I remember it like a Super 8 movie—over- and underexposed, frenetically jittery, awash in the autumnal shades of early Kodacolor—though of course my family made no such films when I was a kid. We had no money until later, and by then the fad of Super 8 had passed.

I remember spending the afternoon by myself in my last change of clothes—shaggy cutoffs and a green T-shirt handed down from my cousin Andy—while my mom was over at Aunt Lucille's place doing mountains of laundry. My sister Tilly had gone along, and I would have been forced to go too, except my father was supposed to be home from the rigs any time, and I had wailed and cried and bargained to be able to wait there for him. Dad had been working on the rigs all winter, three weeks on and two weeks off, and whenever he came home he brought treats for us kids. Sometimes it was pink popcorn in a box, with plastic power rings or tiny mazes or whistles wrapped up in the bottom, and other times it was a doll for Tilly and a toy gun or a slingshot for me. Once it was even a game called Operation, where you had to reach inside the body of a man and pull out his liver or his spleen or his kneecap without touching the sides of the holes. We never knew what Dad would come up with. And because the suspense had got me worked up to the point of nausea, I was willing to bargain away several days' worth of extra chores in return for the privilege of waiting. Finally Mom agreed, either because she thought my presence might discourage Dad from getting too deeply into his rum and Coke or because she just couldn't take my whining anymore. She piled the laundry in the backseat of Aunt Lucille's Plymouth and then the three of them—Tilly, Aunt Lucille, and Mom—hovered back down the driveway, waving like they were in a float at the Stampede parade.

I waited in the yard, sitting among tufts of quackgrass and foxtail and mats of creeping charlie, tinkering with the remnants of a Meccano set I had got for Christmas, trying to make something—a bridge, a tower, a baseball bat—out of four yellow girders, three red ones, and half a dozen blue bolts. Nothing I made looked like anything, but I continued the quest for some kind of resemblance. I wanted to be a builder man when I grew up, to be like Uncle Harv and *work the high steel*, which Uncle Harv had only done for three weeks in Toronto but still it was the highlight of his life. He never got tired of telling the stories. "Standin' there in the forty-mile-an-hour wind," he would say, "and twenty-inch I-beams sailing back and forth on the crane cables and tryin' to eat your lunch without heavin' it all back out on the guy below, I tell you it was a treat. If you can do that you can do any goddamn thing, was what I told myself. So once I proved I could do it I said fuck this proverbial noise I'm finding a job that don't make me want to puke."

Uncle Harv's favourite word was "proverbial." He pronounced it like a swear word, and as a kid I thought maybe it was one. Perverbial. "So there they were," he liked to say to his men friends out in the workshop, "doin' the old perverbial on the piano bench, when all at once . . ." Or when the family was going fishing up north and Dad drove maniacally over the whoop-de-doo hilltops, accelerating at the crests, Uncle Harv would wink and say, "Oooooeee, don't that get ya square in the perverbials?"

For a few years I wanted to be Uncle Harv. Except without the belly.

I sat there in the prickly grass under the aching sunlight, making nothing much at all out of the remains of my Meccano set, wishing for a Spirograph or a skateboard for my birthday, wondering if I was adopted like my friend Gordy, and if so, how would they know when my birthday was? I decapitated dandelions with a flick of my thumb, singing *Had a little baby but his head popped off!* I watched the black ants molest the nodding spheres of the peony buds beside the porch, two or three ants at a time, clinging there unmoving as if sniffing the flower prematurely, or maybe boring down into it, sucking out its goodness before it could bloom. I shook the ants off one bud and sawed it in half with my jackknife and beheld the miniscule pink pleats inside, ready to unfold, like a parachute before it opens. Then I cut into several of the bleeding heart flowers and explored their delicate chambers, their nascent ventricles empty of blood. And when I was finished those dissections I peeled an old golf ball that I'd found in the porch, cutting into the broad smile that my father had sometime whacked into its weathered skin, pulling back the flap to expose the windings of thin thin rubber band, which I slowly unravelled from the shrinking ball, backing my way around the yard as if marking the way out of a labyrinth.

The ball had nearly shrunk to its dense black centre when I saw something lumbering up the gravel road that led out to our driveway and past that to the bridge over to the reserve. It was a car, of course, but so unlike any car I had ever seen that I had to wonder if it was something aeronautical, or a space probe or a robot of some kind, sent there on an exploratory mission. It was the most outlandish green, a green that stood out against the grass and the poplar leaves and the dark shadows of the spruces like an altogether different colour, an unnamed one yet to be discovered in the spectrum: a pulsing green, a plastic one. And it had huge black stripes along its muscular flanks, stripes that looked like armour plating, exoskeleton.

It rumbled along the gravel road and I stared, with a tenth of a golf ball in my left hand and half a mile of rubber filament knitting its way from my fingers across the yard. Where would a car like that be going? I knew virtually nothing yet about cars, except what I had gleaned from the Stonehenge of wrecks in our back forty and the moving wreck that my parents drove, the old International truck with its gaping holes in the floorboards that you had to keep your foot over in rainy weather unless you wanted to be sprayed in the face. What I did know about cars was that one like this green monstrosity would have no business out here on this road; it must be lost or prowling or involved in something illegal.

But believe it or not it was turning in at our driveway, and I saw the flash of sun off the polished wheels, the cut of chrome against the dun switchgrass at the road's edge, and as it straightened out again a gleam slid over the body panels like a wash of foam, the crest of a wave, and I heard the deliberate rumble and resonance of tuned exhaust, the engine pulling at even revs, just above idle, firing out an announcement of its potential, like the low growl of a dog at his food when you get too close. There was a man at the wheel, wearing aviator sunglasses and a white T-shirt, and his left arm was out the window, his fingertips just touching the cupped shape of the lime-green side mirror, as if to hold the car back, to say, "Steady girl, steady. Don't lose your cool."

The man held a cigarette in his other hand and he was steering with the heel of that same hand, and his smile was like the wizened golf ball I had just unravelled, an impossible beaming—and suddenly I understood the Kool-Aid commercial about *That big wide happy, ear-to-ear Kool-Aid Smi-i-ile*, except this grin went even beyond liquid refreshments of any kind: it was the pure and radiant and beautifully egocentric smile of a man with a new car. Unmistakeable even to those neophyte males who had never seen it. Part of the genetic code.

I knew I wasn't supposed to talk to strangers in cars, but what could I do in my own yard anyway, and this guy was probably looking for directions back to the highway and out of this hole and he would probably say, "Hey, little man, I'm looking for the road back to California where I came from, how's about you help me out?" And anyway I knew it would look odd to run away now; the guy might realize nobody else was home and start helping himself to our nonexistent valuables. So I didn't move at all, except for my eyes tracking this green missile that keened to a stop less than thirty feet away from me. The driver had cranked the steering wheel a second before stopping, so the car was nosed slightly off the driveway, showing off its angles.

"So?" the man shouted over the clamour of the engine. "Whatcha think, Bud?"

Then the cigaretteless hand came up to that buoyant face and drew the sunglasses down so the eyes could peer out over the lenses, and I felt a tremor in myself, a charge of duodenal energy as I studied those dark blue eyes and that jaw and the wavy black lubricated hair and the mosslike, unruly eyebrows. I picked these features one by one out of the face and arrived at the inescapable conclusion that the man I was staring at was my father.

There. In that phenomenal humming beast. Its cylinders idling out the rhythm of a message: *gonna gonna gonna gonna gonna gonna gonna gonna.*

At first I could only think about what was missing. Where was our old Chitty Chitty Bang Bang truck? Where was Dad's Imperial Oil ball cap, and his plaid flannelette shirt, and the oil-mud that usually coated him from head to foot?

What was most obviously missing was the perennial expression of puzzlement on my dad's face, the look of loserhood, of inconsequence: the sense that he was doomed before he started. I had never been able to pinpoint that aspect of my father before, but now that it was gone I recognized its former omnipresence. Albert Aloysius Fontaine had always looked like he was the butt of someone's joke. Years later I would be able to recognize it in the family pictures: my father's vague owliness, his air of incipient dissatisfaction with himself and his lot in life. The sense that he was looking at a place two feet in front of the camera rather than directly into its measuring eye, as if he was embarrassed at being caught there in the past, left behind in history.

But now, as of this moment, that look of my father's was gone.

I had never even dreamed about cars at this point, had never thought to covet the Mustangs and Barracudas or even the Oldsmobiles that blew by us on the highway every time we drove to town in the old truck. The arrival of this car was like something from the *Richie Rich* comics I read at Danny's house, or something from TV, where such transformations were possible. It had no connection to my ideas of my own bland future.

"Well?" my dad said (yes, it *was* my dad), and he held his palms up toward the general magnificence of the car.

"Whose is it?" I ventured.

"Whose d'you think? Someday yours, maybe, if you're good. I got a deal on it over in Lloyd—the guy who owned it had to go to jail."

Someday yours, maybe. That phrase would rattle around in my memory for years, but at this particular moment I barely heard it, so amazed was I that my dad had told me about the car's previous owner, had spoken to me like I was not a kid but a compatriot, a buddy.

"What was he in for?"

"Grand theft auto. Just kidding, don't go popping your eyes out like that, they'll stay that way. So where's your mom?"

"Aunt Lucille and Uncle Harv's."

A hint of my father's old hangdog expression had flickered in his eyes when he asked the question, but once it had been answered he was back in full possession of his new self. He notched the shifter into gear and leaned forward on the steering wheel.

"Well then. Guess we might as well go for a drive."

The car sliced a wide arc around the yard, its undercarriage raking the long grass, and I discarded the sticky remains of my golf ball just in time before the huge green gate-like door swung open for me, and I climbed up into the black vinyl cockpit, and then we were gone, in the sudden Vesuvius of the igniting engine, the snap of acceleration banging the door shut. I had no chance to absorb the space-age ambience of gauges and lights and buttons. Everything was gravity, sitting me up straight in the leatherette seat, and then tossing me over onto the bare arm of my gearshifting father, then fling-ing me back. The slewing of rear wheels in the dusty slurry of gravel, and then the squelch of pavement and the eye-watering rush of air forcing itself in the windows, stealing the breath from my nostrils. And finally, when the acceleration tapered off, a cruising peacefulness settled upon us, a satori of speed, a harmonic convergence of motion and vibration and the sibilant whish of tires singing beneath the unending vituperation of the engine. It was built to run, this machine, it wanted to go flat out, like a thoroughbred on the way back to the stable.

"Not bad, eh?" my dad yelled.

It was all I could do to nod. I could barely see the road out the windshield, could mostly see the black precipice of the dashboard and the dusty blue sky, and between them a narrow band of asphalt wagging in the distance, radiating the heat lines of a mirage. For all I knew we had launched ourselves into the sky—except that when I looked out the side window I saw the smudged sideswipe of the whistling landscape, the reserve houses following each other like the backgrounds in a Flintstones cartoon, and then the tiny cemetery at the top of the lookout hill, and then more of the inter-changeable houses, and then trees. My dad was squinting out over the hood as if train-ing a gunsight, leaning back in his seat, steering with his right arm held straight, his fist clenched atop the wheel, like Superman flying. And grinning still. I could have sworn in that moment that the two of us were the same age.

We drove out past the sawmill where my dad and his brothers had been denied employment at least a dozen times, and then past the government experimental farms where they hadn't even bothered to apply. We sailed past Grandma and Grandpa's farmhouse without slowing down, and did the same at Uncle Harv and Aunt Lucille's, where I had expected we would stop to pick up my mom. Instead we turned north on a grid road, past the gymkhana grounds with their rickety white grandstands, and crossed the river again on a rusty steel bridge, and we came out of a pine forest into a large alfalfa field with a spindly oil derrick poking out of it, which my dad pointed to and shouted, "See? They're even drilling *here*!"

And we kept on rolling, criss-crossing the district on backroads and highways, blowing past other vehicles toddling toylike along the shoulders—the two of us, father and son, waving and laughing as we slingshotted by. I sensed that my dad would never again be so reckless, and the car would never be so loud and so green and so perfectly rancorous, and for these reasons I abandoned myself to the ride without the slightest bit of fear.

What I remember most clearly about the ride, though, is not the velocity but the slow and rumbling ambulations through town at something approaching the speed limit. Watching people watching us, cataloguing the looks of disdain and admiration and alarm the car inspired.

"Rubberneckers!" Dad would say, and tromp on the accelerator.

No one had ever looked at us before, except maybe to feel sorry, or to laugh. *There go those Fontaines again, sad case.* But now people could hardly tear their eyes away. The parking meter lady gawked at us as we cruised down Main Street, and so did Mr. Jayco out sweeping the sidewalk of Jayco's Sporting Goods. A family of five stood paralyzed outside the Dairy Freez, their unlicked soft-serve cones leaning like torches in the wind. A Mercury full of teenagers honked. Three separate old ladies pinched their faces at the onslaught of green, and one of them wagged an index finger. While we were gassing up at Jerry's Spray 'n' Serve, the gas jockey made eyes at the car, caressing the wheel well with one hand as he worked the nozzle.

"Hey Eddy!" he called to the guy inside. "Check out the Superbee!" And that was the first time I heard what the car was called. I whispered to myself, "Superbee, Superbee, Superbee," while the young men studied the car's insignias, the airfoil wing on the trunk lid, the flared nostrils of the hood scoops.

"440 Six Pack," my dad said to them, almost casually, as he propped open the hood and they gazed inside. I couldn't see the engine from my seat, but I peered between the hinges at their idolatrous faces. They looked like a Christmas card I had seen, of the Three Wise Men staring down at baby Jesus.

All this time, fuel kept funnelling into the bottomless tank.

Finally we were rolling again and I had a Mars Bar and a cream soda for supper, and I cradled them against my bony chest because I had promised for god's sake not to spill. And just when I thought I had already reached the pinnacle of my life, we pulled up at Parkton's only stoplight and there on the corner was David Turner, the grade four kid who had won all the ribbons at field day that year, and who was captain of my intramural team, the Dusters. A flashing walk light beckoned David Turner but he didn't notice. He stood there with his arms dangling past his pants pockets like decorations, staring at the car, his mouth forming a silent syllable: "Hoooooooo!"

And then he recognized me. He didn't wave or even nod his head, but our eyes connected and I saw the hitch of recognition there, the current of awe. I sensed the car around me like a garment, an aura, and that was when my father's phrase *maybe yours someday* came back to me for the first time. And then, before I could think to dispense a smile or a nod or some other bonbon of association to David Turner, the light changed and we were charging up Main Street toward the train station.

When we finally turned off the highway toward home, dazed with momentum and clamour, my dad took his foot off the accelerator and we idled along the gravel driveway for a while, neither of us speaking. Halfway down, Dad veered off into the alfalfa field, keeping a clump of lilacs between us and the house. Through the leaves we could see that the porch light was already on, even though the sun was still high.

Dry grass clattered under the car as we idled past the falling-down workshop, and suddenly I saw where we were going: the graveyard of wrecked cars at the edge of Mr. Holman's oat field. There were eight vehicles altogether, rusted right down into the ground: trucks and cars that had belonged to Mr. Holman's hired men over the years, or maybe even to some of his town friends who didn't have the luxury of their own car cemetery.

Dad swung the wheel and we pulled in next to an ancient windowless jalopy. He switched off the ignition, and the engine almost refused to die, as if it believed it might

161

be left there forever with the rest of the hulks—but finally it was silent and we sat there for a few seconds, adjusting to the idea of stasis.

"Alright," Dad said then, and reached for the door handle. "You better go play out back, while I break the news to your mother."

In the years between that day and my teenagehood, I would go on to learn everything about the car. I would haunt the magazine stand at Dalke's Drugs downtown, and buy (or sometimes steal) any magazine that mentioned the Superbee or its cousins, the Dodge Charger and Plymouth Roadrunner. I would memorize the statistics of the 440 Six Pack engine: its bore and stroke, its revolutionary multi-port carburetion, its 300 horsepower and 290 foot-pounds of "stump-pulling" torque at 6200 RPM. By the time I was thirteen I would be able to recite the transmission's gear ratios, and I would know by heart every option the car had come with: the Hearst Pistol-Grip shifter, the dished steering wheel, the Super-performance axle package and the 4.10 Dana 60 rear-end, the Rallye wheels. I would learn that the car's distinctive colour was called Sublime Green, and that the other colours available that year had been Yellow Jacket, Rallye Red, and In-Violet.

But in those first moments alone with the Superbee, just after my father had left for the house to talk it all over with my mom, I knew nothing about the car except that it was my future. I was afraid to stay with it at first, and I walked halfway toward the old workshop where I'd left my bike before I turned again to look back at the machine, coruscating there in the bloodless sunset. I wasn't supposed to play among the dead cars anymore, ever since I cut my hand on the old grain truck's fender the previous summer and had to get a tetanus shot. But the Superbee held me there by its green gravity. It drew me in. I huddled behind a smashed-up, cross-eyed delivery van and watched my dad high-stepping through a stand of wild oats toward the house. I knew my mom would be out soon to look at the car, and I wanted to see her face when she did, wanted to witness my own astonishment re-enacted there, and perhaps even to read in her features the meaning of this momentous event. Because now that the whirl and thunder of my first ride had receded into memory, I was more and more certain that the car was going to change all of us, as it had already changed my father.

I had never seriously contemplated the prospect of things in my life changing, except in incidental ways. Of course I would grow up and progress through the grades at school, and some day *work the high steel* like Uncle Harv. But even then, I believed, I would still be living with my family in the same old ramshackle rental house with its ragged tarpaper siding, and my sister would still be three years old, and my parents would continue to smoke Sweet Caporals and drink rum at the kitchen table almost every night, playing cribbage with the same greasy deck of *Viva Las Vegas* cards and telling the same stories about the same neighbours and relatives. *Fifteen-two, fifteen-four, and there ain't no more.*

But now my future was as wide open as the yawning throat of a 440 Six Pack carburetor. It could take me anywhere. If something like *this* could happen, what else might occur in the coming weeks and months? Maybe David Turner would be my friend in school. Maybe Chrissy Durocher would give me a kiss like she did to Marlon Torchewsky in the coatroom the previous fall, though I would never tell anyone if she did. Maybe no one would tease me about floodpants and stinky hair, and the boys wouldn't give me charley horses or threaten to make me eat yellow snow. And maybe a camera crew would appear at my family's broken-down front steps and a man in a suit would announce, "You, Julian Gabriel Fontaine, have won the big big draw . . . A MILLION DOLLARS and free Pink Elephant popcorn every day for the rest of your life!"

The car radiated maybes.

"Eeeeeeeooooooooowwwwwwmmmmmmmmm!" I said, and swung my arm in a wide horizontal arc past the Superbee, as if it was a Hot Wheels miniature and I could hold it in the palm of my hand.

It regarded me with frowning pugilism. How different it felt to watch the beast from a distance than to be inside, enveloped in its green menace. I moved toward it, drawn unerringly to its ballistic, wide-nostrilled, predatory front end. I didn't dare touch it. Heat levitated off the hood, and the engine clinked and ticked underneath, as if tapping to get out. It smelled of grease and rubber and the peppery stink of burning insects caught in the grille.

I progressed down the car's smooth flank to the place behind the rear fender where the two wide racing stripes met and surrounded the Superbee insignia: a yellow cartoon bee, leaning forward into the wind of its own momentum, smiling a sidewise grin of glee and concentration, with a hint of smugness that said, "I can't believe I'm getting away with this!" The bee wore goggles and a racing helmet with pert antennae jutting out of it, much like The Great Gazoo. And its most prominent features were the two huge rubber-burning dragster tires affixed to its abdomen, churning so furiously they had gone elliptical. On the bee's back were his folded needless wings and an enormous hood-scoop mounted on an engine block. This thing was all motor and traction and sting.

With my index finger I traced the bee's outline on the body panel. And once I had touched the car again it was only a matter of seconds before I cupped my hands beside my eyes, leaned down onto the glass of the driver's-side window, and became my father: shifting through the rabid gears, dancing on the pedals, roaring over the back-roads and humming along the town streets. I imagined slowing down to whistle at Chrissy Durocher as she walked on the reserve road to her grandma's place, and I thought of the way she would smile, a brief unveiling of her white white teeth as she blushed and glanced down at the roadway, and the car kept flying past, abandoning her in its wake, and she looked up and waved timidly just before it reached the horizon. Then, still glowing with the memory of Chrissy's coy little cup-handed wave, I aimed the green beast toward town and idled up Main Street to stop at the traffic light, where David Turner was still standing.

Gonna gonna gonna gonna.

163

/ THE DARK PART OF THE SKY

/ BY JONATHAN **BALL**

My earliest memory is of socks. My feet bare, my mother scolding. The socks were a day old, a present from my grandparents. A day old and already ruined, by my mother's standards. A mother's expectations are higher than a child could ever dream. It is a miracle that they continue to love.

The world is full of holes. They appear in socks, they eat through leaves, they arise in the ether itself, blossoming and elastic in the spaces between things. They flourish in our memories. The past is not the past at all, existing only in photographs and half-remembered, half-invented utterances.

The look on my mother's face. The trembling in her voice. *Reality is threatening to consume itself, and with it, us.* Bend your knees, say your prayers, beg forgiveness. Lord, deliver us from entropy, let now not be the hour of our deaths. Mary, gracious Mother, mend my socks.

When I was growing up, Sundays were Church, and Church Sundays. There was no important difference between the two. They began each week, set its tone, dictated its content. Sunday morning, mother awakened my brother and me without fuss, breathing our names on the backs of our necks.

"David," she said. A fine mist, drifting down.

I turned to her, eyes blurry with sleep, but she was already gone. Bending down to my sleeping brother on the lower bunk. "Joshua." Even so early, she already sported her Sunday best. "Come now. You can't sleep all day."

We longed to prove her wrong. I was the later riser, lingering in bed while Joshua showered. I read. In those days, before the caterpillars came, I read young adult mysteries. The books had simple plots, about money stolen or scammed. The criminals were clever, but not as clever as the young detective. Near the end of each book, our hero revealed the circumstances and motivations surrounding the commission of the crime. Once proven guilty through these logical manoeuvres, the criminals shrugged their shoulders and admitted defeat. They never tried to escape, appeal, or deny the charges.

Even so young, I was something of a skeptic. But I found these stories comforting. I liked thinking there were mysteries in the world—mysteries that could be solved, shelved and moved beyond.

While we showered and dressed, mother made breakfast. The meal depended on how we acted in Church the previous Sunday. If we were quiet, attentive, if we sang our best, we were treated to pancakes or French toast, fragrant and drowning in syrup. If we took a particular interest in the sermon, she served crepes bursting with strawberries that, in the summer, still smelled of our garden's dark earth. But if we grew bored, or otherwise distracted, we ate cold cereal or sugarless oatmeal. Once, during a rather long sermon, I produced a silent but unmistakable yawn. The next week, we were ushered off to Church in a rush, without pausing for breakfast at all. Joshua hated me for days. We were never punished separately, and so had to police each other.

After breakfast, mother went out to start the car while we hugged Father good-bye. Father never came to Church. Neither of us asked why, it seemed so obvious. Church was the House of God, to which we paid weekly visits. Our house, where we spent every day, was the House of Father. It was only proper for each deity to maintain his own residence. I dipped my fingers in the font and crossed myself before God welcomed me into His house, and when I arrived home I knocked three times on the locked door and waited. There was silence. Then the staccato drumming of Father's long fingers, followed by a hard rap and the click of the door unlocking. All people and all places have their rituals.

I liked Church. Church in a small town is not the same as Church in a city. In a city church is not capitalized. Since moving to Toronto, I have only been to church once. The water in the font was cold. I don't remember the holy water ever being cold when I was a child in small-town Brussels.

I liked the *mystery* of Church, that word the priest always used when he talked about God. *These are the mysteries of God,* he said, and I leaned forward to listen. He told the most strange and wonderful stories then, of transformation, of miracles. When the caterpillars came, he spoke of *plague.* After which he attempted to explain the meaning of these stories, and it was then I struggled to sit still, keep my eyes open, stifle yawns. These explanations did not satisfy me. God was not a mystery like the ones in the books I read, something that could be explained away by connecting a few dots.

But if God was, indeed, a mystery, he could be solved, explained. The priest believed this, it was obvious, but his conclusions were too reductive; he ignored large parts of the stories to focus on other, smaller parts. Mother echoed him. My brother was nine, almost two years younger than me, and found it impossible to pay attention to anything, even God, for over half an hour. But Father, by not attending Church, signalled to me that he had already solved this mystery. However, he avoided the subject. Whenever I asked him questions, the room grew quiet. "Ask your mother," he said, but she was the one who had stopped speaking.

The caterpillars came slowly at first, trickling into the world, a few tears preceding the flood. That spring, as I approached my eleventh birthday, I began to notice webbing in the trees. One night, while Father was eating a late dinner after a long day working at his brother's sawmill, I began to tell him about these odd clumps of webbing. He stopped eating, put down his plate, moved to the doorway and began putting on his shoes. "Show me." I looked at Mother, but she looked away, and began to run water for the dishes. I pulled on my shoes while Father rummaged in the laundry room for a can of bug killer, and then led him to one of the small trees planted to screen off our yard from the neighbours.

"Up there." A small clump of webbing stretched from the trunk across three branches. Father took a long look, shook up the can, and sprayed the webbing until it dripped.

From then on, Joshua and I were my father's soldiers, on the hunt for tent caterpillars and their "camps." Father called them "army worms," and we took to calling them worms too, though we didn't draw the word out with the venom that he did. Our time playing in the town became more serious, and wherever we went we investigated the trees before beginning our games. Anything we found was reported to Father that night over dinner.

He was fanatical in his hunt, emptying can after can, but must have known from the beginning that he was fighting a losing battle. With each nest he demolished, his resolve diminished instead of increasing, hope fading in the face of hopelessness. When Brussels awoke one day to find it was being eaten alive, he didn't raise a single eyebrow in surprise. Instead, he walked through the house, closing all of the blinds— an oracle whose prophecy had come to pass, no longer in need of its vision.

Caterpillars clogged the streets. They caused accidents by obscuring road signs. They ruined footwear, guts soaking into the material, which cracked amber flakes and smelled like rotten meat. They stripped trees of their leaves, of their essence. The hunger of the worms was exceeded only by their number. Hundreds died every day, rose again in the night. They crawled into every conversation. *The worst it's ever been. An epidemic.* They were bold enough to invade my dreams, night-time phantasms of zombie caterpillars crawling over my skin. One night I woke shivering from such a nightmare, only to find myself face to face with one of the infernal worms. My father had failed. The world was no longer safe.

I began writing, then. It began as an offshoot of my reading, as I put away my simple mysteries in the face of more complex ones. I dug out the set of encyclopaedias my parents had bought for me a few years ago, finding them at a garage sale and thinking I could use them when I started high school. It occurred to me that I knew nothing about the caterpillars, and that if I learned more about them I might be able to think of some way to deal with them. As it turned out, later, it was my failure to understand the worms even after this research that spurred me into action. But then, while reading, I found one entry suggesting another, and as I leapt from volume to volume I found it difficult to remember all the things I was learning. So I got my mother to buy me a small spiral-bound scribbler, where I recorded interesting facts and bits of trivia about the caterpillars, and anything else I found interesting.

Even after the caterpillars were gone, I read and wrote until the notebook was full and I needed a second one. Just before starting this second book, I became interested in astronomy, fascinated by the idea of Earth as a small sphere amongst other spheres, something never discussed in Church. This second book I divided into two sections. In the first I noted various bits of trivia. The second was reserved for definitions. I liked astronomy because the words held such power. Among them were the names of gods, and simple gods at that, pinned to the sky in constellations, like dead moths in display cases. These gods did not move. They offered their bodies to me, exposed themselves to every light. They were immense, and strange, but not unimaginable like the God I was used to.

It was not until many years later, while in university, that I stumbled upon my most interesting bit of trivia. In the centre of the Milky Way galaxy, at the heart of our small section of the universe, lies a tremendous black hole known as Sagittarius A*. At the very centre of this black hole exists what is known as a singularity, a point of compressed matter so dense that its gravity collapses all nearby matter and light into itself. This singularity is incredibly small, almost infinitely so, though it contains a mass estimated at 2.6 million times that of the sun. The remainder of the expansive Sagittarius A* is a void in which nothing can exist without collapsing into the singularity. Once anything moves within the proximity of the black hole, passing what is known as the point of no return, it is absorbed into the singularity.

Or so the theory goes. All science is theory, something which frustrated me as a child, but which I have made my peace with now. Another theory I found fascinating was that of the Big Crunch. After time inestimable, the universe will collapse into itself. Worlds will collide. Galaxies will merge. Presence will be absence, the cosmos will be void, collapsed into itself, save for a sort of universal singularity, a dense point containing all energy and matter. Every drop of rain, every beam of light, every word ever spoken, every once-living cell, all will become one. But only for an instant. The moment such perfect unity is achieved, a critical mass will be reached, and in one Big Bang the universe will rise, phoenix-like, yet again—as it has perhaps already done.

But this is only one possibility. The Big Crunch can only take place if there is sufficient matter present in the universe. Scientists have no accurate way to measure all the matter in the universe, but attempts to do so suggest that in fact there will be no Big Crunch after all. The alternative possibility is that the universe will continue to expand eternally, dying a slow heat death as it does, slowing to a crawl and then a final, cold and silent stop.

If these measurements are correct, our only hope for renewal lies in the existence of dark matter. Theorists are divided on the subject of its existence. Just as I wonder about the spaces between the stars: what lies there, in the dark part of the sky?

It was midday, and the sun blazed, but the curtain was drawn over the lone window in the room I shared with my brother. I used to like to look out at the sky, but I kept it drawn all the time now. The worms had suction-cup feet. They clung to the glass, writhed across its flatness. If you dropped them in water, they skipped across the surface tension to safety. Unholy soldiers, marching in mockery of the once-Lord Jesus. They called to me in my dreams. *Come out amongst the waves. Outside. You will not drown, as long as you have faith.* I stayed seated inside. I was almost eleven, too old for miracles.

I read encyclopaedias, my new Bibles. The door creaked. My breath stopped. I raised a book, to bring it down upon any fuzzy intruder. But it was only Joshua, and I began to breathe again.

"What are you doing?" he asked.

"Reading. You?"

"Nothing." He fell into a chair. "I'm sick of these stupid caterpillars. I want to go outside."

"Then go outside."

"It's disgusting."

"I've been reading about these things. *Malacosoma disstria.*" I liked the hiss of the Latin. "There's a different kind in parts of the us, and if pregnant horses eat them the baby dies."

"I wish *they* would die."

"They will, if it gets cold."

"It won't get cold for months. After school starts."

Joshua swung his feet, bored. Waiting for me to think of a diversion. But I was not in the mood for diversions. I wanted *solutions.* I sat on the edge of the bed, looking into the darkness of the heating vent in the floor below. And somehow, from somewhere terrible, something rose.

"Come on," I said, stepping down from the bed.

"Where to?"

"I'll show you." I left the room and Joshua followed. I led him to our parents' bedroom. They were gone, Father to the sawmill and Mother out shopping, but still we walked on our toes.

I rifled through their nightstands, pulling a pack of matches out of the drawer, a relic from my father's days as a smoker. "What are you doing?" Joshua asked.

"Just get dressed. We're going outside."

Joshua balked. "This is the dumbest idea ever."

"I haven't told you the idea yet."

"I don't care."

"Put on your boots. You might want to wear a jacket too, in case they start jumping from the roof."

"No." He stood in the hallway while I pulled on my rubber boots. "I'm not going."

"I need your help." I didn't, but it felt important, somehow, that he be with me. "Do you want to get rid of these things or not?"

Joshua looked down. "I guess so."

"Then get dressed. Better put on some gloves too."

Bundled and sweating, we lingered in the hallway a while before getting up the nerve to open the door. Caterpillars exploded into my vision. The trees were barely visible beneath the squirming waves of worms. They walked in sheets across the lawn, stepping over one another in the search for food. Some were balled together, worm on worm, as if they were so ravenous they had resorted to cannibalism. My heart sank. How could the two of us be any match against the demons? They were legion.

"Follow me," I said. Steeling myself, I began to walk toward the garage, a separate building on our mid-sized lot. I turned back to Joshua, who still stood in the doorway.

"What are you waiting for?"

"The garage is the worst place of all. They're raining off of it." He was right. The largest of the trees lining our yard hung over the building. Caterpillars fell from the tree in a visible torrent, onto the building and down to the ground.

"We'll run in, really fast. They aren't many in the building itself. Pull your jacket over your head." I glanced down to see caterpillars crawling up my boots. "Hurry."

I pulled my own jacket up over my head and ran toward the garage. This time, when I looked back, Joshua was following me. Caterpillars squelched beneath us. Their clinging corpses made our feet heavy and their innards made our footing treacherous, but we managed to reach the garage without tripping or falling.

Once safely inside the building, we inspected each other's jackets for caterpillars, flicking them away with our fingers. Along the back wall was a row of jars, filled with different types of nails and screws. I unscrewed one of the jars, dumped its contents onto a neat pile on the ground, and handed the jar to Joshua.

"We're going to empty all these jars," I said, "and then we're going to fill them with caterpillars."

He nodded, and began emptying the jars. Not asking what we were going to do next, after the jars were full. Thankfully. I was afraid he would ask, not what but why. That was a question it seemed wrong to answer. I had ideas, but not reasons.

I still do not have reasons. When you are young, you do not need a reason for anything. You think of things, and then you do them. Some of them make your parents smile, and some of them make the devil proud.

We spent the next hour repeating our actions. Jars were filled, matches struck, and fire dropped onto the unsuspecting caterpillars. They burned quicker than I thought they would. Thin wisps of black smoke, smelling of chlorophyll, rose from their bubbling, popping bodies. In death, the worms coalesced into a single molten mass. The sludge coated the jar, growing thicker and blacker. Their bodies fell away, melting together, so many collapsing into one.

I don't know how many of the caterpillars we managed to kill before our mother came home. She didn't scream, so we didn't notice her at first. She'd left the car running near the house and come looking for us, to help with her shopping bags. I heard Joshua draw a sharp breath, and turned to see him facing Mother, who stood near the garage door, silent and staring. She looked broken, like a beaten dog. I hurried to snuff out the burning caterpillars, as if to erase them. She stood in the doorway for what seemed like a long time, eyes moving from jar to jar, moving over us, unable to rest on any particular thing.

I turned my back to her, to see what she was seeing: a row of jars, laid out with cold precision, and inside each a smouldering black mass no longer recognizable as ever having lived. A single jar held the next batch of victims, a horde of suffocating worms, climbing the walls in a futile attempt to escape. Their desperation was palpable, a stench as strong as the odour that rose from their burning bodies. Maddened, they crawled up the smooth glass only to hit the lid, fall back, and begin to climb again with renewed fury. In the jar I had just snuffed out, a few still-living caterpillars were mired in the sticky blackness, struggling against the gelled corpses to tear themselves loose from a death they had never before known.

I was saddened, then, by what I had done, but it was only when I turned to see Joshua, matches in hand, that I began to feel what my mother must have felt.

When Father found out, he scolded us for ruining his jars and playing with matches, and in my mind it was because of this, because his reaction implied sympathy with our behaviour, that my mother divorced him two years later. She never set foot in the garage again, parked her car on the street even in the middle of winter.

Our attempt to liberate the outdoors resulted in our confinement indoors for the next few weeks, and in the cancellation of my birthday party. I still got a present, a shiny black perfect-bound notebook and a book about the solar system, but I wasn't allowed to have them until school began. And though I regretted my actions, they seemed effective. We couldn't have killed enough of the caterpillars to make any real impact on their numbers, but nonetheless they began to retreat, morale shattered, perhaps. Within a few days, only skeletal trees remained to document their passing. Not a leaf was left on the limbs bordering our lawn.

Reality appeared more fragmented from then on. Everywhere I looked I could see that the world was not whole. The worms had shown me the corrosion awaiting all things, and although they had departed, eyes opened could not be closed again. I sat on the edge of my bed, staring out the window into the night sky, looking not at the stars but at the spaces between them.

I was quiet then, as I am now, remembering, writing this. I thought about worms then, but now I think about black holes, of the void at the heart of the world. And I tapped my chest then, as I tap it still, like I used to knock on my father's front door.

When the gods died, they went up into the sky, but they couldn't fill it. The emptiness clung to the stars, moved between them, and still it keeps forcing them further and further apart. As they move out, away from each other and from parts of themselves, they slow down, grow tired and cold. And they were gods. What will happen to me? Already, in my chest, I can hear it thud hollow.

/ SEASONAL

/ BY SARAH **KLASSEN**

The machine chews on grass or what's left of it
after a season of heat.

From the deck a woman, a plate of pasta on her lap,
monitors with obvious intent the boy

who follows the machine, a power mower
neither too sleek nor absolutely obsolete.

Yellow jackets practise their usual buzzing around
savoury or sweet. Half-eaten pasta tempts them.

The boy pursuing the machine tempts them too
and the woman who watches the umpteenth

turn, a noisy direction change the boy guides.
He pretends to ignore the woman observing

his moves. Does she think she's got a clue
what's going on in his brain? He's impatient,

bored with the back and forth, the machine's
incessance, yellow jackets circling and circling.

Should someone pay attention?
Should the woman shift her gaze

away from the boy and his aging machine, escape
the annoying buzz, scan the anonymous distance?

She takes her plate back to the kitchen, pours coffee
sloppily as if she's bothered by the constant

motion under the sun. Most likely she will order
the boy when he's done turning and turning

to find the paper nest wasps build (over and over,
according to prototype, with ingenuity)

and with whatever it takes
put an end to it.
Please.

/ UNTITLED

/ BY SARAH **KLASSEN**

With what to compare this
abstraction? What in the world
is like it? Might be
a dance of burning leaves, blue fire,
or the silk swirl of a seldom worn
garment a doting lover gave.
There is no chaos in this free shimmering.
No confusion in the blue and yellow. It is
the rare quiet of reflection the afternoon evokes
before the light dims. The memory
may find no phrase for it. And yet
the eye believes
shades of motion thus embodied will not pale
and the pure notion
of light
will be remembered.

Living Memory (Diptych)
Maria Chevsky, 1988 (Wax and oil on canvas)

/ TWO CROWS

/ BY SARAH **KLASSEN**

I heard twa corbies making a mane
             (Anonymous)

A pair of crows perched like closed books on the weathered fence.
They are reading me. Leaving me uneasy. All morning
they flapped up and down, distraught
parents, feeding their wide-mouthed fledglings
nested in the elm whose juicy leaves feed canker worms.

I am on the deck munching a tuna sandwich. I have stopped
clapping away dull-witted rabbits from my lettuce. Crows.
Whatever grows lures gluttony. Whatever lives is ravenous.
Legions of forest tent caterpillars, fat slugs, aphids
in the hollyhocks. Across the dust-choked lane,

my neighbour, paper-thin from breast cancer,
brings her book to the window. After a winter of surgery
and chemo, volumes of radiation, light swims through her.
Only a miracle, her doctor says, will shrink the canker in her chest,
and only sleep silence the crows' loud conversation,
blot out (her words) the hungry shadow of black wings.

/ from KADDISH

/ BY DAVE **MARGOSHES**

This sequence of dialogue between two old brothers, Zan and Abe Zachman, is from my novel "Kaddish," which I began while I was living in Winnipeg as writer-in-residence for the Guild, 1995-96. Ten years on, I'm still working on that novel!

"Pass the bread."

"Pass? It's right there. You got a sprained arm, maybe?"

"Okay, okay. Bread like this, the least you could do is pass. It ain't Gunn's, you know."

"Gunn's? Gunn's Bakery?"

"What else?"

"On Selkirk?"

"Where else?"

"In Winnipeg?"

"Abela, take a look at me. It's Zannie, your brother, remember? What else would I be talking about? Gunn's Bakery, Selkirk Avenue, Winnipeg, Manitoba, Canada."

"So how could it be Gunn's? It ain't Gunn's. It's Superstore."

"Superstore! That ain't Raber's Grocery."

"Again with what it ain't. It ain't Raber's. Why should it be? It is what it is, not what it ain't."

"Gunn's was better, believe me. So was Raber's."

"Gunn's was good, sure. This is too. Raber's was good, but it was small. And Raber always marked up too high. Superstore is big. Raber's in the winter had oranges. Superstore in the winter has oranges, melons, apples, grapes . . ."

"Just like California."

"But this ain't California. Again with what this ain't. This is here, now. Why not tell what this is?"

"What this is? This ain't the old neighbourhood. You remember Civkin's barber shop?"

"Remember it? I got my hair cut there ten thousand times. How could I forget?"

"And the conversation? Always, the old men in the morning talking about yesterday's *Tag* like it was today's. Philosophy, art. Playing chess."

"But would they buy the *Free Press* from you?"

"Not on your life."

"'War coming,' it says in *Der Tag*, that's yesterday. 'War breaks out,' in the *Free Press*, that's today. But will they buy the *Free Press* from you?"

"No, they sit and talk about the war that's coming."

"That's you."

"That's me?"

"Like those old men at Civkin's."

"What, I'm reading *Der Tag*?"

"Not exactly."

"What exactly?"

"Yesterday's news."

"What about it?"

"You're reading it . . . you are it."

"What, because I'd like a piece of decent rye bread?"

"Because this is here and you're still walking down Selkirk Avenue like forty years haven't passed by."

"Fifty."

"Fifty? Sixty, you mean."

"Why stop at sixty? Seventy."

"Exactly, seventy years and you're still there, like nothing's happened."

"So? It's not such a bad place to be. This is better?"

"Not better. This is this. That was that. This is where we are."

"And that's such a big deal?"

"A big deal? What, to be alive? Yeah, that's a big deal, Mr. Big Shot California. Maybe to you it isn't. To me, it is."

"That's not what I meant."

"So what you meant?"

"Never mind."

"Now it's never mind. First you're on Selkirk Avenue by Civkin's barber shop, now you're on Nevermind Boulevard in Hollywood, California."

"Another place that's not so bad to be."

"I'll take this place."

"This place! Is there a Gunn's? Is Civkin's down the street?"

"Now you're really talking *meshuggana*. Civkin's was two blocks over."

"I'm meshuggana? It was just down the street, past the Queen's Theatre."

"Wake up and drink your coffee, Zannie. That's Misha's on the Gunn's block."

"Misha's?"

"Sure. With the picture of the fireman's dog in the window. What that fireman's dog was doing there, I never knew. To ward off fire, maybe. West from Gunn's, the Queen's Theatre, a hardware man every year a different name, the *Jewish Post*. The other way, Saidman's Seeds, Kneller the carpenter, Rabkin the dentist, Kirk's deli-catessen, Misha the barber, Manitoba Upholstery, Raber's on the corner. Across the street . . ."

"Okay, okay."

"Civkin's, two blocks over, the other way."

"So why'd we go so far?"

"You're asking me? Pop liked Civkin's."

"So how come you remember all this so good? I'm the one who's there, you say, you're the one who's here."

"How come? I don't have a head full of garbage, that's how come. I don't think about it, that's how come I can."

"Can what?"

"Think about it, Mr. Big Shot. When I have to."

/ BY MÉIRA **COOK**

#60

Westward ho ho ho. Trudgy with weariness
off the gimlet shift and longing
for the vicious rounding of a little sleep.
But how to get home again, homesweet

east-best and wee wee wee (all the way).
And she without her wings, without key
or compass or ruby mittens. She lost. Alas,
alack lacks she volition, verily

so tired, you see. Mired in the high
mucky-muck of toil & trouble, wan
and wondering, by the bus stop palely loitering.
Who owns this night the city?

Grain merchants, oilers and bankers, cutpurses,
rogues. I trow, some slithy tove
or other in an office tower 'bove Portage & Main.
The golden lad highballing his legislature

or Worm the Conqueror? She walks
to disown. The möbius spool
to spool of earth & sky, no joints showing
unpremeditated snowing

and then the lighting of the lamps.

#18

Blinks the hazy orange eye
of a no. 18 cross-town in which an old party
cable-knitted to a flecked rectitude
faces inwards profiling his spruce coin.

Above her dozy lapse
the Heinz baby food baby
agape with joy. Mood Gush
to the Last Spoonerism! Gathers the bus

and rattles them as stones into
one pocket: an old man, tired girl, that beamish
tot shiny as pate. Full
holy at last, one family, at least

for another two stops. Advertisement
for Madonna & Child, St. Joseph gazing benignly on
while the past tenses—perfects itself
in the future's radiant pigment. What the city

offers tentatively, tenderly,
late at night and far away from home:
a stone in the shoe, the body's metal-
fatigued chrome, presentiment of kinship

between strangers.

/ MIMSIE AND BOY-OH

/ BY MELISSA **STEELE**

For dinner, Boy-Oh liked a can of white albacore tuna, drained and turned out onto a large white dinner plate. He would drink a glass of milk with it and have maybe some pickled beets or a few green olives but never on the same dish. Beet juice or olive brine could not bleed into the pure pinkish white blandness of the tuna. In the fifty-five years of their marriage, Boy-Oh's dinner had always been thus. At first, Mimsie, who was too young to be married and knew nothing about cooking, welcomed Boy-Oh's ironclad consistency. It was only during the dinner party years that the full shame of Boy-Oh's particularities rained upon her. These were the fifties and the sixties, years of turkey à la king and lime Jell-O moulds, years when Mimsie had cajoled and carped and begged to get him to eat like other people, to try other foods, to vary his diet. Mimsie had become a great hostess and the slab bungalow with its picture windows and expansive L-shaped living room/dining room (the first such bungalow to be built on Waterloo Street south of Corydon, a street that is now completely filled in with similar bungalows) was perfect for entertaining Boy-Oh's business acquaintances or poker buddies or the aunts and uncles and cousins and later the kids and then the grandkids. So many times Mimsie had planned and prepared feasts that were consumed by all except Boy-Oh, who only went to synagogue for his boys' bar mitzvahs and for whom it seemed his only religion was his perfectly cylindrical meals and his drive to take care of his own. Boy-Oh had been a successful businessman; he had taken over his uncle's clothing business and turned it into a thriving blue jeans factory. In the early days, he sold to the Hutterite farmers and other small-town dwellers in rural Manitoba and Saskatchewan. When Mark took over the business, the blue jeans became chic high-fashion items that sold for hundreds of dollars a pair in boutiques in Los Angeles and Manhattan and Montreal and even Tokyo, though Boy-Oh maintained a line of farmer's overalls that he still sold in the rural general stores. He himself never wore or even owned a pair of blue jeans, but he provided for his family and that gave him the right to have a plain simple dinner prepared for him nightly by Mimsie. He had been healthy except for his spine, which began crumbling in his middle age, and some angina that caused him sporadic pains in his chest and forced him to wear a MedicAlert bracelet and carry emergency pills in his trouser pocket. By the age of seventy-five he was doubled over at an almost ninety-degree angle like a human pretzel, and more than once Mimsie found him gasping, sweating and even producing tears of agony and clutching at his heart in that made-for-television way that made both of them laugh once he'd swallowed the pill and recovered.

Mimsie's father's job had been delivering the *Winnipeg Tribune* to newsstands and drugstores before sunrise six days a week. For some mysterious reason, that was the only job he could get. Mimsie's mother had been a sad, angry woman who could love only sons, not daughters. She used to hit Mimsie with a hairbrush or just slap her with the flat of her hand. Mimsie's mother had worked as a cleaning lady and a babysitter for a rich family, the Carters, who lived in a big brick house on Wellington Crescent. The Carters had only sons, so Mimsie thought her mother must have enjoyed them very much. When Mimsie was nine, she came down with chicken pox and so did her mother and her sisters and all the Carter boys. Everyone remarked on how odd it was that Mimsie's mother had never had chicken pox before. They said it as though someone must be to blame for this oversight. Mimsie remembers her mother saying, "Little Mimsie brought home chicken pox first. I guess that was this one's little gift to me," and pointing her swollen finger (every part of her was swollen from the chicken pox) at Mimsie. "She brings them home from school and before you know it, we're all at death's door." Maybe her mother didn't really say that or didn't mean it if she had. Maybe that was her mother's way of making light, of laughing at her own fate as a way of trying to run around it or jump over it. Maybe Mimsie's mother had said nothing at all and the memory was just Mimsie's brain working so hard to try keep some detail about her mother that it made that up.

What was more unusual than a grown woman getting chicken pox was that it killed her. It took only a week. Mimsie was nine years old, recovering from chicken pox herself, and her mother was dead. Now the only money coming into the house was her father's newspaper delivery income. The house belonged to them, inherited from her grandparents, but they had nothing else. They ate only bread and margarine and matzo ball soup for dinner six nights a week. On Friday night they had kugel with raisins and walnuts and more soup. Starting with Mimsie, the girls all had to drop out of school at age thirteen to get jobs as hired help to support the family. Mimsie had loved school; she loved tests and reading and the smell of chalk and she hated looking after Mrs. Anderson's spoiled rich brats and cleaning her so-clean-you-could-eat-off-them kitchen floors. She hated it, but she did what she had to do until finally Boy-Oh rescued her from a life of drudgery.

Mimsie met Boy-Oh at her friend Lily's house, but it took Boy-Oh several years to notice Mimsie and then to save her. Boy-Oh had lost his parents when he was a teenager, and Lily's parents, who were Boy-Oh's much older brother and sister-in-law, had taken him in. He'd had to move from Montreal, where he'd grown up, to Winnipeg, where he knew nobody except his relatives. Lily's parents were average middle class, not well off, but they offered Boy-Oh a chance to study—free room and board if he could make his own tuition. He was two years older than Lily and had no use for Mimsie and Lily at first. Lily was Mimsie's best friend and they spent most of their free time together at Lily's place, imagining their futures as wealthy housewives, planning subtle tricks to play on the Anderson children, like adding a hint of mustard to their peanut butter sandwiches. Boy-Oh was formal with Mimsie, not rude, but hardly friendly. Mimsie thought he had a brotherly disdain for her and Lily. Mimsie took to helping Lily tease him in small, silly ways. They would hide his economics text or sneak into his room and turn all his socks inside out. Whatever they did to rile him, Lily and Mimsie remained invisible to Boy-Oh. He was just too serious, too driven for little-girl foolishness.

Then, one day, when Lily and Mimsie had just turned sixteen and Boy-Oh was almost nineteen and almost finished his economics degree, he offered to walk Mimsie home. Mimsie was shocked but flattered. The two of them said nothing to each other the whole three blocks from Cathedral Street to Machray. When they got to her house, Mimsie said, "Thank you, Boy-Oh, for walking with me."

Boy-Oh said, "Lily is a pretty girl, but a royal pain. Did you know you are a million times prettier than Lily and only a junior pain?"

After that, he walked her home whenever she came over to see Lily, and she came as often as she could. Boy-Oh told her about his plans after college to get into his uncle's clothing business. Mimsie told funny stories about the brats she looked after and their parents. The couple she worked for now since the Andersons let her go, the Mackenzies, treated her like she was a slave girl. They avoided her eyes when they told her what they wanted her to do. They made her turn her pockets inside out and show them the inside of her handbag whenever she left the house. Their last girl had stolen from them and they were done with trusting servant girls.

Mimsie often reminded herself how grateful she was, how blessed she was, while she dumped Boy-Oh's can of pink tuna onto his plate or when she made him his coffee and bagel every morning. When you are rescued from a terrible life of mind-numbing work, hunger and constant humiliation, you should feel fantastic every minute you're alive after that. You should, and Mimsie tried to feel that way. If anyone asked her she always said what a good life she had and she told anyone who would listen what a good provider Boy-Oh was.

After they had been married three years and Boy-Oh was getting established in the business, Mimsie started to feel violently ill. She lay in bed in the mornings and couldn't even get up to put Boy-Oh's bagel in the toaster. She refused to sip the juice that Boy-Oh brought her and wouldn't go into the kitchen to answer the phone when her friends called to see how she was. Mimsie went to doctor after doctor. One doctor put her on a cleansing diet—nothing but broth for three days. That was okay. She didn't feel like eating anyway. Another wanted her to take ice baths and then brisk walks. She balked. Another thought she had "women's trouble" and wanted to cut out her uterus. Boy-Oh said that was absurd. Instead he offered to buy her a lot and build her a bungalow. A cousin of a friend of his was developing the south part of River Heights. Their bungalow was the first house built on Waterloo Street south of Corydon. Boy-Oh got a discount for moving into a house on a street with nothing but prairie grass the rest of the block going north and all the way to Roostertown going south. When they invited people over, they always joked, "You can't miss it. Just look for the house at the end of the farmer's field."

Mimsie and Boy-Oh's house was on a corner lot with huge windows facing south and east. The kitchen had teak cupboards with magnetic cupboard door closures. It had built-ins and a breakfast nook. The benches in the breakfast area were done in turquoise padded vinyl. After the children were born, Mimsie had orange shag carpeting put in all through the living room—huge and formal and only for special occasions—and the television room which was for living in. There were five bedrooms and three bathrooms, each one with turquoise fixtures.

Mimsie loved the house so much that it cured her of her mysterious ailment. There was so much to do with decorating the house and inviting Lily and her husband, David, over for bridge and having the family over for Shabbat, and Boy-Oh's Wednesday night poker game, now held at their house, that she had no time to be sick.

While all these good times were rolling, Mimsie and Boy-Oh had three children, Mark, Daniel and Sherrie, all by cesarean section. With each pregnancy, Mimsie gained more weight and then lost even more in between. With Mark she gained thirty-five pounds and by the time he was six months old she had lost forty. With Daniel she gained forty-five and then lost fifty. And so on. She loved to eat during her pregnancies and these were the times she learned to be a brilliant cook. After each baby was born, she fell into deep despair—years later her grown-up daughter Sherrie explained that now they called that postpartum depression and they had medicine to make it lift—and she would give up eating almost completely. While she was pregnant, foods of all varieties appealed to her, but after each birth, she wanted only cigarettes and sweets. She smoked like a demon and sucked on Starbursts and everyone complimented her on her amazing ability to regain her youthful figure.

These were the fun years, the years of dinner parties and nights at the theatre and the symphony and the opera, but they were also years when Boy-Oh worked hard and came home late. He would often arrive home after eight o'clock when the children were already in bed. Mimsie would prepare his can of tuna and present it to him and he would barely grunt in acknowledgement. Mimsie would fill the dead air between them with chatter about Lily's most recent argument with David, about the menu she was planning for the next big get-together, about what horrors Mark had committed against Daniel, about what darling thing Sherrie had said. Boy-Oh was exhausted from making money so that she could have all the things she wanted, Mimsie knew, but there were times when it felt like she was married to a large lump of dough. Boy-Oh had not been particularly handsome as a young man, but he had been strong and feisty and he had known how to make her smile. Now, in the supposed good years, Boy-Oh was getting soft and pudgy. His features were melting into one another. His eyes were now red-rimmed and droopy and his teeth were yellow and chipped. The smell of cigar on his breath that had once given her a charge now reminded her of an ashtray, a large metal ashtray overflowing with butts next to the spittoon at the Viscount Gort Hotel, where Boy-Oh had his staff party every year.

Boy-Oh would perk up when they had company for bridge or poker or even a family dinner. He would joke with the children and tell dirty stories to the adults. Boy-Oh had natural warmth and he was generous to a fault with friends and family. Everyone adored Boy-Oh to the point that Mimsie nursed a secret pain because their love for Boy-Oh was all about ignoring her, not appreciating all she did as a host, a mother and a wife and all she could have been if her life had been different, if she had had an education, if she had studied music, if she hadn't been saddled with all the domestic responsibility. In short, if she hadn't been born a woman.

Mimsie loved her children. She was proud of them and thought they were better at most things than other people's children, but she was not a natural as a mother. Plus she had her children at a time when little was expected of mothers and children were supposed to be polite and grateful and generally invisible.

Mark, the oldest, was tough and strong and smart. He was a whiz at school and good at sports too. He liked to torture his brother Daniel and also insects. He dissected live insects, saying he was born curious and wanted to see how a three-legged ant (three on one side) would get around. He liked to offer his arm up for a mosquito to take a drink. Once the mosquito had settled in, Mark would pinch his arm so that the mosquito was trapped at the trough. The creature would drink and drink until its body became taut and until it finally exploded. With Daniel, Mark liked to twist his limbs or rub his face on the carpet or tickle him until he threw up. The best was tickling because Daniel seemed to enjoy it, at least he laughed hard enough, so that when he finally puked on Mimsie's precious carpet, it was Daniel's fault, not Mark's.

Daniel was skinny and smart, more school-smart than Mark, but terrified of most things and most people. He was gullible and believed in ghosts. When the boys were a little older, too old for tickling, Mark liked to whisper in Daniel's ear that he just heard the ghost of Levin Schipper rattling his newspapers in the closet in Daniel's room. Levin Schipper was the neighbour boy, two years older than Mark, who died mysteriously while delivering papers one very cold January afternoon. They found him frozen on the school steps with his eyes wide open, the kids all said, just like the little match girl from the Hans Christian Andersen story. Mark had wanted Levin's paper route but Mimsie said absolutely not. She still carried the shame of being the daughter of a newspaper delivery man and she didn't want Mark following in his footsteps. What if soul-numbing poverty skipped a generation? Plus she couldn't get the image of poor, industrious, dead Levin out of her head.

Mimsie wished Mark weren't so mean to Daniel, but she liked his go-getter attitude and she liked his curly hair and his smile, both like Boy-Oh's had been when he was young. If Boy-Oh came home from work before the children were in bed, she would tell him the terrible things Mark had done to Daniel. Boy-Oh would remove his belt and drag Mark into the den, where he would try to whip some kindness into him. Mark refused to cry. Boy-Oh would hit him only on his buttocks and his back, not wanting to harm him, but it was infuriating the way Mark just took it and took it. "Hit me harder, Dad," Mark would say. Or, "You hit like a silly girl, Dad. Come on.

Put some muscle into it." Sometimes Boy-Oh would try different straps—a wide white leather belt with a rhinestone-studded buckle that belonged to Mimsie, the fly swatter, or the paddle from the basement ping pong set. The fly swatter drew blood and the paddle left large lumpy welts. Boy-Oh was furious, but proud of Mark's tenacity. He hoped one day Mark would take over his business. "Hit me harder, Old Man," Mark would say. Boy-Oh would. Finally Mark would cry out, "Enough." He would scream and stagger backwards and then fall down and beg for mercy.

Boy-Oh would help Mark get up off the floor. He would hold him tenderly while he cried and say, "You're made solid, son. You're going to do great things in this world."

When Mark had regained his composure, he would stand up straight, pull himself away from his father's embrace and spit into the carpet at his father's feet. Then, if Boy-Oh wasn't too tired, he would have to start the whole lesson all over again or, if he'd had a long day, as he usually had, he would just stalk off, saying, "A son should respect his father. You're lucky to have a father to disrespect." The older Mark grew, the harder it was for Boy-Oh to break him down. Finally, when Mark was twelve, Boy-Oh beat him until he passed out. It scared Boy-Oh. He could see that the only way to win with Mark would be to kill him. When Mark came to, Boy-Oh said, "Son, you're almost a man. From now on, it will be up to you to act like one," and he never beat him again.

Boy-Oh never beat Daniel because Daniel was so quick to cower and whimper. All Boy-Oh had to do to discipline Daniel was to glower at him. Boy-Oh tried to hide his preference for Mark, but how could Daniel not know that he was weak and Mark was strong? When Daniel came crying to Mimsie, she tried to push him away. "Grow up," she would say. "There's no Pulitzer Prize for being a crybaby."

When he was small, Daniel would cling to her anyway and Mimsie would say, "Go and play or I'll make an outy out of that belly button." She would grab onto some part of his hard, round, toddler tummy and squeeze. If he wailed more after this, she would carry him to his room for a time-out. If he controlled himself and got quiet, she would reward him by letting him sit on her lap and bury his face in her chest. She was tiny and bony so there was nothing pillowy soft about her embrace but he liked to breathe in the smell of her and wipe his tears against the fabric of her slippery satin blouse. If she and Boy-Oh were going out later, his tear stains on her blouse would make her angry again. She would push him off her lap and say, "That's it," in a voice that sounded like the end of the world.

Daniel would flee to Majda, the nanny and cleaning girl. Majda was a teenager like Mimsie had been: young, poor, skinny, orphaned and foreign-looking, except Majda had terrible skin, while Mimsie's had been her best feature. Unlike Mimsie when she had looked after the Anderson children, Majda acted like a kid herself. She preferred playing Go Fish with Mark and Daniel and the baby, Sherrie, to doing any actual work. Mimsie always had to get after her to clean the bathrooms and to do other jobs. She brought the children chocolate-covered ginger candies that Majda said came to Winnipeg first on a huge ocean liner and then on a mile-long train. She said these candies had travelled halfway around the world just so these children could eat them.

185

Eventually, Mimsie had had it with Majda and her little-girl ways. She fired her and replaced her with Anita, a stern, older woman who was tolerant of well-behaved children but lived for winning the war against dust and grime. When Sherrie was a teenager and at her most vitriolic, she would scream at her mother, "Majda was the only woman who ever mothered me, who ever loved me. I wish Majda was my mother, not you."

"At least you have a mother," Mimsie would answer. "And a father who spoils you." Boy-Oh did spoil Sherrie. He brought her purses and jewellery whenever he came back from a trip and gave her whatever she asked for so long as she giggled at him and called him the best daddy in the world. From an early age, she knew how to work him. Mimsie wished he had been tougher on Sherrie—not beating her, she was a girl after all, but at least demanding respect. Mimsie had wished and wished for a daughter. The whole reason they had a third child after two cesareans, when the doctor said it would be wise to stop there, was so that they could have a little girl. It was amazing to Mimsie how much grief this little strip of ingratitude and demanding bad attitude brought into her life in comparison to the boys who had their troubles but never faced off with Mimsie the way Sherrie had from the day she learned the word "no." Sherrie was a terrible brat, but she was also a musical prodigy. She started playing the violin at the age of four. By the age of eight she was practising two hours a day and winning music competitions against kids twice her age.

The children grew up and disappointed their parents in various ways, but none insurmountable. Mark got into Yale but dropped out after two years to become a landlord. He explained to Boy-Oh, as if he, Boy-Oh, knew nothing about the business world, that all the easy money to be made in the world was in real estate. Boy-Oh refused to co-sign for any of Mark's loans, but he did take him on as a manager in the business and eventually let him take over. Mark married a woman Mimsie described to anyone who would listen as "high maintenance." Alana spent her time redecorating and working out and eating tiny bits of Salisbury House bran muffins. Those bran muffins were like Boy-Oh's tuna to her: sacred and exclusive. She and Mark had twin girls but Alana turned them against Mimsie early on. When they did see her, they treated her like the hired help.

Daniel moved to Minneapolis and studied law. He graduated at the top of his class and worked as a taxation lawyer for two years, but then he became so agoraphobic that he had to move back home. He moved in with his parents and Mimsie and Lily sent him on numerous disastrous blind dates. He became an expert poker player and was eventually banned from Boy-Oh's poker nights because no one could beat him and it wasn't fun for Boy-Oh and his buddies to lose all the time. Daniel lived at home for the rest of his life, and, as his parents aged and grew frailer, his natural meanness, always kept in check by his timidity, came into focus. He liked to jeer at Mimsie when she forgot things or repeated herself and he snarled at all of Boy-Oh's ideas, small or large. He complained about Mimsie's cooking and Boy-Oh's way of shuffling along, slowing everyone down whenever he took him out to the barber or the grocery store or for coffee and toast at Harman's, the lunch counter near the blue jeans office that Mark ran now.

Sherrie was a crazy teenager, in love with George Harrison and mini-skirts, and stealing various things like lipstick and bibles even though she had a pipeline to Boy-Oh's wallet whenever she wanted to buy anything. She made it to university somehow and then ran off with her music professor and married him. For a time, Mimsie and Boy-Oh were step-grandparents to three teenagers. They were ragamuffin, aimless, dirty children, but they liked Mimsie's cooking and appreciated Boy-Oh's gifts of Chanukah gelt and decks of cards. Mimsie and Boy-Oh loathed the professor but at least he was Jewish and had a good job. Also, he was crazy for Sherrie until she broke his heart by running off with his friend, not a music professor but the conductor of the Winnipeg Symphony Orchestra. Sherrie played in the symphony for a time but Mimsie and Boy-Oh rarely attended because they would have to look the whole time at the backside of the conductor who had ruined their daughter's life. The professor was twenty years older than Sherrie, but the conductor was thirty years older and bald and alcoholic and pompous and a nasty drunk. His idea of a good joke was to tell Boy-Oh and Mimsie about the cue Sherrie missed at rehearsal and then to offer a toast to "beauty and incompetence" while he chuckled like a woodchuck. Finally he got so drunk at a Shabbat dinner that he wouldn't sit at the table for the meal but instead staggered around the house singing and belching and whacking Mimsie's knickknacks with his baton until many of her precious trinkets were smashed on the floor. Boy-Oh told him to get out and never come back. Sherrie left with him, and didn't talk to her parents for months, but eventually even she couldn't take life with the conductor anymore. When she left him a few years later, she and their daughter moved to Halifax to play in a string quartet there.

At seventy-nine, Boy-Oh was in a lot of pain because of his spine, and the doctors had put a pacemaker in a few years back. Now he spent his time watching poker or golf on the sports channel. He still had a few friends over for Wednesday night poker, but too many had died and some of the ones that were left had trouble seeing the cards or remembering what was what. He and Mimsie still played bridge on Friday afternoons with Lily and David. It seemed Lily got all the good cards. Boy-Oh joked that after almost sixty years, it was time for their luck to turn. Boy-Oh's hearing was going and that was affecting his luck.

For Boy-Oh's eightieth birthday, Mimsie planned a big bash. She cooked hors d'oeuvres for months ahead and froze them. She invited fifty people and hired Anita's daughter to manage the kitchen for the party. In the old days, a party like this would be commonplace, no big deal, but it took a lot out of Mimsie now and Boy-Oh told her she shouldn't be making such a fuss. This party was important to Mimsie. She wanted Boy-Oh to practise his stretching and the exercises the doctor gave him so that he wouldn't be quite so stooped. She wanted him to be cheerful and flirtatious and she still held out hope that for once, on this special occasion, for her sake and for all their years together, he would not demand his round serving of tuna but would partake in the feast with all the other guests. This was an insane hope, as Sherrie pointed out when she confessed it to her on the phone. "The thing about Dad is, he can't change.

You should know that by now," she said. Sherrie would be flying in for the party and bringing her grown daughter, Shoshana. Mark, now divorced from Alana and remarried, would be there and so would Sarah and Rachel, the twin granddaughters, Sarah now a lawyer in Miami and Rachel married to an acupuncturist and soon-to-be mother of her own twins.

The day before the party, Mimsie was crabby and exhausted. In the morning, they went to the Salisbury House for breakfast with Daniel and Mark and all the visitors from out of town. Sherrie and the grandchildren were staying with Mark so that Mimsie wouldn't work too hard looking after them all. Mimsie and Boy-Oh had a quiet afternoon, Boy-Oh watching poker on television and dozing and Mimsie making cottage cheese pie and talking on the phone to various people about last-minute arrangements. Daniel was home but in his room watching his own television. Living at home all these years had made him behave like a sulky, sleep-deprived, albeit paunchy and balding teenager. He refused to eat with his parents and was barely civil to them most of the time.

At five-thirty, Mimsie put Boy-Oh's can of tuna under the electric can opener and then squeezed the liquid into the sink and transferred the tuna to a bare, white plate. She took a spoonful of cold beets out of the jar and put them in a bowl. She put Boy-Oh's meal on the kitchen table and called him in. For herself she took a slice of the still cooling cottage cheese pie she'd made for tomorrow night's birthday party. Because she couldn't help herself, she cut a sliver of the pie and put it on Boy-Oh's plate next to his tuna. "Supper, Boy-Oh," she called. She had a bite and called again, louder this time, "Boy-Oh! Time to eat."

Boy-Oh shuffled in and sat down in front of his plate. Before he could say anything, Mimsie started to talk. "For once in your life, Boy-Oh," she began. "It breaks my heart that you've never once tried my cottage cheese pie."

Boy-Oh looked at his plate. The pie, because it was still hot, was slightly runny and some of it had oozed across the plate and was merging with the round arc of the tuna. "I'm an old man, Mimsie," he said. He took a few bites of the tuna.

Mimsie took another bite of the pie and said it was perhaps the best she'd ever made. Boy-oh refused to look at her. He took a small forkful of the pie and put it in his mouth and swallowed. "It is good, " he said. "I'm just not that hungry tonight." Boy-Oh stood up and carried his plate and the bowl with the untouched beets over to the kitchen sink.

"After sixty years, is it too much to ask that you have a little pie?" Mimsie said, her voice croaking.

"I'm an old man," Boy-Oh said and he walked into the den and sat down in his chair opposite the television.

"At least finish your beets," she called after him.

Boy-Oh died peacefully in his sleep sometime that evening. Mimsie found him in his leather chair in the den with the remote in his hand when she came in to ask him to get ready for bed. The emergency response team tried but couldn't revive him.

Mimsie was delirious, still planning for the party and talking as if Boy-Oh was just being his usual stubborn self by refusing to wake up. Mark's good friend Evan, who was a doctor, stopped by and gave Mimsie some tranquillizers.

At the funeral, Mark broke down completely. He said his father was the best man he had ever known and he pledged to look after his mother and Sherrie and everyone else in the family now that his father was gone. Daniel tried to comfort Mark. "You were always the favourite son," he told him. "You were the one Dad loved."

"Why did I fight him so hard?" Mark asked. "Why couldn't I have just given him a little of what he wanted?

"Fighting him was what he wanted," Daniel said.

Mimsie, whose edges were rounded from the pills she was taking, leaned on Sherrie as they made their way over to the corner where Mark and Daniel were talking. "Here are my boys," she said. "My grown-up boys."

"Here's our Mimsie," they said. "Our one and only Mimsie."

/ QUEPOS, COSTA RICA
APRIL 16, 1997

from "Tasting the Dark," a novel

/ BY MAGGIE **DWYER**

Rona Kay-Stern paid Ishmael the four dollars in US funds. Four singles. The mini-
mum charge for using the Internet access at the International House of Pancakes in
Quepos. She counted them into his outstretched, pink-palmed, grimy left hand. He
grinned and as he bobbed his head in thanks; his dreadlocks writhed in the stifling air.
Rona was relieved to see that he was not doing the cooking. The thought of those
braids waving over the stove was nauseating. The culinary duties were the province of
his cherubic, bronze-skinned wife, Eugenie, a *zaftig* gal who was singing joyfully in
Spanish over her batters.

Ishmael and Eugenie came from San Francisco. Long ago now, they said in unison.
Their café was crowded for its hearty breakfasts, which were served out on the narrow,
cement-floored patio at the side of their house. It closed for lunch and reopened at din-
ner. When asked, Eugenie was vague about the time and the menu for the evening. We
do offer a special every day, she said. Depends, she added with a laugh, who can say
what will be provided?

The Internet access was set up on an old kitchen countertop in what must be their
living room when the café is closed. On three sides of the room were low hard couches
in what Rona thought of as waiting-room style. They were upholstered in turquoise
vinyl and softened by fabric-covered pillows in African prints that featured elephant
heads and giraffes running through grassland. Fearsome-looking dark wooden masks
glared down from dull gold-coloured walls. The back half of the room was screened off,
floor to ceiling, by draperies in a black and brown zebra-stripe print. Ishmael swanned
back and forth between the folds of these drapes with menus and trays of water glasses
and cutlery. Eugenie herself came out to mark down the food orders with a rundown
pencil on a notepad made of stapled-together paper scraps. She looked her customers
straight in the eye and nodded her approval of their selections. She greeted all she knew
with a beaming face and a cry to let me hug you up brother or sister. These regulars
were clamped to her bosom with a delight that made other customers feel second class.
They spoke in jargon like some esoteric religious cult. Rona heard them talking about
Gurdjieff and Sufistic dancing. Sunnies rather than moonies, she thought.

While she waited for her turn at the computer, Rona watched a thin twenty-some-
thing Québécois who was typing at a furious pace. When stuck for a word, he rhyth-
mically slapped his bare tanned thighs, right hand over right thigh, left hand over left,

and sang *merde, merde, merde,* running up and down a familiar scale as if trying to harmonize with himself. She remembered seeing him the day before with a group of kids at the kayak rental place over at Manuel Antonio beach.

Rona waited so long, she had to ask to use the bathroom. It was surprisingly clean (though she knew her standards had shifted after seven months in the Third World). She examined her tanned angular face in the mirror. No major damage visible after months of tropical sunlight. She wet the tip of her index finger on her tongue and smoothed her high arched eyebrows. She had let her hair go while they were travelling. It had grown out to grey at the temples. Ben had cut it once and now it was grazing her shoulders again. She had lost ten pounds over the winter and looked slender in her long cotton skirt. She admired her full breasts and smoothed her pale blue T-shirt over them. She pulled out the tortoiseshell combs that held her hair and twisted it back with her hands into a French roll. She turned around and examined the back of her head by looking into the mirror over her right shoulder. She felt content, happier perhaps than she had a right to be.

The walls around her were a vibrant, rich pink. It was like being inside a watermelon. She had felt safer as soon as they crossed the border into Costa Rica. It was a relief not to worry about the drinking water and to eat whatever appealed.

Rona persuaded Ben to have brunch at the cybercafé so she could check for email. She hoped for one from Georgia Lee, at home in Winnipeg, up north in frozen Canada. When she got online, it took only seconds to see there was no new mail from their daughter. She sat trying to calm herself, recalling that she and Ben had agreed, as he said, to "back off" and let their daughter live her own life while they were away. Georgia Lee refused their offer of a gap year in Israel—that's only a really big reservation for Jews, isn't it? No place for me there.

They set Georgia Lee up in her own funky apartment before they left Winnipeg early in September. Ben had a full sabbatical year from his position as department head in political science and they had spent it, as planned, touring aid projects in Belize, Honduras and Nicaragua. All places associated, in her mind and now in her experience, with life lived, not without dignity, but under primitive and chaotic conditions unlike anything she'd ever seen.

Costa Rica was their last stop. A chance to relax and, though Ben was working on his notes, it felt like a holiday. Or, more accurately, a working holiday. This was a designation that Ben enjoyed. We live in oxymoronic times, he declared. They rented a little white stucco house outside the town of Quepos that had a primitive kitchen and a functional bathroom. It did not matter. They had managed their money easily in the Third World and now had lunch and dinner out each day.

She could see her husband on the patio hunched over one of his notebooks on a glass-topped table amid the leavings of their brunch. She wished she'd brought her sketchbook. She would love to capture him now with his bull neck and square Roman skull rising above the collar of his white cotton shirt. He had a heavily muscular torso and short powerful arms and legs that ended in wide square hands and feet. His deeply

191 ∎

tanned balding head was bent over his work, his broad shoulders prominent under the thin fabric of an old white dress shirt stretched tightly over his back. His longish white fringe of hair and full beard and his golden eyes deeply set under his furrowed brow marked him as a man in his early sixties. In his sixty-third year, to be precise.

She hurriedly sent an email to her brother Mark at his office. She tried for a casual tone. Have you seen our little *bubeleh*, she wrote? And added, you know, no news is not good news for mothers. The last eight words were written in upper case. He had promised to be in contact with Georgia Lee every week. Mark was not an ideal choice as guardian for their daughter, but as their only close relative in Winnipeg, he was their obvious option and his condo was only a few blocks from her apartment.

To delay telling Ben that Georgia Lee had not written, she looked up the Winnipeg weather. She knew that this would please him. Both the idea that she could easily find their hometown newspaper's web page and the pleasure of knowing that the temperature in Winnipeg was in the low minus range. That their city was firmly in the cold grip of winter while they idled in the sun. It intensified his pleasure to know that they were escaping the familiar communal miseries, that they were not among its shivering citizens with their nostrils frozen together. Granted a reprieve from block heaters and wind chill.

How sweet it is, he said. His delight in having twelve months of warm weather was constant. He announced that this suited him. I've always thought that, psychologically, I needed to experience the four seasons. I am happy to acknowledge, he added, that I was wrong.

Rona asked herself why Georgia Lee had not written. She made up a list of possible reasons for the neglect of the promised weekly letter. Was she too bogged down with end-of-term reading or papers? Was there a new boyfriend? There had been a six-day gap in their communication over the Christmas break when Georgia Lee had a bad dose of the flu. Rona was so worried that she had sent Mark over to check. Ben had downplayed her anxieties then, too. He was right. A silence can mean any number of things. Rona told herself to consider only innocuous reasons. An eighteen-year-old should be, was, capable of looking after herself. She mentally reviewed Georgia Lee's daily schedule. No classes before 10:30 a.m. The online newspaper reported that Winnipeg's skies were clear; the temperature was a tolerable plus one degree Celsius with a predicted overnight low of minus three. Daylight Saving Time was making Georgia Lee's mornings brighter. The blizzard of snow dumped on the city ten days ago had quickly melted and the annual threat of spring flooding was under daily appraisal. Dikes were being constructed and the swollen Red River was reported to be an ominous sight as it flowed toward the Manitoba border. The potential for a deluge of Biblical proportions was greater this year, the newspaper report indicated, due to the over-saturated condition of the ground late in the previous fall.

Rona imagined Georgia Lee dressing in layers to walk from her apartment over the bridge across the frozen river, past the statue of Taras Shevchenko brooding over the side lawn of the Legislature grounds, a lone crow perched on one of his epaulets of snow, and on to her classes at the university. She imagined her daughter in long underwear decorated with hearts and flowers covered by two sweat tops, skinny-legged blue jeans, her down-filled parka, toque, mitts and a scarf tied over her mouth.

Mothers can't know everything and Rona didn't know that Georgia Lee had reinvented herself soon after her parents left town. Changed her name to Georgie. Cut her hair in a chin-length bob with short bangs and dyed it jet-black. Long black skirts and black sweaters replaced jeans and sweat tops. Casual went punk. A dime-sized silver hoop set with a piece of rose quartz dangled from her pierced navel. Doc Marten boots replaced moccasins. An old grey Persian lamb coat from a thrift store topped off her new look. Value Village chic.

Her extracurricular activities changed, too. No more dance classes at the old church on River Avenue. Now it was dancing at Die Maschine, the after-hours club in the Village, and most weekends, a session of theatre improv with the new friends she met through Chick Fontaine, the skinny platinum blond who worked with her at the video rental store kitty-corner from the coffeehouse at River and Osborne. Chick had the palest skin; you couldn't see anything Native about her. She said it was her grandmother who was Métis and she liked that. I'm like a long-lost cousin to Louis Riel. It was cool. She was an art school student, and she had made dozens of videos, including a series on the seven deadly sins. Georgie starred in the one about lust.

Rona looked out through the doorway again. The intense sunlight bleached the patio of colour; she had to squint to see Ben. Now his body appeared foreshortened, his face was in deep shadow. He was engrossed in deciphering and transcribing his handwritten notes, an onerous task usually accomplished by his patient secretary, Helga Neustaedter, who could easily turn his self-titled "snail trails" into intelligible English. Rona watched him tapping away on his laptop computer for a minute or two before she went to tell him that there was no word from their Georgia Lee. She had not written since April fifth. Eleven days ago. He looked up at her and she felt his golden gaze assessing her. He could not see the ache that sat behind her breastbone. Only its reflection in her dark eyes.

Rona knew that if she brought up the topic of returning home earlier for Passover, Ben would refuse to discuss it. Before they left Winnipeg, they'd debated the fact that, in this sabbatical year, they would be away from home for all the major holidays. September 1996 to June, 1997. It was only one year of many.

"We'll take a year off," he said. "In circumstances like these, the Lord forgives."

"What do you care?" she countered. "Aren't you an atheist?"

"I do not have the same sort of need for transactions with the spiritual world that you have. As you know, other concerns shape my life, my world. Rationality, not religious superstition, should be your guiding force." Ben prided himself on the limits he placed on his Judaism. He had reduced it to a loose cultural affiliation of humanistic traditions and seasonal feasts.

He smiled at her and continued, "You won't be able to find any matzo in San José. No matzo, no *charoset*, no gefilte fish with fresh *chrane*, no carrot *tzimmes*, no *farfel* kugel, no *chremsleh* with prunes inside, no compote, no macaroons, no Red Rose tea with lemon, no nothings. That sounds like a punishment worse than the ten plagues, doesn't it? But you must realize that you cannot carry your house with you on a trip like this."

That was his way: to smile and look away from her sorrows. He had nothing to offer in consolation. This discussion had been going on for the full extent of their married years. Twenty-seven years of compromise but no real consolation. She knew that was not an entirely fair characterization. Though on some days it felt right. No one thing could fulfill all her needs. He usually listened patiently as she spoke about her feelings. He gave as much as he had and when his sympathies were exhausted, he looked away. He did care. He knew she believed that he did not understand her. What he did not understand, and he knew this, was her need to factor her sorrow into every day of her life.

He had two fine sons from his first marriage. Avi and Lior were strong like their mother, Rivka. Neither of them needed any mothering from Rona. Over the intervening years the boys had been polite but aloof on the rare occasions when they all were together. They made aliyah to Israel with their mother twenty years ago and Ben accepted the span of ocean between them as the price of his divorce. He found a refuge in Canada and made a new life with Rona. There was no point in looking back, no point in missing other places, other people.

That she was unable to bear a living child did distress him for her sake. Being barren had a deeper meaning for her. She said she was not a real woman. The potent spirits of their two unnamed stillborn sons lingered in the shadows of their marriage bed. Two pale wraiths that mocked their union. And she longs for them, her lost babes.

He was interested in finding workable solutions. That tenet was central to his carefully drawn *Weltanschauung*. He was a product of his 1960s doctorate from Columbia University and he fully endorsed the familiar all-American attitudes that knowhow and a can-do attitude will overcome any obstacle. He appreciated that their problem required a solution and embraced the most viable, and then currently popular, option suggested. He proposed that they adopt a child.

A number of his colleagues at the university promoted the idea of adopting Aboriginal children from bleak inner city houses or the northern reserves. All firmly believed their theorem: that it was a good thing to offer the benefits of middle-class life and make a safe home for children who otherwise would lead impoverished lives. These earnest professors hoped to strengthen the birth communities by fostering a generation of leaders who would use their talents to help their own kind. Native communities were to be helped like Third World countries. It was an avenue for social change that appealed to the domesticated sixties radicals now safely ensconced in tenured positions on pacific Canadian campuses. He had no idea then that Rona would live in constant fear that something would happen to their child. He did not know that she would be the centre of their world.

She was eight days old when she came to them. The little girl they named Georgia for Ben's favourite song, "Sweet Georgia Brown." That was the first song he learned to whistle successfully. He did it to annoy cousin Moishe, his aged guardian, who detested popular music. Lee was her English name for the Hebrew Leah. Rona talked Ben and the new Reform rabbi into allowing an official naming ceremony at the Temple. She looked a little like Rona, whose Russian ancestry was evident in her broad high Slavic cheekbones and crimped black hair. Strangers, who looked at their warm olive skin and dark hair, presumed that she and Ben were the natural parents. Why didn't your mom give you any of her curls, they asked Georgia Lee. The illusion lasted until she was twelve and puberty brought its astonishing changes and undeniable indications of her Aboriginal ancestry. Over her teenage years, her skin tone faded to tan and she grew tall enough to look down on both of them. She developed a graceful way of carrying herself thanks to her dance lessons and grew her straight black hair to her waist.

After her twelfth birthday, she informed Ben and Rona that she no longer wished to go to Hebrew school to prepare for her bat mitzvah. There is no point, she told them in a new, definite tone of voice. She said she did not know who she was but she knew she was not Jewish. There was no bat mitzvah.

Georgia Lee convinced Ben that she needed to see her adoption papers. When she found out the truth, that her mother was Native, she asked to visit the reserve at Footprint Lake. Ben took her the following spring. Rona refused to go with them. They found remnants of her family, a granny, her mother's uncle, a few cousins and an aunt who remembered that her niece Ruby McKay had a child in Winnipeg. None of them had thought about that baby in many years. They did not recall that the child was a girl.

"After a while," the aunt said, "well, not to say you forget. You keep it deep in your heart." She smiled at Georgia Lee. "We would have loved you if we'd known where you were. We never saw you." They did not know the name of her father.

Georgia Lee saw that her granny's eyes were filling with tears. Dark brown, almost black, soft eyes moist with her old woman's sorrows made fresh again.

Ruby had been dead for thirteen years by then. She got drunk and sniffed up and was found frozen in a snow bank outside her own front door on her twenty-second birthday. Harvey Spence, the band councillor, who added this last piece of information, also told Georgia Lee that her mother was a lively girl who made friends with the wrong crowd. She went south to Winnipeg to study at the beauty school on Portage Avenue. That was all they knew.

Georgia Lee knew the space for a father's name was left blank on her birth certificate. Not literally blank but the word unknown meant the same thing to her. She'd never felt half so lost as she did then. That's what she told Ben. "I'm a lost member of a lost tribe."

195

/ ETCHING IMAGES

/ BY CAROL **ROSE**

is there a language
for women's ritual

or must we grunt
pre-verbal

using whatever
is at hand

an old conch
thigh bones, a twig

etching images
in the sand

are there words
waiting to be exhumed

ancient utterances
taboo & crusted in fear

filtering memories
through fire & smoke

/ CONVERSOS*

/ BY CAROL **ROSE**

during the inquisition women
hid hebrew prayer books
(like jewels) in the folds
of their skirts, lifted those
skirts for men familiar
with the rituals, secret
ceremonies performed
in darkness, shutters
latched, curtains drawn
candles lit in airless rooms
where blessings (in spanish
portuguese, or ladino)
were chanted to melodies
never heard in daylight.

at the entrance
to their homes
the women placed
madonnas (female guardians)
who watched those who passed by
especially strangers.
inside the heart
of each statue, a talisman
tightly rolled scrolls
(unseen mezzuzot)
embedded in the bodice
of mother mary's dress
protection against
the loss of memory.

in springtime
(during lent)
the women scrubbed
their ovens, prepared
them for the baking
of unleavened bread
& roasted lamb
foods cooked in silence
a sacred rite performed
by the women, kept alive
(despite persecution)
in the hearts
of their children
for over five hundred years

* conversos = the converted ones
Jews & their descendants who were baptized by force,
but who secretly continued to practise their faith.

/ MIDNIGHT TRAIN

/ BY LAURIE **BLOCK**

Gloria has found Jesus. It's taken a long time, a lifetime, to bring her to her knees but not for obvious reasons; not because she's a woman or that she's Native; certainly it's not on account of the jailhouse tattoos on her knuckles, the insults to her beauty and the damage to her liver that she's opened her heart to the good news. It's because she finds herself alone at the worst possible time, alone except for doctors and nurses in their immaculate uniforms, alone except for friendly volunteer visitors and the ragtag handful of musicians, hired to sweeten the final days of the terminally ill. The sickness has sharpened her memories, exposed her soul and left her twisting and tumbling in thin air between this world and the next. High above the centre ring she needs something she can grasp. With no net below her and no guarantees in sight she prays for Jesus to comfort her with his two strong arms, to catch her and carry her beyond fear and suffering to a place where it's simply easy to be, where she won't hurt anymore. Because grace can be difficult and she has so little time and not enough strength to call on Him by herself, she's joined a church, an evangelical Main Street congregation called Living Springs or Fruits of Faith, something with a flock and a pasture, a river to cross and a vineyard where there's plenty for everyone. I hope it works for her.

Pay no mind, I can't help myself. I've always been a skeptic, mistrustful of those who brandish truths that are golden, sticky and far too sweet, like marshmallows at the cosmic weenie roast. But this is definitely not the time or the place. This is about Gloria and she deserves all the hope and consolation available to her. She's on the eighth floor, Palliative Care, and she's dying.

For Gloria, faith came like a seed catalogue, arriving with the landlord and a sheaf of overdue bills in late February. As the cancer began its dance with her, when she was still ass-deep in snow and darkness, it brought hope, bright glossy pictures, promises in living colour. Down the hallway there's a place like that, a lounge with hanging plants and homey furniture. A corner of peace that is in, but not of, the hospital, that faces the morning sun high above the ancient coupling of two muddy rivers. Beyond the dirty business of the traffic below, the trains and cars and the white puffs of smoke from the crematorium, you can imagine what was there once and still moves along the borders of dreamtime, through the unspoiled wilderness of memory. Grasslands and lakes, rocks and trees reclaim their ancient title to the horizon; the creatures that once inhabited the night come near to smell the source of the waters, to drink the mists of

199

the morning. If you could only look deep enough you could roll back the canvas on Creation, restore the prehistoric inland sea and the wandering clans that spoke and drummed and danced at its margins. Such a welcoming place for a story to begin and to end, among the fierce and tender ghosts who knew it before it was measured, fenced and parcelled out in print. But this is my construct. I am drawn to the old legends and the ring of original words around a fire, but Gloria's holding out for Christ's golden kingdom and the rapture to come.

Today there are no patients in the lounge, no wheelchairs pointed at the window and over the ruins of the burnt-out Cathedral. Here at the end of the hall, outside the rooms of fear and hushed release, two musicians are rehearsing. Guitarists hired to bring comfort to the dying, but sometimes it's simply impossible to face them; to present your self to a stranger in extremis with nothing to offer but sound. Sometimes you've got to take cover and so, cloaked in their instruments, they have engineered an escape into music, leaning into each other and laughing like lovers, guitar to guitar in naked sonic delight. A secret language trails from their fingers, majors and minors, chords and hooks, an acoustic intimacy I can't hear and don't understand.

Gloria comes to sit muffled inside her bathrobe, the metallic taste of medicine on her tongue, a Bible in her hands, the smell of du Mauriers rising from her long black wig. I used to think it was her own, that Indian hair was so strong and healthy it could survive the chemotherapy as well as the genocide, but I know better now, having walked in on Gloria in her baldness one day. I confess I felt embarrassed, even aroused at the sight of her, alive and dying, the naked vulnerable head, her unadorned and fragile beauty. As the illness progressed her wardrobe had changed. Gone were the tight jeans that hung from her hips, the black T-shirts and fuck-me boots, her denim and leather forsaken, abandoned in the closet. She wears the uniform of the terminally ill now, hospital blue envelops her difficult breath and her dancer's body as it fades towards whiteness, cleansed of colour like clouds in the sun, like bones on the forest floor. Fuck, what a time to think about sex.

Leaning out of private shadows, Gloria brings her face inches from the girl with the guitar: *Lois, play me "too blue to cry"* but Lois isn't listening, she's climbing those crazy strings who knows where, she's riding every note to ground zero. Gloria won't let go, insisting *Low-wiss* but Lois still can't hear her, she isn't there, she's gone deep to where the wound is, deep past the birth cry to the song of Genesis, the sound of water separating from clay, of wings and claws and bellies slithering over grass, inching towards a name. I force myself to say something, I actually have to lean over and put my hand on her shoulder, give her a gentle shake, a waking. *Lois, you need to play Gloria the song you promised. Now.* I don't have to add *because she's here on borrowed time.* It's enough to bring her back, the bass line of imminent death lifts Lois out of the interior of her instrument and into present time. She adjusts her capo, clears her throat and sings as smooth and sweet as if she were spooning honey down a sick child's ravaged throat, as if she were already on her way to hillbilly heaven, night riding between gigs along a blacktop highway in a baby blue convertible; a Cadillac with the stars out, the top down and Hank asleep in her lap.

Somewhere around the third verse, Gloria joins in, picking up the tune and belting it out with all her heart and what remains of her lungs:

> That midnight train got painted blue
> and I'm so wasted I might fly.

And so what if she stumbles on the lyrics and bends a few notes out of shape? That's only the drugs talking, thickening her tongue and thinning her thoughts as if they were hair. That's pain highballing along the cerebral cortex like a rogue locomotive while consciousness gets bumped onto a deserted siding. Besides, what with the moonlight and machinery and a lone bedraggled bird whistling into the wind, this song is her life story. She's sung it, God, she's lived it a thousand times over. Now it's her time to sing lead and so the rest of us join in and follow her to the end as if it were not only her last request, but her show; a grand finale, something she's prayed and practised and paid for. Gloria sings as if all she needed to recover was some backup, a little whisky and smoke and a feel for the blues, a bit of Ronstadt and a bushel of Patsy Cline. Once she warms up her voice is surprisingly strong.

Maybe it's only dying that makes it sound so real or maybe she was always out there, Gloria wailing as if she were waiting for winter, the last bird in a leafless forest while that relentless train rumbles by her nest, all feathers and clatter and alarm. As if she were late but could still catch it if she sang with all her might, that she'd soon find it waiting for her uncoupled at the edge of town with the smell of cold steel and shooting stars, the sparks curling from childhood fires, the flavour of raspberries and stolen cream on her tongue. The twang as a promise snaps, the high harmony when the screen door slams in a room at the end of the hall. Hurting music, but don't get me wrong. It carries absolutely no weight what I think, how I find this music cloying and unbearably shallow. What counts is Gloria, how she holds all those notes from beginning to end, the rags and ribbons of her sorrow and her strength.

One of the nurses closes the door to the ward with an exaggerated and deliberate motion, a mime of respectful silence as if Gloria is singing too loud, as if she might kill the sleepers on the other side or make the dying dance their way into the elevator and out, into the night. But there's no danger of that. We cover a bit of soul, sample some R & B and a spiritual or two, but after three or four songs Gloria's played out, her head slumps, her eyes cloud over and she has to be helped back to her room. That's not the point; there are times when a healing is not the same thing as a cure.

Days later when I stop by her bed, there are no more songs left. Her voice has shrunk to a soft, scared hush, like leaves against a window fogged by smoke and disease, darkened by the fear or the morphine, the interchangeable parade of solicitous white faces that peer into her doorway in the hopes of doing something, anything in the middle of the night. We start talking about our youth and the wild times, about God and spirit and the importance of family. Anything but death. I push a little harder, trying to find out if she still has any connection to traditional beliefs. I'm fishing for a teaching or at least a story from the elders, wisdom from the sweat lodge, something from the medicine wheel, but she won't deliver. When I mention the Creator she snaps at me, *That's the Devil talking*, and changes the subject, asks me what I want most from life. That's easy, too easy maybe. I want what everyone's dying for, deep inside. I want to keep what I have. I want to do good and find God and love fully. When Gloria asks me to pray with her, I experience only a moment's queasiness, a brief discomfort in my gut like I'm about to try on someone else's underwear, that I'll appear ridiculous, in drag. It's not me but hell, she's at death's door and what kind of person would refuse a dying woman?

I perch on the edge of the bed and Gloria takes my hands: *Oh Lord*, she says, her voice rising and quavering with fever, *lift this good man to Your side, open his heart to Your Light, his ears to Your Truth and wash away his sins. Reveal to him a path through darkness and let him come to sit at Your feet. Teach him to sing Your praises and serve as instrument of Your Perfect Will and, through the grace of Jesus Christ Your Son, let him live in love eternal. Forever and ever, amen.*

Gloria closes her eyes, propped upright and silent among the pillows, exhausted from the physical demands of prayer, the energy it cost. What else is left for me to say? That life is hard and dying unimaginable, that all a human being can do is show up, speak their truth and not be attached to the outcome. *Gloria*, I say, *I am deeply moved and honoured by your prayer and I am privileged to be with you in your journey but I also need to be honest with you. I believe in God, Gloria, but not the way you do. I am a Jew.*

Jewjewjew, it's all Gloria hears, the millennial tolling of the Jewbell shivers her pentecostal timbers. She sits up straight and tall and, with no mean effort, lifts her hands, palms out and fingers apart, rolling her bright black eyes back to a better world, a place of ecstasy. She throws her head back moaning *Halleluia Jesus, I've saved a Jew.* I restrain my laughter, bite the lip of the resident critic, resist the temptation to whisper in her ear, *Lady, this Jew ain't that easy to save.* She's the one dying and who am I to give her the news? By what right do I set myself apart from her life and her death, her music and her prayer? By what right pity? By what right fear?

/ NEW WATER ZEAL GOODBYE POEM

/ BY MARVIN **FRANCIS**

deer strides over water like a
child
on a mission

deer slides across southern cross
announces northern boss

roots hanging thompson
mae north
looks down into the pacific
seeks fresh water poets

she's a northern rose
anne of a thousand beers
thinks about it
a woman for all reasons she is a skin
skwawker full of zeal
leaking real

new land grab   ancestral agony
volcanoes new constellation
same old story

sheep instead of moose 'cookie'
4 legs observe from the bush
watch through the water signs
look into those shadows
northern word shark   loaded with southern poetry charms

watch the maori land
scape by with
these weird final words:

nothing has buns like a
deer

/ CHILDREN OF THE CEMENT

/ BY MARVIN **FRANCIS**

my childhood background stretches
landscape wild beyond sight beyond the NWT beyond me

      come see our beer bottle forest, it grows bigger
      brown xmas trees for sale or refund or to break
soft rabbit sounds, loud tracks reverb
can it be a . . . wolverine, a lost trapper?
      tracks on the arms, in the neck in the eye
      long lost dad jumping like a bunny
water games, do you know the hair/thread snake of northern water?
fish rainbow gleam, homemade fishing rod, cattail weaves, self
      fire hydrant delight, rainbow peons, stray cat running
      fish for spare change, food bank animal
baby ducks familiar, run free as long as you can, as you want to
tree ripples wind ripples love ripples

      baby duck, gimli goose, apple jack, ripple wine,
      runs over souls, mallard breakdown

          see the men pour over the child
          see the cement harden
          hypodermic sand toys
          see the
          children of the cement

/ TEACHING IN THE INNER CITY

for adam billy ken frank jesse matthew rick
richard emmanuel and the others

/ BY BRIAN **MACKINNON**

sometimes you imagine you are teaching with whip and chair training in a circus
cage crack the bull whip to keep the father-beaten angry wounded young bulls
human male animals at bay

you crack the whip with assignments over the heads of these young outlaws
show them the booze-free drug-free chair for homework get them to jump through
crowd-pleasing educational hoops when you know full well by their snarling they
don't want to jump expose them to various theatrical books stretchers like mark
twain's *huck* running from pa into the adventurous world expose them to great
stories throughout the ages and dramatic poems and how to write poems and life
story short stories and how to probe for voice for individual voice to locate and utter
the complexity of their feelings songs of experience to bleed out the bad blood so
they can begin to breathe and heal

they hate it when you juggle several hats do a song and dance create a little essential
energy dare to show a few vital signs add a little life a little life-stirring vitality to the
proceedings of the hungover the drugged the sleep deprived the violated the depressed
and downtrodden members do a little all-the-world's-a-stage monty python's flying
circus up on the classroom tables invite them to climb up and perform centre
stage they're not ready yet act like a total dionysiac clown imitate them buffoonlike
to make a point *he's a goof he's lost it* recite a shakespearean soliloquy *a tale told by
an idiot* with fire and ice *he's a shakespearean freak or a clone man* or get big and
passionate over words over *big words* over them *he's using those big words again* give
them ringmaster tongue-lashings to transform the pain to perform and build a life
they think *their cool teacher* has *lost his cool got jarred, eh* become a *nerd face*

205

they want to kill you *if i had a gun i'd shoot the bastard* snaps the sneering son of
an absent wheeler-dealer drug dealer social worker father as he gleefully fires
imaginary bullets from his right hand steadied by his left for a direct hit complete
with shooting sound effects and the realistic jerking motion of the firing handgun
kick *i just want to kill 'im shitfuck he's high on words again i just want to kill 'im just
really want to pound him* growls the huge son of an absent drunken father a one-time
fists of fury brawling cursing dark-eyed black-faced coal miner now a crane operator
who parties all night far away in a distant third world country *just really like to pound
him out make mincemeat of 'im once and for all if he was a chick teacher i'd want to cut
off his tits* he laughs and chuckles joyfully

sometimes with hardly a moment's notice one will come charging through the
circus metaphor with a vengeance like a 240-lb bull ape fullback crying *bull crap
bull shit* toss aside your whip and chair with furious playful paws fear ignites and
rushes wildly tastes like bitter bread you swallow it whole

i'm going to grab 'im he wants to grab you and throw you an older male body around
the classroom slam you over the desks tables and word processors up against the
walls and bookcases jump on you to feel a father

they want to cry and gnash their teeth they want to throw you crashing to the earth
so they can gain strength and power they want to wrestle you dangerously and
mythically to punish a sober father to share a young son's pain a terrible thrashing
relentless pain

the son of an absent father i receive the attacking body wrestle back hold the body
try to sustain grapple the prodigious force as my body is hurled into a classroom
door wood splinters try not to get hurt try not to hurt call upon all my middle-aged
tenacity all my male journeys to counter the power of lost angry youth try to give
him a challenge be a worthy opponent find inner strength gain some determined
vantage try to hold him with all my might try to hold him like my baby son

add male humour to defuse the nasty avenging inward struggle *hey what is this sport
or entertainment* psychic humour for psychic surgery feel the fury subside after the
physical struggle it's a young rebel's laughter and *i could'a gotchu now let's arm wrestle*

sometimes they can't reach you can't reach anybody so they simply smash their fists
swiftly without hesitation into the school's brick walls

bleeding hands to clear momentarily a male adolescent mind of its uncomprehending
agony

i shudder to see it

/ CHICKEN

/ BY JESSICA **WOOLFORD**

dusk and we are down
town   the street straight ahead gritty
sagging houses strung out on either side

some kid leaps
from the sidewalk

soars   into the air

rolls his body through it
a diver entering a pool
though william avenue will not embrace him
and surely he does not expect it to

maybe this is all
he expects: his body less
body than rusty burr
wire weed tumbling along tar tongue

stop the car
I get out / watchers angling their eyes
from pitted doors and ailing porches / approach the kid
his back to me   ask are you ok?

he staggers up all the time
looking elsewhere (where else?)
I'm ok
his voice a pebble on a well wall

trips away from me
and my what happened?

moves slowly down the throat
of the alley one
quick glance back for

207

gone

/ HUNGRY

/ BY DAVID **BERGEN**

I'm on my bike near Sargent and this guy Patty is running his mouth off at me. He's wearing blue and his hands are in fists. He looks like my dog. His mouth is open. I tell Patty to shut up and he doesn't so I call on him and he says something about Tiff Trinkett and takes off down the street.

It's a good afternoon, my day off at the car wash, no afternoon classes, so I go past the school and sit on a curb. At 3:30 Tiff comes out holding her books. She's with Jennifer. Jennifer's talking, Tiff's laughing. Then they're standing in front of me and I look up at them. There's a white cloud, like scissors, in the sky.

Tiff's got something written on her chest, close to her bare shoulder. It says, "Freak."

"What the fuck," I say.

She shrugs. Says Hazel wrote it. She scrubs at it with a fist.

We go to Subway. There's an old woman with blue shoes and a dirty coat. The old woman has her face in her coffee. Swings her short legs. Jennifer buys a sub and we go outside and share a drink. Jennifer says her brother got a job at Western Glove.

"Sewing jeans for little girls' asses," Tiff says.

"Fourteen bucks an hour," I say. Then I tell her that Patty was calling her down. Getting nasty.

"Prick," she says.

I know she knows Patty. They were together two months ago and then Patty's brother wanted in and Tiff ran. But I don't speak. Just smoke and look at the writing on her chest and I think about this time in Geo when we were doing the layers of the earth and I brought in a display made out of food. Graham crackers for the crust, raspberry Jell-O for the core, other kinds of Jell-O, sugar, margarine. I have always been intense about marks and projects and my father, happy to see this, cheerleads me in my schooling and he helped me build the Jell-O piece. So, I brought it in for a display and during the class we gobbled up the earth piece. Used plastic spoons and jiggled it off the plywood platter to our mouths. Mr. Harrison said it was great, just great. One hundred per cent. He shook my hand. Then he talked about the age of the world. He took out these soil samples and pointed at the layers and named them. Lots of hard words that sounded like he was stuttering or maybe trying out a poem.

"Mr. Davis," he said. "What's this?" He pointed at the middle sample, middle layer. I said, "Dirt."

"No, no, no, no, Mr. Davis. It's both your past and your future." And he laughed. Then he passed around some black rocks that were sleeping on cotton inside little glass cubes. "Be careful," Mr. Harrison said. "These are four billion years old." He was terribly excited. And his voice went up and down, all music-like, and I didn't hear the words, only the sounds he made.

Tiff and I leave Jen and go to my place. It's a tiny green house behind the food bank. My father went into the food bank once and he came back with canned corn and scalloped potatoes in a box and a bag of rice. He didn't know what to do with the rice so I ended up using it for another project, music class, where I built a hollow instrument out of paste and newspaper and poured the rice inside.

My house smells like bacon and I know my father had a big lunch and then left for work. Wanda's there. He's sitting on the couch with Harry, my dog, and they're watching *Terminator*. Wanda showed up one day a couple of months ago. Just sitting on our couch eating chips. I asked him who he was and he mumbled something and then I asked him where he was from and he said Wanda. Little black kid with a mother who works three jobs, and when he's home alone he's scared and so he hangs at our house.

"Hey, Wanda," Tiff says.

He looks up and then back at the TV.

"I saw your mom, Wanda," I say. "She's home. You can leave now."

He says he wants to finish the movie. I make him a peanut butter sandwich and tell him to go home. He gets up and shuffles sideways and then out the door.

I sit down and Tiff sits on my lap and says what she wants. Leather couches, a fifty-seven-inch HD Sony, a tight little foreign car and an espresso machine. She closes her eyes and dreams about a tiny white cup with foam spilling over it. She wants a pair of hipsters from Below the Belt. She keeps talking and her mouth twists when she gets greedy. "You getting a stick," she says. Then she kisses me. Her breath all over my face. Harry's lying on the floor, watching us.

She opens my jeans and goes, "Big stick." She has a shiny green thong and a red bra and looking at her I think, Christmas. So we fool around, but we don't do it. It makes her too sad when we do it. I have little tricks to change her mind, like I'm the cat and she's the mouse, but I haven't caught her for the last while. "C'mon, Sandy," she mumbles, and we float. After, we put our clothes back on and we sit on the couch and eat popcorn and watch TV.

When my older brother Jack comes home he looks at us on the couch and then he goes in the kitchen and fries some eggs. He steps back into the living room, holding his plate, his fork up in the air like a spear. He eats slowly, watching us watch TV.

Tiff swivels her head from Jack to the TV and back again.

"It's all good," I say.

"How are ya, Tiff?" my brother says.

Tiff sits up. Puts one hand up near her neck. "Good, Jack. Everything's good."

My brother nods. Then he tells me that the boys at Midtown want me to work tomorrow morning.

"I got school," I say.

"That so."

He asks Tiff where I was today.

She doesn't know. She looks at me with her wet eyes and says, "At school?"

"Yeah," I say. And I tell Jack about Mr. Harrison and the soil samples. About the Jell-O and graham crackers, which isn't really true, because it happened two months ago.

When I'm done, my brother nods and says, "You're such a loser."

At Midtown, I vacuum. Two minutes to do the front and back, shake out the mats, clean the trunk, and put everything back together. If I'm too slow, I lose a buck a car. If Earl finds gravel under the mats when he's wiping down the inside with Armor-All, he takes another dollar. Six o'clock we get a fifteen-minute break and I smoke two and a half cigarettes and listen to the boys talk. They think I'm shit. Jack's little brother, a cracker.

By the second month Earl's still beating on me. He calls me down, or hits me with the broom, and the gang laughs and then they all turn away. I'm bigger than him but he's got his buddies, and so I always walk away. One afternoon, he catches me coming out of the can and he gets stupid and says, "What's up do you think you're solid then come fight me."

I laugh.

He spits and says, "Let's go."

I say, "I don't care." I throw my hat on the ground and hit him first, knowing that surprise is everything and it is. I give him a few more good shots and with each one his eyes open, like he's waking up and he doesn't know where he is. I leave him sitting on the ground, leaning against the garage door. His hands are flat on the ground, like he's trying to stop himself from falling through a hole. After that day, Earl leaves me alone. I settle into work and I'm free. Nobody's on me and I fall in love with the tang of the cars. You open the door and wham, it's handsome, smelling like the lawyer woman who stands at attention in the sunshine, talking talking talking on her silver phone, hand swaying at her hip. Oh man. Sometimes, when it's slow, I push my nose against the leather and breathe deep and think about Tiff and me rollin'. Still, it's a shit job, but the money's good, and it keeps me away from Jack in the evenings. I tell Tiff never to go over to my place on her own. Jack's a scrub, I say.

Mr. Harrison takes the Geo class to his house one day after school. It's a big house with a sunken living room and leather couches and we sit there and watch slides of his trip to a place called Machu Picchu. There's a slide of Mr. Harrison standing by some ruins with his wife and daughter and they both look good. They're smiling, the daughter is blond and she has great legs, and Mrs. Harrison has green shorts, and Mr. Harrison is wearing binoculars and a grey hat with a wide rim and he's pointing off at something behind the person taking the photo. Then there's a shot of Mr. Harrison in a Speedo on a beach and we all laugh and make fun of him. Later, he brings out food, little bits of quiche, and wieners wrapped in dough, and taco chips and punch. Outside, beyond the picture window, there's a pool. I go the bathroom. It's painted dark red and the towels are rusty coloured and soft and the Jacuzzi is red. On the cabinet there's a bowl. It's copper inside and black outside and on the bottom it says Burma. I put it in my jacket pocket and then go back to the sunken living room where Mr. Harrison is talking about deep sea fishing and taking Gravol for seasickness and sleeping through the whole expedition. He says the word *expedition* carefully, as if it were a word with a lot of meaning.

I get home late and walk in the door and I can hear the snap of something, very regular, a crack and then a sharp spitting sound, like a whip. Then I hear Jack laugh and a girl's voice goes "Oh, oh, Jesus," and I know it's Tiff by the way the *us* in *Jesus* goes up and up. They're in the living room. Wanda's there too. He's standing against the wall, his head really black against the light paint, and his eyes are wide open. Jack is standing across the room and he's holding a pellet gun that's been shortened and he's aiming it at Wanda. He fires, the pellet hits the wall just above Wanda's right shoulder, Tiff squeals and claps, and Jack, when he sees me, touches the barrel to his chest. "Fucking circus," he says. "And I'm the ringmaster."

I ask Wanda if he's okay. He grins. Yeah, he's all good.

"Just his head left," Jack says.

I tell him to stop.

"Whoaa," Jack says. "Whoaa." And he raises the barrel and pulls the trigger and the pellet enters Wanda's left eye and Wanda doesn't shift, doesn't say anything, just puts his hand up to touch his face, as if he were checking for something. His mouth opens and closes, but no sound comes out. Tiff moves around the room, arms in the air, lost in the music.

I go to Wanda and say, "Hey, you okay?"

He nods. Shrugs. His mouth moves, but still there's no sound.

"Here." I take his hand away from his eye. No blood. This is good. Blood means damage. His eyeball is whacked though. Out of control, like a marble in a bowl.

I hold up two fingers. "Look here," I say.

His eye rolls left and all that remains is a white ping-pong ball. He sighs and lays his head against my shoulder.

"Fuck," I say. I sit him on the couch and go to the kitchen for a rag and some water. When I come back Jack is going, "It's cool. No problem, Wanda. Everything's cool."

There's the tiniest trickle of blood coming out of the corner of Wanda's eye. I dab at it. My hands are shaking.

Jack says, "He'll be good. The bullet bounced off."

"Uh, uh," I say. "It's fuckin' in his head."

"Don't think so. Maybe it went through." Jack touches the back of Wanda's head. "Did it?"

Wanda looks up at Jack. His good eye is big, almost happy. "Hungry," he says.

"There ya go," Jack says. "You're hungry. What'll ya have. Pizza Pop? Cheerios? Ice cream?"

"Hungry," Wanda says.

"Shut up with the fucking music, will ya?" Jack waves a hand at Tiff, who slides across the room and stands with her back against the wall, right where Wanda got hit. She smiles sleepily.

I take Wanda's hand and pull him up. "Here." I pull him toward the door and he follows easily. Nothing wrong with his walking.

"Where ya going?" Jack's voice is hard.

I don't answer, just take Wanda's arm and lead him outside and down the stairs onto the sidewalk and we go up together to Notre Dame and stand at the bus stop in the darkness.

"I'm gonna take you to the hospital, Wanda, okay?"

He's holding an orange towel to his hurt eye and so I can only see one side of his face and that side twists up and he grunts and he sounds like Harry when he's sad or wants petting. So I pat Wanda's curly head and say, "You're good, man. All good."

"Hungry," he says.

"I know. I know. Me too."

He says it again, "Hungry," and then we're on the bus, sitting near the back, and the word keeps jumping out of his mouth.

"Hungry."

"Hungry."

"Hungry."

The people on the bus are watching. They're disgusted by this chanting noise and so I turn away from Wanda and pretend that I am not his.

We go to Children's, where the nurses do their serious look thing and one nurse, fat in blue pants that are too short, asks a bagful of questions while Wanda sits there dying. Then I am alone in a room. A stethoscope and a white coat on the door. There are all these beautiful clean objects on the desk. Beakers, sticks, cotton balls, a little black bed with paper laid out over it in case you're bleeding and shit. A poster on the wall showing pink lungs and black lungs and at that point I want a cigarette.

The door opens and in comes a thin nurse. She's holding a chart. Her arms are bare. She's got a great ass. I can tell because her green fatigues or whatever you call them are tight and show off the hollows at her bum. She's married, or something. A ring and she smells like bath powder and her hands are older like she's done dishes a lot, or maybe changed diapers. I can smell her goodness and I think what it would be like to be married to her.

She sits close and says that Wanda's hurt bad. He can't talk, so I'll have to talk for him.

"Hungry," she says. "What's that?"

A cloud opens above me. The thin nurse is with me in a large house, twenty-five rooms at least, and we are sitting by the pool drinking cognac out of snifters. She is leaning into me and her mouth opens and she talks softly.

"Can you tell me his name?" she asks.

I shake my head.

"Hungry. He keeps saying that."

She is wearing nothing. I am wearing nothing. The pool has green lights. The cognac is making her voice slow down. "Do you know his name?"

"I don't know him. He got hurt, I found him, I brought him here."

Her eyes are the colour of the pool.

"Whose gun was it?"

"I dunno."

"So, you found him and brought him here like the Good Samaritan."

"I don't know what you're talking about."

My wife holds up her long fingers and shows me the lines in her palms. "Where do you live?"

I give her Mr. Harrison's address and make up a phone number. Then someone turns out the green lights, and the pool and the twenty-five rooms and the oily cognac all disappear and my wife sits up and says, "Good." Then the fat nurse leans into the room and makes a soft noise and the thin nurse stands and leaves and I am alone. For five minutes I sit and wait and nothing happens, no-one comes back, and when I step out into the hall it is silent and empty, and it's like everyone has died, the thin nurse, Wanda, the fat nurse, the woman at the desk, and I turn and follow the green line down past the elevators, past the security guard, out the exit, and into the night.

When I get home, I enter through the back door and I can hear loud music and voices and when I come through the kitchen door I see Tiff naked and sitting on my brother's lap and he's naked too. They're both facing the TV and Jack's arms come around Tiff's front and hold her tits. She's singing or something and he's singing too. They don't see me. They're on the couch and I can see them from behind and the side. I watch and then step back into the kitchen. The cast iron frying pan is on the stove, the one my father uses to fry his pickerel and bacon. I pick it up. Mr. Fox, the Phys Ed teacher, taught us just last week the rich kid's game, tennis, how you're supposed to keep your arm straight as you swing through and hit the ball. In the kitchen I take a few practice swings with the frying pan. Then I go into the living room and aim at my brother's head. I lock my elbow and say, "I saved your ass." He looks up to find my words and he sees me. His eyes are like two yellow balls of surprise, and just as he's about to call out, I follow through with this mad swing that Mr. Fox'd be terrifically proud of, and I catch one of those balls dead centre, and I can feel it, a perfect hit, and I know it's a winner.

213

/ from HOW MEMORY WORKS

/ BY CLARISE **FOSTER**

2.

in winter the trees here not all that different from the black & limbless trees our
father woke to find every morning as he rubbed at his cold-burnt feet—with wooden
hands afraid to take his boots—his socks off—for the snow—for the march—for the
war—for the freezing no one planned—for the enemy no one thought would fight
back but came in waves just the same like forest grows up one side of a mountain &
down the other—the enemy rooted in the countryside—next to rivers—in city streets
until soldiers like our father were forced to run helter-skelter like thieves or chickens
cornered—some with their heads blown right off while others lost what little sanity
anyone could salvage at 25 below with wind sniping at them—a siren storm of
bullets—broken branches—the ice of enemy fingers in a war that wasn't supposed to
be a war—their own fingers crossed & bleeding & hoping it would soon be over—
hoping they would soon go home

3.

home for some becoming a place where the enemy continued—to loom leaving faces
planted—screams—like the burned out hulk of limbless trees—like shadows rooted
—always somewhere just beyond a hail of bullets—the sleet of dreams where
weathered fingers still stuck to the insides of gloves & feet marched—marching
under the dark weight of guns—under smoke belching—the long & terrible
marching of those too young & those who could never march or love quite enough to
undo the memory of all that blood spilled—the memory of women held in the midst
of all that fighting who could never be held close enough—women with all those
daughters & sons strangely featured & abandoned to their father's dust because
what else was a mother supposed to do

6.

& how it seems i forget every spring—how long it's been since my brother's death—
forget the way it seems the trees forget winter until it's winter again—the deep
freeze always out of the blue & the day in march it comes back to me on a wave of
ice & dirt curling up—like the sea curls—sometimes hair—my brother's hair—when
he was young—the colour of earth & unruly & later grey as the wave of snow & dirt
curling up from the curb where the wind has left it to remind me—understanding
suddenly this is how memory works—like the ocean—like a game of hide & seek
where the little girl in the middle of it all tears a leaf from the neighbour's geranium
plant—makes a promise to herself—suddenly knowing what it means to have a
father home from the war—a brother who will succumb to a terrible disease—that
everything she loves will be lost like a drunk loses her gloves her favourite toque in
the snow on the way to the bar—understanding that this is the way the world turns
upside down & that like the dull ring of morning sky perched on the tip of her
heart—like the trees that will one day line the boulevard outside her house she will
have no choice but to bear the weight—

/ APOLOGY TO BETTY

/ BY ALISON **PRESTON**

When I was out for a walk in my neighbourhood recently, I noticed a house up for sale. For the rest of that day I could think of little else but the former owner of that storied house and the magic and fun she added to my childhood.

Maybe every neighbourhood has one. In my part of town, the Norwood Flats, her name was Birchdale Betty. And whether she deserved it or not, she was targeted by the kids in the neighbourhood with never-ending pranks.

In winter her house and yard were lit up with more decorations than any of us had ever seen in one place. We hadn't seen a lot. She had Santa and his reindeer, a nativity scene, angels, and lights to the tops of all her evergreens. When we were very young it seemed as enchanting as Eaton's corner window, as awe-inspiring as a drive down Wellington Crescent. And it belonged to us.

Summer meant a riot of flowers that bloomed all season long with dwarfs and bird-baths and fawns and flamingoes living charmed lives in the midst of the shrubbery. The lawn rivalled putting greens anywhere. That grass was an invitation to us kids to sully it in some way and sully it we did. Betty often stood guard on the corner of her property warding us off with her glares and her shouts. One scientifically minded boy concocted a poisoned brew that he poured on a patch of her lawn one night after dark. It left a large sinister-looking dead spot that took four seasons to heal itself.

As a kid I believed that I lived in the best neighbourhood in the world. We walked everywhere: downtown, Old St. Boniface, my grandma's home on Stradbrook Avenue, and across Birchdale Betty's lawn. Of course, days lasted a lifetime then and summer was forever. We had the time during our walks to stop and rest for a bit while we ate entire ice-cream cakes out of their boxes.

After years away I came back to Norwood and bought a house. It took me a while to settle in again, with all the worries and busyness of grownup life. But there was something comforting about coming upon old friends living in their parents' homes or in houses just down the street, about finding a former neighbour behind the desk at PhilosoTea, a rewarding little bookstore on Taché Avenue, and about riding on the number 53 bus (it was called the Coniston in the old days), where I often ran into the mums of kids I used to know.

Birchdale Betty was still there, too. But her yard had gone to seed, decades-old dwarfs were lying on their sides in need of paint and Betty herself looked as if her long-hinted-at dark side had taken over. We rode the number 53 together more than once and I was scared that she would recognize me as a grown-up evil child of the fifties and sixties. I was afraid to meet her eyes.

As a youngster I thought her summer garden was magical, like the Christmas lights, but a thirteen-year-old is a different breed. My friends and I made up a song about her. It went something like this:

> J-U-N-G-L-E, jungle, jungle la-a-dy,
> la-di-da, la-di-da.
> She has flowers spring and fall and we're gonna PICK 'em all,
> la-di-da, la-di-da.
> She has pumpkins, big and small, and we're gonna SMASH 'em all,
> la-di-da, la-di-da . . .

You get the idea. There were more verses but they got pretty mean and I can't bring myself to share them. It was a nasty song and we sang it at the top of our lungs on her quiet corner where she worked so hard to create something that she thought was beautiful.

She called the cops. When they asked me my name I was so nervous I couldn't pronounce it.

"Auieein Preueiin," I tried.

"Pardon," said the cop.

I gave it to him again, the same. Finally my friend, Kate, stepped in and said crisply, "Her name is Alison Preston." Good job, Kate.

The Norwood Flats occupy a D-shaped tract of land, with St. Mary's Road as the straight line of the D and the Red River as the bow. Lyndale Drive follows the river from the Norwood Bridge back to St. Mary's further along, just before the start of Old St. Vital. The newer houses in the area were built just after World War II on land that was once a golf course. My dad discovered the neighbourhood in 1950 when he came over during the flood to help lay sandbags behind the houses on the river side of Lyndale Drive. It was that year that Lyndale was built up with dirt from what is now called the flood bowl. That dike saved the neighbourhood and the flood bowl became home to baseball diamonds and football fields and the swimming pool that was our answer to California's surfing beaches when we were young teenagers. God, we had fun!

Anyway, my dad was taken with the Norwood area and we moved onto Ashdale Avenue in 1953 when I was almost four years old. I remember that day; I wasn't getting enough attention.

There were two ash trees planted in front of each house on the boulevard. Small trees then, big trees now. The fathers of two of my friends helped to plant those trees. The fathers' names were Ray Thagard and Ed Oldershaw.

I think Birchdale Betty was there before we were. I can't remember her not being there. Our parents tried very hard not to encourage us in our pranks but one wonderful mother helped us out one time that I remember. My friend and I were sitting at her dining room table cutting out letters from a magazine to paste on paper and send to Betty through the mail. We were struggling for a suitable phrase.

"How about: Frost is on the pumpkin?" my friend's mother tossed out from the kitchen as she slid a cake into the oven.

It was perfect. Hallowe'en was around the corner and as usual, Birchdale Betty celebrated by placing hundreds (I'm not exaggerating) of pumpkins around her yard.

A quiet prank and one that caused no real harm, but still . . .

I'm sorry, Betty, wherever you are.

The main difference in the neighbourhood from then to now, to me, anyway, is that it was quieter then. Leaf-blowers and weed-eaters hadn't been invented yet. Push mowers made their muffled clattering sound now and then, here and there. People were satisfied with the size of their houses and construction sounds were at a minimum. The odd garage went up and sure, Birchdale Betty vacuumed her trees, but she was just one person.

I remember the feel of those faraway days. I can picture the newborn pavements and hear the shouts of kids playing baseball on the D. I can taste my mum's crabapple jelly; it was better than any I have eaten since. And I won't forget what it was like to bury my face in the pink peonies that lined our back fence. They don't make peonies like that anymore. Or maybe it's just that young girls grow old and days past are truly gone.

/ THE COAL CHUTE

from "The House Outside," a Gothic novel

/ BY DUNCAN **THORNTON**

In college, Tannis and Cameron and I were among a group of people who took turns sharing an old house, the sort of old house whose owners didn't mind how badly students looked after the place as long as they weren't very demanding themselves.

It was drafty, very drafty. The heating was dodgy. In the winter, frost built up along the floor beside my mattress (I had no actual bed). Sometimes the water in the kitchen sink drained out quickly enough that you could watch; other times it moved at a rate that was quick only in geological terms. But there was no calling the landlord until the floating bits of potato peel weren't moving at all.

He didn't care how many people slept in a bed, or whether they smoked while they were there, or what they were smoking, so the attention sort of evened out.

There weren't enough lights on the ceiling. There weren't enough power outlets on the walls. When you had any two things in the kitchen switched on at the same time, the breaker tripped and someone had to go down into the basement and try to remember where the box was.

The house had been lived in by students for decades. Whoever had been the last person to get permission to repaint the bathroom had chosen purple. One of the painters had gotten bored and decided to paint freehand concentric purple circles on the back of the door, and we kept a box of darts in there so you had something to do when you were constipated. But whoever had done the real work had clearly not bothered to get a ladder, and had painted the walls only as high as they could reach.

Then, right at the end of the project, someone must have become dispirited or inspired enough to get a chair from the kitchen (you could always tell which chair it had been) and use it to paint a message on the ceiling that could only really be read when you were having a bath: *I loathe purple*. It might have been Tannis.

All kinds of things were hidden away in that house. When you went to flip the breakers, you might run across framed honest-to-god amateur psychedelic paintings. In the cupboards there were unopened packages of Freshie left over from the '70s. But in the dim living room, there had been a huge old oak wardrobe. The sort of wardrobe, someone pointed out at almost every party, that might open into Narnia. That was never me. I was never high or drunk, just bored. "Mister Rational," Tannis said once, when she was pretty far gone. "Won't even have a little smoke-up. Likes to watch the

219 ◾

rest of us get stoned. You're so fucking superior." You see, that was one of those times it was her fault we had never slept together.

Of course, after decades of students like Tannis, it might be that just being in the house was all it took to make you a little stoned. Anyway, on one of the last days before I moved out to begin a more grown-up life somewhere else, after the term was over, after the after-term parties were done, I was the only one in the house. And I was a grown man, a rational man.

But there was a part of me that wondered: *What if the wardrobe does take you somewhere? And you never even bothered to check? How hard would it be just to step inside for a moment?*

I didn't step inside. But now, after I woke up from my bad dreams, it occurred to me that I might have failed, at that last moment in the hippy house, to be an empiricist. To make just one little test. And now, in our own house, with this unknown task, with my wife and our ailing son upstairs, maybe there was something that simple I needed to check.

The coal chute.

I did not turn on the basement light. I found my way downstairs with a flashlight from the junk drawer in the kitchen.

It doesn't have a dirt floor, our basement. There are big oak pillars that hold up the house, and stone walls with crumbling mortar, and nooks and crannies and a crawl space under the porch, and a cracked cement floor. But you wouldn't call it finished.

At the bottom of the stairs I took a moment to get my bearings.

Then I turned off the flashlight, and it was very dark. Once or twice, I'd been with people developing film in darkrooms, when people still took pictures that way. In a darkroom, you could wait as long as you liked, but your eyes would never adjust well enough to see anything.

The basement was almost that dark. Except, after several minutes of standing there by myself, I did notice a little flame, a very little flame, the pilot light behind the furnace grill.

Other than that, nothing.

Kat would have been able to see something, I was pretty sure. But Kat didn't like me anymore. Even with fictional beast-women, sex always gets in the way.

I hoped I wasn't going to hear anything either. And I really hoped I wasn't going to feel anything.

Probably the light touch on my face was a cobweb.

Just a light brush across my face, under my nose. I'm not the panicking kind, but there in the blackness, it seemed some sort of panic might be the rational response:

Brush whatever it was away with a big sweep of my left arm; scream; turn the flashlight on with my right hand and use its beam to slash at the darkness.

If I had thought it was a burglar, that would have been the right thing to do. But I held myself down, kept still. It was just barely possible, like keeping back a sneeze.

I wanted to shudder at least, but I kept that down too. You enter Narnia by hiding in the wardrobe, not by thrashing and yelling. I would have to enter the darkness gently.

I made a slow sweep with my left arm that cleared the thing from my face. My hand just felt it, just barely felt anything at all, almost too powdery and insubstantial to notice. A spiderweb, the smallest thing, but one of the things we understand are scary from our youngest days. Death, abandonment, spiders.

Suddenly I became conscious of all the spiders I had ever seen in our basement, or any basement, or anywhere at all. In my hair, possibly, or going down the back of my collar. I held down that shudder, too. That would only have been the start of it, and I had to hold my shudders in reserve. Spiders were just the beginning of the things that might crawl in the darkness.

I slid my sock-clad left foot forward, low, almost touching the floor. Then the ball of my foot did touch and I slowly rolled my weight onto it, and then made another very small step with my right, all in the blackness.

A dozen slow steps maybe, and then I could feel the wall was near my face, smell the crumbling mortar, the dusty stone, the old wood that covered the coal chute where a long time ago I had dreamt I had followed Kat, like Alice down the rabbit hole.

I closed my eyes. Breathed the darkness. Cleared my mind. Reached up for the little doorway. Felt for the wooden latch, grabbed it, and just then there was a roar of flame, and the fan started up, and then the furnace and the ductwork began to tick with the heat, and I tried to turn the latch, but I already knew I would enter no dream-world.

My nails could feel the latch—it was painted over. Thickly. Long ago. This coal chute hadn't been used since the gas-lines had gone in, most of a hundred years ago. Mr. Rational had finally made the test. Probably that big wardrobe hadn't really opened onto Narnia, either.

I switched the flashlight on, opened my eyes, and crept back up the stairs.

When I got into bed that woke Julia, of course, and she turned her head and opened her eyes to look at me. She didn't say anything.

"Maybe I took the wrong turn a long time ago," I whispered. "Maybe the wrong things are no longer an option."

Under the covers, she took my hand and squeezed it hard. "We need options," she said. "Find your way back and then take the other path."

"Sure," I said. "No problem."

But I had no plan.

An inventory I hadn't realized I had kept ran through my mind. Pills. Ropes. Knives. A broken window we kept in the garage. No, those things were for a different project, a last project that would be just for me.

I had no plan for anything, but I had known since I climbed out of the river that I would have to follow procedure now; follow depression hygiene:

Keep some good place, some right moment tended.

Otherwise be here and now.

Otherwise, don't remember, don't think back.

If you look back at things while he is prowling, all you will hear is the black dog.

All you will see is the story of how you came to be this miserable.

So I would need to keep an inventory of Julia and Sammy in my head all the time, right up near the surface. Not as they were now, but in that ideal time I had made for them. Sammy when he still smiled. Julia when she still trusted I could do the things I said.

Soon it was morning.

I had lost my feeble hope that I could close my eyes and find a magic door that would let me find Sammy as he should have been, that would let Julia feel joy again. And I had no plan to replace it.

/ THE LAST TO BREAK

/ BY DAVID **ELIAS**

Sunday afternoons the children played outside while the father took a long nap on the living room couch. The mother went upstairs and stayed there. They would see her, sometimes, sitting at the window with the curtains pulled back. But today was an especially sunny, warm day, and she was busy in the kitchen, preparing a lunch for them to take. When she was done, she put on her favourite yellow dress and she and the children drove all the way across the valley to the edge of the river while the father slept on. When they got there, they spread a blanket under one of the large shady trees and sat down to have a picnic.

The children ate everything, but the mother said she wasn't hungry, and after a while she got up and walked slowly over to the edge of the river and stood very still. The children watched her from the blanket. After a while they got up, too, and went to stand at the edge of river, but farther up the bank than their mother. They took turns throwing dead twigs and branches that had fallen from the trees into the dark water.

"What's something a river never does?" said the girl. She was always making up riddles.

"What?" said the boy. He could never guess the answers to any of them.

"No. You have to repeat it. Before I tell you. That's the rule."

"Alright. What's it never do?"

The boy had just thrown a branch far out into the water and he was watching the lazy current take it. He wanted to wait until it had floated past the spot where his mother was standing before he threw in another one.

"You're not saying it right," said the girl. "You have to say it the way I did."

"What's something a river doesn't do? There."

"Change direction," said the girl. "It only ever flows one way."

"A river meanders," said the boy. "It curves back on itself. So then it's going the other way."

"But it always turns back again," said the girl. "The way it was meant to go. The sticks we throw never come back."

The boy looked past his sister at the mother, still standing on the bank with her arms folded. Beneath her feet, the stick he had thrown into the river floated by on a dark glossy mirror of water. The way she looked in her yellow dress and dark sunglasses made the boy think of a sad movie star.

223

"What changes but always stays the same?" said the girl.

"Another one?" The boy didn't want to answer any more riddles. "If I get it right can we stop?"

"Well?"

"The answer is the same," he said.

"Then say it."

"A river. That's the answer."

"Yes, but why?"

"I got it. I was right."

"Only if you can say why."

"That's easy. Because the water moves, so it's always changing. But everything else doesn't." He was looking at the wide easy curve of the steep banks. At the tall old trees along the shore. Just then the mother turned away from the water and called over to them that it was time to go. They packed up the picnic and folded the blanket and drove all the way across the valley back to the house.

When they got there, the father was still asleep on the couch so the boy left the yard and walked all by himself out into the pastures and fields that surrounded the farm. He liked to explore. He liked to find things out. For a while he wandered in and out of the small stands of willow and maple that grew there until he found a dead robin hanging upside down from the electric fence that ran along the creek. Its claws were still curled around the barbed fence wire as it swivelled a little, back and forth, in the light breeze. A thin, blackened strand of copper wire ran from one of the claws down into the damp grass. The boy could smell singed feathers and flesh. The robin must have landed on the fence with the copper wire wrapped around its leg and electrocuted itself. When he leaned closer he could hear the carcass crackling and sizzling. The electricity was burning a hole into the side of the bird. He knelt and peered into the small organic fire. Saw organs and tissue there, glowing like embers. Wondered what the charged glow of his own insides might look like. The way they burned sometimes. With the jolt and buzz of something. Just like this. When he sat across the kitchen table from the father. How it seemed as if he were staring intensely into a fire. How it always ignited the boy's insides. Made him want to combust.

He left the burning bird and walked farther into the thicket of willow and birch saplings. He decided to take off his shirt. He wanted to feel the warm breeze on his exposed skin. He looked down and saw how the sun dappled the pale flesh on his boyish chest. He decided to take off the rest of his clothes. To walk naked among the small trees. He wanted to think of himself as a creature. To move like one. He heard some chirping and followed the sound. The way a creature would. He discovered a nest in one of the lower branches. Inside were five newly hatched robins with their eyes closed and their beaks open wide. He saw that they were as naked as he was. That they had only the first beginnings of feathers. He looked at their swollen, mottled stomachs. He could see right into their bodies through the translucent skin there. See the blue and red and green organs.

They became agitated. "They think I'm their mother," the boy said out loud. Their scratchy squawking intensified and their beaks opened even wider as they swivelled their enormous heads from side to side, trying to be fed. The boy wondered if it was their mother hanging upside down on the fence wire, smouldering. He reached into the nest and lifted one of the baby birds out carefully. Cradled it in the palm of his hand. He tilted his palm a little one way, then the other. Each time, the hatchling sensed the change in equilibrium and tried to compensate. Then the boy tilted it farther and farther and the hatchling spread its naked wings and scratched awkwardly at his palm with its soft claws until it tumbled out and fell to the ground. It landed on its back and rolled awkwardly onto its side, wings and legs flailing, trying to right itself. The other hatchlings were quiet now. They were listening to the pain and surprise of their lost sibling. To the raspy, vulgar frenzy of it.

He was one creature and the hatchling was another. He understood its helplessness. Its nakedness. He lifted a bare foot and lowered it slowly over the hatchling until he could feel its naked warmth against his skin. It pulsed and tickled there in the strangest way. He brought more weight down. Pressed the bird deeper and deeper into the moist earth. The squawking became a muffled cry that was barely audible. The sound of it so small. Like something coming from far, far beneath a blanket, deep inside a night. He felt a small scratching against the bottom of his foot. The creature was desperately trying to dig its tiny claws into his flesh. It was trying to get him to stop. He pressed harder until he could no longer feel even the tiniest prickly tickle.

And just before he lifted away his foot he understood that he had wanted this. Had planned it. Before he ever ventured into the countryside that afternoon. Before the trip to the river with his sister and his mother. Before he woke that morning. Somewhere in the deepest part of the night, in the darkness, he had already imagined how the little bird would feel, hot against the cool skin on the sole of his bare foot. How the canopy of leaves and branches would look when he tilted his head up. How the blue sky beyond that would do to him what he had done to the bird. Mock and mock him with its brightness. Kill and kill him with its endlessness.

He squatted down next to the warm, dead bird. Saw that some of the ruined organs had burst through the translucent skin. He knelt closer. Caught the odour of its tiny death in his nostrils. The moist smell of it, fresh against the mulch of old leaves. Then he trembled. With a strange dread of regret. Sighed. Because he knew he was lost inside that regret. Inside the immensity of its future.

Not far from the thicket where the boy knelt, a big black car came gliding down out of the hills. The girl was playing with a kitten out in the yard and was the first to spot it. She ran to tell her mother. The mother said how she hoped it wouldn't be their yard the car decided to pull into but the girl knew that it would be. Just as always, the car rolled to a silent stop in the middle of the yard and stayed there. That was always the worst part. The way it just stayed there. The way nobody ever got out. The girl stood in the doorway of the summer kitchen. She could see them in there. Five or six of them. Waiting.

After a long while, one of the wide doors swung open and a man stuck out his leg. Crushed a cigarette under his brown boot. Then a back window rolled down far enough for the girl to see a woman's face inside. The woman was dark-skinned. Black-haired and black-eyed and the girl, with her blond hair and fair skin, wondered what it would be like. To have eyes and skin and hair the same colour as her thoughts. The kind she had when she got tired of trying to be good all the time. She thought the woman in the back seat of the car must have them, too. They must all have them. To just sit there that way. Scaring her. Scaring her mother.

"Why do they always come here?" she said to her brother. He was back from his walk and now he stood next to his sister in the doorway of the summer kitchen.

"Because they remember," said the boy. He was thinking about the stories he sometimes heard. How the land they lived on once belonged to other people—people like the ones in the car. How they'd gone to live up in the hills.

Just then the mother walked past them out of the summer kitchen into the sunshine. She stopped a few feet from the car and held out a small, clear bottle. The children knew that it was a bottle of dandelion wine. Other times it could be Wonder Oil or even vanilla extract.

"She always gives them something," said the girl.

"She says it's like medicine for them."

"Why do they need medicine?"

"She says they just want to forget."

The man's hand reached out through the partly open door and took the bottle from their mother gently. Then the door closed and the car glided slowly out of the yard.

"They're like a river," said the boy. He was thinking back to the picnic they had been on. "The way it remembers. All the way along to where it's going. It still remembers back to the beginning. To where it started from."

"Not if the river dries up," said the girl.

"Then the riverbed remembers. And the banks and trees. Even the sky."

"Sometimes I think it's him they're always waiting for," said the girl. She was thinking about the father asleep on the couch inside the house. "It's him they want."

The girl went back into the house and walked very quietly into the living room and sat on a chair across from the father. She sat very still and watched him as he lay on the couch with his back to her. Then he stirred and turned over and rested his head in the palm of his hand. He opened his eyes and looked right at her. Wiggled two fingers at her. She got up off the chair and walked over and stood in front of him. His other hand rested on his hip. She looked at it. It was calloused and scarred and blackened under the nails because he worked all day in the blacksmith shop across the yard. He worked with iron and steel. She reached out and let her small hand hover over the back of his. Over a small red scratch there. There were always scars on the father's big hands. This one looked fresh. She lowered her hand and ran one finger lightly along the edge of it. He pulled his hand away slowly and turned over so that he had his back to her again. She stood very still for a long, long time and listened to his even breathing. Finally, she turned and left the room but something stayed there. Hovered in mid-air above the place where her hand had been. Something she had left behind. That would always be there now, mixed in with his even breathing and the rising and falling of his chest. He would wake up and feel it as a light breeze against the skin on the back of his hand.

The girl had only wanted what the boy and the mother wanted, too. What they all longed for. For the father to shine down on them. Like the time he took them all to the JC Penney store in Walhalla, North Dakota. The mother had wanted to buy clothes and dishes but the father had bought a television set for them to watch instead. When they went to pay for it there was a pretty young clerk at the counter. She was as pretty as the girl hoped she'd be one day. And she was also very shy. Then she made a mistake and the father put his hand on hers and said sweetly that it was quite alright. The pretty young clerk was so happy she began to glow.

The boy looked at the mother, standing there next to him, and saw that his mother's heart was breaking. And he knew why. It was because the father was doing to the pretty young clerk what he never did to her anymore. To any of them. He was shining his light on her. Then he looked at his sister and saw that her heart was breaking, too. His was the last to break. But right there in the JC Penney store in Walhalla, North Dakota, they became a family of broken hearts.

That evening, when it was time for the mother to go out and milk the cows, the children went out with her. The barn full of cows was not quite warm and not quite cold. They watched the way she grabbed the warm cow's teats with her cold winter fingers. The way her pale wrists rubbed against the shiny udder of the cow.

"The milk is still alive in there," said the girl.

Living, it squirted from the teat into the galvanized pail between the mother's thighs. They stood on either side of the mother and watched the milk sing into the bucket, high-pitched and urgent, until the bottom of the pail disappeared into white and the sound became frothy and liquid. Now the mother began to sing. If teardrops were pennies and heartaches were gold. The milk cried into the bucket. The boy put his hand on the wall of the cow's stomach. Felt it swell. Tighten. The cow sighed and two streams of steam gushed from its flared nostrils. The girl placed her cheek against the bulging great roundness of the cow's warm stomach. Listened to the machinery of its interior. To the gurgling and grinding of its digestion. She waited until the cow sighed, and when it did, she sighed, too. She lifted her head away from the cow's side, and turned, and placed the other cheek there. All this time the milk frothed into the pail. Then the mother stopped her milking. She lifted her hand and placed her hands on the side of the cow's stomach. Rested the palms there. The steaming cow turned its head and stared at the three of them with one big brown eye. Blinked down at them. Chewed.

"We are creatures," said the boy.

"Just like this cow," said the girl.

"We are the same," said the boy.

Then it was winter and they were in the basement of a church, walking between rows of tables and chairs. "He didn't used to be so bad," the children heard a woman say. The woman was sitting on one of the chairs. There was bowl of sugar cubes on the table in front of her. She had just picked one up and dropped it into her coffee.

"I don't know what's got into that man," said the woman next to her. She was large and round and her black dress looked too small for her big bosoms. She had her hair in a bun.

"Too much time in that blacksmith shop, if you ask me."

Arranged evenly along the tops of the tables in the church basement were sets of cup, saucers, knives and spoons.

"All that smoke and steel."

Set along the middle of the tables were plates of orange cheese chunks, cut-up sausage and large trays of fresh-baked buns.

"All that grime and dust."

The lady in the black dress was sipping coffee from her cup very loudly and taking enormous bites out of a bun she had picked up from one of the trays.

"It turns a man's heart black."

The children didn't want to hear any more so they moved along, in behind the chairs, eavesdropping on people as they made their way from table to table, stealing sugar cubes and sucking on them while they listened. Eating bits of cheese. Slices of baloney.

"Her with all those cows to milk."

"He ought to get her a machine."

"It would be different if it was him that had to do the milking."

They were eavesdropping on some other people now.

"Lord knows what he's building in that shop of his now."

"It won't come to anything. It never does."

"What will she do?"

"What can she do?"

"Such a sweet thing, too."

"And look where it's got her."

The next day was Christmas Eve and the mother got up very early in the morning and started cleaning the house. She worked all day. She scrubbed everything from top to bottom. Inside the cupboards and out. Up the stairs and down.

"Tonight is Christmas Eve," said the girl.

"Tomorrow is Christmas Day," said the boy.

"We will get a present."

"Our mother will give us each one."

"The house will be so clean."

"She wants to make it shine."

"Like a star."

"Like the Christmas star."

They could hear the mother in the other room, humming to herself. She hardly ever hummed anymore. They had forgotten how happy it made them to hear it.

"She's cleaning everything up," said the girl.

"It makes her happy to clean it so well," said the boy.

"She's making it new."

"Everything's new at Christmas."

"Everything starts over."

While the mother hummed the children stayed close enough to hear her, but not so close that she knew they were listening.

"She's like a bird," said the girl.

"No. She's like the sun on water."

They started to hum, too, quietly.

"And the house is like a boat on the water."

"A boat that sails over everything."

That night when the boy went to bed, the cold came down out of the rafters of the house and compressed his lungs and pressed against his heart so that it could hardly beat. He could hardly breathe with the mystery of his solitude. He decided to pray very hard. He put his hands together above the covers and closed his eyes and turned his face up to the ceiling. As he prayed he moved his lips but did not make any sound. He didn't want his sister in the other bed to know he was still praying. He prayed and prayed until he wasn't sure whether he was still awake and praying or asleep and dreaming that he was praying.

He imagined his heart as a small treasure chest, with a lid that locked. He unlocked it with a key he took from under the mattress and opened the chest and inside was the colour of red velvet or gold cloth. When he opened it, tiny music came from down inside. The melody was familiar and he hummed along quietly. Then he was getting out of bed on Christmas morning and he wasn't cold anymore and he went down the stairs and there was a tree. Decorated with yellow ribbons. There were lots of presents under the tree and the father was standing in front of it with his hands on his hips and laughing like Santa Claus on a Coca-Cola sign. He had a red Santa cap on his head. He had white gloves on his hands.

When the boy woke up his hands were still folded together. His face was still turned up to the ceiling. His eyes were closed. His lips were dry. His body was stiff and rigid and tired. He couldn't remember what he had been praying for all night long but he could remember all the way back to summer and the way his mother had stood next to the river for so long.

When he got downstairs, the father was still on the couch. The mother had put a paper bag of chocolates and a paper bag of peanuts on the table in front him. There was a bowl for the shells. While the children opened their presents, the father sat up and began to crack open the peanuts, one at a time. He began to eat the chocolates. The children had seen their mother buy them at the store. The one down the road. It was the kind of store where you could buy jelly cookies out of one bin and nails out of another. The peanuts and chocolates had been in two big wooden boxes with a scoop in each one. The mother had scooped the peanuts and chocolates into separate paper bags and the storekeeper had weighed them on his scale.

While the children opened their presents and the father ate the chocolates and shelled the peanuts the mother sat on the floor next to them with her legs folded under her skirt and watched them. They rustled the wrapping paper but above it they could hear how he broke open a peanut. How he put the kernel into his mouth. They heard how he crunched it up. When he put a chocolate in his mouth, they could hear him smacking his lips.

After they had opened their presents they went outside to play behind the blacksmith shop. That was where the machines were. The ones the father spent all of his time building out of steel and iron. The ones he never finished. They found one that was shaped kind of like a boat and pretended to sail far out to sea in it. The water they sailed on was pale green for the boy, but a deep violet blue for the girl. The boy put up sails and took them down. The girl watched for dolphins and whales. Sometimes she looked for land.

They never went into the blacksmith shop but even today they could hear the father inside, pounding steel with a hammer. There was a window they could peek through if they stood on a crate, but the panes were so blackened with soot and grime that all they could ever make out was shadows. Today they listened at the door. They could hear him in there. They could hear the sound of metal banging and clanging. Of hammer on steel. They listened to the father's effort. To the sureness of it. The will.

"Things are being bent," said the boy.

"Things are being broken," said the girl, just before she went back inside the house.

But the boy stayed. He had decided that today he would sneak into the shop while the father was welding. He knew the sound the arc welder made. The way it crackled and sizzled with angry power and harm. And he knew that when the father was welding, he had to wear a big black mask that pulled down right over his face. There was a tiny black window on the mask for him to look through, but when he pulled it down and started to weld, he wouldn't be able to see anything else.

The boy knew all this because he sometimes snuck into the shop while the father was away and tried the mask on. Slipped it over his skull. It was heavy and cold and far too big for his head. He would pull the visor down and look through the black glass panel at nothing. There was nothing to see. Even when he took the mask to the door of the shop and stepped out into the sunshine to look up at the sky. But then one day he had tried looking directly at the sun through the black glass. Then the sun looked like a tiny pale disk. It looked like the full moon. It had no power over him. That day he learned he could tame the sun with a piece of black glass. He also discovered there were tiny blemishes on the surface of the sun. The sun was not perfect. He thought what it would be like to wear the mask whenever the father stared at him with such violent intensity from across the table. And how he could use it to tame the father's eyes.

When he heard the welder start up he crept through the door into the darkness. Into a lightning storm. He could see the father hunched over. Where the tip of the welding rod touched the steel there was a holocaust of fire. A volcano of smoke rose up from it, and red molten liquid dropped down onto the floor beneath. The boy stared into the small, impossibly bright sun. His eyes wanted to close but he forced them to stay open with his fingers until his naked eyeballs shuddered. Until tears ran down his face. He looked upon the holocaust. The destruction of darkness was complete and utterly terrifying. So this was what the father had really been doing all this time. Making a small sun to stare into. To shine up at him.

That night, not long after the boy had gone to bed, a thousand sharp grains of sand attacked his eyes. Left him screaming in his bed. His eyes were fires of their own. He wanted to tear them out. He writhed on the small cold bed. Then he could hear the mother standing over him. And the sister. And even the father. This must be what it's like at a funeral, the boy thought. The way they are standing over my body.

"What is it?" said the girl to him.

"My eyes," the boy said. "My eyes."

The boy felt his eyes frying inside the sockets of his skull. They had become two itching, throbbing suns of their own.

This is what the robin must have felt, he thought. This is what it feels like to be consumed by fire. Then he opened his eyes and he could see everything. He felt the strangest kind of comfort. Of joy. He looked up at the mother. The sister. And the last thing he saw was his father's eyes. Shining down on him at last.

/ WHORLWIND

/ BY DAVID **ANNANDALE**

Callahan was being annoying again.

"If you'd seen it, then you'd know what I was talking about," he said. Again. By Heath's count, this was the seventh time.

"Yeah, well, as previously indicated, Richard, I haven't seen it."

"You have to. You absolutely have to." No point using sarcasm on Callahan when he was on a tear. He wouldn't notice a truck smacking his forehead. "It's . . . It's . . ."

And round the circuit one more time. Heath sighed. He leaned back in his chair while Callahan groped for the words. Heath sipped his coffee. They were sitting in Bar Italia. Outside, on Corydon Avenue, the Sunday evening traffic drove by, windshields reflecting the dull glare of the streetlights. Exhaust fog billowed into February clouds. Heath was bored. The novelty of Callahan's inarticulate enthusiasms had worn off years ago. But Callahan's deep pockets had powerful charisma, and Heath wanted some of their nectar. So he sat and sipped and waited for Callahan to get on with it.

"You've got . . . I mean . . ." Callahan blinked. He waved a hand in front of his face as if batting an insect away. "On my mother's grave, Don, you haven't lived until you've seen this thing."

Finally. A full sentence, even if it was larded with Callahan's usual clichéd hyperboles. Callahan picked up his own cup, coffee untouched and lukewarming, and took a gulp. Heath watched and tried to swallow his contempt for the ridiculous. Callahan and his stupid Colonel Sanders moustache and goatee, moustache peroxide blond, goatee henna red. All that and a priss-priss suit, perfect knife creases and pink bow tie. Ludicrous enough on a young man. Insupportable on a twit in his fifties. At least he didn't use a monocle.

"I take it, though, that I am going to see it."

"Well . . ."

"You want it."

"It isn't a question of want." Callahan was calming down now that they were circling close to actual business. He rubbed at an eye, fighting with an eyelash.

Not a question of want? Yeah yeah. "It's a question of need."

"Exactly. Exactly. Couldn't have said it better myself."

That's because that's what you were going to say, you prat. "You've already tried buying it?"

"Of course. Would I be here otherwise?"

"You tried hard?" Heath always asked the question. He did so partly because it put the guilt back on the client, and made Heath look like the ethics king. But he did it mainly to get a sense of how high he'd be able to set his price.

"Like I've never tried anything in my life." That was the one thing Heath liked about Callahan: the no-holds-barred honesty of wholehearted stupidity. He was always good for serious change, a rare thing in the limited Winnipeg market. But it only took a couple of Callahans, or Callahan only a couple of times a year, to keep Heath comfortable. Much easier being the big fish in the small pond here than having to face the competition and shoot-me-now cost of living in Toronto or New York.

"So this is a go?" Heath asked. Make the client say it.

"Yes. Yes. Get it for me."

Heath nodded. He flipped open his notebook, picked up his pen. "So who has it?"

"His name is Garfield Rutherford."

"Where does he live?"

"Near Roseisle."

"You saw the tapestry at his place?" Heath asked.

"Yes yes, I already told you." Callahan struggled with the eyelash again. "I was there yesterday."

"And he got it where?"

"Brittany. At an auction a month or so ago. Some inheritance thing."

Heath knew the deal. Heirs to an old-line aristocracy land the castle, handed down from Great-great-aunt Marie, and the thing is an albatross. Unless you sell it off piece by piece, that is. Ching ching, he knew the tune of that siren song all right. "Rutherford's loaded, I guess?"

Callahan shook his head. "No. Not that much, anyway. That's what makes me sick. He bought it for practically nothing."

"Family didn't know what it was worth?"

"God, does anybody know what it's worth? I think you, Rutherford and I are the only ones who even know it exists."

The logic of Callahan's story was disappearing down the twists of its own convolutions. "Then how could he buy it?"

"He didn't buy it. He bought another tapestry. Some sorry piece of junk. Wasn't even Flemish, and don't even talk to me about Arras. But when he got it home, he found that what he thought was one tapestry was really two, with the junk one sewn over the other. He pulled them apart and . . ." Callahan shook his head. "I can't believe . . . I mean the odds . . ." His words abandoned him again, fleeing as he worked himself up over the injustice of it all. "So?" he asked.

Heath moved the coffee cup in a circle, spreading out the ring on the table. "Local jobs aren't a good idea," he said. He kept his expression unhappy and doubtful. Now he was haggling, dangling the bait of uncertainty in front of Callahan's face. Maybe I'll do this for you, maybe I won't. Maybe you'll get your treasure, maybe you won't. How badly do you want it? You want it really badly, don't you?

Callahan was frowning. His hand fluttered near his eyes, waving at imaginary midges. "Please," he begged. "I'll triple your rate."

It took an effort for Heath not to blink. Callahan's need was the most naked he'd ever seen. Triple? He could take the year off after a job like this. More time for his own projects. Maybe have some luck, start reducing the number of gigs altogether. "All right," he said slowly, still keeping up the front of deep doubt. Inside he was grinning at a good evening's work.

He had the grin at the surface when he reached home. Home was in a converted warehouse in the Exchange District. It was a studio whose only sectioned-off area was the washroom. The rest of the space, in all its expansiveness, was the domain of art. Jill Conley looked up from the mirror she was polishing as he walked in. Heath crouched down beside her on the futon, still grinning.

"Okay," she asked. "Whose canary did you swallow?"

"Dick Callahan's."

Conley chuckled. She picked up the mirror, a small, perfect oval, and slipped a hook through one end. "That can't have been too hard. Name me someone more eager to bend over. How much you taking him for this time?"

Heath told her. She stopped laughing.

"What do you have to do?"

"Snatch a tapestry."

"Oh sure, something light and easy to carry."

Heath waved the problem off. "It's not that bad. I've done cabinets, after all. I think I can handle this."

"I guess. When do you have to fly out?"

"I don't. The target lives in Snow Valley."

"A local? Oh geez, Don."

"I know, I know." He held up his hands: don't blame me. "Just this once, though. And at that price, I figure it's worth the risk. Serious time off after that." He looked around. "Then there'd be no problem getting this done by deadline."

Conley's eyes glinted, wistful. "That would be nice." She stood up and carried the mirror over to the Project.

"How many did you do today?" Heath asked.

"Four." She hooked the mirror into place.

"Four," Heath repeated, the enormity of what remained sinking in. He straightened up and walked around the Project, feeling that daily mix of pride and despair at what they were trying to accomplish.

It was a dance of his paintings and Conley's mirrors. His canvases, neon-industrial meditations of violet and orange, both surrounded the mirrors and created their structure. The mirrors, a legion of reflecting perfection, hung from cat's cradle tentacles. There was still what seemed an endless road of paint and shaping of glass yet to go, but Heath could already feel the touches of the endgame of the Project. Colours and light spiralled and spun, interwove and captured. When the last of the paintings was done, when the last mirror was hung, the viewer would be trapped in a vortical spectrum, whirled and twisted by a wind whose force was vision, whose movement was illusion.

They'd been working on the Project for a year now. They had fantasies of the Venice Biennale. Pipe dreams, Heath knew. But that didn't stop him from wanting, and it didn't stop him from hoping. He had earned his pragmatist stripes, so hope was allowed, wasn't it? The life of the visual artist was an oratorio of poverty, nuanced by brief ritornellos of grants, usually just enough to set up the next chorus of lack. Vicious circle problem: how to earn a living and still have enough time to work? Outside-the-box answer: theft. It turned out Heath was very good at it. Conley was philosophical about the solution. It was a shame to waste talent, she pointed out. Heath chose his assignments carefully. He never robbed museums, only other collectors. The public good was never harmed, went the rationalization. He was more a market lubricant, speeding up the transfer of property from one pair of elite hands to another. It was all kept in-house. Nobody complained. Nobody could: nine times out of ten, the target objects had been stolen in the first place.

Still and all, a sabbatical would be nice.

Conley stepped back from the Project. Eyed it hard.

"What're you thinking?" Heath asked.

"That it doesn't look any different than it did this morning." She brushed some hair from her eyes.

The hair—long, fine, floating, siren—called Heath over. "That doesn't mean it looked bad this morning." He traced a finger down Conley's cheek.

She smiled, leaned her face into his hand. "I didn't say it did. It just didn't look finished."

"Time enough."

"Barely."

"We'll do it." He put an arm around her waist, turned her gently into his chest.

She reached around and gave his butt a squeeze. "You really thinking about art right now?"

He tried to think of something clever to say.

There was wind as Heath drove out west on Highway 3, but it wasn't strong. It was just breath enough to push the snow in serpentine whispers over the road, white-on-black shiftings, mirage-insubstantial to the wheels of his car. The sky was clear, the moon nearly full. Heath didn't mind the light from the sky. He knew how to use shadows, and his headlights would announce his arrival less stridently in the country if the night stopped short of the absolute.

Snow Valley: the valley without a mountain. West of Winnipeg, west beyond Carmen, just beyond Roseisle, was where the prairie came to a sudden interruption. There was a slight roll to the ground, and then down the road went, into a winding depression, and magically there were hills. And in the hills, there were houses.   NO TRESPASSING signs were lone sentries standing guard at the end of gravel roads that were barely more than paths. Heath smiled when he spotted the sign he knew marked Rutherford's property. Rutherford's road was so small it was impossible to spot without the warning. Heath wouldn't be able to trespass without the help of the admonition not to.

He turned right into Rutherford's land, wheels bumping hard as they sought the grooves in the packed snow. He drove in just far enough to be invisible from the main road, then killed lights and ignition. He sat and waited for his eyes to adjust to the night. No more noise now, no more light. He had a flashlight in his parka pocket for when he was inside the house. Outside, he could see the moonblue glow of the snow.

He got out of the car and started walking up the road. He stuck to the tire grooves, but the snow, treacherous with minus-twenty rigidity, still squeaked and crunched beneath his boots. He didn't like it, but that was the reality of risk in a dead-of-winter job. In brittlesnap cold, sound whipcracked and travelled for miles. At least there was still a bit of a wind, whispering to itself through the trees, sussurring over the drifts, doing its bit to give him a bit of background white noise. He walked slowly, varying his rhythm, trying to sound less like a prowler, more like deep forest restlessness. Rutherford's house came into view, lights off, asleep and dreaming. It was a giant wooden A-frame, rich man's hillside rustic. The living room windows were two storeys high. Heath hoped Rutherford's heating bills were obscene.

The shadows around the front door were wrong. Heath stopped, his body reacting before his mind had consciously registered trouble. He stood motionless, breath held, ears straining and eyes wide wide wide. Nothing came at him. Nobody yelled. Trouble all the same though. He looked at the shadows. They bothered him, teased with the deep nausea of a bad surprise. What, though? He couldn't see anyth—

The wind found the energy for a solid gust. Heath heard a door creak.

No breathing now, none at all. Do Not Move. He waited for Rutherford to come charging out with a rifle. He waited for career apocalypse. Seconds tick tick ticked. His blood began to pound in his ears. His lungs complained. He wondered just how long he was going to have to wait for that apocalypse.

The shadows didn't move. Heath let his breath out. His antennae retracted. Things were still wrong, but they didn't seem like trouble. He started walking again. As he approached, the shadows began to define themselves. He reached the front porch, and the shadows, with a snicker, gave up their mystery. Heath's heart started to pound again. The front door was open. It swung a few lazy inches, whinging, when the wind gusted. It couldn't swing shut, though. Not with a body lying in the doorway.

Heath stood on the porch and paused a good minute before he made himself look more closely. He felt the pull of the inevitable and the bad, but he allowed himself the faint hope of resisting just that little bit longer. Then he knelt to see what it was that he didn't want to see. The body was that of an old woman, or so he guessed from the bun of white hair. She was lying face down, and her head seemed unnaturally flat, too close to the deck. Knowing he was making a mistake, knowing he was kissing many nights of rest goodbye, Heath grabbed the hair and lifted the head. The face was gone. The front half of the head had been hacked away by axe and madness. Heath gulped, dropped the head and stumbled back down the steps, consigning the horror to the shadows.

He didn't head back to the car. He stayed at the foot of the steps and wondered just how much of an idiot he was prepared to be. Instinct, common sense, self-preservation, fear: all the smart impulses told him to go. Now. The only thing keeping him here was greed, and let's get real here: Callahan was offering him a partial sabbatical bonus, not mortal danger pay. So come on. Let's go. Let's go.

He didn't. That most bone-dumb and extinction-prone of all drives was holding him fast. Curiosity kept him there. Curiosity made him peer at the darkness of the house as if squinting would tell him anything. Curiosity made him start back up the steps to the corpse. Curiosity made him pull off a glove, reach down and touch the body.

Cold. Icicle and marble, old death cold.

Curiosity made him take the stupid risk. He turned the flashlight on. Nobody jumped out of the shadows, but he saw a pool of blood gone black and frozen. Heath turned the light off, let his eyes readjust to the dark, let his stupid side argue with the rest. The reasons to run were still very good. Even better were the reasons not to leave any trace that he had been here.

And yet.

He answered the call, the call of a spiderlurking mystery in the house, the call that would brook no denial. Come and see. Come and see. So he did.

He turned the flashlight back on and stepped over the body, into the house, into the still image of violence done and death triumphant. His light was a diameter of jagged revelation, shining off shattered furniture, broken glass and Jackson Pollock blood. Things had been smashed, things had been torn, things had been burned. There was very little still recognizable. Heath could tell that a pile of stuffing and sticks probably had been furniture, maybe a couch, but beyond that, expensive or cheap, high taste or low kitsch, his imagination had no guide. Everywhere he looked, identity and art, as if equivalent threats, had been erased.

He found the axe at the foot of the stairs. Lying beside the axe was the other body. This was an old man, and Heath guessed it was Rutherford. His face was broken, soft and purple, as if it had been smashed repeatedly into a wall. Heath saw some teeth on the ground. Rutherford had sunk his fingers knuckle-deep into both his eyes.

Heath eyed the stairs. No stopping now, he thought, and climbed. In for a nickel, in for it all, and he still had a tapestry to find, or at least evidence that Rutherford had destroyed it too. If he had, then the narrative arc of the house's violence would be complete and Heath could leave and start work on forgetting.

Rutherford hadn't touched the tapestry. Heath found it in a room at the end of the upstairs corridor. The tapestry took up most of one wall, and there was nothing else in the room. As Heath stood in the doorway and shone his light over the tapestry, he knew why only it was here. Nothing else could stay here. Any other presence would have been blasted, shrivelled and withered by the woven force on the wall. The tapestry was a rondo of majesty and pain, gold and red twisted into the muscle of torture. In the centre, a gryphon triumphant sank talons into the body of a unicorn. In the background, tears of blood plummeted, downpour, from a sky of screaming gold. And surrounding the slaughter, more tears, more weeping. Mourners noble and serf stretched their mouths wide to the ripping limits of grief. Their hands, taut claws, were raised to empty sockets. Through the empty sockets, the sky wept.

Heath drew closer, closer yet, his eye spiralcaught by the detail and the vortex of the art. Gryphon to unicorn to mourners and hard yank through the sky, vision spattered by blood, to gryphon again. And more too, more that he couldn't identify from a distance but that had him frowning from both pain and Stendhal Syndrome awe. He stumbled forward until he was almost touching the tapestry, and then he saw what it was that was sucking him in. The tapestry was a lie. Its form was impossible, violating any definition of the art form it purported to be. There was no warp here, no weft. The threads obeyed no grid, no pattern that would permit the tapestry to be. Instead they twisted and spiralled, whorled into the patterns of a demon's fingerprint. The closer Heath looked, the deeper the hook went, and the faster and harder his eyes rolled around the violence. A maelstrom groove trapped them. Locked in, his eyes whipped back and forth, over and around and past the gryphon's beak, and around again and in, and the movement was so fast he felt himself fall into fully conscious REM.

The pain, deep beneath his eyes, pineal specific, came at a vicious whiplash turn. It was stiletto sharp and ice harsh, but it wasn't a stab. It was a *yank*.

Fade to white.

Full day when he came to, his head throbbing to the beat of a lead drum. He blinked a few times, trying to clear his vision, and wondered whose floor he was lying on. The return of memory was the cue to panic, and he was on his feet so fast the rush of blood from his head almost made him pass out again. He rubbed his eyes, held his palms against them until the world felt steady, then looked around. The tapestry marched into his vision and he looked away before it could clamp its jaws around him again. The light from the window hit his head like a diamond hammer, but he could see clearly. A hair dangled in front of his eyes and he brushed at it. It stayed put, barely visible irritant.

Time to go. Long past time to go. But not without his prize. Callahan could take his tapestry and hypnotize himself straight into eternal flame, and Heath hoped he would. But he wanted his money even more now. He'd earned it ten times over. He found a chair in the room next door, dragged it to the tapestry and used it as a stepladder. He controlled his eye movement as he approached the tapestry. He avoided staring, held himself to flickering glances, never staying in one spot, just seeing enough to do what he needed to. The flickflickflick hurt his head, but not as much as another descent would. When he managed to unhook the tapestry and it slumped to the floor, folding over itself, hiding its glory, he took what felt like the first true and good breaths he'd had since arriving in Snow Valley. He brushed at the hair in front of his face. It had been joined by a twin. Neither left.

The rear of the tapestry was easier to deal with. There was still the faint radiance of disease, but Heath didn't have to avert his gaze any longer. He rolled the tapestry up, and he wasn't gentle. He might as well have been manhandling shag carpet, but he didn't care. He hated the tapestry, and anyway he doubted he could hurt it. It was strong and flexible as if newly formed of steel thread, yet his touch recoiled from a slickness that could only come from the dark smugness of great age. He hated it.

He hated it as he hauled it from the house, hefting it over the blood and the bodies. He hated it as he stumbled down the drive to his Tercel and stuffed the tapestry into the back seat. He hated it as he turned the keys in the ignition, ready to blame the tapestry for the dead click sound of a battery drained by cold. But the car started, and didn't get stuck in the snow, and took him onto the road and out of Snow Valley.

He hated the tapestry all the way home to Winnipeg. Yes, he did. And the hatred hadn't diminished one iota by the time he rolled in. And yet. Yes, and yet. He and the tapestry had been through a fair bit together now, and damn it, it was his enemy. He pulled up to the warehouse and looked in the rear-view mirror at the tapestry. He glared at it, hating its satisfaction. It was a gauntlet, a thing to be defeated. He brushed at his eyes. There were more hairs now, off-focus flaws in his vision, unscratchable itches. He couldn't make them go, and then he remembered Callahan swatting at the air. He felt cold. He felt epiphany: not hair in his eyes, but thread. He felt hatred flare. He snarled at the tapestry and hauled it out of the car.

Conley rushed to the door as he stumbled into the studio. Her face was pale, her eyes sunken from lack of sleep. "My God, what happened?" she asked.

Heath flung the tapestry to the floor. "Picture the worst and then some."

"Did you get caught?"

He shook his head. "I wish."

Her eyes widened. "Then what—?"

"Later. I have to see Callahan."

"He's been calling all night."

"You don't say." He glanced at the rolled-up tapestry. His challenge. His war. Not Callahan's. He clawed at the air, trying to part the gathering threads. His eyes, not Callahan's. But maybe Callahan knew something. Maybe he had keys to mysteries. Perhaps not. It seemed pretty obvious that Callahan hadn't looked at the tapestry as long or as closely as he had. He wouldn't have been telling Heath he had to see it. And the threads must have been gathering in his sight more slowly. "I'll be back in a little while," Heath said. "I'm leaving that here." He pointed at the tapestry.

"Why? You don't think he'll pay you?"

"No, it's not that. Listen, you have to promise me something. Don't look at it."

"What?"

"Promise me, Jill. Don't unroll it, don't touch it, absolutely and for sure do not look at it. It's bad. It'll hurt you."

"Jesus, Don."

"I'm not kidding."

"Did it hurt y—"

"Yes. Promise."

"Promise."

And so to Callahan's. He lived on Wellington Crescent, Winnipeg's domain of old and big money. The drive there was difficult. The threads were getting thicker, more entwined, and beginning to move. Spider legs quivered at the horizon. So he drove slowly to the road of elms and mansions. He slowed down to a crawl as he approached Callahan's address. The house wasn't set back as far from the street as many of the other homes. It sat in what was still a "yard" and not "grounds." The house was big, though, two tall storeys of grey stone. The top floor was dominated by a huge half-circle window. There was movement behind the window. Heath stopped the car and looked. The movement was jagged, fluttering. It was Callahan. Dancing.

Heath stared. Callahan waved his arms and seizure-spun, St. Vitus's dance in overdrive. He whirled and smashed against the window, whirled and smashed again. His arms banged the glass, struggled with the air. His head shook back and forth in a madness of denial. Heath stood and watched and did not approach the door. There would be no answer. He stood and watched, stood and watched, and after five minutes of jigjigjig and smash, Callahan finally broke the window. The glass plummeted to the ground, spears sinking into snow. Serrated teeth of a giant shark remained in the window frame. Callahan's dance paused for just a second, and then he slammed his face down into the upreaching glass.

Heath was whining as he scrambled back into the car.

The drive home was even slower. It was all he could do to keep his hands on the steering wheel and not claw at the veil that was coming down over his vision. The threads had colour now, the viscera red and viscera gold of the tapestry. They twitched with the beat of an arrhythmic heart. The road was becoming a phantom, insubstantial behind the growing strength of the threads. And yet more was happening now, so fast, so fast. The sky, when he looked up, was no longer winter grey. It was a uniform gold, smugly waiting for the tears to arrive. Heath wondered when he would begin to dance.

The threads picked up a new trick as he was closer to home. They twisted into a rope, and acquired a definite direction, clearing the lower left of his vision, but blacking out everything else completely. Heath stopped the car three blocks from the warehouse. He couldn't drive anymore. He got out and walked, stumbling against walls, frightened and angry, feeling the foghorn call of death, but feeling also his hatred reaching transcendence. The tapestry was going to burn.

One block from home he saw the direction of the rope. It was flowing straight and true into the warehouse door. He ran forward as well as he could, and when he stepped into the building, he saw the rope, laughing, twist upstairs. A terrible thought, then: had Conley looked? *No no no no*, mantra and prayer. Up the stairs, up the river current of the rope, his last space of vision shrinking yet further. "No no no *no*," a spoken roar as he burst into the studio. And there, stumbling back, not Conley but a mummy-wrapped victim, the threads not a rope but glistening muscle suffocating her, not a rope but a squeezing fist of red and dripping gold.

She had looked, oh god oh god oh christ she had looked. He ran towards her. When they banged together and she went down, his hands touched the threads, actually *touched* this time, and in their reality he felt flesh. "Wait wait wait," he told her. "Oh Jill, oh Jill, get you out, get you out." Cut you out. But how? And before he could look around the tapestry stepped up the attack, and new spider legs scrabbled into the last of his vision, and he had seconds before the gryphon's final curtain came down on him.

He lunged at the one thing he knew he would find, and he collided with the tentacles of the Project. It shattercrashed to the floor, and he didn't need to see to find the tools of liberation now. He was surrounded by the daggers of broken mirrors. He grabbed one in each hand and crawled back to Jill. Blind now, all gone but tears of gold and smiles of red, his ears pounding with the pulse of the tapestry, he reached forward until he felt the flesh, and then he began. He cut deep and dragged hard.

His vision cleared when he struck bone. His hearing did too, but Conley had stopped screaming by then. After that, there was nothing left for him to do but take the mirrorshards to his face and join in the mourning.

/ from THE LAST MAN AND WOMAN ON EARTH

/ BY RICK **CHAFE**

ACT ONE

(Two chairs, a therapist's office. Anthony and Lisa are in mid-session.)

LISA: *(pause)* . . . And . . .

ANTHONY: *(pause)* And . . . ?

LISA: And . . . I have a gun.

ANTHONY: So you're . . .

LISA: Yes. It's just . . . I'd rather . . .

ANTHONY: Rather . . . ?

LISA: Use pills.

ANTHONY: *(pause)* You'd like me to *prescribe* . . . ?

LISA: Yes.

ANTHONY: And if I don't . . . you'll go home and blow your brains out?

LISA: Yes.

ANTHONY: *(pause)* I'm sorry, I've forgotten your name.

LISA: Lisa.

ANTHONY: Right. Lisa. Have you considered—

LISA: I've seen shrinks for years. Drugs, shock, everything.

ANTHONY: Have you thought about—

LISA: I've asked seven doctors this week, you're the last one.

ANTHONY: What about having somebody with you. *(pause)* A companion.

■ 242

LISA: When I . . . ?

ANTHONY: Someone to hold your hand or read something from your favourite book.

A/CROSS SECTIONS: NEW MANITOBA WRITING

LISA: I don't have anyone.

ANTHONY: To sing to you. Bring over my cat for you to hold. Anything you want.

LISA: You?

ANTHONY: Yes.

LISA: Why would you do that?

ANTHONY: Because I can't believe you're not afraid.

LISA: You've done this before?

ANTHONY: This afternoon a patient of mine jumped. I thought I was helping. But if someone really wants to . . . what can anyone do? I've seen it dozens of times, and been no help whatsoever. I think it's time I really helped.

LISA: Reverse psychology really bugs me.

ANTHONY: When you walked in here today, something said to me: Now.

LISA: But. You'd go to jail.

ANTHONY: The first woman I ever knew who killed herself was my mother. An awful, lonely, despairing death. I can't change my mother's life. But if I could change the way she died. Well, of course I would.

LISA: *(pause)* You'll give me pills?

ANTHONY: I can't.

LISA: Then what are you talking—

ANTHONY: I'm not a psychiatrist.

LISA: Your sign says—

ANTHONY: Psychologist.

LISA: Psychologist . . . ? Oh shit.

ANTHONY: I can't prescribe.

LISA: What a goddamned week I'm having—

ANTHONY: I have a different idea for you, this will work just fine—

LISA: What a screw-up. You must think I'm a total beginner—

ANTHONY: Here. *(He takes out a transparent plastic bag and duct tape.)*

LISA: What.

243

ANTHONY: We'll use two and tape it tight, so there's no air leaks.

LISA: A plastic . . . ?

ANTHONY: It's actually a great home method—simple, very effective, much safer than a gun, easy to stop if you change your mind . . .

LISA: I want pills! I want this to be easy! Why can't something just be easy for a change?

ANTHONY: You didn't come here just for pills.

LISA: Right, here we go. You think I want to be talked out of it. I'm leaving.

ANTHONY: Not talked out of it, but what? Seven doctors—what are you looking for? Not pills. To let someone know? To share your burden? To get *permission*? What if you could find one doctor who didn't say, "This is wrong, don't do this, we'll fix you?" What if a professional told you this could be a valid choice? You haven't been looking for pills. You've been looking for permission. This is clicking for you, isn't it? That little click of recognition? Lisa, it's never easy, not for anyone. But maybe you can change that. Society is almost ready for this, we're right on the edge of change. If you let me help you, I will fight all the way to the Supreme Court, in your name and my mother's. So the next person who has suffered like you will have a right to a dignified death. You think your life has been meaningless. Maybe you can have a meaningful death.

LISA: So . . . we would just . . . do it here? Right now?

ANTHONY: Here, your place, wherever you want, but the first thing to think about is our case. We want to have the strongest possible case. Are you with me?

LISA: Okay . . .

ANTHONY: Good. Now it'll be a jury trial, so what will really influence them, god only knows but in Holland this is legal already, so based on that example there's a number of criteria we should definitely try to meet, okay? Ideally of course we would first have a long-term therapeutic relationship—

LISA: Well, we don't.

ANTHONY: A year or two would be great, but six months would probably be reasonable—

LISA: Well, we can't.

ANTHONY: I understand your urgency, three months would really be pushing it; for now let's at least agree to the first month—

LISA: Tonight.

ANTHONY: Tonight?

LISA: I'm doing it tonight. I told you that.

ANTHONY: Yes, but the circumstances have changed slightly since then, I think we
            can agree on that—

LISA: I don't believe this.

ANTHONY: You think I'm trying to stall you, I can see that—I'm not, I assure you—

LISA: Fuck. *(begins to leave)*

ANTHONY: *(blocking her path)* It's a crucial step in the process, it's legally essential . . .

LISA: Don't touch me.

ANTHONY: Which if you think about it makes sense—It's your mind, I'm not try-
            ing to make you change it, but we have to allow time for the possibility
            that you might—

LISA: Move.

ANTHONY: Which is also my first responsibility as a therapist, which makes it not
            negotiable—it's morally imperative—

LISA: *Morally?*

ANTHONY: Morally *and* ethically, I can't even consider helping you if therapy isn't
            part of the process.

LISA: *(taking the plastic bag)* How do I do this—double-bag and duct tape,
            that's it?

ANTHONY: *(taking the bag back)* No more information. You commit to one two-hour
            session a day for two weeks. Take it or leave it.

LISA: Not even close.

ANTHONY: Three hours between now and Friday.

LISA: I'm dead by midnight.

ANTHONY: This is really—

LISA: *(finger to temple)* Bangbangbang!

ANTHONY: Fine! *(He pulls out a tape recorder, sets it on the table.)* Just you me and
            the jury, your therapy starts now. *(He hits the record button.)* Why now,
            Lisa? Why today? Why can't you wait just one second past midnight?

LISA:	*(beat)* It's my mother's birthday.
ANTHONY:	You're kidding.
LISA:	No.
ANTHONY:	You're angry with her?
LISA:	Yes.
ANTHONY:	*(pause)* You're focusing a lifetime of pain into one act of revenge.
LISA:	Yes.
ANTHONY:	A lifetime of depression, a life devoid of significance, this is your last desperate attempt to redeem through your death this tiny shred of meaning.
LISA:	Yes.
ANTHONY:	Lisa. Linking the end of your life to your mother's birthday is petty and spiteful; it won't redeem your death, it will trivialize it.
LISA:	That's right and if you're not helping just say so.
ANTHONY:	You are absolutely determined to go home and commit a lonely, horrible, dangerous suicide? *(She stares at him. He motions her to answer.)*
LISA:	Yes! *(He gives her the thumbs-up.)*
ANTHONY:	Then given your desperate state, I will agree to assist you, on the condition that you stay with me until midnight for one last therapeutic intervention.
LISA:	Midnight? No!
ANTHONY:	Eleven-thirty.
LISA:	*Six*-thirty.
ANTHONY:	I need three hours, absolute minimum.
LISA:	I'm not spending my entire last night in this disgusting little office.
ANTHONY:	It isn't possib—
LISA:	I'm not asking—
ANTHONY:	I will be facing a jury over helping you in a matter I believe in to the depths of my soul, *would you please give me a little leeway?*
LISA:	*(beat)* Three hours and I walk out any time I don't like what you're doing.
ANTHONY:	And . . . you can understand I must be absolutely sure I'm not helping

you to do something that you might not do if I wasn't helping. So when you say you're going to kill yourself tonight, is there any chance that if I refuse to help you, you might decide not to?

LISA: No.

ANTHONY: You're sure you won't chicken out? Or decide to give it one more day to think about it?

LISA: Absolutely not.

ANTHONY: Okay. Final offer: In return for you agreeing to three hours therapy, and promising to keep an open mind to the possibility of not killing yourself, I promise to help you kill yourself tonight if you promise that if I don't help you, you'll kill yourself for sure.

LISA: Deal.
            (She moves back to her chair. Anthony turns off the tape recorder and paces.)

ANTHONY: *Oh my god.*

LISA: What?

ANTHONY: Nothing—that was excellent. *Oh my god.*

Lisa;   *What?*

ANTHONY: Well, we've just entered into a bit of a pact with the devil, haven't we.

LISA: You're not some very weird kind of Christian, are you?

ANTHONY: Of course not. It's just that the price of any dubious act is doubt. And *three hours?*

LISA: You *agreed.*

ANTHONY: Yes, because it was great! You were totally convincing. It's very important that it's clear to the jury that you are giving me absolutely no choice and you were *beautiful.*
            Oh my god, I shouldn't have turned off the tape. Never mind. We've got three hours to convince a court that I've interviewed you thoroughly, I've come to know every corner of your life, which will be tough but we can do it. Right?

LISA: *I* don't know . . .

ANTHONY: Yes, we *can.* And that you've convinced me that your suffering is irremediable—you'll talk about your pain, all the doctors and therapists you've seen, all the drug treatments you've tried, yes?

LISA: Yes . . .

ANTHONY: That your wish for death has been long present.

LISA: Yes.

ANTHONY: And that you are competent to make the decision to take your own life.

LISA: Yes.

ANTHONY: More conviction.

LISA: *Yes.*

ANTHONY: Fantastic. Oh my god.

LISA: Stop saying that!

ANTHONY: I'm sorry. It's just that we're making history in one hell of a hurry.
            We're charging ahead, no more turning off the machine, ready?
            (He sits, turns on the tape.)

/ from A ROSE

/ BY DEBORAH **SCHNITZER**

spill

a walkrough day iced sidestreetssmells bad wind. This should have been a pleasanter
town. In the advertising you will always see that it has been. Flat but spry. Cold
building character. Winter sun. Cedar in burlap dresses. Lots of preparation for
the Christmas season. Custom-made lights for the downtown whose cross streets
drive motorists mad. And prizes. For the best decorated. Chamber of Commerce
beautifications troubling a rather tainted core. When isn't there. Natives, immigrants.
people lament. But you can drive by. Windows rolled. Remember Detroit At least here
Nohandguns in the glove compartment. Bullets rare. Usually knives, broken bottles.
Might be worse. Maybe Maybe not. Everybody's got an opinion. They're entitledEven
jews. Too many of them. Run everything. Remember what they said in Germany. Oh yes. But there's a
Calvary Temple. Can't be too bad. Family values. Pamphlets on rehabilitation for gays.
Lots of opportunities to fit in.

Jeanette doesn't read the newspaper any more. Same old. Same old. She can't get
it straight though she understands everything. The Titanic. Research prizes. Cultural
capital. Hierarchies. Wonderful ways to insult the down. Bolster elites. That's what
they call them at the university. The really important people. Nice Nice factories. Lots
of money. Most of the stuff's never read but passes To a good job. A pet. The special
ones advertised in the breeders' journal which she's seen in salons, might even
subscribe to. People can get a way with Upgrades. Soft bark, no bite, retractable
claws, noclaws, minx tail, hand-held sizes, fur that knits. Take tips. Think about the
clone job that superscientist pulled off with dogs in Korea. Not a fake at all. The
West's just envious. We're stuck with pigs, maybe rats. Hard to know. Pretty soon,
everything's adjustable. Botox in the men's room, where the condoms used to
beDildo dispenser Talk about never having to leave the house. You send a freak. One
of those virtual representatives. Your own emissary. Can go everywhere for you. Do
everything. You stay home. Play computer games. Join fascist organizations. Cruise
porn sites. Plugged. Your own music. Nothing to get in the way of what you want.
Private clubs. Parts. Any body at your finger tips. Lifesize dolls you can buy. The
internet. Made to order. Even the clitoris. Pretty reasonable. Customize. That's the

ticket. What you want you get. Think of the toys. Won't even have to queue on boxing day to buy the shit that falls apart in the cart.

Inside the script she's always composing, Jeanette can see the two of them across the street, struggling between the shops, especially Millie, the younger, more tentative, giddy. Gertrude barrels. Older. Jeanette likes how she distinguishes them. Their dress shop bears the brunt of her grasp. In the name: A ROSE. In the front foyer whose wild mysticism she cannot at the moment begin to explain Jeanette can see feel Millie's fall before it happens. Too far away to be of any immediate help. Gert so preoccupied with rummaging her purse, she does not hear the draft of Millie's sinking form behind her.

But Jeanette does.
Pulls
an
old
ski
jacket
stuffed
plum
in
the
clo set.   R   u   ns.

Suddenly hearing   Gertrude turns very slowly slowly because she's been expecting disaster. Six nights out of seven dreams of dead babies and things gone missing, especially the mock lamb's wool which disappears in a cavern posing as a renewal organization with stunning portraits her friend who is not a portrait maker suddenly produces, staked endless round the base of the room where her coat should have been but is no longer and she left sleeveless and alone

What have you done. What have you done   What are we going to do.

Millie biting the arm of her navy coat. Gert pushing toward her fallen Biting too. The inside of her own throat. Hip. It will be the hip and that will be the end of it. In their seventies. The hip will do them both in.

Wounding the snow bank
Jeanette can see this. She cries out.

> Gert. Call an ambulance.
> I'll stay. Go on. Do it.
> Quick. I won't move her.
> Just make the call.

don't fall.

Millie cannot see Speak. A terribly wrong. Fearsome pain torments. She bites harder.
The navy coat will turn islet before this morning turns to noon. Jeanette doesn't
know what sound she'll make.

It'll be okay Millie. You just see if it isn't. Contessa's calling the hospital. Millie.
I won't let any one hurt you. Millie. Come on. Millie dearest. It's okay.
Everything. You'll see.
The ambulance will be here in a minute.
They know what to do.
Everything's going to be okay.
Gertrude can take care of things.
I'll help. I'll help. You know I can help. Millie.
Hold on.
Don't cry.
Please don't cry.

How can Millie not cry. Jeanette is crying wiping her nose sleevewise. Denting the
ice. Puddling. This is the time for a cigarette. It won't do to light one. She can't
resist. Millie smiles. Knew Jeanette couldn't quit. They wait. Jeanette's down on
one knee, bracing Millie's shoulders with her arm. Stroking the side of her face,
whispering, stubbing the butt with the edge of her boot, not but two puffs into it.
She can tooquit. Just not now. Would light another.

Show off.
They were
only a few steps away from making it inside. Safe where they have been for almost
fifty years. The coffee on. A couple of adjustments to the pink cashmere stole pawing
that last mannequin whose shoulder droops with age. Millie's quite fond of the way
the mannequins are falling apart.

Sees them as her sisters except
She gets to leave the shop at night,
chinese whenever she wants. cookies in the fall when
hand made canadagoose cutter cookies because
she likes their **v** in their sky serves them justso
on white fancy dancy plates found on sale at Cherry Tree Lane with a wing
spread of its own actually. Meant for Christmas dainties sweettea but
Mildred always running counter to her Six on the Enneagram Counter-phobic.

A regular resistance fighter in the kitchen though recipes scare her and she does
not understand food in any useful way. Will serve a mish mash of this. That. Mostly
considers values, serving pieces. A pansy, artful, in the early summer to decorate,

251

always scrounging in the garden thinking only pretty. Impressed easily, repeatedly when Gertrude reminds her that what they really have on the go is an herb garden. Gertrude is always careful with the 'h' which further pleases Millie very much Millie proud ofGert

Likes the way the h works with rollingpin eyes flat cackle spread along the counter panes in a hot kitchen with Such a plop and sizzle. Millie's greatness sparkles a festive season even when she has the blues. About the way things were. About the heavy hands that tossed her out at sixteen, slamming the door. Her uncle fluttering in the living room curtains opposed to the harsh measure but with a runnel stained by drink. Always smaller than he needs to be. Mildred understood.

Still does. Onlysees him at the Shoppers on Henderson wearing that gaberdine with the yellow scarf. Classy. She appreciates this pleat in him even when he'd soiled things by caving in, dropping down the spiral staircase in the third house, giblets in hand for the damn dog whose nostrils rank, drooled more than the speckled tongue every one claimed distinguished the breed.

Enough.

Jeanette's reaching for the snow to bring her back. A light wash round the mouth. Come on Millie. Don't fade.

As long as she's got the receiver in her hand
Gertrude cannot lose sight of Millie spilled
on ice. She can give the address and the
details. Flick the lights by the counter where
she stands with the minty coloured phone
and the pink flamenco pen that someone left
as a joke after a fitting that didn't go well.
As long as there is a concrete step to be
taken. This practicality A source of joy in
their relationship really for Gertrude—what
with Millie tending toward hesitant,
however mystical her other properties.
Once 6
foot high,
Gert can
dial clear.
Though
when 911
hangs up
she stays
on the

line can't
imagine
how
she'll turn
back to
the front
door and
Millie's
inside
screaming
down a
thigh that
won't

hold.

Suddenly, the siren scrapes the line of traffic toward the left. Pushes Gertrude
       down three front stairs
           to Jeanette and the cradle she's made   for Millie's
                                        head
                                      and
                                    ne
                              ck.
I cannot breathe Gertrude. I Cannot breathe. You've got to
           tell them I cannot breathe.

In Millie's eyes Gertrude reads panic. Out loud she names what Millie won't tell.
Tears and urine. By Millie's left leg.

They know sweetie. They know. They will help you. They know what to do. You're in
shock. That's what it is. Don't cry lovey. Please don't cry. Jeanette. Tell her not to cry.
She has to remain calm. If she keeps on crying she's going to exhaust herself.

Please make her stop crying.   I
                                                        C
                                                        A

cannot.

We've got her
ma'am. Just step back
a bit. HoldWe're
going to check some
thingsShe's taken quite a fall.

Of course you're scared sweetheart. Don't worry. Cry if you need to. It's okay.

They are so kind. Quiet. Making eye contact. Sure
that Gertrude is in charge. Careful with Jeanette.
Coaxing her to let go. They check everything out.
Move back into the ambulance. Whisk the stretcher.
Make adjustments againstthe snow bank.

Yes. It's a metal plate you see and we can slide it right underneath.
OkayThis will only take a second. Be as calm as you can. This isn't
going to hurt. We're going to slide you onto the metal plate and then
lift it ever so carefully and put you on the stretcher. You see. Like
this. Just like this. The metal slides. And there are these hinges on the
stretcher. Nice and easy.
Yes. That's it. Your friend's here. We're going to take you to St. B.
It's closest. Your friend can ride with you.

Your friend. Always that wet word.

There's the closing of doors. Gertrude stands even as she tries to sit down.
Jeanette waves the way she used to when Robert took off on his bike.

Elbow bent, hand turned once to the outside thumb.

She calls after. Though the doors are closed and the siren's started. "Don't worry. I'll
turn the lights. Put a sign in the window, close the door. You can call me at home. If
there's anything." The last so quiet, so unexpected from Jeanette who's usually fuck
this and fuck that.

Inside, they can't hear her though Gertrude is nodding. Millie is nodding. They are
both wet.

/ DEATH OF A PET

/ BY MAURICE **MIERAU**

One morning blood began spurting
        from the cat's eye—
a tumour in his brain it wasn't hurting
        or anything I

picked him up, he was fat with age
        and we went to the clinic
in our car, the cat in a cage
        and then on stainless steel

where he died, purring slightly
        more dignified than millions
of other deaths, intimately
        smelling and feeling

his own body, expecting it
        more than I will,
resisting nothing, neither passive and lit
        up with distractions, nor futile,

not fighting his own intimacy
        with his last breath
the needle sinking be
        -neath, eyes closing, death,

and the transaction went through on Visa,
and we left quicker than he did.

/ NEWS, SPAM, TAGS

/ BY MAURICE **MIERAU**

In Nigeria a local rapper tried stealing the first-class seats on a chartered jet belonging to 50 Cent and his posse.

I saw a beer bottle on a street's furrowed snow, brown and obscene, reflecting Christmas lights.

<html><font color="#ffffff">

her round-shaped ipaq looks around however
A given white soft frog got an idea.

A Winnipeg architect pleaded guilty to child porn possession. He said it was difficult to spend time alone.

The salmon-farming company says that GM salmon are like more fuel-efficient cars, and that efficiency is desirable.

Our hairy odd shaped mobile phone adheres.
A well-crafted recycle bin scowls.

At Buckingham Palace, a man dressed as Batman climbed onto a balcony to demand more rights for divorced fathers. He will face no charges.

Desire wraps itself in freezer paper, in stained sheets, in holding back, in tongues intertwined and spines aligned, in the low bandwidth of the telephone's murmur.

His noisy soft round car runs.
The children's small boat shows its value.

In Canada someone smashed the window on our car and took the stereo, the power amp, the subwoofer from the trunk.

In China a thousand farmers lost their land, without compensation, so a highway could be built.

Any white caw sleeps.

Her silver baby smiles at the place that our tall house stinks.

</font color="#ffffff"></html>

/ BY SYLVIA **LEGRIS**

A is for . . .

Apoplexy: from the cerebellum up you are paralyzed with irrationality

(Inferior colliculus!   Inferior fears!). Sheet-snarling sleep and when morning comes you are Alektorophobic . . . *bock bock bock* . . . Chicken-Brained; Chicken-Livered; Rhode Island Red-in-the-Face Chicken-Little Shit.

Arithmania: Choking on ridiculous calculations. Turn each article of clothing (counterclockwise) 3 times before you put it on and you will be the best-dressed fool in Hell. And the hottest. When you take your sweater off hold your breath for a count of 20, followed by a recitation of *I am bad I am bad* 4 times. Screw it up and Hell's thermostat rises a degree. Go back to the beginning and collect 200 new reasons why the door might still be unlocked even though you checked the lock how many times? Five. Once, because that's what normal people do; twice, because twice isn't unreasonable even for a normal person; three times, just for good measure; four times, because maybe you only thought you locked it the previous times; five, because it doesn't make any difference how many times you do it because you're still bad and you are still going to Hell! . . . *1* . . . *2* . . . *3* . . . *4* . . .

Apotropaic: The trick is to stuff your mouth with elephant garlic and pretend the glass is half empty. Never trust the meniscus. Measurements and math will deceive you at every turn (see above). Turn turn turn . . .

It's like stirring a vat of doom and gloom in the opposite to what you normally do direction.   (Breathe seven sighs of relief that you're not in the Southern Hemisphere because who knows how the Coriolis Effect could upset the Flush of Disaster.)

/ CEDILLA

/ BY MARK **MORTON**

Chapter One

One day, for no apparent reason, Harold woke up unable to concentrate.

Chapter Two

He couldn't read a novel, not even a short story. He couldn't get through one of the "Life's Like That" items in the *Reader's Digest*. Two weeks ago he began to read Ezra Pound's "In a Station of the Metro" but interrupted himself three times to go pee, once to get a mirror to see if the mole on his left shoulder had grown or darkened, and twice to make sure that the neighbour boy hadn't ignored the sign and slipped a flyer into his mailbox. Thanks to those forays, and a myriad of other thoughts that seized his attention, it had taken him an hour to read the first line of Pound's poem.

Chapter Three

And it was getting worse. "Maybe I should call a—" he thought to himself, or tried to, but another thought pushed in, and he began to wonder if he were exactly six feet tall, like the Irish said Jesus was, and set out to find a tape measure, but was distracted by a loose thread on his cuff. As his fingers moved to the thread, he thought of the word "exponent" and how it denoted both someone who advocated something, and also the power to which a number is raised. He began to remember his friend Laura, who tuned her violin with the hum of a fluorescent light, but then Laura vanished as his attention span shrank again, shorter and shorter, until his thoughts were like TV static, thousands of fleeting pulses firing through his brain, black-and-white noise, fractals of memory. As his thoughts became more slender than protons, the fragments of words erupting in his head became mountain ranges, his tiny self suddenly lost its footing, and he began to tumble into the crevasse that gaped between the double "e"s in the word "between." But as the duration of his thoughts diminished and approached the limit of zero, their number increased toward infinity. He was falling, falling and thinking—literally—of Everything.

Chapter Four

Harold's fall was broken by the "r" in the word "number," which happened to be type-set right below the double "e"s of "between." Had it been any other letter, he probably would have ricocheted off and plummeted down from line to line, careening off vowels and consonants like a pinball, until he slipped right off this page and out of existence. But the top of the "r" had serifs, which snagged his leg like a tree branch, and held him fast. "Ouch," Harold said, opening his eyes and unwedging his ankle from the serifs. "I wonder where I am?" As you can tell from his question, Harold was thinking of himself, rather than of Everything. The impact of his fall had shaken Everything loose from his brain. He was back to his old self, the self he had always been, or pretty close to it. The one difference was that he still remembered thinking of Everything, and as you know that is bound to have an effect on a person. He could still see and understand connections between impossibly disparate events and ideas. For instance, he knew that his mother's life had once been saved by a shoe salesman who had mistaken her for someone else and had stopped her on the street to tell her that the new Vicinis were now in stock. Harold knew that the few moments his mother had taken to nod and smile politely to the salesman had changed the drift of her life: she had not stumbled three weeks later, as she otherwise would have, and fallen throat-first onto an iron stave of the fence outside of St. Margaret's Chapel. Harold knew, too, that an old man in Etobicoke had once unwittingly prevented the most perfect love in the world, when he sank tiredly into the subway seat next to young Mia Soletti, forcing Andrew Birkholz to sit across the aisle, too far away to do anything but stare at her dark-eyed beauty. He knew that Mia Soletti would marry an actor four years later, and that after their first and only child was born with a cleft palate, she would never forgive herself for a one-night drinking spree (four margaritas) when she was three months pregnant. Harold retained these vestiges of Everything, and many others, but they seemed like movie trailers, not like fragments of being.

"I wonder where I am?" Harold said again. He stood up on the top of the "r" and glanced around. He appeared to be in a white cathedral, with what seemed like huge black table legs suspended above him. To the right and left a broken, black line stretched into the distance like Hadrian's wall. Beneath his feet was an inky black surface, the texture and consistency of chalk. "I appear to have fallen into my own text," he mused. It may seem surprising that Harold was able to divine this fact so quickly, but as a child he had read how a bear with a very small brain had once climbed up the sentences of his story in order to reach a honey nest at the top of a tall tree.

It was—or rather is—at this point that I decide to introduce myself. "You are almost correct, Harold," I say. "You are indeed in a text, but the text is mine, not yours."

Harold raises his head and squints off the page to where I am sitting. "Who are you?" he cries in a voice so shrill and tiny that a mosquito would drown it out. "Why can't I see you?"

"I'm your author," I explain. "You can't see me because I exist in three dimensions, and you are merely a two-dimensional character. If I were a better writer, able to create three-dimensional characters, we might see eye to eye. But I'm not."

"Perhaps you could revise me," Harold suggests. "Give me a few interesting quirks that would flesh me out. Or maybe an editor could help."

I am taken aback by Harold's suggestion that I need an editor. "Thanks for the advice," I tell him curtly. "But to be honest I'm now finding myself more intrigued by the young and dark-eyed Mia Soletti. She still remembers the quiet subway-gaze of Andrew Birkholz. I think I will write about how they continue to live in the same city, and sometimes their paths almost intersect, but never close enough that she catches sight of him, or he of her. I will write how her heart instinctively aches as he drives by the building where she works, and how she lifts her head and pulls aside the blinds as if she can see her destiny written in the sky. I think I will write of her, rather than spend time revising you."

And with that, I turn the page, abandoning Harold, and begin to pen the most beautiful novel about unrequited love ever written: *Written in the Sky*. The novel becomes a bestseller, and I appear on Oprah on two occasions.

Chapter Five

When the page turned, darkness fell upon Harold. Unable to climb up or down from the letter "r" of the word "number," he languished in a box of my manuscripts for a long time, first in my attic, and then—after I died—in the Provincial Archives where my papers were cached for safekeeping. Bit by bit, the vestiges of Everything that Harold held in his mind faded away. "They fade," he said to himself, "like a summer cloud. They melt like snow in water. They vanish like a smile." He went on like this for years, building similes with the vestiges of Everything, staring into the darkness with his head resting on the left-hand serif of the "r" that had become his home. Then one day it petered out. Everything was exhausted. His head was empty, and Harold began to think of nothing—not Nothing, but simply nothing. "I wish I were dead," he didn't think to himself. "I wish I had never been born," he never cried out. The nothing in his head was too absolute, too pure, to permit such thoughts, to permit any thoughts. For Harold, time and joy, words and pain, ceased to be.

Sometimes, in the spring, if you lay your head upon the ground, you can hear thunder rumbling in the earth. It goes on for hours, getting louder and louder, closer and closer. It's not really thunder, nor is it an approaching freight train. It's life reclaiming what winter has taken. It's crocus roots uncurling and stems pushing up to the surface. It's the sun riding toward noon. That's what happened to Harold one day, eight years after he thought of Everything and slipped between the "e"s of the word "between." Without lifting his head or opening his eyes, the first thing he felt was the light: beautiful white light, streaming into his text from all angles, warming the "r" he lay upon. Then he heard it. At first it was so faint that he could find no word to name it. Then, as it grew louder, the first word came:

263

"thunder," then another and another—"rumble," "riding," "noon." With that, his eyes opened, and then his heart. The thunder grew still louder. Memories began to flood his being: a blue button, a father's hands, a caress, a glimmer of hope. But these memories, he knew, were not his own. "What is happening?" he wondered as the rumbling grew louder and the images, the memories, flashed faster and brighter through his mind. And then he realized: his text was being read. A reader's gaze was approaching, perhaps only a few paragraphs from the word where he lay. And not just a gaze, but a consciousness, comprehending the words, remaking his story, creating meaning by fusing her—it must be a her—own experience with his text. The rumbling was now a tornado roar. She was almost at him. He could feel her breath on the page, he could see the words to the far left jostle and heave as her eye took them in and extracted their syntax. Another dart of the eye and she was upon him, beholding him, becoming him—

"HAROLD?" This was thought, not said. She glanced up from the page, a small smile playing across her lips. She hadn't thought of Harold in a long time. I wonder where he ended up, she thought to herself. I wonder why he just up and left and why would he pop into my head here of all places, here in the archives, which he would have hated, just like he hated everything old, like my gramma's mixing bowl, which he said made the cake taste dusty, and my violin too, even that time I brought it over to his place for his birthday to play him that Bach piece, "Sleepers, Awake," and he couldn't get over how I tuned it with the fluorescent lights, and how it was older than my gramma, and he picked it up and smelled it, and crinkled his nose and said that it smelled like evaporated sweat, and I told him that's why I like it because people have sweated over it, they've poured their lives into this violin, at least five people before me, and the last one, Evelyn, who taught me how to bow like Yehudi Menuhin, she still comes over every fall when she's in town and asks to hold the violin though she never plays it now, not with her hands the way they are, twisted and swollen, hands that would make Harold wince; I know, because he used to love my hands; not you, just your hands he always said, but I think he did love me or could have, or at least I used to think that, once especially after he massaged my fingers and even after the cramp was gone he held my palm and closed his eyes, and said no one not even the rain has such small hands, which made me smile, and then he told me that was a line from a poem whose title he couldn't remember, and then I said to him love can change like a look on a face, and told him that was a line from a poem that hadn't been written, which seemed to puzzle him, and the next thing I knew he had let go of my hand and was getting up to get some ice and when he came back we watched the news about how Iraq had invaded Kuwait, which wasn't the last time I saw Harold, though it was the last time he massaged my hand or the last time he meant it, but maybe one day he'll come back and we can talk like we always did—

—she thought, and then returned to her reading, her eye running forward from word to word, and the rumbling, the jostling, the thrust of life that had shaken Harold to the quick began to recede like the end of thunder, and then the page was turned and the awful clutch of darkness fell again.

/ POEM IN THE POSTMODERN AGE

/ BY ROB **BUDDE**

part here, part there, past
his prime but plugged in,
Poem tries hard to do the right thing

the paradigms of midday
traffic just look bad
but remain in motion; Poem sighs, edges out
on his refurbished bicycle using
proper hand signals and a dash
of theatre

Poem is off to the printers and he
is an informed shopper,
rubs the linen texture between his fingers,
and looks for post-consumer
recycled paper whenever he can

the Age thinks it's in transition but
Poem knows there is no such thing

if the moment exists,
an object is hurled out of a crew cab
and the object "certainty" is not in flux

it hits him in the forehead, beneath his
properly adjusted helmet, and Poem
falls beneath the wheel of what

when his eyes open Poem looks up at
a kind pizza guy
cradling his head in his lap;
there is something familiar there but
publishers are a restless lot and
Poem must hurry out of consciousness

he winks to the bystanders and takes
one final breath, there

/ IF YES IS THE APERTURE

/ BY CHARLENE **DIEHL**

1. *if yes*

if, if
yes
is the aperture, open
in dream,
a hesitant yes, if
yes is the opening,
the aperture opening,
a promise, a breath,
the quickening
if, if
yes is
the light, the pale
open light and the gathering
promise, a breath
in the yes,
if
yes is a dream,
a dance
toward if in the quick of the
dream, if yes
is the breath and the pale
open light, if
yes,
if yes
is an aperture
bursting with light, if
yes,
if yes is a promise
of breath in the green,

if yes to
the quick,
to play the breath
open, green in the dance,
the rapturous leaning
if yes, an aperture
quick
in the light, if yes,
if yes is a promise,
if yes is the play of the breath,
the rapturous
breath in the dance
to the quick, if yes
is an aperture,
an if
in the rapturous dance
of the light, if
yes, if yes,
and promise will play
if yes

2. *if no*

spring is today, a green wind, sudden breathing. the woman
on the corner slides her arms from her coat. she slips off her
shoes and dips her toe in the slush. spring is today, the
middle of march, a great green breathing. the bus is
nowhere. she stands in the slush and lifts her face to the
warm hands of the sun.

spring is an argument. the woman in the hands of the sun
sways in the slush, reckless with love. her fingers stretch for
the great green breath on the corner, they play the pale light
of the middle of march. the bus is nowhere. spring blows in,
the sun reaches down, the woman blooms in the middle of
march.

the bus is nowhere, but the woman is here, her face open in
the sun. spring is today, the middle of march. her hands fold
and fold the sudden air. the shoeless woman sways in the
maze of today. she swallows it all. the reach of the sun, the
invention of spring. she catches it open, swallows it all.

spring is an argument. if no, tomorrow will snow. the bus
will be nowhere, the slush will be rigid with waiting. no
great green breathing, no swaying woman, hands lifting the
maze of her heart. the sun will not lean down, kiss open her
face. spring is an argument. tomorrow will snow, and
tomorrow will snow, if no. if no.

3. *if yes*

if yes, if
yes is a promise, if
yes is the rapturous
dance of the breath, if yes
is the aperture, the face
in the sun in the
promise of spring,
if yes is a promise, a
dance along breath,
if yes is an aperture,
a kiss, a maze
in the breath
of the light, if yes
is a voice,
a wish,
a kiss,
if yes is a thread
in the maze of your
heart, if yes
is a folding, a lift
in the air,
if yes is a rapture,
the shatter of spring,
if yes is a maze,
a breath,
a promise,
if yes is the shatter of
rapturous spring,
if yes
is the sun in pale open
light, if yes
is the aperture,
spring,
rapture at play,
if yes is
the aperture,
if yes is spring,
if yes,
if yes is
spring,
if
yes

/ ORANGES, 1956

/ BY SHARON **CASEBURG**

Ten days on board the *Seven Seas*.
She becomes preoccupied with oranges
hungers for their citric bite in her mouth
can't sleep, becomes weak-kneed
when a fellow passenger
tells her about North American fruit.

Day one:
the ocean knocks the ship about
each swell sending passengers
and their baggage tumbling.
Oranges are all she can stomach
she grabs one as it rolls by.
Elsewhere, in the ship's lounge
the village boys from Rastatt and Karlsruhe
sit on the floor, slide back and forth
in time with the waves. Keep hold of their bottles.
Weissbier spills only down their throats.

Day two: no better.
The Atlantic is angry.
Tired of ferrying immigrants on its slick back
it makes the voyage difficult.

On day three she scores the peel with a penknife
separates each section
dislodges them one by one, skins them, licks them
lets juice flood her throat.
In the lounge, the boys are still on their bottoms
bottles still in their hands.

Day four: she gouges her thumbs into each end
stretches the rind from the flesh
tosses the white pith overboard to feed the fish.
Bright rubbish stars.

Her weight loss shows in earnest by day five—
sunken cheeks, dark-rimmed eyes.
Afraid her waiting sister won't recognize her—
will mistakenly greet the plump schoolmistress
from Baden instead—
she doubles her efforts to eat more fruit.

On day six she is cut off. No more
oranges in the hold. No more
sweet juice on her tongue.
She is reduced
to eating lesser fruit:
woody apples and dried plums.

Days seven through nine become lost days
everything bright and blurred
she spends her feverish hours in her cabin
the boys stay in the lounge, still drinking beer
don't even realize she's missing.

Day ten arrives, she's free, rushes down the gangplank
heads past the train station and its car to Winnipeg
heads for the market and a bag full of oranges
to eat on her way to the prairies.
Fruit junkie now, she spends her last coins for the citrus
misses the train
her sister wearing her Sunday dress
still waiting on the other end.

/ TIDE POOL

/ BY SHARON **CASEBURG**

Our child should be conceived near water
this I say knowing full and well
that the ocean's green skin
is too far from our bed
and that the smooth glass of inland lakes
is only potent after storms.

Though even here, in the centre of the country
it is possible to become like shorebirds
collect the necessary items for nest-building
in the bottom of a galvanized pail.

It is possible to find what I need in you.

Even if you are still beachcombing
piecing yourself together—
your retrieval random, dependent on
things as fickle as the weather
and your determination to excavate
each shallow midden we encounter.

What's left to find, we can find together.

Pregnancy and the notion of absolution
absolutely appealing
we locate every mass of water
within a 100-kilometre radius.

Means for life to evolve
secure within the tide pool of my body.

/ WHAT TO EXPECT WHEN YOU'RE EXPECTING

/ BY ALISON **CALDER**

If you fall, your child will have fits;
if you spy through keyholes, your child will squint.
If you climb over carriage-shafts, your child will be bandy-legged.
Make water in a churchyard, and your child will be a bed-wetter.

If you eat speckled eggs, your child will be freckled;
climb under a rope and your child's cord will twist.
If you carry logs, your child's penis will be large.
If you see a mouse, your child will be marked.

Your child will steal if you climb through a window.
Your child will drink if you spill beer on your clothes.
Your child will be pale if you shroud a corpse.
Your child will hunger if you look into a grave.

If you're frightened by cats, your child will have paws.
If you dream of rabbits, you will deliver a rabbit.

/ SOOTERKIN, MY TWIN

/ BY ALISON **CALDER**

Dr. John Maubray . . . believed that Dutch women were disposed to bring forth an evil-looking little animal, which they called *de suyger* or *sooterkin*. . . . The sooterkin sucked all the infant's nourishment, like a leech, and the child was dead and dessicated when it was born in such unpleasant company. Dr. Maubray even claimed that he had seen and delivered a sooterkin. . . .
— From *A Cabinet of Medical Curiosities* by Jan Bondeson

sooterkin, my twin
how oft I see you in dark corners of this room
so like our early home, a hot dark womb
the stove that bade us rise like bread
from our undreaming sleep

when our mother bore us
into this bright place
we shrieked to be returned
and when the blood-smell weakened
I ope'd my eye to spy your figure gone
and none remarking

my baby's mouth then had no tongue
to say that you had been

the rat inside my crib, the kitten found
on my frail chest, I knew that you yet were
and still I had no tongue

and though I grew
I grew not fat, a pale reed-girl
and hollow, o
my dark sister
       I see you by the fire
       I see you by the stair

our cord yet binds us

a clot upon the bedclothes, the mark
upon my breast of four small teeth

I think you have a thing of mine
I am coming to call it back

/ UNTITLED

/ BY KATHERENA **VERMETTE**

a baby's cry
rises up into the infinite
night
unanswered

the music's too loud
the party's too good

below her
voices meld into desperate bass, cheap
rhythm, below her
words are lost
in the din

but from this distance
her cry is clear
it resonates into the sky
finds its pitch
against the stars
she is strong
already
she is

a
ca
pel
la

/ OUTCAST

/ BY KATHERENA **VERMETTE**

heavy with the day, my eyes
haven't opened yet, weighed
down with thick
cloud just above my brows
the sky is sinking
further and further, it's going to crash
into the earth, into me lying here
listless like gravity, waiting
for the collision, i am
the stolid sky, waiting
a swollen belly housed by soft
bones, wrapped with glowing skin, a child
in June, an infant,
an egg, waiting
for the perfect Spring moment
to crack

/ SPILLING OVER

/ BY HEDY WIKTOROWICZ **HEPPENSTALL**

Sandra reaches into the greying pink gym bag. She fumbles with a round object, yanks it out and stands there with a fresh roll of duct tape in her hand. "My boyfriend's," she sighs to the grocery clerk. She scoops her red-cheeked toddler onto her hip. "Just a second, Nigel. I'm trying my best here, baby." He can't hear her over his cries, so she continues to herself, in her head: I'm trying. I really am. And tomorrow, once we've got everything ready, we are goin' to the beach. I'm not Bsing this time. Let's just get the shopping done and we're that much closer.

The clerk holds her arms straight on the checkout counter, her nails doing little pushups. Her fingertips blanch from pressure when Nigel's scream climbs to a new pitch.

For Sandra, going to the beach—a real beach, not the kind with a cement pool surrounded by sand—means driving for at least an hour on the highway, any direction, with the windows rolled down and the music cranked up, and the full force of summer moving through her. Something about spending a hot summer day on a beach opens her up, allows a breeze to move around inside her tight spaces, untangling them. What the breeze doesn't reach, the water runs into and through, her body like a muddy sponge being dunked into fresh water, time and again, until the dirt gets washed away. Then, like a worn white shirt, she lies down in the sun, lets its heat sear its whiteness into her, down deep to her bones. She loves the way it seems to bleach away the yellowness of living in cramped quarters, where others have lived and layered their smells, only for others to come after them and add their own stench of living. Gonna get there. Gonna get there. God, do I need to get there. Can't wait to see their tender little tushes all caked with sand. Who knows? Maybe it'll make Stewie a little jealous and he'll want to come with us next time.

Sandra continues to poke through the gym bag that's become her diaper bag. What it offers in space, it lacks in compartments, so the many odd items stashed in there are rarely in the same place twice. Her hand jabs through disposable diapers and a stained receiving blanket. Receive what? she wondered when her aunt gave it to her as a "must have." The only thing this sucker has received is gobs of spit-up and drool lately. Without her realizing it, her still-buried right hand flips Stewie "the bird." After all, he's the one who talked her into using the gym bag reject for a diaper bag.

"Look at how much you can stuff in here"—his words, bad stains that won't fade away—"and look at the strap on this thing. It's way tougher than that cottony

279

shit that always got rubbed away on that expensive diaper bag you used for Ramona."

The expensive bag that he had run out and bought for Ramona, when Sandra gave him the news. That day, he walked his lanky bones, those long puppet arms of his bouncing right along, over to the Bay downtown. Back then, Stewie had only a hint of those creases running up his cheeks, but she's sure that those lines were firmly set on either side of his mouth, filled with good intention, holding the corners of his mouth up into a smile. They've become so loaded, those lines on his face, deeper now, and reaching up to his eyes. She imagines that if he would let her touch those creases, trace them like the ravines on a trail map, her fingertips would learn more about Stewie than his words would ever let on.

He bought her the best Fisher Price diaper bag he could find, like everything a kid would need in life could be packed into that thing—or maybe so he and his kid could be ready to bolt at a moment's notice. Stewie does have a tendency to bolt when he feels the heat. So now she's stuck with Stewie's version of the new and improved diaper bag. She knows why he really wants her to use it—because he never would. The colour reminds her of Pepto-Bismol–pink playdough that's been left out overnight—that powder-pink shade that you get when you find it under the kitchen table the next morning. Sure, the gym bag is strong, but your chance of finding what you need quickly is like your chance of getting through the checkout line and having enough left over to buy an extra pack of smokes.

"Finally," she announces, feeling the familiar bite marks along one side of the Tupperware lid. She pries it open with her right thumb, while bouncing and balancing Nigel on her left hip. Please God, don't let me spill all the fishy crackers. She stuffs the orange fish into Nigel's mouth. It works. His cries morph into wet mouthing sounds that lead to a gooey trickle of drool out of the right corner of his mouth. "Good boy." You do want to go to the beach after all, don't you?

"Poor little guy was starving," says the clerk, voice laden with years of customer service training.

Sandra is tempted to say something snotty back to the clerk, but instead she tightens her lips and pays her. It's one of the few times when she doesn't have to go through the godawful exercise of deciding which items to weed out as "not absolutely necessary," cinching her bill down below the hundred-dollar mark that she gives herself for a week's groceries. Sometimes it's easy—the mini-marshmallows disguised as cereal have to go. Other times it comes down to toilet paper or tampons. Usually the toilet paper wins—more versatile.

Sandra gets a whiff of sour milk from Nigel's sleeper, and she remembers that she has to do the laundry soon. Her dread for laundry day has a way of spilling over, sudsing its way into the grocery store. Only apple juice or the syrupy stuff disguised as apple juice—whatever is cheapest. Kool-Aid stains like a bugger and orange juice is just too damned expensive. Macaroni with margarine, unless she is absolutely sure that she's seen those plastic bibs around the house—then she might risk buying the marked-down, dented can of spaghetti sauce.

Sandra loads two of the grocery bags on the storage space below the stroller and picks two evenly heavy bags for either side of the stroller handle. She finds a way to tie them so that they counterbalance each other. The handle of one of the bags rubs back and forth against the label that reads: *Warning—do not load heavy objects on handle*. She puts the last bag into the actual stroller itself. She sits Nigel up and bunches his legs against his body. Most of the time Nigel seemed unfazed by this invasion of his space, often making a game of pushing his feet against the plastic. Sometimes he just lets them move randomly, and other times he kicks them to some internal beat, smiling at the crinkly rhythm that seems to come from his toes.

During the fifteen-minute walk back to the apartment, Sandra relives the fight she and Stewie had last week after her trip to the laundromat. She'd come home exhausted. The smell of the front foyer was stronger than usual—as if another film of stench had been layered there recently. It was all she could do to plop the kids in front of the TV and fry up the fish sticks that had been on sale because the box had come undone and had to be taped shut.

Stewie came in, beer on his breath, a looseness to his voice.

He started in. "Fish sticks on Friday. Whadya think I am—a goddam Cathlick or somethin'? I could smell that shit a mile away and if I knew it wuz comin' from here I wouldna been rushin' home."

"I think what you're smelling is called shithole—like the one we're living in!"

"Ya, well . . . I'm out there bustin' my ass night and day to put a roof over our heads. But if you'd rather live in a cardboard box, then go right ahead . . . lots more . . ."

"Okay babe, can we cool it a bit?" she said as she motioned towards the kids, but Stewie ignored her. He'd been doing that a lot lately.

"Lot more fresh air in a cardboard box, ya know, and a stale loaf of bread'd be better than goddam fish sticks anyway." The vertical lines on his face reminded her of deep cracks dried in mud.

"Listen Stewie, I just had a real shitty afternoon and if you don't want to eat the goddam fish sticks, don't!"

Stewie raised his voice to mock hers: " 'I had a real shitty afternoon'—it's not like you're doin' brain surgery round here all day. I mean a few meals—if you can call 'em that—and a little stroll to the laundrymat once a week?"

"You have no idea how I bust my ass around here. Yeah—do a little laundry. When's the last time you did a little laundry at that rat-trap laundrymat? Well, I'll tell you what it's like."

"Here comes the sob story."

" First you find all the rotten, stinkin', pissy, shitty, barfy clothes lying around here. Then you got to load 'em into a garbage bag—that is if you can find one—and hope to hell that it holds all the way there. Then you gotta carry it there for three blocks with two whiny kids in tow. Yup, two little angels who want to push each other into traffic, that is when they're not picking up dried dog shit or pulling down their pull-ups and trying to 'do like a dog' and piss on the fire hydrant. Ramona actually did that today.

She had her pants off and her butt to the red thing, and then she bends forward while she's squatting—so she can watch herself pee! Yup, and that's just my 'stroll' to the laundromat."

"Yeah, yeah, yeah . . . well, you guys eat your fish sticks. I can't listen to this bull-shit anymore. I'm outta here!" And he bailed.

"Why are we doing this?" she says to the door. It always just stands there. Grey. Quiet. Not bothering anyone. Shutting out so much crap, but shutting enough of it in too.

"We got a car—we got a car!" says Sandra from the front passenger seat. Her friend Corrine is driving her new boyfriend's old Ford. The fender is wired to the body of the car and there are small splotches of rust along the lower half of the vehicle. It has to be at least ten years old, but it looks like it can go the distance.

Nigel and Ramona chatter in the back seat.

"Caaa, caaa," repeats Nigel.

Ramona strings her excitement into a song: "We're going to the beach, to the beach, to the beach . . ."

Sandra joins in. "We're going to the beach, because we got a car!"

The summer she'd met Stewie, she'd talked him into playing hooky from work one day. It was the first time he'd seen her in a bikini and the first time that she'd seen so much of him. It's the little things she remembers most—the way he placed his hand against the small of her back as they walked towards the lake to go for a swim. That hand of his stretched across her back, wanting its way into her. Something about it made some part of her want to answer back to it. She arched back into his hand, a faint counter pressure, and was rewarded with the feel of his hand pressing deeper. Then, after swimming together, the way he didn't use a towel, just shook the water out of his hair, then lay back on his towel, beads of water shining on his arms, his chest. That day with Stewie made her love the beach even more.

She's never managed to get the kids to the beach. The summer after Ramona was born, Sandra accepted that she would have to take a summer off from her annual ritual—Ramona was just too young and wasn't doing much more than lying on a blan-ket and kicking her feet, or nursing. So she let that summer slip by, promising herself that she would go the next year, when Ramona would be old enough to walk.

The next summer Stewie broke his leg and money was tighter than usual. But she almost got there. She was planning to go with Stewie's sister. The day before they were leaving Sandra was down to her last twenty, which was the cash she had been stashing away for her day at the beach. She figured that a twenty should be able to cover the cost of everything—the gas, those greasy fries that she would drench in vinegar, and ice cream, of course. She'd been squirrelling it away one dollar at a time, sneaking the money into an old envelope and sliding it into a hole in the lining of her box spring. Stewie never looked under there. He'd go out with mismatched socks or without underwear before he would have thought to bend his long bony legs and check under the bed, where, more often than not, there would be a stray sock or a pair of day-olds.

So she'd had the money, but they were down to a jar of mustard, some stale crackers from the food bank, and a can of Chicken of the Sea. She was a little afraid to open that tin. The label was faded and beginning to shred along the bottom. What was in that tin anyways . . . chicken or seafood . . . or some gross mixture of the two, laced with botulism by now? Sandra figured she could've managed to get by herself on stale crackers and mustard until the next family allowance cheque arrived, but she knew that Stewie and Ramona would start in on each other. The edginess of hunger made both of them feed off anything annoying. Stewie had already started.

"Does she have to be so bloody messy when she eats those crackers? Look at this . . . mogey bits everywhere. No wonder I keep finding bits of crap stuck to the bottom of my socks . . . and in my shoes. Chunks of goddam toast inside my shoes some days. Shouldn't we be teachin' her to eat the frickin' food instead of chucking it around?"

Ramona stopped eating the crackers. She was pounding her fists on the tray of her high chair, looking at her mother and calling "Down . . . down." Her clamped fists splayed more cracker crumbs to the floor.

"Get her out of there, will ya!" he yelled to Sandra. "And you," he said pointing to the child, "stop being such a messy little shit."

Ramona's fists froze to her slightly parted mouth. She made a jerky, snuffing noise, the sound of tears being stifled by fear. Finally Stewie turned away and Ramona's tight lips unleashed a loud cry.

"I'm outta here," said Stewie. He grabbed the twenty-dollar bill that Sandra had just laid on the counter and turned for the door.

"Hey—you just can't . . ." The slam of the door cut her off in mid-sentence. Stewie wasn't about to be told what he could and couldn't do. So, just like that, her day at the beach, dead in the water. She never knew how long he'd be gone. She did know that she had to phone Diane and tell her that she couldn't make it.

"Hi Diane—yeah it's me," she started.

"Hey girl, looks like pretty good beaching weather we got ourselves today."

Sandra answered slowly, "Yeah, I know. Here's the thing. Mona just blew her groceries all over the kitchen and she's all cranky and hot."

"No way."

"I know. I'd strangle her if she weren't so damned pathetic today. You know how much I needed this."

"Aww shit. Well, don't worry. I'm sure we'll do it again sometime," Diane said, trying to console her.

"Yeah, like in another ten years or so. Anyways, I gotta go. You guys have fun. And I'll get there when I get there."

"All right," said Diane, making it sound like it wasn't all right at all. "You guys gonna be okay? You need anything from the drugstore?"

"Naah. I think we just need to sleep."

The summer after that, Nigel was too little—six months old—and it was just too hard to drag a two-year-old and a baby to the beach.

"Let me tell you, Corinne, four years is too long to wait for all this."

"Four years too long, if you ask me."

"And look at us. It's happening. It's really happening."

Nigel didn't have a great sleep last night and Sandra hopes that he'll fall asleep once they get moving. He doesn't. Every high-pitched word, every jerky movement of his mother's head, hands and jaw seems to stir him awake, like some manic episode of *Sesame Street*. He looks a bit like an astronaut all strapped into the seat like that. The car has a toddler seat already attached, as if it's really meant to happen this time, like her luck is finally changing.

Sandra catches a glimpse of the beach umbrella in the back seat.

"Would you believe I got that beach umbrella for a buck?" she says to Corrine. "It's missing a spoke, but other than that it works fine."

"You're the woman."

They hit the perimeter highway and take the exit labelled North Grand Beach.

"North Grand Beach, baby! Here we come!" says Sandra, sounding more like a teenager than she has in years.

"Whoohoo!" whoops Corinne after her. The kids chatter and squawk along in the back seat.

"Tunes, girl. We need some tunes," says Sandra, fiddling with the FM dial until she finds some music that grooves to her mood. She rests her right arm along the open passenger window and lets the vibrations from the speakers tickle her skin and tease her lips into a smile. She closes her eyes and lets her head fall back into the headrest for a whole blessed song.

Then from the back seat: "Ow! Stop it, you little . . . or I'll . . ."

Nigel doesn't stop, but cackles at the reaction he gets from his sister. His hand tightens around the beach umbrella and he pushes it into her leg again.

"Owwwww!" repeats Ramona and she reflexively whacks back at his hand, making him drop the umbrella.

Sandra's mouth recoils. "Stop it! Both of you!" She hates it when they fight. Hates it even more in the cramped space of this car. She especially hates how it's clawing into her moment, dragging her back into the place she is trying to slip away from.

Nigel is crying from his sister's slap and Ramona scrunches her face at him.

"Geez, you guys. Cut the crap back there or you'll be sorry," yells Sandra. Nigel is still crying, cheeks flushed, and he's tossing his head from side to side along the edge of the back seat. He starts bucking his body forward and back, raging against the straps of the car seat.

Sandra turns the music louder, hoping the radio will drown him out just long enough for him to scream himself out and fall asleep. Ramona uses her fingers to plug her ears and is staring out the window counting cows. Nigel stops crying, but his restlessness moves back into his right arm, the one nearest his sister. He grabs hold of her shoulder-length black hair and yanks.

"Oooooowwwww!" yells Ramona, louder than before. "Mooom, Nigel pulled my hair!"

"Pull over," says Sandra, with the authority of a cop. Corinne doesn't argue. She signals, brakes and slows towards the shoulder. While the car is slowing down, Sandra searches through the diaper bag as if the solution to the kids fighting is something she can pick up and turn on. Her hands run through the things in the bag as if they are eyes scanning a grocery list. Soother—he doesn't take it any more . . . red striped after-dinner mint starting to powder at the edges—might choke on that . . . juice in his tippy cup—could work if I can stop him from throwing it somehow. Damn . . . damn . . . what else? . . . what else? The car reaches a stop. Crackers. Where the hell are they? Again her hand feels the roundness and she brings out the duct tape by mistake. "Duct tape—yes, duct tape." She takes the duct tape and the tippy cup and unbuckles her seat belt.

"Sandra, whatcha gonna do with that?"

"Just what needs to be done."

The kids sit like statues in the back seat, eyes open, mouths shut. Sandra opens the door on Nigel's side and begins to unwrap the package of duct tape. Nigel stares at his mother as if she's a wild animal at close range.

"I know you're tired," she says after biting through the first piece, "so I'm just gonna do a little somethin' here to help you settle down." She bites through a second piece. "You might not like it at first, but . . ." she lets the words dangle there and her hands take over. She pulls Nigel's left t-shirt sleeve towards his elbow, then secures his upper arm to his body with a strip of tape. She does the same to his right arm. Nigel cries and thrashes his legs, but there is little else he can do. She uses the third piece of tape to attach the tippy cup to his right hand. She makes sure there is just enough movement in his right arm to allow him to bring the juice cup to his mouth.

Sandra takes his right hand and brings the juice cup to his mouth for him. When the juice reaches his tongue, his lips close around the spout and he begins to suck. The scraping sound of Nigel's sucking can be heard above the sounds of passing cars. Sandra gets back into the front seat of the car.

"I guess I gotta stick to the speed limit now," says Corinne, starting the car back up.

"Yeah, I guess you do," says Sandra.

They continue down the highway, gazing out the window as they drive, strangely comforted by the rhythmic drag of the sucking noises from the back seat. Sandra closes her eyes. She imagines that the sipping sounds are the pull of the waves on the beach and she lets herself float away a little further with each one.

/ DUCKS

/ BY SALLY **ITO**

Of plastic or rubber,
they are fixtures around the tub.   Seika
plays· floating them on the shared pond
of our bathing as we splash together—
          two birds in the shallows.

You are the mommy duck, she declares,
          planting the largest one near the stretch-marked plain
of her birthing,
          And I am the baby!

The smallest yellow one is launched,
          bobbling, nodding, quivering
towards me.

                    All the nested down
of my wings   stirs
          not for flights of imagination   but for the shape
of this smaller self
          returning to its mother

whose body,
          once melting with the skies
has been now claimed   for a season
          by its young.

/ BLUEBERRIES

/ BY SALLY **ITO**

Someone has hauled these
through the dark night
down a lonesome stretch
of northern Ontario highway.

By the time they reach the table
where my toddler's hands pick and fumble
to bring their sweetness into her mouth,

they are well-travelled souls.

All I can think of
      is the rumble of midnight
and star-shine that carried them these
      few hours before the market's opening.

How they were gleaned from
      wooded fields, by strange hands
and kept cool in a box
      shaded by trees.

Blue, sweet tender night,
      your passing has never brought
more succulent boon than these,
      night sky's dark gems
glistening in the morning light.

/ SHERBROOK POOL

/ BY ALEX **MERRILL**

It's the end of Christmas vacation and I'm at Sherbrook Pool watching my daughter and her friend swim. For two weeks the wind chill factor has been at minus 40 and holding.

This factor has not been a factor anywhere else I've lived. That covers a lot of places. I've learned since moving here that wind chill is NOT the temperature on the thermometer but the temperature of what it *feels like before* you lose all feeling. The weather announcer says it like this: *It is minus 32 today, but with the wind speed at 60 km per hour, it feels like minus 50.* And then she adds: *A good day to stay inside.*

Wind chill measures how many minutes it takes your eyeballs to freeze stuck or how long it take your thighs to turn to ice stumps when you don't wear long johns under your jeans. It measures at what point in the winter you are driven to keening and gnashing of teeth and joining a cult. Wind chill is Winnipeg code for too f-ing cold.

Wind chill explains why I'm sweating up in the bleachers at Sherbrook Pool in December. I forgot to bring a sleeveless T-shirt and cut-offs, advisable because it's a sauna up here. I haven't figured out how to wear summer clothes under a parka. I've settled for taking off my boots and socks.

The pool is almost empty. It's the regular swim time, an hour and a half to the free swim. During the regular swim neighbourhood kids usually line up at the entrance waiting for the free swim, and sometimes there's too many to get in and the pool attendants have to turn some away. The free swim is the best deal around here, otherwise known as the poorest postal code in Canada. It's so cold today there's no one waiting for the free swim.

My two girls play and one woman does laps across the deep end. A bored lifeguard slouches in her plastic picnic chair by the door.

Sherbrook Pool is a no-frills pool. The name POOL says it all. It's not an aquatic centre or an athletic complex. It doesn't offer tai chi or yoga or Pilates or aerobics or Falun Gong. There's a small weight room upstairs by the bleachers but that's it. The pool itself is a plain rectangle with cracked tiles all around the edge. There's no diving board, just a rope to swing across the deep end and a one-metre-wide red rubber cap hanging over one corner of the shallow end. It looks like a giant diaphragm, the birth control kind. On request, a lifeguard will flip a switch on the wall and this rubber cap will rain recycled pool water over your head.

Outside, Sherbrook Pool looks like a utility building with rusty brick and grimy windows across the basement. It is a utility of sorts, an essential service to a neighbourhood where parents don't have the resources to drive their kids across the city to the deluxe Pan Am. The entrance to Sherbrook Pool says PUBLIC BATHS. When I first moved here and saw that sign I imagined this was a real bath house, like the places where Bette Midler started her singing career in New York. It still has the feel of the era when it was built, 1912. My father-in-law and lots of people's parents learned to swim here.

Inside on the bleachers I sweat it out, gratefully. People have told me, people born in Winnipeg, that you dress in layers and you'll be fine. They say *If you're active, winter here is not a hardship, it's an opportunity.* They say *It's a dry cold.* Winnipeggers are a curious mix of stoic and quixotic. They have to be, I guess.

This is my third winter here. The first was unreal, unreal in the sense that there were only two weeks of severe wind chill before we headed into spring. I said to a Winnipegger, the man I moved here with, *This isn't so bad. What's all the fuss about winter?* He'd cringed for me then, he told me later.

Last year the snow started in November and the wind chill stayed between minus 30 and 40 in January and February. The temperature see-sawed like a maniac into April. On the balmy days I was giddy with gratitude. When it turned arctic again, I felt bleaker than I would have if it had just stayed cold all along. May was the real heartbreaker. We still had snow May 24 and the ground was frozen until June.

June.

I thought since I lived through that, any kind of winter would be manageable. I was becoming a bit of a Winnipegger, I thought.

This year we had our first snowfall in September, winter was well established by November, and now here we are at Sherbrook Pool.

There's barely a blip on the pool surface. At the deep end the woman's doing laps, doggedly. From the change room two more girls have appeared, recent teenagers, it looks like. They hunch over, arms crossed, shielding their chests and bellies from invisible onlookers. Like cats to water, they pick their way down the steps into the shallow end.

Up here in the chlorine steam I perch on hardwood benches ten inches wide, not enough to engage the average adult butt in any one position for more than thirty seconds. To survive here for an hour and a half you must shift position often, standing up every once in a while.

The narrow benches are a small price to pay for an afternoon of bliss. As soon as I get to Sherbrook Pool I feel it. Being at Sherbrook Pool is like being at the airport early, or like being on a Greyhound bus. There's nothing to do but read and daydream unless someone sits beside you and tells you their life story, which isn't going to happen here today.

Someone has donated recent copies of *Elle* and *Vogue* to the Pool. I grabbed them from the table downstairs. These are rare finds. Typically at Sherbrook Pool there's

289

Maclean's or *Homemakers*, old *Swimming Worlds* and Canadian Tire flyers. To have *Elle* and *Vogue* is a mystery. Who would have brought these here? Once I found a current *Oprah* with the subscriber's address on it—a dentist from Kansas City. I pictured the dentist and wondered how the magazine got from Kansas City to Sherbrook Pool. I thought of tearing off the address tag and writing her to ask.

I sip a tepid Tim Hortons and flip pages. The Dior ad on the back cover of *Vogue* is an underage girl with Angelina Jolie-size joystick red lips and matching red dress in a v shape veering from clavicle to pubic bone. She's holding up a handbag in the shape of an old-fashioned iron with belt buckles all over it. The handbag with all its buckles looks like a chastity belt.

I look up at my daughter and her friend gliding through the water porpoise-like from the shallow to the deep end. Someone from the '60s warbles over the sound system, their words bouncing across these old walls.

I don't want this afternoon to end but I do know that when I leave here I'll feel able to face the cold again. I'll feel like a new woman. That's what happens at Sherbrook Pool.

The black tiles painted on the green pool bottom ripple under the water. A fortyish woman with black goggles strides water to the slow soul of Lionel Ritchie. I watch her for moments more and drift off thinking of some pun about women and the deep end.

I believe that women my age love this pool.

When I'm here Tuesday night for my daughter's lessons, I watch a class of older women in swimercise ski through the water in slow motion while Eric Clapton croons. They crank up the old music especially for this class. The women laugh and talk while they're striding and bopping as if they were having coffee together. This class is for anyone who doesn't worry about bikini line waxes or what they look like in the shower. *You're all gorgeous!* I sometimes want to shout at the women in the pool.

It's close to the end and my daughter has asked me three times already—*Please, Mom, can we stay longer?*

No problem, I say.

And me, I say to myself, can I stay here for the rest of my life?

The lifeguard calls out to the girls and I wonder what she wants with them; they aren't horsing around. She leans over the edge of the pool and shows them how to make water spray through a pool noodle by sticking it over one of the pipes pouring into the pool. The girls watch and giggle. Then the lifeguard points to the red diaphragm on the ceiling and goes to the wall and turns it on. The girls shriek and jump under the spray. I want them to stay like that forever.

The two other girls rise out of the other side of the pool. They're a couple of years older than my daughter. They have budding women forms, breasts getting obvious, hips getting wide. They tiptoe over the tiles to the change room, stooped over, still protecting themselves from unseen observers.

My daughter yells up at me, *How much time do we have left?*

I wonder if this means she wants the time to be up? Or not?

Five minutes! I yell down.

At that moment one of the two older girls slips and catches herself on her way to the change room. The other one grabs at her and she slips too and they giggle as they disappear down the stairs.

I pick up the magazines, pull on my socks and boots and coat and head down to the change room. I have to go through the underground tunnel, a half-lit hallway with exposed low-hanging pipes and chunks of peeling paint. There's a hushed feel in here, a sense of communing with a century's worth of ghosts.

In the change room I sit down on a bench to wait for the girls, sweating, having too soon donned my winter stuff. The girls' voices ricochet off the shower room walls and mingle with reggae piped in from above. Hard to make out the words, exactly. It's something like *Everything's gonna be alright, yeah.*

/ STALKERS

/ BY MIRIAM **TOEWS**

My friend Carol and I were sitting in Rae and Jerry's lounge, drinking champagne cocktails and talking about our various failures and disappointments. Rae and Jerry's is attached to one of those '50s-type steakhouses, on Portage Avenue in Winnipeg. We really like Rae and Jerry's lounge because it's almost entirely red and we are given chocolate mints after our drinks and also allowed to take a red pen, engraved with the Rae and Jerry's logo, on our way out.

The big topic of conversation for us was my eighteen-year-old son moving out. A couple of days earlier he'd moved into a house downtown with two of his friends. I'm happy for him, he's happy, too, but I'm also feeling a little like: Hey, how did that just happen?

Carol's known my son for maybe about half an hour less than I have known him. I got pregnant with him when I was young, twenty-one, and she showed up at the hospital right after he was born, with a big bottle of champagne that she had to sneak in. We shuffled over to the nursery where he was lying under a bright lamp and we stared at him through the glass and she whispered: Oh my god, Miriam, oh my god.

"I'm kind of bummed," I told her.

"Yeah, I know." she said. "It's weird, isn't it?"

"I mean, it's good—he's happy, he's loving it, but it's—yeah, I miss the kid. His big shoes. His clank clank clank."

"What?"

"His weights."

"Yeah."

"And it's more just sort of you know—have I been a good enough mother?"

We ordered another round of champagne cocktails and then I told Carol how my son had been at home (our home, my home, his old home) earlier that evening picking up some stuff and had mentioned that he and his friends were having a housewarming party later that night.

"Like, tonight?" Carol asked.

"Yeah—like, now."

"You weren't invited?"

"Well, when he mentioned it I went, 'Oh no, I don't have a gift, can I still come?' And he said really sweetly that the party was more for their friends, less for their parents."

"Ah."

"Yeah."

"Right now?"

"Yup."

Carol and I finished our drinks, eventually, and wandered out into the giant dark parking lot and then sat in the car holding onto our red pens and chocolate mints. I was giving her a ride home, even though I probably shouldn't have been driving at all. It occurred to me that my son's new home was more or less on the way to her place. Okay, well, maybe just a little bit out of the way, but not much.

"Hey!" I said. "Do you wanna drive past his house?"

She said yes.

We weren't hearing any of those voices that sober forty-one-year-old responsible, even-keeled, emotionally mature parents generally rely on to guide them through the morass. Nope, we were sixteen all over again, giggling, feeling energized suddenly, with an exciting adventure ahead of us—driving late at night past the house of a boy we both really liked.

We drove down a bunch of back streets, behind Portage Avenue, until we got to the one he lived on and as we got closer to the house we said things like: Oh my god, I can't believe we're doing this. This is sooooo stupid. What if he sees us? But of course we kept going, and then there was his house on the left side of the street, all lit up from the inside, lights blaring, music blaring, a zillion kids, it seemed like, getting out of taxicabs and walking in through his front door.

"They're taking cabs," I said to Carol. "They're more responsible than us."

"We're pathetic."

"I know. Look, is that him?"

"It *is* him. He's talking to someone."

"Is he laughing?"

"I think so."

"He looks happy."

"He does. They all look happy. Look at them."

We drove around the back and looked in those windows too, the kitchen and back porch windows, and saw more kids standing around talking and laughing and arms going up in the air, down again, heads shaking, the fridge door being opened, fingers snaking through hair, big grins, high-fives.

Then we drove around to the front one last time and looked through the big living room window and I saw my son still standing under a very bright light, talking, laughing, so much bigger now than when Carol and I stared at him through the glass wall of the hospital nursery.

We took off, feeling sheepish but pleased, and I dropped Carol at home and then went home myself. My husband was out of town and my fifteen-year-old daughter was out with her friends. I'm definitely not going to make a habit of doing this, I told myself. I sat on the couch in the dark and slowly ate my chocolate mint. I put my red Rae and Jerry's pen into my pen container on the kitchen counter, and went to bed.

/ ONCE SUMMER COMES

/ BY DONNA **GAMACHE**

Come in, come in. It's good to have you visit me. Have a chair. You don't mind if I stay where I am, do you? I just lay down for a few more minutes to rest my bones, and I must have fallen asleep.

I had another visitor earlier today. At least, that's what the redheaded nurse said when she brought my supper. Actually, I don't recall an earlier visitor, but I guess she knew what she was talking about.

"How nice of your niece to visit," she said. "Where does she come from? A fine-looking woman she is."

I shrugged and didn't answer. She must have me confused with someone else. I've just got the one niece, William's sister's girl, and she's not seven yet. Or she wasn't, when I saw her last. What *is* that girl's name, anyway? I can't remember, but she only started school last year.

The nurse stood beside me, so I finally started my supper. I wasn't hungry, but you know how it is. If you don't eat, they'll stay with you all night. Why don't they let me eat at my own pace? And as much or as little as I want? Why do they watch me all the time? Once summer comes, and I'm out of here, I'll take my meals when I want them.

I used to eat more, of course, and it showed a little, I'm afraid. But I needed to eat more then. When you're hoeing the garden and shovelling grain and milking cows, you need to keep up your energy. It's only when I came here that I stopped eating.

I fooled them for a while. I used to eat in the dining room with the others, and I'd carry my purse with me. I'd sneak the meat and bread into my purse, and I'd throw them out the window later. I was on the ground floor then, and there was a tabby cat used to come below my window and eat what I threw out. I watched for it every evening, when the others were in the lounge, watching television.

What made them suspicious, I wonder. Did someone see the cat? Anyway, then they started checking my purse after every meal. Or they made me leave it in my room at mealtimes. Now, of course, I couldn't feed the cat anyway. They've moved me to the third floor, and I take most of my meals here. They watch me like a hawk, too.

Do you like my new housecoat? It's a pretty shade of red, isn't it? Someone gave it to me not long ago; I don't remember who. Maybe it was for my birthday. Or was it Christmas? Anyway, they took away my old one, said the sleeves were frayed. It was still comfortable, but you know the way some people are—as soon as something's a little worn, they toss it out and buy a new one.

We never do that, on the farm. We just make do with what there is. And William's really good at fixing things up. Just last month, he fixed my washing machine. — That *was* last month, wasn't it? Or was it? Sometimes, I'm not sure about time, in this place. It's hard to keep track of the months in here.

But I do know something—the nurse changed the calendar yesterday. "April first today," she said. "That's it for March." I let her do it. One month here isn't much different from the rest. Not like at home, of course, where each month is different. In March, I have the seed catalogue out, planning my garden. And in April, William's cleaning grain, just *waiting* for the snow to melt. I wonder if he's doing that now?

Then May will come, and he'll be on the fields from dawn to dusk. He's not the best organizer in the world, though, and I work with him whenever I can. Will they let me out of this place soon, I wonder. He might need me. Maybe, once summer comes, they'll let me go home.

I've worked with William ever since we got married, except when Tommy was just a baby, and the spring I was pregnant with him. Oh, that was an exciting time! We'd waited so long for a baby—ten long years, and three miscarriages I'd had. We could hardly believe this baby would make it. I spent most of April and May lying in bed. I didn't even plant a garden, and William didn't have time. But he managed the seeding alone, and for the next few springs, too, when Tommy was little. But now Tommy comes with me, if I'm working outside, or sometimes we leave him with William's sister.

Did I mention to you about the cat I used to feed? It was a pretty one, but not as friendly as our farm cats. We always have half a dozen or so around the barn. I hunt for the kittens every spring, and Tommy helps me. — But I'm not supposed to think about that. That's what the nurse said when I asked if William was feeding my cats.

I can't feed the tabby one now I'm on the third floor. Did I tell you that? And the bars on the window don't help, either. Could you ask the nurses to take those off? I asked them, but they just shake their heads. Anyway, I guess it doesn't matter; someone always stays with me while I eat.

Can you stay a little longer? Maybe we could ask the nurse to bring us a cup of tea. I'd make you one myself, but they won't let me keep my kettle anymore. Not since I scalded my leg. When *was* that, anyway? One day last week, I think.

Look at that nice sunset. I'm glad I have a west window; I've always liked sunsets. Sometimes if William and I have time in the evening, we sit outside and enjoy the view. Once Tommy's asleep, of course. Such a busy little boy, he keeps me running all the time. Some days, I can't keep up with him. — But I guess I'm not supposed to talk about that.

Did you hear that song on the radio this morning? The one about springtime and forty below? It made me think of spring blizzards. There was one in the spring the year I was sixteen. Came on April the fifth, and we didn't get the road open for a week. It's a good thing Mother had lots of flour on hand.

Then there was one in late April, two years after I married William. He had to dig his way into the barn to feed the cattle. The snow was so deep we couldn't let them out to the watering hole, and we gave them snow. Do you remember that year? I asked the nurse if she lived around here then—but she just laughed as if she didn't believe my story.

But the biggest snowstorm was last spring, and you know what it was like. Tommy was so excited at all the snow! — Oh, I forgot. "Don't think about that," the nurse said.

Why doesn't William bring Tommy to see me, do you suppose? Are there rules against children visiting here? It seems like such a long time since I saw either of them. — Oh well, I'll probably be out of here in a day or two more. Just as soon as I get my strength back. Maybe William's waiting till then, to come and get me. He'll need me, once seeding starts. Or afterwards, once summer comes.

April first already. It won't be long until the crows come, then the robins and blue-birds, and then the warblers and swallows. I like *both* birds and cats? Do you find that strange?

The robins always build a nest in the maple outside our bedroom. Sometimes they start chirping before there's a hint of daylight. Tommy and I like to stand inside the window and watch them feed the little ones on the nest.

That's what I was doing last week at that window, you know, looking for nests. "Trying to jump," I heard the nurse say, and that's why they put the bars there. But really, I was just leaning out to look for nests, and to see if there were any flowers below. I'd forgotten it was winter.

How do you like my hair cut this way? The girl came last week, and she said it suited my age to wear it shorter. I don't know why she said that. I'm only thirty-five yet. Or is it thirty-six? I know I look older, but that's because I haven't been well. Maybe that's what she meant. Well, it's better short, when you're sick in bed, I guess.

Do you like this wallpaper? The walls were yellow on the first floor, but I like this wallpaper, with roses all over it. Such bright colours, you can almost smell them. I've always loved flowers, but the nurse said I can't have them here anymore. Not even arti-ficial ones. Something to do with a wall, and a broken vase. I don't know what she meant. Maybe you could ask her to change her mind.

Wild roses are what I like the best—or used to. I had a few of the earliest ones in the house last spring, the very end of May. William and Tommy picked them in the west pasture and put them in my pink vase on the kitchen table. But someone wrecked them later, I think, crushed them till the thorns brought blood.

Do *you* like flowers? I always enjoy taking a walk to pick the wild ones. Tommy likes to come, and sometimes Janice, too, if she's over for the afternoon playing with Tommy. — Janice, that's her name; why couldn't I remember it before? And why did the nurse say my niece was visiting? If Janice can visit me, then there aren't any rules about children, after all. But why wasn't her mother with her? If she can come alone, why not Tommy?

Could you ask someone about that? The nurses always give me strange looks when I ask. Or they say something about "facing reality," whatever that means. They shouldn't use that technical jargon; they know I don't have the education they do.

I'd have liked to take something after high school, but there wasn't any money. And then I started going with William, anyway. We married when I was just twenty. In the beginning we figured we'd have a big family, but it hasn't turned out that way. Just Tommy, that's all we've managed.

Oh, William dotes on that boy. We have to watch we don't spoil him. Such a live wire he is, always getting into things, or going places we don't expect. Or repeating things he's heard us say. Just a typical five-year-old, I guess. I wish he'd come to visit me. I wish they'd both come.

Could you stay just a little longer? There's something I want to talk to you about, something I don't usually mention. But if it's April, then it's time for spring blizzards. And it was the blizzard's fault. No blizzard, no flood, I know that.

April 20th, that's when we had the snowstorm, more snow than there was all winter. And since it was so late, it melted fast and all at once. "The river will flood for sure," William said. But it didn't happen till the end of May. The river is really slow and winding, so it takes the meltwater a long time to come. May 28th we expected the crest, at least that's what William said.

"What's a crest?" asked Tommy, but I was busy and didn't answer him. I'd explain it later, I thought.

Do you like that picture for April on my calendar? Too bad about the mistake on the year, though. It's thirty years wrong! Why did the nurses give me one with a mistake? Could you get me a proper one, do you think?

But I was talking about the crest. I should have explained about the crest, when Tommy asked. And I should have watched him better. But you know how it is when you're busy.

I told him he could hunt for kittens in the barn loft. The striped female was obviously thinner the night before when I did the milking, so she must have delivered. I told Tommy to check in the west loft. I never thought he'd go near the river. He'd been told and told to keep away from it.

No, no, don't stop me, please. And don't leave yet. Let me talk. The nurses say I shouldn't remember if it bothers me, but if it's spring, I *need* to remember.

He hadn't been gone long—fifteen minutes at most—barely long enough to find the kittens, I thought. But maybe he never even went to the loft.

I was looking out the window when I saw William dash from the tractor shed, where he was working, towards the barn and beyond it, running like I'd never seen him run before. I thought he'd heard a cow bawling, or something.

I followed him on the run. If there was a cow in trouble, he might need help. Only it wasn't a cow. And I was too late. We were *both* too late.

I couldn't believe how much the river had risen overnight. Clumps of ice swirled around in the dirty grey water. And both of them, struggling and flailing, just a little

297

DONNA GAMACHE

downstream from the barn. But just as I got there, a tree branch knocked William, and they both went under. *Both* of them!

I tried to wade in after them. But the water was so cold, and so fast. And the crest was so high. I couldn't even swim. If only I'd learned how to swim, maybe —

And how about you? Can you swim? You should take lessons, you know. I'm going to, when I leave here. William and Tommy and I, we're all going to take lessons. Once summer comes, that is.

/ MEAT

/ BY MARGARET **SHAW-MACKINNON**

"Hurry up!" I holler, up the two flights of stairs. "Get down here, Victoria! You're going to miss the bus."

Every morning we go through this hassle. What's wrong with this family?

"Alex, where's your knapsack?"

"*I* don't know," he drawls. At eleven, he has an attitude. He turns his back on me, picks his jacket up off the floor.

"Well, where did you put your knapsack yesterday? I have to put your lunch in it!"

"I won't eat meat, not after that TV show!"

"You will eat meat! You have a corned beef sandwich, and you'd damned well better eat it."

"I won't! The meat's mixed up with cow poo! That scientist lady on the show said so. It's disgusting."

"That's only in ground beef, not corned beef! I don't have time to make another."

"I won't eat it!"

I see what he sees: cow carcasses hanging from hooks; muscular men thrusting knives upward from pelvis to rib cage; guts spilling onto the floor; truck loads of ground-up cows—ground beef; hamburger patties made up of countless dead cows, a haven for bacteria; the resulting E coli displayed in Petri dishes.

Why did I let him watch it? What kind of terrible mother am I?

It was one of my weak, exhausted moments, when I plunk down in front of the television to escape and find myself riveted by any horror that unfolds before me. I told Alex to leave the room, but he stayed, and I was too tired to argue. Now I'm paying for it. Furious, I whip out some bread and jam, knowing Alex, knowing that if I make him take the meat sandwich, he'll throw it out and say he ate it.

"Alex, you jerk! I'm making another sandwich. Now get your knapsack, young man! Check for it upstairs! And get Victoria down here."

I yank the corned beef sandwich out of the lunch bag, throw in the jam sandwich. I leave Victoria's sandwich, feeling only a twinge of guilt. She won't care, and I don't have the time to make two jam sandwiches. I swerve around the kitchen, scanning for the knapsack. I hear screaming upstairs, as Alex confronts Victoria about "The Time." The knapsack is slouched under the kitchen table. I shove the lunch bag into it.

"I found your knapsack, Alex," I yell. "Now both of you get down here, or else I'm coming up! The bus will be here in five minutes. You have to the count of three!"

Alex flies down the stairs, glares, shoves past me. "She won't come!"

"Your milkshake is on the hall table. You have two seconds to drink it." I call up the stairs again. "Victoria, I said you have to the count of three! One! Two! Three!"

I take the steps two at a time, find Victoria in her room, fiddling with an elastic hopelessly entwined in her Cool Girl doll's black wool hair.

"What are you doing?"

"I want to wear this today," she says, pulling weakly at the elastic.

I grab the rag doll, throw it across the room, the green and white striped legs somersaulting through the air. It hits the wall, catapults onto a fluffy pillow, a pile of legs, purple mini dress, the forever smiling face. I seize Victoria's wrist, pull her up. She bursts into tears.

"Don't!" she cries indignantly. "Don't touch me!"

I am shamed by her hurt, but I am too stressed to ease up, and she's late all the time. I put my angry face into hers. "How dare you say, 'Don't touch me!' I have to get you downstairs somehow. You know the bus will be here any minute! You can't be late for school!"

Alex calls from downstairs. "The bus is here! Is Victoria coming?"

I glare at her. "Thanks a lot!" I spin out of the room, down to Alex. "No, she's not. I'll have to drive her—again!" I hold the front door as he leaves. I soften my voice, bring it up an octave. "Have a nice day." A child should never leave without some words of encouragement.

"'Bye. Love you, Mom."

I turn and take the stairs back to Victoria, who is red-faced, defensive.

"Now, you get downstairs. See what you've done? I have to drive you. And I have such a busy day!"

And I do. I have to tidy the house to have the family over for dinner tomorrow for Carter's birthday—a huge job, given the mess. Then I have to drive all the way downtown to pick up a cheque from a client to deposit it immediately, so that the cheques we've written don't bounce. Then I have to meet with a new design client, after which I should work on the other two projects that I have going. Before the end of the school day, I need to shop for groceries and make supper. Once the kids are home, I have to feed them, help them with homework and get them to bed. And of course, Carter's job is so impossibly demanding, he'll arrive home, large as life, only after the dust settles.

At the school, Victoria trudges up to the door, her long hair held in place with two heart-shaped hair clips, her fluorescent pink knapsack heavy on her back. She turns and waves, blows me a kiss that I return. We've made up by this point. She disappears into the rest of her day, which I hope will go better than its beginning.

At home, I head for the kitchen to make coffee, reach into the cupboard for my Royal Brew. I take out an unbleached coffee filter—bleached filters eventually kill you—fit it snugly into the plastic drip tray. Plastic gives you cancer. As I spoon in the dark grounds, the soothing aroma blends with, temporarily neutralizes, my sense of despair and defeat. I go to the sink, turn on the tap, listen to the rush and slosh, stare into the reflection of sunlight in clear water as it splashes into the carafe. I fill the coffeemaker, press the button that glows orange for "On."

Turning, I see the crumpled plastic bag with the corned beef sandwich in it. I'll eat the sandwich for lunch. Alex is right, of course, meat is disgusting. We should become vegetarians. Whenever my life simplifies, becomes more what I want it to be, we do eat mostly vegetarian food, but it takes more planning and preparation time. So when I get busy, back to meat we go.

That show was really something. The cow dung does get into the meat. The odd piece of meat accidentally falls on the filth-covered floor. A poor worker, exhausted and brutalized by the work, picks it up, unthinking, throws it on the line.

Those slaughterhouse workers are unbelievably good-looking, sculpted upper bodies, arms elegant with sinewy muscle. Of course they would have to be strong, cutting the massive bodies of cows apart. Even so, I didn't expect them to be beautiful. They should be dancers, lifting fairy-shaped women off the ground, twirling them about in tales of romance. But no, there they are, stuck inside buildings that house the horrific inner workings of our Hamburger Kingdom culture.

Why are those men willing to work there? How did their mothers fail them? Why aren't they in the upper offices, their gorgeous bodies tucked into nice three-piece suits? Eating vegetarian lunches. What are the pathetic childhoods that lead to such traps?

I open the fridge, pour cream into my Hunter green mug, and wait as the coffee continues to flow into the carafe.

I look around at the mess that is everywhere. *This house is a pig sty,* my dead father and I bellow together, our voices rising in unison out of the dark windy cavern we share in my mind. He would know. He'd actually been in a pig sty. Growing up on a farm, tending the pigs was his job. At the time, his stepbrothers laughed at him. Now, at eighty, one of them, prosperous, still strong, cries like a baby when he thinks of my father, his early death. "Poor Willy. You don't know what he had to go through to put himself through law school. Up at five o'clock, tending the pigs. He was no farmer. Not like me. That's why he died young, you know. He was worked to death."

He died at fifty-five of a heart attack. We, his children, were stunned. How could our arch enemy, our dear and furious father, with whom we wanted to fight endlessly until he might learn kindness—how could he die?

"This house is a pig sty!" he would scream at my mother.

"What's wrong with you kids? You'd think you were brought up in a barn!"

"I work hard all day and come home to this?"

The coffee is ready. I pour it into my mug and take a sip. I reach into the kitchen broom closet for a duster and glass cleaner and head for the living room. I'll start there.

I survey the room. Cushions are out of the couches, on the floor where Victoria and her friend left them, part of the fort they were building. Blankets, toys, two empty glasses with slicks of chocolate milk on the bottoms. My papers are piled up in corners. There are dust bunnies under the loveseat. What are we doing wrong? I pick up a jacket. I know what we're doing wrong. I've been working nearly full time for the past three months. This always happens when I work. Two parents working, two young children busy with school, and everything goes to hell. Of course. How could it be any different? Who can pick up? No one. There's no money to hire a cleaning lady, with all the other bills to pay.

I head over to the drum table, inherited from Carter's mother. The table is crowded with objects that are covered in a fine layer of dust. I put my mug down on a coaster and proceed to dust the lamp, the lampshade, several small framed photos and figurines. I pick up the large family photo taken before Mom died. What a group! There are my six siblings, their six spouses, all the grandchildren. I'm there, with Alex, a baby on my lap, Carter behind. I gaze into my face. I look so young, serene, with my clean-cut features, upswept chestnut hair.

But I remember that day and know what lies behind that frozen smile.

We were late as usual. My pantyhose ran, just as I was putting them on. I rifled through my drawers, finding only other pantyhose with runs in them. I had to dash out to get a new pair. Carter was in the shower when I left. When I came back twenty minutes later, he was still naked, lying on the bed, talking on the phone!

I hissed at him. "Carter! What are you doing? Get off the phone! We're late!"

He motioned for me to be quiet, grabbed a pen and paper, wrote the words, "Dad—from the Mayo."

Annette, Carter's stepmom, had found a mole that had changed on Carter's dad's back. Unwilling to wait two weeks to see his family doctor, he'd phoned the Mayo Clinic in Rochester where he could be seen immediately. He refused to take chances with a mole that might be cancerous, and besides, money was no object. It was his opinion anyhow that the Mayo offered the best care in the world and he'd always indulged in an annual check-up there. He'd been gone for two days. We were awaiting the news.

I pulled on my stockings, went to Alex. I had to wake him. He whimpered. I quickly changed his diaper, put on a new undershirt, stuffed him into the tiny black dress pants, put his chubby arms into the white dress shirt, pulled the red stretchy vest over his head, adjusted the green bow tie. I ran a comb through his fine wisps of blond baby hair. I cooed and cajoled to help him make the transition out of sleep. My anxiety mounted. We were almost ready, and I could still hear the low murmur of Carter's voice in the other room.

Yes, I *was* worried about Carter's dad, but my siblings, as enraged by tardiness as my father had been, would kill us. And what would the photographer do? Cancel the shoot?

As I entered the bedroom, Carter laughed. "That's great, Dad! Good for you to get in a round of golf! A hole in one!"

A hole in one? "Get off the phone!" I grabbed at Carter's arm. He pulled it away, whispered, "Wait!"

I stood there, heart pounding, unable to act.

"Dad, well, I'm so glad you called."

His dad's voice rose and fell on the other end of the line.

"If anyone knows what they're doing, it's the doctors at the Mayo."

Again, the voice poured on, without lapse. I shoved Alex into Carter's one free arm. Alex started to cry.

"Well, Dad, it's been great talking to you. I guess I've got to go now. The baby needs me."

We were forty minutes late. My oldest brother confronted me at the door, with others glaring from behind.

"What is your problem? How could you keep six families waiting? Mom is so disappointed in you. We're just lucky the photographer doesn't have another shoot scheduled right after us, but even so, we've wasted his valuable time! And the kids are out of their minds with boredom! You always do this. What's wrong with you?"

"We had a call from Carter's dad at the Mayo, about his mole. He has a melanoma, you ass!"

"Well, that's sad, but we matter too! You could have phoned or something."

Acquaintances look at the photo, comment on our large lovely family. The surfaces are perfect. Every child is beautifully dressed, in draping wool dresses, velvets, ribbons, little suits and bow ties. Every mother is elegant, hair gleaming, tasteful dresses, strands of pearls, chains of gold. The fathers appear prosperous, healthy, square-shouldered in expensive suits. Mom, in the middle of it all, smiles a genuine smile, being a good-natured person. She has already forgiven me, is so sorry to hear about Carter's dad.

I return the dusted photo to the tabletop, feel the squeeze in my heart that says, "They are gone"—Dad, Mom, Carter's dad. I turn quickly, settle on the next task— wiping fingerprints off the French doors. I spray blue cleaner that beads and drips. I catch it and polish with slow circular motions.

It starts innocently, I think. The cows begin their lives out on the range. They have a good life during their youth, although youth has been considerably shortened due to the use of steroids. The young cows graze on succulent grasses, under a blue, cloudless sky, in the lazy sunlight of an endless day. I saw this on the television show. I saw the cowboys—rugged, handsome men—commanding large horses, weaving back and forth, herding cattle. Such is the beautiful beginning of the continuum, the worst of which I have so often chosen to forget. At the end of the continuum is an advertising image of a neat circular bun, covered in sesame seeds, the sliver of dark brown meat, succulent, sizzling, transformed, hidden in the lettuce leaves, slices of tomato, special sauce and, hovering above the burger, about to take a bite, is the happiest human face.

I step back to examine the French door, the dark, woodgrain grid work, the panes of gleaming glass. It is then that I see her, trapped, a shadowy, sad-eyed woman, and I do not look away.

/ ANOTHER POEM TO REMEMBER ANYONE'S FAMILY

/ BY CHANDRA **MAYOR**

I.

We lived in a big square house beside the river. The door was red and the shutters were blue and I never played in the front yard because of the thousands of loose pine needles lurking beneath the grass, longing for the soft flesh of my bare feet.

If I played in the front yard anyone at all driving past the house could have seen me, unguarded, smiling. I would have died of shame.

2.

My mother says that those were the years when she had more time than brains. The basement was filled with fabric, ends and discounted prints, rolls left over from her years as a home ec teacher, green and orange and turquoise, a decade out of date. She made all my clothes when I was a child, and I was grateful and embarrassed. Halloween began in September when she began sewing, six distinct costumes, a different one for school, Brownies, skating, parties, trick or treating. Underneath the handmade Little Bo Peep crinolines and lace-edged petticoats and blue velvet lace-up dirndl, my body burned with guilt.

3.

My brother dragged his GT Snowracer across the street to the riverbank every winter Saturday afternoon. The riverbank was steep and treacherous and grown over with brush. He'd position the sled at the top of the precipice, balance his body on it, and careen through the trees, frozen twigs snapping against his face. The blur of bush ended and he'd drop straight down five feet to the frozen river below: one perfect moment of suspension before something broke, the steering wheel, a runner, an arm, a neck. My mother drew the living room curtains closed. *If something happens, she said, I'll hear the screams. I don't need to watch it happen.* I watched out the window of my parents' room, upstairs, as his small body climbed up the hill, dragging the plastic racer on a rope behind him. I waved but he never looked back, never saw me.

4.

My father went to Mohawk for hours at a time. He would suddenly be gone, not in the house, not in the garage, nowhere. When he reappeared at the end of the afternoon, someone would ask him, exasperated, where he'd been. "Mohawk," he'd say, and that would be the end of it. Maybe he had a secret fetish for the swivelling plastic stand of sunglasses, spinning and spinning, light bouncing off the black lenses. Maybe he meant the Mohawk in another town, Morris or Steinbach. Maybe "Mohawk" was code for cocaine and prostitutes. Maybe he just couldn't stomach another afternoon with my mother, or another afternoon with me, made from her body, sullied. Maybe "Mohawk" just meant freedom, cruising the city streets in the two-tone green van, arm hanging out the window, Stompin' Tom blaring, pretending to be in the old convertible T-Bird, robin's egg blue, leather seats, anyone at all sitting beside him, laughing.

5.

I had a playhouse in the back yard. My father built it, with dutch doors and real windows, a row of cupboards along the back wall. My mother decorated it, pink curtains and a cot with a pink bedspread and a pink paper lamp, a fragile globe hanging from the ceiling. Lucky girl, it said to me. Lucky, ungrateful girl. There were thick-legged spiders building webs in the corners, and trails of ants on the floor. It was my house, but everywhere I looked I saw my parents' hands, my mother's eye, my father's ruler. One afternoon my friend Lisa accidentally ripped the pink paper lamp. My stomach burned and my throat sealed off and the blood pounding in my ears made me deaf. I never let anyone into the little pink house again. It squatted in the back yard and my father kept mowing around it. Every morning when I left for school it stared at me reproachfully. I looked away, concentrated on the garage full of tools, the lilac bushes at the edge of the yard, the tiny black beetles in the garden.

6.

We sold the house or we didn't and lived there forever. My parents divorced or they stayed the same, orbiting each other endlessly in the kitchen, happily ever after with a van in the suburbs. The pine tree in the front yard kept growing, year after year, untrimmed and shadowy, a dark green unwelcome presence with razor sharp fingernails. Every winter a snowman appeared on the front lawn and no one talked about it. My brother broke his neck every January on the river and I was the only one who ever saw it. I jumped every time the clock ticked although it was only the big hand that ever moved, rotating endlessly through 2:00, my father gone and my mother sitting beside the back door, a plastic green suitcase on the deck beside her.

/ A TRADITIONAL FAMILY EASTER

/ BY MARGARET **ULLRICH**

I made a loaf of soda bread to serve with the corned beef and cabbage on St. Patrick's Day. I don't know why I did it. I'm Maltese. My husband's German/Swedish. Not a single Irish person among our ancestors. Then, on March 19th, I made a lasagna and cream puffs for St. Joseph. I'd be twenty pounds lighter if I just ignored holidays.

Yeah, right, like that'll ever happen.

I'm a sucker for holiday traditions. And, just like Christmas, Lent and Easter are loaded with traditions.

Lent is the time to really clean the house. Ah, spring cleaning. Scrub and wax the floors, wash the windows and launder the curtains. Everything from cellar to attic is clean. After being sealed in tighter than a drum all winter, who could argue with giving the house a good cleaning?

Lent is also a time to cut back on the calories. Let's be honest. Who doesn't want to drop the pounds gained during December? Between the fasting and the exercise we get from cleaning house we should be able to fit into the clothes we wore last November. Alleluia!! Religion can be good for the body as well as the soul.

And then there's Easter, when Christians celebrate Christ's resurrection. We attend church in new outfits. Little boys in little suits and little girls in fluffy dresses and shiny white patent leather shoes make families look like Hallmark cards.

Easter has more customs than the Bunny has eggs. A popular tradition is to gather together and share a feast. Over the centuries women have made this a glorious occasion with beautifully decorated eggs, colourful coffee cakes and sweet breads.

And that's where Easter goes to hell in a handbasket.

According to tradition, an angel appeared to Mary to tell her that Jesus would arise on Easter. To show her joy she baked bread to share with her friends. And to make it more special, she put an egg, a symbol of life, on the top.

Now, I have to admit I don't know what I'd do if someone told me that a recently deceased relative was rising from the dead. I guess baking bread is as good a thing to do as any. The only problem is that over the past two millennia something got lost in translation as that bread recipe went from country to country.

During my earliest years in Corona, Easter was Italian. Palm Sunday was the Day of the Olive. Small blessed olive branches were offered as tokens of peacemaking. For Easter breakfast we had Colomba di Pasqua. Colomba is bread shaped to look like a dove, the symbol of peace, and covered with almond paste and almonds.

Easter dinner also had traditions. First we had manicotti. That was followed by a roasted whole baby lamb with a mixed salad, sautéed spinach and roasted artichokes. For dessert there were cream tarts, cookies, spumoni, nuts and roasted chestnuts. The adults had coffee.

Then my family moved to College Point, which had been settled by Irish and German families. They had their own Easter traditions. Since Easter was not as commercial as Christmas, we were able to follow our own customs.

When I was seven I had to follow the Church's rules during Lent. I ate *kwarezimal*, an almond cookie that was topped with honey and chopped pistachio nuts. Ma said we could eat it during Lent because it didn't have fat or eggs. For Maundy Thursday Ma baked bread in the form of a ring. It was sprinkled with sesame seeds and pierced with roasted almonds. Our Easter dinner menu was the same as it had been in Corona. But Ma baked a Figolla, a Maltese sweet bread with a marzipan filling, instead of making a Colomba di Pasqua.

A Figolla was harder to make than a Colomba. The dough was rolled about one centimetre thick. Then Ma cut the dough into pairs of Figolli with a Figolla cutter. They looked like a large letter J, but the stick part ended in a fish's tail. On one side of a Figolla she put jam and marzipan. Then she covered it with the identical shape as if she was making a sandwich. After the Figolli had been baked and cooled they were covered with coloured icing and piped royal icing. Then an Easter egg was placed on top of each Figolla. For the final touch a cardboard woman's face was inserted into the mound of the J.

The odd thing about Ma's Figolla was that it was a mermaid. I asked Ma why a mermaid and not a dove and she said, "I don't know. It's our tradition."

Well, you can't argue with tradition.

In College Point, as Easter approached, the bakeries filled with cross buns, pretzels, braided almond loaves, Easter cookies and marzipan treats. There were also decorated sugar Easter eggs that had a hole in one end. When we looked into the hole we could see tiny bunny villages. Ma knew about the cross buns. Since Malta was part of the British Empire she had eaten them in Malta, too.

We brought samples of our mothers' baking to school. There were lots of pretzels. Since they didn't have fat or eggs, they could be eaten during Lent. I brought *kwarezimal*. After I explained that the almond cookies didn't have fat or eggs either, my friends agreed to try them. I liked the braided loaves that were spread with almond paste. They reminded me of Colomba di Pasqua.

Easter was a simple celebration with our traditional foods eaten in private. There weren't any problems until the year Ma's brother Charlie married an American girl. Ma invited Charlie and Liz for Easter. Aunt Liz wanted to learn more about Maltese customs.

Pop told his oldest sister, Aunt Demi, that we had invited Charlie and Liz. Aunt Demi was worried that our branch of the family was becoming too American. So, Aunt

Demi decided that she would come to dinner to make sure that Ma kept everything kosher.

Then Aunt Dina, one of my Sicilian aunts, heard that we were inviting company for Easter. Aunt Dina always took things personally. She was insulted. Why hadn't she been invited, too? Ma invited Aunt Dina, Uncle George and their children. We had enough folding tables and chairs to seat everyone in the yard. As long as it didn't rain, Ma thought it would be a nice family dinner.

Easter Sunday morning the sun was shining and the lamb was roasting on a spit in our yard. The tables had been set. Aunt Liz was taking notes and learning recipes. She had brought cross buns and a Jell-O mould. The only thing missing was the centrepiece. Aunt Demi had told Ma that she would bring a proper Figolla.

It was the biggest Figolla I'd ever seen. The icing was as thick as my thumb. While Aunt Demi was placing the Easter egg on her mermaid, Aunt Dina marched in and pulled a Colomba di Pasqua out of her tote bag. The Colomba had a three-foot wingspan. There was barely room enough for one centrepiece.

Fish or fowl, which would Ma use?

After forty days of fasting and scrubbing, Demi and Dina were lean, clean, Easter tradition machines. They glared at each other.

"What the hell is that?" Aunt Demi spat.

"It's a dove, a symbol of peace, you idiot," Aunt Dina shot back.

"It's Easter. We don't need a damn dove."

"Throw that fish back in the sea."

"The Figolla is part of our tradition."

"Since when did Jesus swim with the fishes?"

Waving a knife, Aunt Demi lunged. "Give me that bread. I'll cut it up for sandwiches."

"Over my dead body."

"No problem."

My new Aunt Liz was fascinated by her new in-laws. She wrote down everything the aunts said. Maybe she thought the fight was part of our ethnic holiday tradition. I stayed close to Liz in case she didn't have sense enough to duck. Ma went back to the kitchen. She knew she couldn't reason with her sisters-in-law. Her plan was to hide in the kitchen until the smoke cleared. If they killed each other, it would leave more food for the others.

"Netta, get out here," Aunt Demi yelled.

"I went to all this trouble," Aunt Dina whined.

Ma came out. The men were taking a walk to work up an appetite. Liz was taking notes.

Aunt Demi barked, "Tell this idiot we are using the Figolla."

"It took me forever to make this," Aunt Dina whined again.

Ma tried to be a good hostess. "They're so big. We could put them on chairs near the table."

No luck. The aunts wanted her to choose one.

Aunt Demi announced, "We are having a traditional Maltese Easter. With a traditional Figolla."

"Do you think Our Blessed Mother baked a mermaid?" Aunt Dina demanded. Ma sighed. The lamb was ready. If this dragged on much longer it would be a lump of coal.

Ma said, "I don't care if the Blessed Mother made hot dogs and beans. I'm tired of the whole damn holiday. I'm tired of cleaning. I'm tired of baking. And I'm tired of bread. A few days ago I gave a Figolla to a friend who lives down the street. Yesterday she came over and gave me a loaf of Hallah. So I have another traditional bread from Mrs. Cohen . . . Mrs. Cohen. That's it!"

Without saying another word Ma turned and went back to the kitchen. In a few minutes she returned with the glossy braided Hallah on the platter.

"Our Blessed Mother was a Jew. She would've made a Hallah. And that's what we're having for Easter. It's traditional. Shut up, sit down and eat."

And so saying, Ma started our traditional Easter Dinner.

/ GRANDMA THERAPY

/ BY LIZ **KATYNSKI**

I am not a grandma and I am not in therapy. But sometimes when the many aggravations of everyday life have been grating upon my last nerve, I step back to what I have come to call Grandma Therapy.

I am no Martha Stewart, no Becky Home-Ec-kie. Not by a long shot. But I have to admit that yes, there are times when this woman doesn't mind stepping into the kitchen and doing a little baking.

There is something warm and comforting about the process. There you are, with an assortment of ingredients: flour, sugar, margarine, salt, baking soda and more. Independently they are just stuff in your pantry. Sifted, mixed, blended together, folded or poured into a pan and baked in the oven, they become a delicious little something.

Sure, you make a bit of a mess in the process. There are bowls to wash, clouds of flour dust, slopped batter to clean up. But when your creation goes into the oven, the comforting smell its transition produces warms your heart.

The smell of flour and ingredients, and fresh baking in the oven, reminds me of my late grandmother. When I was a kid, I would spend many an afternoon with her at her kitchen table as she took a bit of this and a pinch of that and crafted it all together to make magic. She made pie crusts without a recipe, rolled and cut cookie dough, double-boiled pudding, and more.

It wasn't just about the end result. It was about the process. She took pride in her craft, in creating something for others. Her efforts warmed her home and left a sweet happy smell in the air.

Those were the days before metric and official bilingualism. She had no idea how many ounces were in a litre, and didn't care. You didn't want to get her started about converting from miles per hour to kilometres per hour. She was a proud imperialist who still believed in the reign of the queen and the importance of recognizing the Union Jack. She was surprised that we did not know the three crosses that made up the British flag's iconic symbol, and that we saw it as British rather than Canadian. That should have continued to be our flag, not that ridiculous maple leaf. She was also surprised that we spoke French, and her old neighbour took up the cause against bilingualism by circulating ill-informed pamphlets in the neighbourhood. Yes, she would say. That's how it is.

Years later, I found one of these, and reading it over confirmed the uneducated, illogical and biased perspective of this neighbour. It was really sad. But as a kid, you are in the background and the adults are in the know. That's just how it is.

My grandma always wore skirts. Think of Edith Bunker in *All in the Family*. That sort of 1950s housewife style, with skirts hiked up to an obscured waist under her boobs—kind of the way the old SCTV character Ed Grimley wore his pants. Sometimes she wore a housedress. She always wore what I would consider dress shoes, with a bit of a heel, and stockings—the real kind with garters, even when it was really hot out.

In the summer months, I loved the feel of the sun on my skin. I would wear shorts. But you didn't want to get my grandma going on how inappropriate such attire was. She often spoke of a time when if you went downtown in shorts, that would be considered indecent and you would be fined or arrested. That always made me laugh. Although looking at old photos of people on Portage Avenue, black and white images of men dressed formally in fedoras and trench coats reminiscent of Humphrey Bogart in *Casablanca*, the women in skirts below the knee, perhaps I could believe it was once so.

After all, at that time, the first tampon commercial hit the television. I think it ran during *Lawrence Welk*. My grandmother was livid. She said the woman chatting about such things in public should be shot.

Imagine if she had seen recent condom ads on television, or the educational pamphlets now being distributed to teach seniors about the risks of HIV infection, and encouraging them to practise safe sex in new relationships. She and my grandpa had their own bedrooms for as long as I can remember.

My grandma and I often put a selection of our freshly baked items on a plate and served them with tea to my grandfather in the living room. He would smile his approval of my creations, even though sometimes I did little in the actual process. Although I did look the part, wearing an apron, something I doubt I have ever done since. Maybe that's because I do my own laundry now. Anyway, Grandpa would be caught up in watching wrestling on his old colour console television, captivated by the cartoon antics of a bunch of sweaty, repulsive men, his butt edged nearly off the cushion of his chair, leaning forward on his cane and waving his hands enthusiastically. If only that television had a remote.

Sometimes I would climb up a ladder into the storage space over the back entry. There, my grandma kept all kinds of things, including a wealth of cookbooks and other resources and supplies for her creations. She also did a lot of sewing in the front sunroom of her small home. There, she had a sewing machine or two, along with a ton of threads and materials and scissors and patterns and designs she came up with herself. She saved more than one of my Home Ec sewing class projects during a weekend emergency visit. But these days, I don't really sew any more other than an occasional repair or button mending. She made us pyjamas every Christmas for years.

A few years ago, I came upon an old handwritten notebook of recipes she had left behind. I remember opening it up and inhaling a bit of the past. The book smelled just like her kitchen. Suddenly, closing my eyes, I was back there—a little girl in awe of her skills.

I was born sixty years, almost to the day, after my grandmother. I grew up inspired by her, and yet two generations apart from her. She was a housewife who raised four children and made ends meet during the Depression. I despise the term *housewife*.

To me, *housewife* has always brought to mind visions of Edith Bunker hopping to attention at her husband's every whim, spending her days detailing the house and living in fear of anyone stopping by and catching a glimpse of any lint on the furniture or disorder in the domain. To me, a housewife was a woman who lived for and in her house, and I always pictured that to be like a domestic prison sentence.

As a more contemporary woman, unlike my mother, it never crossed my mind that I might quit working when I got married and stay home. I had a career. But there the lines blurred, because, in fact, I do stay home. I work at home. I am self-employed and would not have it any other way.

Yes, I take pride in my home. I'll admit that sometimes I find solace in the tedious domestic duties that keep things in order here—laundry, vacuuming, sorting out the clutter. But no, I am not wearing an apron and doing my hair and lipstick first. And I see all of this as a sideline, not a career, not the limit of who I am.

I know one woman who is currently living her dream as a housewife and stay-at-home mom. That's all she ever wanted to be, and she is even younger than me. Her definition of housewife is a positive one—a wife and mother who takes pride in her home and dedicates herself to her home, husband and children.

Not every family can afford to do that these days, and not every woman is up for such a nostalgic role.

I think I will stick to my moments of Grandma Therapy. Today, I might bake some cookies. They will be low in saturated fats, something else my grandmother never worried about. Heck, she didn't have a microwave or dishwasher either. I will take my time massaging the dough into little bits of sweet that will warm my home with the familiar comforting smells of yesterday.

The dough will be like fresh soil in my hand and will keep me grounded.

If I close my eyes, I can see my grandmother at my side, her hair combed back and up with a hairnet, her 1950s horn-rimmed glasses again in vogue, wiping her hands on her apron and smiling at me.

And I will make something, in a pinch.

/ THE EBONY BOX

/ BY LESLIE **SHEFFIELD**

It sat on your dresser like an oyster shell in a
pool of water, lid.clamped on its treasure. Great
great Auntie Kate brought it from India where
she'd been a missionary and saved thousands of
souls, long ago and far away.
What's a soul? I asked, and you said,
It's the part of you that never dies.

Did the great Auntie Kate save souls in this box?

Will they float out, turbanned, black-eyed in a
plume of smoke if I open the lid, maybe rub for good measure?

Let's find out, you laughed, and pried open the lid
to reveal—oh sweet disappointment—
nine more ebony lids. You teased me, pinched the
ring on the middle lid, dropped it as if burned, blew
on your finger, licked it, and finally, with an *abracadabra*,
showed me the treasure inside,
a coil of your fiery wiry Highland hair.

I teased you, picked it up, dropped it as if
burned, picked it up again and wrapped
it around my ring finger.
Can I have the ebony box when you die?

Now the ebony box rests on my dresser. Still
my fingers yearn for its treasure, lifting, rubbing
waiting
for your soul to float out.

/ STARLAND

/ BY BRENDA **SCIBERRAS**

Starland is where we mortals go
to sit upon old velvet seats crusted
with cum, eat bags of rancid popcorn
dream of being rescued from *bronte* by Kong
bitten on the box by Dracula, buriedalive
like the Mummy or scream along
with the Japanese, as Godzilla
crushes their running children.

Starland is where we mortals wish
to be as chinadolldelicate as Fay Wray.
As wonderlustful with twinkling
bigbrowneyes, pucker our cherry
lips & kiss her leading man
the prick from his own neverneverland
dead already from drugs & drink
women & want, who materialized
in the shadows of a wideanglelens.   .

Starland is where nothingisasitseems
only illusion opaque painted on glass,
mounted in front of a camera,
cardboard cut-outs & miniature projection
an eternal lost world
happyeverafter or terrified to death
life in focus or OUT. That's why we're
sitting in the Starland darkened watching
the credits roll by.

/ BELLA VISTA

/ BY BRENDA **SCIBERRAS**

We walk arm in arm in cold
under a canopy of elms,
snow crunching beneath our feet
down Wolseley to Maryland.
Entering the Bella Vista, an aroma
of garlic wraps us like a blanket.

Behind black-rimmed glasses,
the waiter ushers us without hesitation
to our usual table along the banister.
The ambience of this factitious place
makes me want to travel to faraway lands.
Tucson paintings surround the room,
bordering a pair of candelabras
each absent one light.

Not the usual crowd of single seekers
at the bar, or content couples at tables,
no gamblers behind the curtain.
Tonight is different, it's All Saints' Day,
only a few faces familiar,
reflecting in the mirrored wall.
Peter Jordan's gang laughing
over pitchers of beer,
Patrick O'Connell with guitar in hand,
waiting to serenade us, with blues or folk.

The band sings "Amazing Grace" &
"Will the Circle Be Unbroken"
echoing memories of an earlier time,
of pews & penance.
We drink down our red wine
skip the calamari & slip back
into cold night air.

/ BY PATRICK **O'CONNELL**

I love the way she runs those lights
in her thunderwear and rocket boots
singing you're going to miss me
when I'm gone
and then she runs another light
and I'm not sure what to say
except I'd love to pop her clutch
and there there she goes again

as all those autumn leaves blow by
like some old long lost shoes
tap dancing in the street

/ UNTITLED

/ BY PATRICK **O'CONNELL**

O it's all the loops and leaps of it
and the way you tango me neatly
toward the Little Dipper of our bed
so to the moon in our open window
shake those sheets out in the air
while the crocked clock
tick and talk, tirelessly it seems
just to end our dream time
the lilt and curve and wash of it
and star parts coming home now
like we knew they always would

/ UNTITLED

/ BY PATRICK **O'CONNELL**

There it goes again
wafting through my mind
that U.S. Cobra Gunship
guns fully blazing
blasting 7 holes in my rubber duck
and yes I know what happens next
I get shot by the CIA,
so please George
I'll do anything you want
I'll get a Stuka Dive Bomber
and bomb whatever you want
the way I Stuka dive my baby
every second night

/ MANGO, WITHOUT YOU

/ BY LORI **CAYER**

it seems pitiless, to perform this act
alone, without you watching, waiting for it

mango drops its fit into my hand
bends me gently at the wrist with its wet weight

my blade so smooth the first slice gives it
up like a hand beneath lycra   it fits

under bellyskin—like our first kiss—curve
and turn, it slicks its bare side belly down

into my palm, barely holdable
perfumed and undressed I try to stop

to save some sweet for you
but one cannot stop halfway with mango

tongues of fruit
oysters of fruit

the secret colour of my mouth
unfaithful

/ GOSSAMER

/ BY ELIZABETH **DENNY**

I'm looking in a cheval mirror wondering why my reflection looks so smoky when the air is perfectly clear. Maybe it's the white gossamer veil on my black hair, or the fact that I'm wearing a veil at all. I never thought I'd get married. Or it could simply be the fact that it's a cheval mirror. Two months ago I didn't even know what a cheval mirror was.

Looking down at my toes I see the bright red chipped paint and though there's no one else in the room, I curl my toes under my feet. The carpet feels soothing on my tired soles.

I look in the mirror again and this time, I see my plaid shirt and faded denims. It's not just my black hair that contrasts with the veil, it's the whole picture. The delicate white canopy bed shows up behind my reflection and I want to love it. Except I can't shake the image that someone hosed the whole bed down with whipping cream.

My head is in such a thick fog that I hardly hear the light tap on the door. Even though I don't know who it is, I'm embarrassed at the absurdity of my own likeness. I rip off the veil and creep toward the door.

I can hear someone shuffling back and forth.

"Who's there?" I say.

"It's me."

"What do you want?"

"Nothing . . ."

This is the absolute last thing I need about now. What the hell is he doing here and who let him in?

"It doesn't sound like nothing," I say, in spite of myself.

"You can't marry him, Kris," the voice says, trembling. "You can't marry that guy."

"Fuck off, Johnny," I growl. And though my words are forceful, they aren't courageous at all.

I don't hate Johnny. It's just that his brain works like a poor satellite signal. Each message, however pertinent or correct it might be, is delayed. Of course, this is exacerbated by the fact that I know, without opening the door, that Johnny is drunk. I'm no psychic, and to the untrained ear, he doesn't sound drunk. I just know that he is because, well, he often is.

It was two years into my courtship with Geoff and three weeks before our wedding that Johnny decided to tell me how little he thought of my fiancé.

It's not long before his banging on my door invites attention. Which would be fine, if it was the right kind. Instead I hear Karver asking Johnny politely to be on his way and Geoff's father shouting "Get that jackass outta here" in the background. Karver is the butler, who I expect let Johnny in to begin with. I sigh, louder than I intend to, close my eyes, look down and open the door.

"It's okay, Mr. Karver," I say. And before Karver can ask me if I'm sure it's okay, Johnny storms into the room. I nod at Karver and he leaves us alone. I close the door and turn to Johnny. He's clearly taking in my surroundings, the cheval mirror, the canopy bed, the clothing valet, the armoire. He's also right inside my head because he looks himself over in the cheval at the precise moment that I choose to take in his appearance. Faded jeans and a plaid shirt. The irony here is, our mother never dressed us alike. She really despised all those mothers who wouldn't let their twins be individuals.

He looks at me. "Nice," he says and raises his eyebrows.

I take it back. I *do* hate Johnny.

"We're just having the wedding here," I say, in my defence. "Are you drunk?"

"That's original," he says, and his rolling eyes are the exclamation point.

"What do you want?"

Johnny starts to circle the room, opens the walk-in closet, steps in and out, then walks over to the vanity and picks up a scented candle. He sniffs, grimaces and puts it back. Next he draws back the curtains on the French doors, then looks at me. "Nothing."

"Except to tell me not to go through with a wedding you weren't invited to in the first place."

"All right," he sighs. "I'll go."

He gets almost to the door. I don't want him to go and I don't want him to stay. I know why he doesn't want me to go through with this but still, I want to hurt him and the only thing I can think to say that will have the desired effect is, "Geoff wanted you as a groomsman."

Instead of walking out the door he slams it closed and looks back at me.

"That's not fair."

"No, what's not fair is you thinking you can come here and ruin my day."

Johnny flops down on the canopy bed and for a moment, he reminds me of myself a moment ago, in my veil. I sink down onto the plush vanity chair and stare at him. I don't hate Johnny.

Johnny stares at the ceiling, his arms tucked behind his head. Then he springs up.

"Wadya got ta drink around here?"

I don't answer him. Instead I take the nail polish remover and cotton balls out of the vanity and start to make my feet look presentable for my open-toe pearl-encrusted pumps tomorrow.

"Karver!" Johnny yells.

"He shouldn't have let you in here," I say, but I nearly choke on the words.

321 ◼

Karver pokes his head in the door and Johnny tips his hand towards his mouth, signalling for a drink and then mouths the word *beer*. Karver looks at me for acquiescence and to my surprise I nod. Then I flip up my fingers and signal for two.

When Karver leaves, Johnny's smiles, his eyes wide. "Does he just, like, hang out outside the room waiting for you to need something?"

I shake my head. Johnny knows I'm unaccustomed to this and the question is his way of forcing me to say that out loud.

I hate Johnny.

Apparently, Johnny had taken offence to the way Geoff had asked him to witness our marriage. He'd asked him to stay sober, for my sake.

"Fuck you . . . couldn't stay sober for one night. Not even . . ."

Karver comes in with the beers so I don't finish. Still, I shake my head at him in disapproval. He doesn't see me so I get no satisfaction out of it. I really hate Johnny.

"Don't give me that look, either," Johnny says. "Not even for you, right? That's what you were going to say, wasn't it? Not even for you."

"I was going to say, 'not even for my wedding.' "

"Same thing." Johnny springs off the bed. "Hey! Let's get drunk, Kris, come on. You're going to be an old married woman tomorrow, let's live it up."

"No."

"Your man's out doing the stag thing tonight, ain't he?" Johnny asks, and then it dawns on him. "Hey . . . why aren't you having one?"

I just shake my head. "Not my thing." Then I see that Johnny has finished his beer and I've barely gotten a taste of mine. He dashes out of the room and that gives me time to think. I realize that Geoff's sisters and cousins make up my ladies-in-waiting and that I barely know any of them but what I do know is that my friends wouldn't be comfortable in these surroundings. I've been with Geoff for nearly two years and still have a hard time remembering which fork to use when. And I know Charlene and Rox hate that stuff. They'd just see it as pretentious.

Johnny comes back in with two more beers. One of which has lost a third of its contents somehow between the downstairs kitchen and my princess-themed bedroom.

"Way to reinforce a stereotype, bro."

"Angh, they don't need to see me drunk to think I'm just a drunken Indian anyway."

"Well, you are drunk, and you are Indian." I smile and so does he. I don't hate Johnny.

"How many Indians are coming to your wedding?"

I want to go into the spiel: our parents are dead, like drunk-dead (or dead-drunk), and we grew up in the system and we don't have much family and those we have we never really knew. Instead I say nothing.

Johnny finishes his beer and with a simple look asks me if I want my other one. I just roll my eyes and he takes that as a no.

"You know, being rich and white isn't a crime," I say.

"He didn't want me in the wedding party, Krista Lee Pangman," Johnny says. "He asked me to be on my best behaviour. Like I wasn't housetrained yet."

"He just didn't want you to puke on him again, jeet," I say.

"Holeh . . . JEET? Haven't heard that in a long time."

"Well if you're going to be an Indian snob, I thought I'd call you an asshole in our language."

Johnny steps through the French doors and stands on the balcony. "Got any smokes?"

I pull my smokes out from under a pillow and toss them out at him. "Next you'll be asking me for spare change, boi."

"Apple."

Johnny stares at the woods behind the estate. I stare at Johnny's back and watch him light the smoke I need so badly, despite the fact that I'm trying to quit. In looking at him, doing something I really want to do but shouldn't, I somehow realize he can't even call me an Apple.

"We're not even all Red. We're kinda white, even."

"Not even," Johnny laughs. He looks for a butt can and doesn't find one so grinds his half-done smoke against the balcony and tosses the butt over the side.

"Hey sis!" he says, not realizing I'm standing right behind him.

"Ya?"

He points with his lips toward the forest.

"Some good hunting in there, I bet," he says.

"Ya, Geoff and few of the guys are going on Sunday afternoon."

"Eh?"

"Quail."

"Pfft . . . moose, that's what they should look for!"

"You never shot a moose in your life!"

We laugh together and he puts his arm around me. I know he's just worried. And I'm not sure how to convince him not to be.

Geoff and I met in a writing workshop. He was facilitating and I was hanging on every word. He loves my work and he loves where I come from. And I guess he loves me, by default.

"I worried too, you know," I say to Johnny. "At first."

"Huh?"

"I didn't trust it, either."

"Ya," Johnny laughs a soft, sad laugh. "Some of my best friends are white."

I pull out of Johnny's lazy embrace and head back inside. Johnny follows me but heads for the bathroom off the bedroom.

I sit down on the bed and pick up the phone on the end table. It rings barely one full ring when Charlene answers.

"Hey," I say.

"Krista!" she shrieks.

"I know it's short notice but—"

She lets me off the hook. "No, Krista, I told you, it's okay. And Rox really can't stand that kind of thing. We'll celebrate in our own way when you get back to the city."

"I love you guys." I can barely talk.

"Take lotsa pictures, girl."

I hold the phone against my ear for a long time after the click. Then Johnny comes out of the bathroom. Checking himself out in the cheval mirror again, he smooths down his shirt.

"Who's walking you down the aisle?" He asks.

"You?"

Johnny picks up his beer bottle and walks back into the bathroom and I hear the toilet flush. When he comes back the bottle is empty.

He sits down beside me on the bed.

"You think these dudes got anything that'll fit me?"

"Karver will be so disappointed," I laugh.

I love Johnny.

/ TO MAKE A CHARM AGAINST LOVE

/ BY ARIEL **GORDON**

Sit up in a bed of clover that has already
been laid flat by the blankets of lovers
and stood up again
only to have every sepal
stuffed full by bees
pick as many flowers as you have had thoughts
of him today pick too many intend
to let them wither
where they fall

As the sun lips your forehead
the tip of your nose your chin pick blooms
so overblown
so spiky they look as though
they've just woken
snap this thought off at its root
split the stems with the thumb
you used to pick at the paint on the table
of the restaurant where he left you
and you never looked
into his eyes

You will know you are finished
because you will have split a stem so far
you don't know if it will hold
and the wreath is as long as short
as a held breath
push the first flower through the hole
as gently as the last time
you watched him dress and plumes of hair
the top of his head
pulled through
the neck of his shirt

Wrap the wreath around your neck
one loop tight
prickly at your throat
the rest tickle-swaying over your breasts
and the nectar that wafts up to you all day
is the smell
of your love dying

/ COUNTING WHALES

/ BY BRENDA **HASIUK**

Their first conversation was unmemorable.

Clay was doing the crossword halfheartedly behind the desk, not expecting any visitors yet. His pencil was a little sticky with lemon Danish and he was just about to lick it clean when she appeared, luggage in tow.

He watched her struggle to roll the suitcase over the stubby lip of the doorframe. This one had the distinctive gait of the overnight traveller. Usually they'd settle in a little, get their bearings, before coming to pick up their brochures and paw the artifacts. He'd seen it a thousand times before. Here, at the end of the line, they would haul their baggage down from the train and sleepily survey the scene in the morning light, as awkward and self-conscious as astronauts in space suits.

He knew this one was here for the whales; the polar bears were only secondary. The middle-aged ladies always came in August for the whales, packing expensive zoom lenses and taking home endless rolls of film filled with hazy white blurs streaking through blank water.

He hadn't even finished his coffee, still hadn't come up with a six-letter word for *perfume* beginning with "t." "You just arriving?" he asked.

"Yes," she said, still struggling. "Just arrived." When she finally managed to park the suitcase in front of her, it fell forward with a bang.

"It always does that," she said.

Clay swung his boots down off the desk, but made no move to get up. "You got a reservation somewhere?"

The bottom of her suitcase was now covered in a putrid yellow dust from the gravel road. "The Aurora Inn," she said.

He nodded knowingly. "You go back about two hundred metres to the Legion. That's the blue building. Walk back through the parking lot and you'll come up on the back of the Aurora."

Clay turned back to his paper. Almost all the little squares were still blank. Who was he kidding, trying to do the crossword?

"The blue Legion," she said. "Righto."

He looked up and smiled his best, welcoming smile. "You should come back this afternoon. We got a documentary on the belugas playing. They used special underwater cameras that don't freeze up."

327

Before she could reply, he grabbed some keys hanging off a nail. As he disappeared into the back office, he felt a small twinge of professional guilt for not rushing to rescue her downed luggage. Only later would he learn that he could've pushed the thing over himself then walked away, and she still would've come back for more.

Because of the permafrost, the passenger train between the nickel mining hub of Thompson and the arctic port of Churchill offers the only land route, inching along at maybe thirty kilometres or twenty-four miles per hour. This far north, as Marie was to learn, the ground snubs its frigid nose at any kind of human tampering, meaning the telephone wires running alongside the tracks stretch not from sturdy pole to sturdy pole but from fragile tripod to fragile tripod, and the tracks themselves rest only gingerly atop the frozen earth.

It was a few hours into her journey, not long before dark, when the gentle swaying had begun. Already hundreds—or what seemed like hundreds—of Indians who'd poured down the aisles at boarding time, trading coach class seats like they owned them, had poured off again at a place called Gillam. Once, after she'd failed to read the parking meter correctly and her car was towed, Marie had taken a bus in downtown Chicago and the blacks on board had acted much the same way—the smirking, restless young boys swaggering up and down the aisle with their caps turned backwards, the adults chattering loudly across the seats after a long day, passing around bags of food. If Marie had been a chronic thinker, the kind of person who feels the need to string experiences together and draw conclusions, she might have made the connection between the Churchill train and the Chicago bus and wondered what it meant. But as it was, she'd only felt the same things—admiring, envious, excluded. She'd simply watched the Indians noisily filing past on their way out, jostling the remaining tourists with their shopping bags, descending onto the clapboard platform and dissolving into the dusky boreal forest with their bulk packs of toilet paper and new sneakers.

After that, there'd only been tourists left: a few young families playing cards or bickering amongst themselves and a dozing retired couple who'd recently driven the Alaskan highway. At the train station, the couple, Alf and Lydia, had taken Marie under their wing, offering her oversized chocolate bars and bruised apples. They were from California, and reminded Marie of her parents, if her parents had been suntanned and adventurous. "As a single woman, you should've got a sleeper," Alf said. "Hell, we should've got one. We just came through Saskatchewan and they were everywhere, lots of them dead drunk in the street."

She'd lost them in the melee of boarding, though, and was sitting alone when the swaying had begun. In the jarring quiet that followed the Indians' disappearing act, it was almost imperceptible, but there all the same, like the teetering of a still motor boat on glassy water. It was enough to make her regret the chocolate.

"I got a daughter who vomits from walking too fast," her father had said more than once. It could come off as an affectionate jibe or hurtful dig depending on whom he said it to and how he said it.

Eventually, the only way Marie had managed to fall asleep on the dark, swaying train was by emptying out her knapsack and telling herself it would be there just in case. When she woke, the sun was nearly up and a little girl was screaming at her brother to get his feet out of her face.

Marie had turned groggily to the window, squinting into the weak, bluish dawn, and the view hit her like a bucket of water. It was as if the dense, imposing trees had been swallowed up, leaving only a few dwarfish and decrepit versions of their former selves. She'd somehow envisioned snow even though the travel agent had said the temperature highs would range between fifty and seventy degrees this time of year. The agent hadn't told her that it would look like the moon, if the moon had the odd swamp, giant puddles sitting amidst a barren, rocky expanse.

By the time they arrived at the end of the line, her queasiness had turned to all-out nausea.

Lydia had appeared from nowhere and squeezed her arm. "You okay, sweetie?"

Alf winked at her. "I hope they got a decent sandwich up here. The porter sold me a ham on rye last night that tasted like sawdust."

He'd taken her bag and she'd let them help her off. She'd fought back tears, and refused to think of home now that she'd come so far.

She told them she was fine, that she'd see them on the tour boat tomorrow, and had started dragging her new suitcase over the gravel. Marie hadn't expected that a train could make you seasick, or that the trees would disappear in the middle of the night, or that there would be more than one hotel. And what little she'd imagined of the place called Churchill, permanent population 800, had involved mountains and icebergs and reindeer. But she refused to be disappointed by the messy collection of industrial-looking warehouses and towering, rusted cranes of the distant port, by the town's haphazard rows of low, prefabricated buildings—prefab churches, prefab motels, prefab jewellery stores. At the windswept tail of Hudson Bay where few living things dared grow or tread, Marie—executive assistant, suburban girl, co-owner of a time-share condo in Florida, passionate doll collector—had soldiered on.

She'd followed the friendly, bear-shaped signs, their noses pointing the way further and further from the station until she'd reached a structure that was somewhere between a strip mall and a trailer. She'd smiled at the familiar sight of a video store here on the moon. When she'd spotted the ranger in the museum next door, she'd told herself you can always count on a man in uniform to be helpful.

And sure enough, by midmorning, Marie was like her old self again. She found the Aurora easily and liked it at once. It was built like a flower-shaped mobile home, with the rooms extending like petals off a compact lobby complete with a bowl of pepper-mints and a wall of brochures at reception. In her room, she lined up her toiletries along the worn, spotless sink. She explored the surprising array of cable television channels at her fingertips. She ate the remaining snacks she'd bought at the grocery store back in Thompson—a banana, twelve low-fat crackers and a vanilla pudding.

In the afternoon, she headed back to the museum and waited a good hour for the movie to start. There were only three of them in the tiny theatre: Marie and two young Japanese boys solemnly eating french fries in the front row. She waited patiently, listening to the boys' soft, foreign mumblings until the lights finally dimmed.

There in the dark she remembered the piercing call of the killer whale in Florida, the one who'd flipped over so she could scratch its massive, slippery belly. She remembered why she was here as the movie started, and it was just like the ranger had promised. It was as if she was swimming right there with them in their natural habitat, gracefully flashing through the icy waters as swift as the minnows she'd swept up in a pail when she was little.

The belugas are smaller and sweeter than the killers, she thought happily, white as Persian cats, and tomorrow she would touch these, too.

Although he didn't believe in such things, Clay would come to see their next meeting as some kind of trajectory of fate. Janie, his wife, had just left for the city that afternoon, taking both kids with her.

For weeks, he'd been anticipating the quiet, telling himself it was just what he needed: a house without the twins needling each other until someone screamed, without Janie's relentless sighs. But Clay had always thought of himself as a family man. When he walked in the door after his shift, the relative quiet seemed to taunt him.

The fridge whined. The motor of a boat roared off in the distance. A dirt bike puttered to a stop somewhere close. Clay threw his work shirt on the bedroom floor, something that always got Janie sighing, and told himself it wasn't too early to get a drink.

He walked across the road to The Good Earth. He was just finishing his third egg roll and second beer when Marie appeared.

"That's a nice little theatre you have there," she said.

He stared, uncomprehending.

"This morning," she said. "You told me about the movie, about the belugas."

Clay remembered. She was the early one with the downed suitcase who'd looked as if she might cry. She looked about the same age as his third-oldest sister, maybe a little younger. But this one carried her fat just like the oldest, all upper body, like her neck was trying to eat her chin. "Right," he said. "The Aurora. You picked a nice place."

Marie nodded happily, as if he'd just told her she had a nice smile. "That underwater footage was something else."

"I thought you'd like that," he said.

She'd obviously come in with an old couple who were smiling amiably in their old people tourist uniforms: matching pale yellow windbreakers with a peach stripe across the chest. Definitely American, Clay thought, the three of them. They travel in packs.

Alf crossed his arms with a swipe of the windbreaker and looked around purposefully. "They got good food? We counted maybe five or six restaurants, but some of them are pretty pricey."

"It's the shipping," Clay said. "Costs a lot to get stuff up here."

Alf clicked his tongue as if duly satisfied. "I'd expect," he said. "I'd expect."

Lydia squeezed Marie's arm. "We'll get a table, sweetie."

It was still too early for any regulars yet and Clay didn't feel like being alone.

Sometimes when he needed a pick-me-up, he would spend some time with the tourists, invite them over for a beer, entertain their questions, wow them with exotic tales of a life in the isolated North.

"You think they like you or something?" Janie would ask. "They just want to check out the weirdos, look at the freaks who live in the middle of nowhere." But he would shrug her off, tell himself it must be her time of the month and it would pass.

"You going out to see them in person tomorrow?" he asked Marie.

It wasn't like Marie to let herself get this hungry, and the smell of wonton soup left her lightheaded. After the film had ended, the ranger on duty behind the desk, a pretty young thing with pimply skin and naturally blond hair, recommended the Chinese place for mid-priced dinners and happy hour cocktails. When she was halfway there, Alf and Lydia had emerged from a prefab souvenir shop specializing in fox hats. They told her no one should have to dine alone and then dawdled as if they'd just eaten.

My daughter faints if you look at her funny, her father had said more than once.

"Tomorrow morning," she said to Clay. "The girl there, she said you can get right up close in the rubber dinghies."

"Sandy," he said.

Marie looked confused.

"The girl there, on duty," Clay said.

Marie blinked self-consciously, laughing at herself like she should've known better. "Sandy, yes. She told me that. She said she goes out there on the tundra."

She noticed for the first time that the young ranger's eyes were a dark chocolate brown. "Is that what you call it?"

Clay drained the last of his second bottle. "The tundra, yeah."

"She said she goes out there with a tranquillizer," Marie said, "and they shoot the bears who come in too close to town and put them in the polar bear jail. You wouldn't think it to look at her."

Clay smiled and shook his head. "No, that's for sure."

"I'm going on the tundra tour after lunch," she said. His eyes, she decided, were as brown as a springer spaniel's. "There's so many great things to do in just a couple of days."

Clay picked up a bottle cap and examined it as if it were a jewel. "Yeah, it's quite a place."

Marie glanced over at Alf and Lydia. Alf seemed to be frowning over his menu. "Have you always lived here?" she asked.

"All my life," Clay said. He leaned back in his chair and crossed his arms like a schoolboy in the back row of class. "Most of my family still does. Two sisters and a brother work at the hospital, one brother owns the shoe repair, one sister's a clerk at the grocery. My brother probably trapped some of that fur there your friends bought. In winter, I take a leave and go out on the line with him."

331

Marie wondered just how big his family could be. "That must be something," she said, "living off the land. But it must get so cold."

Clay shrugged and leaned back a little further. "Yeah," he said. "I'm going to write a book about the trapping life, about what it's really like."

"That's great," she said. "That's really great." Now she could honestly tell all the doubters back home: everything was nice, everyone was nice, you'd be surprised.

One of the regulars came through the door. Clay had known him for a few years, a refugee from the Balkan wars who'd come up north to find work and lick his wounds.

"Yeah, well, you say hello to the whales for me," he said.

He threw a tip down on the soggy paper placemat, more generous than Janie would've liked, and left Marie there, swooning with hunger amidst the heady smells of batter-fried shrimp.

Six beers and three gruesome battle stories later, Clay collapsed on his couch at home for the night. The kitchen clock ticked relentlessly and he thought about how it always got boring when the Americans started saying everything was great. About young Sandy, who could've been Janie's little sister, or Janie ten years and a hundred pounds ago. About how Janie was right, he was such a liar, from start to finish.

One of his sisters had worked for a while at the Aurora and said one of the house-keepers would sometimes just shake out the sheets and then remake the bed.

The next time they met, something had changed in both of them, something almost imperceptible to even the trained eye. Within twenty-five hours they would both be back, him downing his eighth with two local bush pilots in the lounge, her coming towards them like they were long-lost friends. When the pilots raised their eyebrows to mock him, Clay quickly realized he didn't care and felt suddenly, terrifyingly free.

"You must've had yourself a full day there," he said, waving his finger at her like she'd been bad. "You just eating now? What time is it? It's past nine."

Marie's self-consciousness of the night before was held at bay by the presence of the pilots. She was rarely shy except when she decided someone was attractive, and then it was as if they suddenly spoke some foreign language she couldn't quite follow. Even with naturally blond Sandy, she'd found herself strangely tongue-tied. But both pilots had a substantial belly hanging over their belts, and the one with the hair was in obvious need of a shower.

"I went to the log cabin place," she said, "the one with the bears carved into the tree. I had Arctic char."

"Not bad," Clay said. "Us locals can't afford The Log Cabin. You like the char?"

"It was great," she said. "Not too strong. I don't like it when it's too fishy."

One of the pilots pushed a stool towards her and clapped Clay on the shoulder. "Knock yourself out," he said. "We're playing darts."

Quick looks were exchanged that Marie had no time to comprehend. She stared down at the empty seat. Normally, she was an early riser, in bed by ten-thirty, but some-where along the way to her channel-filled room at The Aurora she'd changed direction in the falling dusk. She'd followed the setting sun, the towering, rusty cranes of the port silhouetted amidst brilliant oranges and pinks, passing packs of children on motorbikes who would never have been allowed to do such a thing in the city.

"You get your fill of belugas?" he asked.

His mouth turned up at the sides, she noticed, boyish and inviting without even trying. "No way," she said. "Oh no."

There was no way she could begin to tell him about the blur of exhilaration that had been her day. About how she'd first gone out on the big boat with the rich French family that had flown in on a small jet, the Japanese man who'd watched it all through the lens of his video camera just like she'd always heard they did, the teacher from the Canadian Arctic who'd sat in shirtsleeves and declared it balmy in the bitter winds, about how they'd all jostled en masse from one side of the deck to another to catch a glimpse of the graceful beings sailing by in whole families of big and little, dozens and dozens of them coming by to say hello then disappearing into the depths before a camera shutter could open and close. Or about how she'd been one of the few who'd paid twice as much to head out in the four-man dinghy, where they'd come right up, curious and chirping, and she'd looked right into their gentle eyes.

Marie caught the elbow of a passing waitress and asked for a glass of white wine.

How could she begin to explain it? She'd never been able to explain when people in the office teased her about her collection. Or when her father asked her what kind of man would want to come over to a whole room filled with dolls. For what was there to say? That she loved to hold each new one in her hands, stroke its tiny features, note its special character, add it to the growing splendour of purple organza and red pouting lips? That as a chubby child she'd loved to swim, had floated on her back in pure bliss as her cousins screamed and screeched all around and for a moment, and in the dinghy today, she'd wanted to dive in and lose herself in the company of such lovely swirling creatures? That when it came to things so pretty, so cute, so perfect, what wasn't there to love?

After her mother left her a modest inheritance, Marie had thought of building a wall-length cabinet in the doll room, but her father had talked her into remodelling the bathroom instead. What do you want to go all the way up there for? he'd asked after she booked the trip. Where do you get such ideas?

Though they were so close, Marie knew he often felt he didn't understand her, that he was forever saving her from herself.

Now, she sat down on the empty stool beside the friendly ranger and hugged her purse to her chest. "I touched a baby one," she said. "I stroked his little nose."

Clay opened his ninth, the twist-top releasing with a hiss, and let the foam settle.

"They're just big fish, you know."

"No, they're mammals," she said quickly. "Just like us."

"Yeah," he said, taking a long drink and wiping his mouth with the back of his hand. Janie had come to call such gestures his rugged outdoorsman act. "But you know what I mean, they might as well be fish."

Marie shrugged. "I just think they're amazing," she said.

Clay grinned and settled back in his chair, starting to feel a good buzz, his eyelids getting that droop Janie had once thought was sexy. When the waitress put the wine on the table, he watched Marie automatically begin to fumble through her purse. Terminally single, he thought. She was wearing walking shorts, the after-forty kind, but her legs were good.

"Where you from?" he asked. "You live in the city?"

Hugging her purse again, she left the wine where it was. "The Midwest," she said. "Just outside Chicago."

Clay whistled. "Chicago. That's a big one. You got the, what do you call it, you got the Million Dollar Mile, you got the rat race."

Marie took a sip of wine and put it back on the table. She hadn't been downtown since a date eleven months ago that had ended badly. "Yeah, we got Millionaire's Mile, we got great museums, we got comedy clubs, we got it all."

Clay was ready to scoff out loud, until it hit him she was sincere. It never in a million years would've occurred to her to mention the gang fights you heard about on the news, little kids being gunned down on their front steps.

He drained his beer and leaned forward across the table, poked her forearm with his finger. "You married? You got kids?"

Marie shook her head. What was there to explain? That she was forty-six years old and her father remained too protective or too controlling, depending on what he was talking about and how he said it? That her date had ordered expensive wine for dinner and alcohol didn't sit well with her? That the complexities of romance had eluded her for no reason she could think of, through no fault of her own?

"My wife, she wants to live in the city," he said. "She hates it here, says she can't breathe, that it's driving her crazy. What does she mean by that? There's nothing but fucking air up here."

His cursing came as a surprise to Marie. She still saw him as the nice young man in uniform. "I think maybe you should go home," she said.

"No, you don't understand," he said. "She's not there, not until next week. See, she grew up in an armpit of a town, nothing there but the jail, but at least this place has character. It's the world-class boonies. I'm writing a book about it, have to start looking for a publisher. She said herself it would make a good movie."

"You should go home," Marie said again. She was quite uncomfortable now, more than was reasonable. She didn't want to hear these things, didn't want to think about what it must be like to live permanently in such isolation, to never go home again.

That afternoon, still flying from the whales and impatient for the tundra tour to begin, she'd wandered past the train tracks, towards a haphazard row of wooden shacks, drawn by something large and red sitting amongst the tall grasses that stretched down to a rocky beach dotted with rotting fishing boats. It was some kind of wooden sled, the kind you might pull with a dog team. As soon as she was close enough, she'd reached out and stroked its peeling paint with a kind of reverence, imagining igloos in winter and round-faced, apple-cheeked children playfully wrestling in their fur coats, until someone had shouted at her, and she'd looked up to see two old Indian women off in the distance, hands on hips, laughing. And though she couldn't make out what they'd said, Marie was sure it had been something rude.

Afterwards, she'd pushed the incident from her mind, spent the afternoon laughing with Alf and Lydia about the utter strangeness of it all—Ranger Sandy looking like a Barbie doll when she stood beside one of the massive rubber wheels of the tour vehicle, the three of them, veteran subway riders, rolling high above the vast nothingness. She'd oohed and aahed with the rest at the sight of a tiny Arctic fox racing prancing across the vast, barren expanse, a pair of caribou bent low to the yellowy lichen as if weighed down by their ridiculously large antlers, even a darling bear cub ambling over the rolling, humpbacked rocks along the coast, looking for its mama. Yet that feeling beside the sled had remained stubbornly lodged somewhere, as if the sun-forsaken landscape would not be denied its date with sunny Marie. Somewhere, the old women with their brightly coloured kerchiefs and wrinkled coffee cheeks remained, laughing and hurtful.

Now, Clay grabbed her forearm, stroking its soft hairlessness, prepared to act more plastered than he really was. "Will you come with me?"

"Don't be silly," Marie said. "I don't even know your name."

"Sure you do," he said. "It's Clay. I'll make you some coffee. I don't bite."

Marie shook her head, but made no move to go. She inexplicably left her arm where it was, remained with this sad, drunk man, just as she'd turned her back on her cozy little room at The Aurora, just as she'd ordered a glass of wine that would make her sick.

"What's your name?" he asked her. He brushed her skin with his thumb, once, twice, three times. "Come on. A cup of coffee."

"Marie," she said.

As soon as they were through the door, he would ease her against the wall in the dark landing, and she would let him. He'd notice her tongue tasted like peppermint, whereas Janie was always fruity. He'd tell himself that this was better, that a cheerful chubby American with good legs was no worse than what he'd been doing, searching the Internet by himself for blondes with small breasts.

Blind and unbelieving, she would let him lead her through the dark to the bedroom, grateful she couldn't see what kind of bedspread the wife had chosen. She'd let him fumble with her clothes, as if her not helping made it okay, close her eyes as he backed away to take off his pants, aware that the warm body before her was just the kind women were supposed to like—broad-shouldered and thin-waisted with the hint of a paunch to make him real, to make him theirs.

Eight minutes would be all it took. The fierce plying and grunting that everyone made such a fuss over, pages and pages of magazine articles, endless numbers of jokes, would run itself out and all that was left would be the two of them breathing side by side in the dark. Less time than it took to boil an egg, she'd think, not unhappily, gazing into the harsh red numbers of the clock radio on the nightstand.

Fifteen minutes later, he would begin to snore, and then almost instantly, with the heady, dangerous freedom born of all reckless acts, Marie would let herself begin to daydream. She would dream of wintering with him along the trapline. Of putting her accounting skills to good use as she tallied the catch and sale of skins beside an oil lamp. Of miraculously having babies at her age that she would carry around on her sturdy back.

The next morning, he would wake to find her watching him, the same guileless, chin-less face as the night before, and would reach for her again out of the aimless desire of the morning. But she would roll away in the weak dawn light, suddenly conscious of the wife's presence in every picture frame and dried-flower arrangement.

So he would shower, and dress, and leave for his shift, as if his plan for dealing with a strange woman in their bed was to go about business as usual. But she would be there when he got back, with supper made in another woman's kitchen.

"I made linguini," she'd say matter-of-factly, as if pretending to be living a life more real than her own. Then he would wonder if he was just hungry, or if it was the best pasta he'd ever tasted. He'd watch her hum tunelessly as she tidied up, her round cheeks flushed red from the stove.

"Stay for awhile," he'd say, pretending for just a moment that he was a kind and charitable man, not a weak man, pretending that he and Janie were a lost cause, that she had given up on him a long time ago because the truth was she was nothing like pretty young Sandy, who was so at ease with herself. Janie was smarter, more intense, too good to be frozen away from the world, eating away her boredom, blaming him for not wanting her anymore, for adoring her too much.

The next day, Marie would check out of the Aurora, and Clay would pretend that he'd never uttered the words *in sickness and in health*, had never heard the word *depression*.

She'd wheel her luggage up his driveway as he stood in the doorway, ready to wave innocently at the neighbours. My mom's second cousin, he'd repeat to himself. Up from the States.

The next morning, Marie would venture out to pick up groceries and bump into Alf and Lydia buying water for the train trip out. You're staying? they'd exclaim. What on earth for? And she would assure them that she was fine, touched by their kindness, their abiding, unalterable concern for one of their own. I just want a little more time, she'd say.

She wouldn't let herself see him naked again, and he would accept what she had to offer. She would cook for him like a doting mother, feeling like a real grown-up for the first time, and he would let her. He would let her proudly show him the doll website and the mockery would die on his lips. She is utterly un-mockable, he'd think, what you see is what you get, and he would tell her things without fear.

I've been out trapping with my brother three times, he'd tell her, just for the weekend, but one day it's going to be a side business, when the twins are older. I can't describe what it's like out there, just man against the elements.

I have only one line, he'd tell her, one fucking line about the aurora borealis and then I'm stuck.

Tell me, she'd say.

It's a place so cold the night sky dances to keep warm, he'd mutter, and she would tell him that this was lovely, that he was lovely, even though she couldn't really imagine such a phenomenon, had only seen pictures that could never quite capture it.

On the fifth day, his morning off, Clay took Marie to see the new upscale hotel going up along the coast. She had been by here once before, on her first day, but had barely noticed the construction site fifty yards out. Instead, she'd been riveted by the sight of mottled sled dogs standing there suckling their pups up on the rocks. Their back haunches were bigger than Easter hams, she'd thought, and they were all in a row in front of their neat little shacks like housewives in an English soap opera. It had been overcast then, the sky and the tide-worn rocks and the Arctic waters all variations on the same muted, bluish grey.

But it was sunny now, almost warm enough to be a real summer morning. They were alone, except for a group of mortar-stained Indian boys huddled together over an empty mixing drum at the side of the road. Slightly bloated after a late breakfast of fried eggs and homemade hash browns, her shirt already damp with sweat, Marie didn't even mind that they couldn't walk arm-in-arm.

As they passed, one of the boys straightened up and grinned at them. She noticed his teeth were crooked but gleamed bright white against his dark skin. "You want to see something funny?" he asked.

Clay ignored him. "The developer's blowing his load on this one," he said to her quietly. "A hundred and fifty rooms and the whole thing is going to be stonework, rocks direct from the beach here."

Marie shaded her eyes with her free hand and dutifully studied the half-finished building, large and lonely in the distance. The bitches were lazing scattered across the rocks now while the gulls circled and screeched overhead. The pups were nowhere to be seen. "The view will be amazing," she said.

She wanted to say something else, something interesting, something to let him know how happy she was, but the boy was shouting again.

"Hey, really, she's going to want to see this. Lady, you want to see something funny?"

Clay shook his head, but Marie turned and squinted. She wanted everyone to know how happy she was. "Sure," she said. "Bring it on."

Then one of the boys flung some kind of weighted rope into the air and a noisy, violent commotion instantly broke out against the blue sky. Two gulls grabbed onto either end of the rope, battling for the raw meat that had been carefully knotted in place, and the boys cheered for blood as the baffled birds charged and squealed, refusing to concede such prime booty, as if prepared to be confused to the death.

Marie stood mesmerized, unable to look away, while Clay imagined taking a rock and bashing in heads—anything to silence the vacant, bravado-filled shouts he knew all too well. Anything to keep such unpleasant intruders at bay.

The night before he'd dreamed of belugas, swimming by in orderly pairs like he was counting sheep. At first it had been restful, until he'd realized he was underwater and couldn't hold his breath like the peacefully gloating mammals. That's when he'd found himself out on the ice alone, his brother, his wife, his twins nowhere in sight, until Marie had woken him.

"You were all twitchy," she'd said. But when he'd automatically apologized for disturbing her, she'd said don't be silly, don't be sorry, it was just a dream, and for the first time he'd understood the real toll of Janie's sadness, catching them up and pulling them both down, down, down in its lonely, seductive eddy.

Now, he just wanted the boys' shouting to stop. He wanted to draw Marie to him and cover her eyes, to tell her that the kids were idiots, that the rope would break any minute, that everything was okay, it was only a dream.

Yet he knew, as soon as he tried to lead her away, felt her chubby elbow stiffen with distress, that it was too late. She wouldn't even look at him, refused to let him touch her, as if this might only make it worse.

That night, the train's subtle swaying kept Marie up again and she was thankful for the Japanese man across the aisle, the one from the boat who'd obligingly lived up to her stereotype of Asians. He'd gone out on the tundra tour five days in a row until he'd finally managed to videotape a polar bear wading through a shallow pond, sitting and splashing like an infant to cool itself. He played it for her in the camera's little viewfinder and they shook their heads at the wonder of it. The guide had told him it was pretty rare to get such a good sighting in August, but you just never knew up here.

They didn't talk about anything important, like the terrible thing she'd done to another woman, fat but beautiful in every frame. Like how she'd refused to even rest her eyes on any images of adorable twin children, like how she could not explain, not to her waiting father, not to her dead mother, not to herself, why she'd let it happen. They didn't talk about how she'd known in her gut where the white-toothed boy and his friends lived, the ones who'd stirred the mortar and tricked the gulls—they lived in those shacks behind the tracks that she'd seen with her own eyes. They belonged to that place of abandoned sleds in cheerful colours, a place more brutal and beautiful than she'd ever imagined, or ever wanted to, where laughing old women stand in the middle of nowhere and taunt you with their bitter wisdom.

That long night on the train, such things remained tucked away with the pale yellow piece of paper in her shirt pocket. Just before she'd left, Clay had written his email address in black fine point, then folded the paper in quarters and slipped it in there himself. But hours had passed, and still she couldn't bring herself to touch it. It seemed too light, somehow, almost weightless, taking up so little space for such a great, hopeless passion.

As dawn broke, the residents of Gillam piled on in the struggling half-light. Already pumped for their day's errands, they didn't bother to whisper amongst the sleeping passengers and this annoyed Marie more than was reasonable. It was upwards of twenty minutes before she managed to will away the stubborn voices and calm herself.

She told herself she would soon be home, only ten hours from her new bathroom with its shiny fixtures and built-in soap caddy. The bathtub had been months on order and when it finally arrived, had been a real pain to install.

The least she could do was enjoy it.

/ IN A TIME OF DROUGHT AND HUNGER

/ BY GERARD **BEIRNE**

Tom has seen it all before. The northern lights wavering through the winter sky, the river ice shearing and cracking with a boom, the intense magenta sunrise reflecting on the ice and soaking through the sky. *This is not it.* This is not what he feels on these nights or mornings. He has heard the crash of the branches as a grey owl breaks loose of its perch. He has, for heaven's sake, lain out on the ice at night on the flat of his back and listened to the hollow thumping of the water below booming like the combined heartbeat of the dead. No, this is not it, either. It is certainly not this. What is it then? What else can it be if it is not the moose Tom has tracked and shot with as steady an aim as is humanly possible, or the brittle frazil ice that melts and shatters between his fingers, or the soft hide moccasins his wife glides through their lifetime in? If it is not this, Tom wonders, what else? *What else can it possibly be?*

Clara, Tom's wife, lies in their enamel bath. The bath is about twelve inches too long for her, and in an unrealistic way she resents it for this. How can this be? she asks herself as she lifts her body for the umpteenth time seeking a more comfortable posture. How could anyone relate emotionally to an inanimate object in such a way? To be stirred to anger is one thing but to actually resent a sheet of pressed metal? No, she thinks, that is impossible. And yet here she is soaping her stretchmarked stomach, feeling resentful. She listens to the cassette player through the open door. The barely audible voice of Patsy Cline as she sings of a lover who has leaving on his mind . . . Clara shifts her neck on the back of the tub. She always has leaving on her mind, she thinks, everyone must have. What other way could it be? Leaving Tom, leaving here, leaving the bath, leaving herself. Sometimes she would like that, leaving herself. Sometimes she almost does. She rises in the bath and looks down upon herself, Clara. She looks at her unkempt hair, her misshapen body. She considers her fruitless thoughts. Despite all of this she can never float away entirely. She remains there like air laden with moisture until her particles become too heavy for the updrafts surrounding her, until she can no longer be suspended, and then she falls, rains back down upon herself. Sometimes this is where Clara thinks she remains, not within herself but upon herself. Not a departure, just a shift in direction.

Clara hears the door bang shut with the wind. Tom is home, she thinks. He is shaking the snow off his boots in the hallway. He is pulling his woolen hat from his head. He is folding his gloves inside of it, and he is coming in.

Tom walks slowly up the hallway. He pushes in the bathroom door. Clara thinks he looks hesitant. He nods at her as though a question has been answered for him. Not who was in the bathroom surely, Clara wonders, and yet, what else? Tom looks like he is going to say something, and Clara waits for him to say it. But then he seems to give up as though he can not find the words or has lost his train of thought. The steam that has fogged over the mirror and moistened the lemon gloss paint on the walls adheres to his brow like perspiration. Clara is forty-one years old. She still loves Tom, but sometimes she thinks he is like the bath. He is too big for her. She does not fit comfortably within him. She feels she has to keep stretching herself, shifting up or down for ease. But even in those moments of ease she knows that further discomfort is certain to follow. And at those times she resents him. Him, Tom. Not a pressed sheet of metal but a human being, her husband. This is their life, then, she reminds herself. Does she not think Tom knows this too?

Once Tom carried a young deer into their kitchen strung across his neck and shoulders. Dead. A stain of blood like red wine, something hard to remove. He shot it right outside their backdoor. It simply wandered into sight from the clump of white spruce and he, as a matter of fortune, had his rifle handy. There was no chase, no sense of predator and prey. It was more a testing of reflexes. Nothing swift, mind. Slow, patient reflexes, a hesitant look, but a bullet pumping into a heart, nevertheless. He took it inside, bled it over the stainless steel sink, skinned it, cut it open and began its dissection. Clara was not at home. This was in the days when their two children still lived with them. If she had been home, this would not have occurred inside the house. But Tom either did not stop to think or arrived at vastly different conclusions to the decisions at hand. In either respect, when Clara arrived with Sean and Elsa, Tom was standing at the kitchen table holding a sharp knife in his right hand and a pulsing liver in his left. A blood stain ran across his right cheek from his ear to the top lip like a gash. This sight, coupled with the stench of death and butchery, stopped all three people in their tracks. And in that instant Tom recognized his wrongdoing. Not so much the mutilation within his home but the slow reflex action he should not have engaged in. He was not living in a time of hunger, he was not short of meat, he should have allowed the deer its escape.

Sean was sixteen then, Elsa fourteen. Now they were twenty and eighteen years old. To Tom and Clara they were uninhibited, promiscuous even. The stench, too, of that dissection within the home. But these are unspoken things. For now there is the stale smell of clammy air in a small bathroom from a hot bath. There is Tom's wife Clara, barely noticeably naked to Tom or herself, the lines indented on her flesh a quiet knowledge. There is Tom moving his hat and gloves from one hand to the next, a faint pang of soon to be satisfied hunger far off in his tensed stomach, moisture on his brow from water that flows outside their door along an array of Precambrian lakes and rivers into their home under pressure through copper pipes. Tom senses something but does not wipe his forehead. Clara's body feels to her, in this brief moment of extreme comfort, soft and pliable. They are looking at one another.

Is this it?

Clara wraps herself in a peach towelling robe, which she tightens around her midriff with its belt. She is thinking about nothing in particular. If Tom were to ask, which he wouldn't, what she was thinking about, Clara would say truthfully that she could not remember. For right now Clara is having thoughts, but she is not consciously aware of them. She watches herself in a mirror, but she does not see herself. She makes no effort to focus. Tom meanwhile moves around the kitchen, his open boot laces trailing the floor, laying tracks. He cuts thick slices of ham with a carving knife and places them between hunks of white bread spread with mustard. He is aware of Clara's presence within the house, but he is not thinking about her. Instead he thinks of a slushy track, muddied, littered with pine needles, leading through the trees. It is a track of his imagination. He has never walked upon it. He chews on the ham and bread, tastes the hot mustard on his tongue. He is ready on his feet. He breathes easily. This is his kitchen.

Clara comes in wearing her slip. She is relieved to find him eating. She walks over and smiles. She stands beside him, and Tom puts his arm around her waist. He rests his hand on her hip. She feels the pull towards him. This is good. This is where Tom and Clara are in this life of theirs. And theirs is not an unhappy life together. Neither Clara nor Tom thinks they have an exceptional life, but they are grateful for how it has turned out. And why not?

After Clara dresses and they have both eaten their fill, Tom tells her about the track. "Is it a dream?" Clara asks. They both sit at the pine kitchen table. Their empty food-soiled plates lie in front of them. "No," Tom says. "It is not a dream. At least not one of sleep. I just keep thinking about it." He shrugs. "A track," she repeats. She asks if it leads anywhere, and Tom smiles. "Is that not it?" he asks. Clara is not sure what he means, but does not inquire further. "Are you there?" she asks him. Tom shakes his head. "No one is there." He is almost whispering now. "It's just a track," his voice raised again. Clara does not know where to go with this. In time she will learn, but for now she can just observe and listen, take her cues from Tom. The importance of this track, this persistent thought, is unclear. Even Tom is unsure if it is relevant or not. "Oh," he says, pushing his plate into the middle of the table, "it is nothing probably." "I am forty-four," he says a moment later. "I know," Clara tells him in a sincere way. "That too is nothing," he says. But both Clara and Tom know this is not true. She has known Tom twenty-six years of these forty-four. The track and Tom's age are not unrelated. In a strange way Clara is well pleased. She is sniffing out the meaning. It is just possible she will get there before Tom.

Clara has never gone on a hunt with Tom. He has asked her many times, but Clara turns up her nose in semi-mock disgust. "Everyone should kill something," Tom tells her often. "No one should go through their life without killing something."

"I have killed insects," Clara once replied. Tom knows this. He wanted to say it is not the same, but he could not. It is not much different. "Well then," he said instead, "the next time think about what you have done." But what Tom really wants is for Clara to kill something large. Big enough so that she can witness the life being taken from it. "Maybe," she joked, "one day I'll kill you." She regretted having said it immediately. It did not sound as she had imagined it would. It was a terrible thing to say. She cried as she apologized. Tom drew her to him and told her he knew she was joking, told her he understood her intention. Clara ran her teeth over her bottom lip and held onto him.

Sean has been out with Tom a few times, but not Elsa. She too has turned down the offer. Sean, however, has never liked hunting. It is too hard for him physically. He does not get any enjoyment from it and has no need to hunt. He is well fed. A growing young man with a huge appetite. He has not hunted in over two years. He tells Tom the only prey he is interested in is the female of the species. And when he smiles as he says it, Tom does not know whether or not to laugh. He is confused by his son's response, by the seemingly abrupt shift in their relationship. For some moments his son has the upper hand. Tom feels at a loss. He does not want to hunt down a son he once had, and yet . . .

Tom suggests a walk. Clara nods her assent. They dress warmly in coats and gloves and hats. It is dusk when they step out the door. They see their breaths condense in front of them, chilled to saturation by the cold air, a suspension of tiny water droplets, clouds.

Tom and Clara have lived in the boreal forest for fourteen of their years together. If asked, they would say they could barely remember anything else. This is clearly not true, but this is how they feel. Tom came to Canada from Ireland as a young boy, ten years old. Clara from southern Alberta. They met as people do. And when Clara was offered a job up north teaching it was unanimous. And now all those years later they are walking arm in arm through the forest, muffled from the cold. This is quite an achievement. Tom has grown to love the forest almost as much as he loves Clara. This is a strange thing for Tom to think, but nevertheless he frequently does.

He thinks now of the forest ecosystem. Dependent on climate. Temperature-limited at its northern edge, moisture-limited at its southern boundary. He thinks of tree mortality by insects, diseases, storms. Natural factors. And he thinks of wildfires, the forest's driving successional force. He thinks of carbon. The forest a source and a sink for CO_2. He thinks of the carbon cycle. Of his life and his death. Is this not why he loves the forest as much as Clara. Is this not justification enough?

His arm interlocked with Clara's feels strange to Tom, as though it did not really belong to him, as though Clara's and his arms were something separate from them, appendages merely to hold them together. He inhales deeply and smells the lush aromas of spruce and pine. He looks down at his feet in the melting snow. Beneath these frozen water molecules he imagines the outcroppings of Precambrian Shield. The grey

343

igneous stratified rock, the orange, green, and pink mosses covering it. This region is gouged by glaciers.

Tom and Clara are frequently silent during their walks together, both lost in their own thoughts. But now Clara speaks, asks Tom if his track is similar to this one. Tom shakes his head, "No." But he does not know how to differentiate between them. Clara waits for more. She is certain more will come. This judgement she can make based on her intimate knowledge of Tom and his behaviour. A few strides later Tom comes to an abrupt halt. Clara is forced to a stop too by the pull of his arm. She turns towards him.

"There is something," Tom says. Clara waits patiently. Tom looks absent, his attention diverted inwards, and yet not totally distracted from Clara's presence. He wants to speak, to finish what he began, but instead his thoughts turn to droughts, the higher than normal seedling mortalities, the fire damage, the tent caterpillar and spruce budworm outbreaks.

What has this to do with it? What could this possibly have to do with it?

While she waits Clara thinks of Elsa. How she could not wait to leave. To put the forest far behind her. "There is no life for me up there," she used to say. No life, Clara thinks. Is that how you say it? And now she looks to Tom. A jack pine of a man. A man who could survive on his own. And yet, she wonders, could he?

Tom refocuses his attention and sees Clara watching him. He sees her wrapped against the weather. He is finding this difficult. He does not have the words to describe this "something" to himself, let alone his wife. "There is something," he repeats, "but I do not know what it is." He hesitates, feels foolish. Yet Tom should know he need not feel foolish in front of his wife. "It is just a feeling." He is still linked to her by their arms. He shifts his weight on his feet. "A different sort of feeling. As though something momentous has occurred, or is about to occur, or is already occurring. Perhaps even something which will ultimately turn out to be trivial." He stops. How could she possibly understand this?

But amazingly, Clara nods. "I understand," she says. And Tom knows she speaks the truth. Against all the odds she understands what he is telling her. He breathes in deeply the fresh chill air, the rich boreal odours. He listens for a sound and hears the clicking of a branch due north, the creaking compression of snow beneath Clara's boots due to the downward force of her body. Although nothing has been settled, Tom is relieved. He is grateful to have met this woman. His mate. To have married her. And he knows Clara has read and understood these thoughts, too. He feels her pull against his arm. It is time to walk further into the forest.

Tom will lie awake at night, and he will think about the forest. He will think in particular about one statistic, how even a warming of 1 degree Celsius could cause the forest to move northward. "How is such a thing possible?" Clara will ask and mean well in her asking it. Tom too wants to understand the reasons but unlike Clara, he has not a single shred of doubt about the possibility. Nothing about this forest will ever surprise Tom. Amaze him, yes. But never surprise. Tom knows some other facts. At night he will think about these, too. How the droughts of the 1980s were among the most severe in North America in the past 100 years, especially the drought of 1988; how rising air and lake temperatures and the lengthened ice-free season caused evapotranspiration to increase and runoff to decrease; how large areas of forest cover were lost to fire and consequently an increase in wind speed could be observed. Tom will think about all of this, but most predominantly he will think about the movement of the forest northward. In Tom's time, a time of global warming, this migration is an entirely reasonable possibility. Tom knows that the forest-grassland transition and the forest subregion are separated by only 2 degrees C in mean annual temperature. Thus an increase in temperature will result in increased evaporative demand, reduced soil moisture, and therefore more severe drought. The forest will die at the southern boundary but can now grow at the northern. Tom understandably will be immensely proud. And why ever not? A forest on the move.

But this is not it, either.

Imagine this if you might. Sean and Elsa standing by the back door of their house, the sun setting in the west, the sky a deepening orange and crimson glow spreading upwards, reflecting across the surface of the lake ice they cannot see because of the trees, the snow eight inches high where they are standing. Within two years both of them will be gone from here. They have this knowledge now and they are fuelled by it. Imagine too Tom and Clara indoors preparing an evening meal of moose stew, Tom energetically cutting through the raw flesh, Clara peeling potatoes. They too possess the knowledge of their children's impending departures. Much of their lives now revolves around this.

Ask yourself, what are Elsa and Sean doing outdoors? Be prepared for any answer. But know this, they are teenagers, young adults. They are filled with a hunger they are unsure how to satisfy.

This night, Clara awakens. Tom, also awake, is thinking of tree ring analyses and palynology, the study of plant pollen, a proxy technique for interpreting the sensitivity of vegetation to past climates. Clara watches him for some time before she indicates her alertness. While she does, she tries to imagine his track. But hard as she may she cannot exclude his presence from it. Whatever path she envisions she sees Tom walking along it. Sadly she sees him walking into the distance alone. What does this mean?

Clara reaches out and touches his shoulder lightly. Tom turns. Clara was afraid she might startle him, but when he looks at her it is almost as though he has been waiting on her touch.

"I was thinking about your track," she tells him.

Tom absorbs what she is saying. He will respond in his own time. "I was thinking of the postglacial forest," he tells her.

345

Clara is intrigued. Tom's thoughts rarely fail to intrigue her. "Tell me about it," she says.

Tom lies on his back and looks at the dark ceiling. He feels the hard mattress against his spine. He does not know what to tell her. In the end he talks about the shifting of the prairie ecozones, how the spruce-dominated postglacial forest migrated northward with the retreat of the Laurentide ice sheet, establishing itself as the boreal forest.

Clara wants to exclaim, "Wow!" But she is all too aware of the inappropriateness of such an exclamation in discussion with Tom. Clara is sensitive to all of this, to the needs of this man she does not fit into but whom she loves. Instead she says, "Tell me more."

Clara rarely demands information of Tom so overtly. Both she and he know that what is occurring right now is unusual. In the circumstances, how could it be any other way?

So Tom, who rarely informs her so overtly either, speaks to her of the climate sensitivity of flowering, of pollination, seed formation, germination and the competitive success of seedlings. And Clara naturally thinks of Elsa and Sean. Soon, however, she determines an alteration in her emotions. Listening to Tom she becomes aware of her arousal. They have not made love now for almost two months. This happens occasionally. Neither considers it a problem. It is not a problem, it is their life. But now Clara is aroused, yet she does not wish to interrupt Tom as he speaks of things so intimately important to him. She bides her time. Tom will soon stop talking. Clara will ask no more of him other than his touch. She will slide her nightgown over her hips and above her shoulders, placing it behind her head alongside the rear edge of the pillow and the headboard. She will reach out and lay the palm of her hand on Tom's penis. And Tom will respond, slowly at first, but shortly a hunger will take over in both of them. They will caress and arouse one another in a way that is as near to and as far removed from the desperate mating of wild animals as is humanly possible.

Unexpectedly Elsa rings and says that Sean and she will be returning for the weekend. It is something they have planned between themselves. Seldom do they come home at the same time, so this is an occasion to be enjoyed. There is an element of thoughtfulness in their planning and both Clara and Tom are aware of this, take pleasure from it. What Tom will most want to do is go on a hunt and kill an animal in celebration, but even he will recognize the unsuitability of this. And so instead Clara will get in the truck and drive to the store, where she will buy whatever meat is available. A fillet of pork, as it turns out. She will prepare a honey and mustard sauce, and it will be well enjoyed by everyone. Tom will open a bottle of red wine he has been saving for an occasion such as this. It is a Chilean Merlot he is particularly fond of. Before the evening is over he will have opened a second bottle and then a third, which will remain unfinished. The evening will be a tremendous success. Everyone will be glad to see everyone, and no one will be quiet or withdrawn. They will all go to their beds contentedly.

The following morning Tom will suggest a walk through the forest down to the shore of the lake. This walk is an old favourite of theirs, and everyone will respond positively to his suggestion. It is not a short walk, so they will eat a good breakfast of bacon and eggs and take ham and tomato sandwiches for later. They will muffle up well and set out. First Tom will walk ahead with Sean, Clara and Elsa behind. Then later they will swap over. Elsa will join Tom, her father, and Sean will step back to Clara, his mother. They will speak of other walks, other occasions, sightings. They will point out differences in the trail along the way. Sean and Elsa will notice and bring to Tom's and Clara's attention an alteration they had not previously seen by themselves. This is why people have children in their lives, is it not?

They will walk between the tall green trees, past the white bark of the trembling aspens, and Tom will fight an urge to share the track that lives in his mind. This is not something his children should hear, but Tom will wonder if they might not be able to bring to his attention something else he and Clara have missed. Something apparently trivial that makes all the difference. Instead he will ask them about life in the city, and for his sake they will not enthuse as much as usual. Tom and Clara will appreciate their consideration.

They will come out on the other side and witness the melting lake ice, submerged in pools, and floes floating on the currents. They will take care as they mount the slippery rock, and all will acknowledge that at least this has not changed.

Elsa, a young woman, and Sean, a young man. Tom and Clara, who have seen it all before.

The night they leave Tom will lie awake, aware that Clara is not sleeping either. And without any questioning from her he will tell her of his thoughts. He will speak of the northern treeline advancing slowly into tundra regions in order to keep up with the shifting climatic zones. He will tell her of the species' differing tolerances, the genetic variations and dispersal rates. How each will have to adapt in its own way to the changing environment. How ecosystems will not migrate as a unit, and how as a result new assemblages, new ecosystems could emerge.

Clara will listen attentively but quietly, giving no indication she is listening. She will listen not only to Tom's words but to his tone. Occasionally her thoughts will drift to Sean and Elsa, but as soon as she notices this she will divert her attention back to Tom. He will be speaking of the slower northward expansion compared with the southern loss of forest to grasslands. And mostly he will speak of the limitations of the tundra. How the warmer temperatures might improve the climate for the woodland, but ultimately might not compensate for the inability of the acid till soils to support the forest. And how the rate of migration might not be rapid enough to keep pace with the climate. How a summer drought with more frequent fires, insect invasions, and shifting permafrost could change the subarctic black spruce woodland into predominantly jack pine. How the grasslands might force the boreal forest from the south and how the inhospitable north might curtail its migration. A forest halted, squeezed out of existence.

Tom will pause here. He will have said as much as there is to say.

347

After Elsa rings to tell them Sean and she will be arriving together, Clara switches on the cassette recorder. She does not wish to listen to Patsy Cline today and instead plays a tape by Judy Garland. She turns on the bath and undresses. She stops to look at her stretch marks in the mirror. In the beginning they were a source of embarrassment to her but now she enjoys them, feels a real sense of pride. With them, how could she ever be alone?

As the hot water rises into the air as steam, Clara lowers her body into the bath she does not fit. The water she displaces rises to cover her flesh. Elsa and Sean will soon be back. She is well pleased. She is looking forward to Tom's return to tell him. He too will be pleased.

She closes her eyes and immediately she feels comfortable. Soon of course this will pass, but for now she can bask in the soothing heat. She can at any moment, if she so wishes, leave herself, rise, and look down upon this contented human being. A woman who can picture a track through a forest, a slushy track, muddied, littered with pine needles, leading through the trees. She sees, now as clearly as though she were on it herself, but there is no one there, no human presence. What Clara feels is something she has never felt before, but something she knows Tom has. She feels the aftermath of a kill, a life that has been taken. Taken by her. In a moment Clara will feel uncomfortable in the large tub and move, be diverted towards the physical relief of her aging body, but right now she lies unmoving amidst the evaporating water molecules. She feels the weight of the kill pushing her deeper into herself, squeezing the life out of her. And although Tom has not yet told her about a forest reaching the limits of its migration, she thinks, this must be it.

This must be it.

/ BY TALIA **PURA**

Scene one

(Paul enters Bonnie's small antique shop.)

PAUL: Oh, this is so cool. This is so neat. Come in here, Ruth, you won't be
         sorry. This is a good one. Was it mentioned in the guidebook?

RUTH: *(enters, obviously bored with the whole thing)* I don't know.

PAUL: Oh, thank you for letting us stop here, honey. I'm having such a nice trip.

RUTH: Yes, Paul.

PAUL: You're having fun, too, aren't you, Ruth?

RUTH: Yes, Paul, lots of fun. *(offers cheek for him to kiss)*

PAUL: Oh, look at this. I haven't seen one of these since I was a kid.

RUTH: Well, we've come a long way since then, haven't we?

PAUL: It brings back a lot of memories, though.

RUTH: Oh no, you don't. Don't even think it.

PAUL: Ahh, Ruthie.

RUTH: No way, not one more thing.

PAUL: But, dear—

RUTH: Not one more old camera, no Depression glassware, no cigar boxes and
         especially no household appliances.

PAUL: But Ruth, you know what the therapist—

RUTH: Don't you dare pull that one on me.

PAUL: Well, he did say that—

RUTH: He said that I should show an interest—

349

PAUL: *(hurt)* Yes, show an interest in my hobbies.

RUTH: Yes, show an interest. Oh yes, that's very interesting. Very nice, dear, yes. That's VERY interesting. But he didn't say anything about letting you actually bring any more junk home.

PAUL: Junk? Ruth. I resent your tone of voice. This is a finely crafted household item. Made in the mid-fifties, I would say, later mass produced in a more durable plastic, of course, but never replicated in terms of its design—

RUTH: ARRRGGG!!!! *(exits)*

PAUL: The sleek sweeping lines, subtly rounded edges, rounded yes, but still crisp and clean. Feel that texture, so smooth, so soothing to the touch. I can smell the fresh orange juice. Pinned to the bed by the patchwork quilt on those chilly autumn mornings, Mom tickling me out of my pajamas, Dad having his first cigarette of the day, just before breakfast, Rover licking my bare toes when they first touch the cold floor, having to pee so bad, I could have—

BONNIE: *(enters)* Can I help you?

PAUL: I'll take this.

BONNIE: Sure, let me wrap it up for you.

PAUL: Sorry, Ruth, I have to have this. It will be the last one, I promise, I do. I— *(turns, sees that Ruth has left)* Ruth? Ahh, ahh, could you hurry, please?

BONNIE: Is something wrong?

PAUL: No, no, I just have to go now. How much is that?

BONNIE: Forty-four ninety-five. *(he throws her money, grabs the bag and exits)*

PAUL: Bye.

BONNIE: But this is too much. I don't need— *(he's gone. She shrugs, puts away the cash)*

/ OBLIQUITY

/ BY SHIRLEY **KITCHEN**

Allison was aware of the widespread, general truth that among single women over forty-five there is a better chance of being struck by lightning than of getting a mate. Nonetheless she felt it was the right time for her to take matters into her own hands and begin a search. After all, she had been on her own for fifteen years in a couples' world that excluded her but sought after unattached men who were needed to balance a dinner table or serve as dancing partners. There was no way she had been able to avoid the almost universal belief among married women that because she was single, she was on the prowl. And she had never been able to think of a way to say, politely, "I'm not the least bit interested in your man." She had started to admire those women of her acquaintance who scanned personal ads, joined dating clubs and went on blind dates. They no longer appeared ridiculous or undignified to her. She felt her chances of connecting with someone improved somewhat after reading in a weather chart that lightning strikes the earth one hundred times per second, nearly three hundred billion times a year. The article didn't say how many people were involved but with that many strikes the odds sounded pretty good.

The secret, she figured, is to come to this quest obliquely. A woman she knew stated within hearing of several people, "I want a man in my kitchen" and arrived home after work a few days later and found just that, only he was wearing a mask and sorting through her silverware. Allison believed, or maybe just suspected, that you got what you asked for. She was always careful in naming what she wanted, but in this instance she wasn't sure she knew. Marriage? Part-time lover? Companion? Housemate? Maybe it was just social acceptance, or someone to drive the car once in a while. Or help fix the plumbing. She knew she didn't yearn for the wild, falling-in-love ecstasy portrayed in popular songs, the pain, the willingness to follow to the ends of the earth and bake bread for him forever syndrome. She thought this happened to people who hadn't found their own niche and so needed another person to make them feel complete. Yet, there was something about a partnership she found appealing, something to do with combined energy, with ongoingness. All of this presented a problem: if her requests were not precise, she wondered how life could interpret and respond.

"Hold yourself in readiness," the Nursing Arts instructor at the hospital used to say when Allison was a probationary student. This state of preparedness often meant there would be an ambulance screaming miles away, coming closer and closer, bringing to her ward a distressed patient who required oxygen, blood tests, x-rays and whose arrival involved waking the intern on call.

Feeling somewhat as if she was walking into another impending emergency, still it was with some degree of readiness that Allison said "yes" when her friend Tanya, getting ready to move to Toronto, said of one of the men in her life, "You've got to meet him. You'll like him. I've been telling him you two were meant for each other. You are so much alike."

An old story.

"Ted? Isn't he younger than I am?"

"So? Colette was fifty-two and Maurice thirty-five when they were lovers."

Except, Allison thought, at that age Colette probably didn't have vertical cracks above her upper lip and her ears wouldn't have started to grow longer.

"He's a gardener," Allison said. "I barely know a primrose from a petunia."

"I'm talking about your creative urges, not species of flowers. He's always juxta-posing textures and colours and materials the way you do with your handwork. You even talk alike. You both use words like assimilation and integration. His landscapes are beautiful. You'll see. By the way he's not a gardener, he's a landscape architect."

As if to further convince, Tanya added: "He's a fantastic lover."

A thought entered. "Is he the one who tied you up?'

"Yes."

Then, probably seeing the look on Allison's face—"Don't knock it if you haven't tried it. It's a matter of trust."

Allison's blind date with Ted lasted an hour and fifteen minutes. She sat in the bar opposite him and willed herself to concentrate on an exchange of personal history, family situations and work. While he talked about designing rock gardens for clients she attempted to figure out the likeness Tanya saw in their philosophies of expanding borders as motive for creativity. It was useless. All she could think about was her friend lying spread-eagled on her bed, leather belts around her wrists and ankles, head thrashing from side to side. No, not Tanya, her, Allison, writhing in anticipation, a male figure hovering, beginning to explore her breasts, belly, thighs. Surely not this gentle-mannered, sandy-haired, ordinary man in cords and Hush Puppies.

She heard herself giggle, a thirteen-year-old, blathering. He was looking at her with what seemed to be puzzlement. Could he read her face? A blank surface, she hoped, swollen underneath with curiosity, anticipation, revulsion.

What had Tanya told him about her sex life, or lack thereof? She moved her glass around to create some diversion and inadvertently touched his hand. She jumped up, murmured something about having to be home by eight, dashed to the cashier to pay for her drink, only to remember she had no credit cards and had given her last ten to her grandchildren for pizza day. Of course she had to be rescued because they wouldn't take a cheque.

She sat in her car, discomfited. Discombobulated, her son's favourite word. Apt, she thought. Expanding borders. Not a chance. What, am I a hypocrite? Being exposed to Tanya's stories for years, she had felt that by listening she too could live on the edge, park her van on the side of the road, blow into a lover's ear. She'd probably make his hearing aid whistle. Never.

When she got home she looked up the word *blind*, as in *blind date*, in her Oxford. The definitions included: to beguile so as to rob of judgment, to overawe; without foresight or discernment, not governed by purpose.

I was emotionally deprived of judgment, she thought. I certainly overreacted. But foresight, purpose. What was my purpose in doing this? Right, she remembered. Social benefits. There were others. Safety issues, for one. She didn't have to be so concerned about her personal space when she was with a man. There used to be religious recommendations for marriage—the control of lust. Surely that has fallen by the wayside. But there are economic reasons as well. Sharing expenses would free up finances for travel, books and music. Yes.

Retired professional, the ad jumped out at Allison several months later as she closed the paper after skimming through the trailers-for-sale listings. *Tall, slim* swm *interested in walking on the beach, reading, travelling. Looking for like-minded* sf *for companionship.*

Two old friends buddying up, she thought. What's good for kindergarten kids is good for seniors. I could hike in the bush without worrying about breaking my ankle and sitting alone until the bears found me. Or the cougars. I'd have help arranging for tickets and not have to go through places like O'Hare by myself. Or climb Machu Picchu. We could discuss *The Da Vinci Code* or the work of Jane Austen, compare the film versions of *Pride and Prejudice*. She answered the ad.

She called her daughter and gave her the number he had given her when he phoned, his first name, which was Norm, and the company for which he had worked as a researcher. Cancanola. More and better oil, hybrids.

"I'll phone you when I get back home so you'll know I survived my adventure. We're going to St. Vital Park, then to that new Thai place on the highway."

He was six-foot-eight at least, not exactly slim—skeletal would be a more apt description. His glasses were out of the fifties, thick, clear plastic frames that covered most of his face and made his ears stick out. His cheeks were sunken over what looked like toothless jaws. Had he been in a refugee camp? She was horrified at his emaciated appearance, but his jacket was a Sierra Design and his pants were grey wool, tailored. She couldn't look at him directly and was glad they had arranged to meet where they could move around. He walked, yes, but couldn't stay outside in the cold nor as he explained, be close to trees, grasses or weeds in the summer because of asthma. Well, he did say he liked walking on the beach, which is barren of trees, grass and weeds.

By the time they finished their smorg she knew he had children who were grown and didn't visit very often, liked swimming, and thought that the women he met through the ads, and there were quite a few of them, didn't really have time to spend

353 ◼

with men. They had a million friends and were busy most of the time when he called. His idea of travelling was to take a car trip to the west coast. He was a scientist and preferred reading journals to novels. Most of her anticipation of shared activities vanished.

However, he was pleasant and willing to talk and by now she could look him in the eyes. They had both danced to the music of Tommy Dorsey and Glenn Miller. They remembered the dry bars and early Elvis. When he invited her out for dinner the following Saturday she accepted and suggested a hotel whose dining room featured a buffet. He preferred to order an entree that didn't include salad, so he asked her to bring him one when she was getting hers. She dumped half of it onto his side plate.

"You didn't bring me any dressing or croutons."

"You didn't ask me to."

"Do you always eat soup?" he asked when she tried the French onion, then the clam chowder.

"I'm learning how to make it," she told him, "so I try out different recipes every chance I get."

She selected portions of fried chicken, Swedish meatballs, seafood casserole, rice and vegetables at the entree bar.

"Do you always eat so much?" Norm asked when she returned with her plate.

She smiled as if she thought he was joking and asked him what he did besides swim.

"Do you do any volunteer work?" she asked when he hesitated.

"Like what? Do you?"

She told him about facilitating crafts at the schools, ushering at various theatres around the city, helping at the food bank.

"I don't want to deal with strangers," he said. He almost threw his fork down on his plate. "You sound busy. That's the trouble with the women I've met. It's not me, you know. You don't have time in your lives for a man."

"Tell me about your apartment," she said, not wanting to pursue the topic of why women didn't have time for him.

He was living in the same block he had found as a mature student, having gone back to university following his divorce. He didn't know who the other tenants were.

"Are you familiar with the housing for seniors?" she asked, kicking herself mentally for the nurturing tone that had come into her voice.

His former partner lived in one and she was always playing bridge, going to art displays and music recitals. In fact she had ended their relationship because she had met a widower who also lived there and liked playing card games.

"So you want another relationship, not just friendship," she stated rather than asked.

"Yes. Don't you?"

"I'm not sure. I think that friendship is more important to me right now. I guess I would just like to spend time doing things together, like going to the theatre or the movies. Cooking."

"You want someone to help you cook?"

I guess I knew when I saw the ad that companionship was a euphemism for commitment, she thought, as she listened to him talk about trying to prepare his dinners; a commitment to get his meals, to be there to fill his hours, to be ready for sex, Viagra induced, probably. She didn't blame him for this discrepancy between the ad and the actual. What can you do? she thought. Advertise for a forever and ever partner? Describe yourself as gangly? That you have wrinkles? That you snore or occasionally pass wind? You complain or are grouchy when you feel left out? You expect someone to look after you? Who'd answer?

"Bring me some ice cream," he called after her when she went for dessert.

"You know the buffet is only a dollar more than what you paid for your salmon and it includes everything."

As she took some chocolate cake and apple pudding with ice cream, which she would give to Norm, she glanced down the future to see what might be in store for her—stealing salads, accounting for a dollar here, a dollar there, explaining her choices. She thought of her granddaughter dancing hip hop and jazz, of how satisfying it had been over the years to watch the generations unfold, giving her life a sense of expansion and continuance, a sense of history. Suddenly playing Scrabble with her ten-year-old grandson seemed very appealing. She was glad she had brought her own car. She apologized for not remembering a previous appointment, thanked him for the dinner and left.

Enough of obliquity, Allison thought over the next few weeks. I'll compose an ad myself. It will read: SF, *mother and grandmother. My days are filled with family, books, film, theatre, wilderness hiking, friends and travel. If you are a* SM *and your life too is full and in order, contact me, not out of need for support or comfort, but out of a desire to explore the world in tandem, knowing a shared experience adds dimension to understanding and appreciation of existence. Open to intimacy if our friendship develops along those lines.*

Will she advertise? She doesn't know. Tell her friends, maybe. In the meantime, "Blessed Solitude," as someone had recently said. There is one thing she is sure she won't do and that is walk outside in a thunderstorm.

/ TRAVELLING HOME

/ BY FAITH **JOHNSTON**

The boarding lounge is quiet. It is strange how quiet a boarding lounge full of people can be. If this were a restaurant there would be a great clamour of conversation shouted over the clatter of dishes and the hiss of the espresso machine. Of course it is only eight-thirty. Most of the travellers are still half asleep.

The man sitting beside Vera is wearing a baseball cap (in mid-winter!) and comes from Saskatchewan. He has been up since four, first driving to Saskatoon and then flying to Winnipeg. And when he gets to Ottawa he will have another drive—to a farm near Hawksbury. He hasn't been home for Christmas in he can't remember how long.

"I know Hawksbury," says Vera. "I lived in Ottawa for fifteen years."

But the man doesn't follow up. Typical. Most men don't know how to carry on a conversation.

"I wonder what the weather's doing down there?" she continues. When she checked in, she had received a warning. The plane might not land in Ottawa after all, the woman said, on account of bad weather. And if it was forced to land elsewhere Vera would be responsible for the cost of her own hotel. But what could she do? It is Christmas. Her carry-on luggage is packed with presents for Winn and a few modest gifts for their hosts (no presents, they said, but she knew what that meant. She is not taking any chances in that department).

Vera tells the man the news about the bad weather and the possibility of landing elsewhere: "And then I asked her where will we land if we land elsewhere, and she said I don't know—the weather's rotten everywhere down there at the moment." It's a funny story. Ridiculous, really. She wants to share it with someone. "Perhaps we'll end up in Chicoutimi," she says.

But the man is not amused. "They've had freezing rain," he says. He heard it on the radio, driving to Saskatoon. Then, once again, he lets the conversation drop.

"Ah," says Vera. Could she tell him some stories about freezing rain, ice storms that knocked out the power for days! Once right on Christmas day itself. No coffee, no bacon and eggs, no toast, and later they had to take the turkey across town to get it cooked. And she had company coming, too. (There was always company for Christmas then—odd people—strays.) But she decides not to tell the man about the Christmas ice storm. If he's from Hawksbury he knows all about freezing rain. And there are limits to how long she is willing to sustain a conversation.

It's almost nine and they should be boarding. Winn will be starting across the Atlantic on another plane now, all drugged up on lorazepam, staring out the window as if her life depended on it. It is a terrible thing—the fear of flying. How her daughter developed such a phobia is a mystery, but there it is. Vera is thankful she has never been afflicted. For her it is always a relief not to be the one in charge. Let the pilot worry, she thinks. Let him (or her!) figure it out.

Maybe the long wait is due to the weather down east. But Superjet always leaves late. They seem determined to squeeze every last body onto the plane. At least half a dozen people are hovering around the counter, hoping for last-minute seats.

When the boarding call finally comes, Vera wishes the man from Saskatchewan happy holidays, throws her knapsack on her shoulder, and wheels her carry-on into a long line of people clutching parkas and photo ID and sucking on coffee in tall paper cups or on bottles of water. The new mania for constant liquid intake strikes her as indulgent and expensive. She has tucked a muffin in her backpack and will wait for coffee on the plane. She will drink her coffee and read and the time will pass and the first thing she knows she will be there (and then, in a few more hours, she will see Winn). If she meets someone interesting, the time will pass even faster, maybe too fast, but usually two and a half hours is enough to learn the essential facts, as much as people are willing to tell. On her travels over the years she has met people from all over the world. Once she sat beside a young man travelling all the way to Karachi to celebrate Eid with his parents. He showed her a timetable (downloaded from the Internet) that told him when he could eat.

Most people like to talk about their work and their families. Some of them give advice. She has been told the best beer to drink in China and the best websites for house rentals on the Riviera. She prides herself on being a good listener. There is really nothing to lose. Even if she has never met a truly interesting eligible man (and how many flights has she taken since Les died? Dozens, surely), she has always come away with the feeling that her world has expanded—or perhaps, more correctly, that she is once again fully inhabiting the world.

When she reaches her row, there is already a man in the aisle seat but no one in the middle. She heaves her heavy suitcase onto the overhead rack, while the man stands aside not offering to help, and then clambers over to the window seat with her knapsack. She extracts her muffin and book, takes off her winter boots, and then tucks both the knapsack and the boots under the seat in front. The baggage handlers are still loading the luggage. She watches out the window as men in orange jumpsuits and ear muffs heave boxes and suitcases of all sizes and the odd plastic bin up the ramp to the plane. She eats her muffin without waiting for the coffee. The plane is a full half hour late taking off.

No one arrives to occupy the middle seat. Incredible, especially at Christmas. "Aren't we lucky?" says Vera to the man in the aisle seat. He is not an attractive man. He is very squarely built (obese would be too strong a word) and is wearing a bright green sweater rimmed with white snowflakes. The poor man hardly has any neck at

FAITH JOHNSTON

all. The crew neck of his sweater rides right up to his ears. And the sleeves are too short. His hands stick out, plump and raw-looking, with not one ounce of grace. But still, thinks Vera, there is something touching about a middle-aged man who would wear such an outrageous sweater. Perhaps his wife or even his mother knit him that sweater years ago (indeed, it looks as though it could have shrunk). Or perhaps he is a man like Les who never thinks of clothes at all. Les wore the same things year after year until they wore out. Sometimes she had to remind him to comb his hair.

She had thought of offering the green-sweater man half of her muffin and decided not to (too chummy), but now she passes on sections of the *Globe and Mail*, for she has managed to snaffle the last one. "Do you have family in Ottawa?" she asks.

"In Gananoque," he replies.

"My God," says Vera, "you will have to drive highway 16! In this weather!" And she tells him about coming up that road in a blizzard, completely blind except for the tail lights of the car ahead, forty kilometres an hour all the way. Frightful!

He knows the road well. His brother is coming to pick him up. "I guess we'll have to take it slow," he says, blinking through his glasses. She can tell he is a very literal man—no sense of drama there.

She is happy to have a good book, for it is an uneventful trip. The coffee is bad stuff (she should have bought one of those tall cups while she had the chance). The stewardess makes two rounds, dispensing cookies or pretzels, whatever your heart desires, and the green-sweater man chooses cookies both times. Then she gathers the cups in a big black garbage bag and announces that today is the captain's birthday, and they all sing happy birthday, dear Jeff—some more heartily than others (it is the fear-of-flying people, thinks Vera, the ones who have already thrown back a drink or three, who sing the loudest). Much to Vera's relief there is no more mention of the flight being diverted.

She feels the beginning of the descent into Ottawa even before the seat belt sign comes on. It is 12:30 Ottawa time, and the temperature there is +2 with light rain. "I hope you brought your umbrellas," says the pilot. A laugh goes up. Ongoing passengers will be given immediate assistance at the gate, he continues, and they may make their connecting flights after all.

Soon they are in the clouds. Then it's down, down, down, through layer after layer of white that becomes muted the further they descend. Like going to the bottom of the sea where the sunlight never reaches. Vera stops reading and looks out the window, expecting to see ground any minute. She knows the landscape—the Rideau River snaking along past the airport to Manotick. There is something reassuring about knowing the landscape. Landings, she knows, are even more perilous than takeoffs, especially in bad weather. But surely the weather has improved? She checks the wing for ice and sees nothing.

Suddenly there is a small opening in the cloud cover below and she can see a patch of ground, part of a field glimpsed so briefly all she remembers afterwards is that it was bare of snow, nubbly with mud—and oh so close. We are down at last, she thinks, but just then the engines roar and they begin to climb steeply up through the clouds again.

Apart from the desperate whine of the engines, the plane is very quiet. Others, too, must be trying to contain their panic. Vera would like an explanation. What has happened? What will happen now? Why doesn't birthday boy Jeff come on the blower with his jolly voice and say "oops, missed that time, but we're all right folks"?

"I think he aborted the landing," Vera says to the silent man beside her. "Why would he do that?"

He offers no explanation. Not even a guess. Somewhere behind them a woman says, "Shouldn't we be down by now?"

But they are still going up! Can't she tell?

The steep ascent finally ends and they are cruising once again. Still the pilot says nothing. Where are they going? It dawns on Vera that being diverted to Timmins or Chicoutimi may be the brightest of the possibilities here. Did she even hear the landing gear descend?

"We could be burning off fuel for a belly-landing," she says to her seatmate. She can hear that her voice has risen a few notes. In a moment tears will take over. She can picture the plane skidding along the runway, sparks shooting every which way. The sirens of ambulances and fire trucks wailing, passengers pushing through smoke and tumbling down plastic chutes. She will not be good at any of this. Already she feels the cold in her arms and throat and the pit of her stomach.

"Do you mind if I hold your hand?" she asks the man in the green sweater. And they reach across the seat where they have strewn the *Globe and Mail*. He has a warm firm hand, and he doesn't let go.

"It would help if you'd talk," she tells him, and they begin. His name is Rheinhart. He came to Canada as a child and grew up near Gananoque. He has done many things in his life and has lived all over the country. He was trained as a typesetter, but then he got an allergy to ink and had to look for something else. For a while he repaired small engines, boats, mostly. After that he was a diamond driller in northern Alberta. Then he met a woman from Winnipeg so that's where he ended up. He's been working in an auto parts firm for the last ten years.

The story doesn't come all at once. Vera offers short prompts (a whole sentence would be too much for her at the moment). The plane continues to cut through murky clouds on its way to God knows where. Still no word from the cockpit.

"Any kids?" she asks. No, they have not been so fortunate, he answers. Fortunate now, she thinks. Fewer people to mourn.

The hand, she realizes, is more important than the talk. It has become her lifeline, her umbilical cord. She remembers walking alongside her mother when she was very young. They would be holding hands and one of them would start the game with three sharp little squeezes ("I love you"). Then the response—two squeezes ("How much?") And finally the answer—a big big squeeze, as hard and long as it could be. It was a secret game, though perhaps others played it with their mothers, too. Perhaps

Rheinhart played the game with his mother in the camp. It was a game that had nothing to do with language.

That there was a camp with a wire fence she knows, although he has said nothing about it. And she can picture him later in a schoolyard (Gananoque, Winnipeg, all the same). He is ten years old and speaks not a word of English. He's a DP (refugee, we would say now, a much kinder word). There he is, standing apart from the others, oddly dressed in knickers and a hand-knit toque, shivering in the cold.

But now he shows no fear. And he speaks English with not a trace of an accent. And his hand is very warm.

"Try to look on this as an adventure," he says. "That's what I do. One day, you will look back at this and laugh."

"I hope so," says Vera, and she notices her voice is steadier, almost normal. It is, surely, a good sign that they have been buzzing through the clouds for twenty minutes since the first aborted landing. No fire, not a whiff of smoke.

And then they begin to descend once again. Vera doesn't look out the window. Her body is angled in the other direction, to a hand in a nest of newspapers. She doesn't let go until a slight jolt indicates they are on the ground at last and everyone begins to clap and cheer. She is still too numb to manage a cheer, but she claps and claps along with the others. The prolonged clapping seems to indicate she wasn't the only one in a funk. Even the stewardess is looking mighty relieved.

When the plane comes to a halt, Rheinhart finds Vera's suitcase and parka in the overhead bin and sets them on the middle seat. What can she say to him? Thank you is not enough and small talk will not do—even if she could manage it. So she precedes him down the aisle, pulling her suitcase. They walk together over the ramp, through the familiar boarding lounge of the Ottawa airport and down an escalator, saying nothing. When they reach the bottom, they stand side by side as a tall, stooped man heads towards them, pushing a walker.

"My brother," Rheinhart explains.

But before the brother can reach them something happens (on whose initiative, she is never sure), and the old man has to wait as Rheinhart and Vera clamp together in a hug that is anything but perfunctory. It is much like the hug that Vera will give Winn later that day. It is the kind of hug that people travel halfway round the world for. When it is over, they stand back, surprised at themselves and still wordless, as the brother steps in.

/ BREAKING THROUGH

/ BY DONNA **BESEL**

Annette woke with a jerk of her head. The clock read 8:45 a.m. Her alarm blinked but did not buzz. She assumed she had overslept but then remembered it was Saturday. Missing work remained a recurring phobia for her, even after twenty-five years of teaching.

Because her bay window faced the rising sun, her bedroom was already filled with light. A few metres away from the cedar deck, the Winnipeg River flowed past her condominium. The river's fresh beauty changed according to season and weather. She often imagined the scene outside her window was recreated daily to surprise and delight only her.

Today, in early December, she stared at the one-kilometre width of water. It lay calm and bright, barely rippling, caught halfway in the midst of winter freeze-up. Each day, the flexible white sheets had advanced further into the centre. Uneven curls of ice grew from the shores.

The barely moving, steel-grey surface disguised the volume of flow. Some parts never froze completely, even in the grip of minus thirty, such was the quickness of the water. But that was upstream, not in her view. The even wider areas downstream could almost be called a lake and always froze first.

The ice's jagged edges sparkled in the strengthening light. If the weather stayed cold, the expanding sheets would join up in less than a week. Jets of mist spiralled from the surface, as if the water were fighting against the release of stored August heat.

The river quickened her senses; she had never seen it so beautiful. Then she remembered all the other days. After another minute of contemplation, she rolled over to the edge of the mattress, then walked stiffly into the kitchen to make coffee. Because this Saturday stretched long and vacant before her, she decided to stay in bed a bit longer. Besides, she wanted to savour the scene framed by her bedroom window, before it evaporated beneath the rising sun.

Not many people she knew allowed themselves such simple pleasures. Like watching river ice inch toward union. Like eating toast and jam in bed. Like reading until she fell asleep again, no matter what time it was. Like drinking as much coffee as possible without getting up to pee.

After the coffee brewed, and toast browned, she returned, with loaded tray, to her king-size bed. With a 600-page murder mystery tucked under her arm, she slid between the sheets and flopped back against the pillows. On mornings like this, she relished living alone, with no obligations. The daily drudgery of a grade six teacher's life faded into the sidelines of her mind.

After she rejected the idea of more toast, she reached down to rub her knees. This was the other reason she preferred to stay in bed. As she kneaded the joints, she thought about her lifelong cycle of pain and gain. At times, her arthritis caused her to become less active. Being less active caused her weight to increase. But, now in her early fifties, she had accepted her limited mobility. By circumstance and/or inclination, she cherished her more contemplative existence. As she ate the last of the toast, she flicked the crumbs onto her carpet. Then she snuggled under the sky-blue duvet and started the next chapter.

One hour and thirty minutes later, the bedside phone rang. Her head had slumped forward in response to the book's stalled momentum and her glasses had fallen off. After she fumbled for the phone receiver, she answered in a woolly-minded mumble. She imagined that she could not hear as well as usual.

"Hello, good morning, bonjour." She patted the hills and valleys of the duvet in search of her fallen spectacles. She had broken three pairs the same way.

The voice on the other end started slowly, and continued slowly. It sounded as hollow and strained as a diesel engine on a winter morning.

"Annette . . . I . . . am . . . so . . . glad . . . to find you at . . . home."

She could not recognize the clenched tones. One of her sisters, maybe, but she could not tell which one.

"Are you all right?" Annette asked softly, as she sat up straight against her pillows. She spotted, and retrieved, her glasses from the outermost edge of the duvet.

"Yes . . . but . . . I wanted to tell you . . . before you heard it on the radio. Or on television."

The stumbling voice had her full attention. She flipped her long dark braid over her shoulder and leaned forward, as if urging the speaker forward, like a rider encouraging a tired horse.

"It's Uncle Anton. He was . . . on the lake. Skating . . . by his house, at St. Francis Park." The speaker gulped hard before continuing. "You know the one they made . . . with the new dam."

Finally, Annette recognized the broken voice. It was her oldest sister, Maria, who worked night shifts at the hospital and usually slept in on Saturday mornings. Annette wanted to make sense of the call, but in her newly aroused muddle, she could not understand why Maria wanted to talk about her energetic uncle and a duck pond. As she waited, she grabbed the end of her braid and combed her fingers repeatedly through the tuft of hair at its end.

Maria was now crying but she kept speaking. Her voice accelerated, as if propelled by the tears toward the conclusion. "This morning, the ice was fine, at least six inches, where he started. He even cut a hole. Lots of other people were out on it. At least twenty or so. He loved to skate on that little lake. But he was only in his sixties. He loved to get outside and exercise. Especially in the winter. Everybody thought it was thick enough. They don't know what happened."

Her voice slowed again. "They just found . . . a big hole. It's as if . . . "

"*Attends, une minute.* Are you telling me he fell through the ice?"

Annette realized Maria was creeping close to hysteria. Once her sister's words had rushed and spilled out so rapidly, Annette had wanted to snatch her back to a more level place, to rein in her terror. It was as if the tired horse she had urged forward had stampeded downhill in a blind panic. But it was now stuck in swamp.

Maria's single-word reply dropped like a brick in a pail of water.

"Yes."

"And they have not found any sign of him. Yet."

"Yes."

Another brick.

"What time did this happen?"

"Around ten o'clock."

A heavy tumble of impacts. The water began to spill. Maria was now sobbing.

Annette glanced at her clock radio. It read 11:36 a.m. Then she quickly picked up a pad and pen from her night table. She wrote down details. They seemed strangely important right now. Or maybe it was the teacher in her, using an automatic strategy to regain control in a crisis. She noticed her hands shook as she wrote, but she pried more information from her sister. The RCMP had already arrived at the park, they expected the divers at any minute, and they had begun to notify family.

Annette's teeth ground when the oddly jarring cliché slid from her mouth. "The only thing we can do now is wait."

Maria was not reassured. Several times, Annette tried variations of the same theme.

Then she attempted a different tactic. After a few minutes, she had almost persuaded Maria, and herself, that their uncle had climbed out of the water, behind some trees, without anyone noticing. He was back at his mobile home, wrapped in a blanket, curled up on his La-z-Boy, drinking tea, laughing and chatting with his cats.

After Maria hung up, Annette could not sit in bed any longer. When she rushed into the kitchen, she realized she had nowhere to go and not much to do. She rinsed out the coffee carafe and wiped up the crumbs.

Despite Maria's outburst, Annette knew her sister would want to keep occupied, and grounded, by telling and retelling. Maria had offered to take care of spreading the grim news. So that meant Annette did not need to phone anyone.

She thought briefly about distracting herself with the murder mystery abandoned on her duvet, but the gory murders now repulsed her. She paced and watched the phone for twenty minutes, until her knees began to twinge in protest. The oversized recliner in her living room seemed like a compromise. She would not be lying in bed,

363 ∎

which felt disloyal and lax, during this crucial interlude. But she could rest her legs. And continue to stare at the phone.

It also seemed reasonable to call some friends. After she called one person, she realized it upset her so much she stopped. The only thing to do now was wait. She hated that stupid cliché.

Thirty minutes later, a flash of motion in her peripheral vision caught her attention. A moving object bounded forward into the middle of her view. Curious, she flipped up out of the recliner and rose to her feet. As she approached the living room window, the dark thing assumed an identity. A white-tailed deer with six-point antlers was in the river, splashing frantically to pull itself back onto solid ice.

Annette blinked, rubbed her eyes, shook her head. She stood transfixed, as if witnessing a car wreck. It looked too surreal, too bizarre, too coincidental to be actually happening.

Again and again, the animal crashed into the edges of the ice and smashed them with the force of its propulsion. After what seemed like an hour to Annette, the deer stopped battling and paddled quietly, just to stay afloat. Then it rested its head on the battered ice. She could see its rib cage heave in and out, back and forth. The tortured gasping reminded her of an incident in her class when a student suffered an asthma attack. They had called the ambulance.

As she stared, she struggled to control her own breathing. On a normal day, the deer's plight would have aroused her sympathies, but the unreality of the two connected events completely overwhelmed her senses. She could not breathe; she could not think. As if she had herself been plunged headfirst into the frigid waters. Immobilized, paralyzed, frozen by panic.

She wanted to go outside to investigate the situation but felt nailed to the floor. Her heart thumped so loudly and powerfully, she crossed her arms tightly over her sternum as if to prevent the organ from breaking loose inside her rib cage.

With a gasp, she collapsed back into the recliner. After a few panting breaths to stabilize her respiration, she tried to hoist herself out of the chair's cushions. But she could not get up. It felt as if a giant hand pushed down on her chest. Smothered her. Squashed the air out of her lungs. Annette succumbed to the squeezing terror, let her body go limp. She inhaled and exhaled deeply several times. Then, in a burst of resolve, she hurled herself out of the chair.

Once upright, she realized she had no idea what to do next. She could not call on her neighbours for help. They were gone for the day, caught up in the rush of pre-Christmas shopping. She narrowed her eyes, considered the option of going out on the ice, but admitted to herself it was not only impractical but ridiculous, even if she weighed much less. The stag was stronger and heavier than any human, with horns designed by nature to be weapons. Also, it was thrashing around in its death struggle, fuelled by adrenaline.

Her mouth suddenly felt dry and toxic. She rushed to the kitchen sink and bent over it, to spit and spit, cough and cough. Her abdomen lurched repeatedly, but she did not vomit. She stood up, turned on the tap, let the water run over her fingers. When they began to ache from the cold, she shivered. Imagined her clammy body immersed in such liquid. She spat once more to clear her mouth and drank two glasses of water.

When the shaking slowed, she turned to her hall closet, beside the back door. After she dressed in parka and snow pants, she thrust her feet into leather Sorels. She did not usually wear such heavy winter clothes, but she wanted to protect herself. She clomped across the living room, slid open the patio door, and stepped out into the mists flying off the river.

As Annette crunched down the steps from her deck and through the skiffs of refrozen snow, she struggled to assemble her thoughts and emotions into a manageable order. She wondered how long a deer could last, the way it was exerting itself. When she thought of its terror, she could not help but remember her uncle. She squeezed hard on both temples with mitten-clad hands and almost knocked off her woollen hat as she tried to press the vision out of her mind. She did not want that graphic picture burned into her brain.

When she reached the edge of the river, she peered at the muted liquid sliding past. The ice appeared to be less than twenty centimetres thick, judging from what she could see from the shore. The stag splashed more violently when she approached, but stopped when she spoke.

"What the hell are you doing in there?"

The animal swung its rack around, to sniff and stare. The large, brown eyes, usually so appealing, conveyed a new emotion. They held a glassy, bloated deadness.

She locked eyes with the animal. "DON'T YOU KNOW BETTER? IT'S TOO THIN!"

Her voice echoed from the opposite bank, bouncing easily in the chilled air. The deer stared at the human for a full fifteen seconds. Annette imagined pleas for mercy, nets, a boat, a rifle. Then she screamed. "COULDN'T YOU WAIT?"

More echoes.

She screeched louder. "NOW YOU'RE GOING TO DIE. AND I CAN'T SAVE YOU!"

After this last outburst, the deer stopped watching her and resumed its battle with the ice. It panted and snorted in sharp breaths as it threw its wide torso forward and upward, achieving nothing except more shattered ice. More scraped-off pieces of hide. Tufts of coarse hair and streaks of blood were scattered at intervals along the edges.

After five minutes, the deer paused. Annette watched the animal repeat this cycle six times, with each scramble getting shorter and each pause growing longer.

She stood motionless. She felt compelled to assist, but no ideas came to her. The deer would die soon, of hypothermia, heart failure or drowning. Or all three. It could not crash around in the frigid water much longer.

The stag's muzzle bled from a wide gash. It thrust its body much lower out of the water now. Its breaths sounded impossibly rapid and raspy in the cool air. A light breeze had come up, blowing the mist sideways. At times, the deer disappeared from her sight.

Suddenly, she thought of an action. Not necessarily a solution, but an action. She turned away, as quickly as the footing would allow, and limped back to her condominium. Her knees grated like mill stones grinding together. The cold air had nearly seized her joints.

When she entered the warmth, through the patio doors, a wave of anxiety almost knocked her flat on the floor. She removed her outerwear, staggered to her recliner, and collapsed.

Once a sense of equilibrium returned, she flipped open the phone book beside her chair. She found the number of the conservation office. It calmed her to believe someone, somewhere, could help. She could rouse assistance, despite her pounding pulse and racing thoughts.

The phone rang and rang. Then she remembered. "Of course, it's Saturday. No one will be in the office."

Once again fighting for normal breathing, she willed herself to concentrate. Her brain had stalled, flooded by the joined images of human and deer thrashing in the water.

"Stop. Think. Think. Alice works at school. Her husband is a conservation officer. I know her number. I can call him at home." She said each of these words slowly, carefully, as if to reassure herself her mind still functioned.

While she waited for the phone to be picked up, she doubted the seriousness of her request. Deer, and lots of other animals, probably drowned this way all the time.

When a man finally answered, her words came in a rush. "Hello, Martin. This is Annette Trudel. Sorry to bother you at home but this is an emergency. A deer is in the river in front of my place."

Emergency. Yes, an emergency. She could scarcely believe the quick but level sounds coming out of her head. As she explained, she unravelled her braid and ran her fingers through the long curls. She wanted the man to come immediately. She doubted if she had enough energy to finish the conversation but conquered her urge to stop, hang up, cry, several times during the call.

"The deer broke through the ice. Now it's stuck in the water." She despised the banal exchange of details. With a sudden surge, she described location, time in water, size of animal.

The officer listened, asked brief, practical questions.

"Are you certain he's still alive?"

Annette wound and unwound the cord of her phone. Wound and unwound strands of hair. For an instant, she became so bewildered, she could not remember which situation she wanted to discuss, the deer or her uncle. The two had fused together. She shook out her hair with her fingers, blinked to stop the tears, and sucked in her breath.

Carefully, thoroughly, she answered the rest of his questions. When she thought of how the officer might react if she bawled, she could feel herself sliding toward a fit of giggles. It was only a deer, after all. She breathed in deeply several times, to shore up her imploding composure.

Martin ceased talking for few seconds. Then he spoke clearly, in a baritone, professional voice. "There is really not much we can do. It's best to let nature take its course. Whatever is going to happen will happen."

"But, what about . . ." Annette interrupted him, and halted. He might wonder why she sounded so agitated.

He repeated his last statement.

"You mean there is absolutely nothing . . ." she interrupted again, and stopped again.

Suddenly, it felt as if someone had poured a bucket of warm massage oil over her shoulders and kneaded it into her vibrating muscles. Her neck uncoiled its tendons. The heated flood of relief surprised her. It was only a deer, after all.

Martin said, "If the stag is going to die, he will. It's a part of nature. But he might also get out of the water."

She thanked him and said good-bye.

His placid, reassuring voice was exactly what she needed. She sat beside the phone for another thirty minutes, staring at it, as if she had to memorize the numbers and letters for a test. It did not ring.

She finally got up and looked out at the river. The milky sun, now high in an overcast sky, played hide and seek with scudding clouds. The deer was gone.

At first, she thought the current must have sucked it under the ice. Then she saw an indentation in the snow, on the ice, closer to the other side of the river. Where a large body could have dragged itself up and across. As she squinted to penetrate the dancing mist, she decided to believe she saw faint imprints of tracks leading toward the opposite shore.

She did not know exactly why or how, but she felt ready to face the phone call. She wrapped herself in a knitted blanket and waited in her recliner.

It did not come until later that night.

/ HOSTAGE

/ BY KERRY **RYAN**

you try to hold your breath
for spring, but all through march
it snows and snows, and winter's still
got you—coughing and gasping—
under his long, white thumb

every time you step outside
he lays claim to another chunk,
and you learn to keep your wasting self
inside these rooms until
someone pays the ransom

you spend your days
fondling the houseplants, eating
their soil by the handful and visiting
scent of earth under your fingernails
every few minutes

you would negotiate if you could, give up
if it would end the standoff, but there's
just no reasoning

so you play along, waiting to be released
from the season, cured
of this long, recurring illness

you try to hold your mind steady, keep it
from twisting away in these last few days
by remembering the precise blue of a robin's egg

/ GRUDGE MATCH

/ BY KERRY **RYAN**

this winter is a feisty old man
who won't cede easily
to gangly, adolescent spring

late into march winter still scowls
under his woolen cap, snarls at puddles
and pokes them with his cane

he jams up the sewer grates,
turns meltwater back into ice,
laughing as he imagines kids
slipping in rubber boots, cars sliding
sideways into telephone poles

spring tries hard to please—bringing back
geese and blue skies, spending hours
each day chipping away at the snow
only to have winter dump
all over him again each night

but spring is right back up
on its feet, doesn't know any better,
doesn't know that winter plays dirty,
that he'll scratch and bite right up
until his last, rancid breath

spring is unfazed, has time and youth
in its corner, and soon grows confident,
sends winter teetering
with one good wallop of sunshine

/ THE HERO, THE VILLAIN AND THE SHMO

Speech given to the Manitoba Association of Teachers of English, Provincial Special Area Groups Conference, October, 2003

/ BY SHELDON **OBERMAN**

The mayor was supposed to give the keynote. And when I was asked to replace him, my first thought was to come up here and declare a cut in taxes, more money for education, and an urban reserve for artists and librarians.

But of course, I wasn't given his power, only his responsibility. It's a bit like being a teacher, it's middle management—lots of responsibility but not so much power. Though, we have some power, and to some, especially to our students, we have quite a bit of power.

It's power I want to talk to you about—the power of being an authority, a positive authority, or perhaps a negative authority and about those who must face our authority, struggle with it, learn from it, and in time, inherit it. After all—isn't that what we want for our kids? To grow up and to take over? That's a big expectation. And it's a long and demanding journey, a heroic journey.

It's this latest book of mine that started me thinking about heroes. *The Island of the Minotaur; Greek Myths of Crete*. The book is full of heroes. It's set in that mysterious civilization that came before the Greeks—The Minoan Civilization on Crete. It lasted 1500 years yet it was destroyed in a single night by a volcanic explosion much like Atlantis [is said to have been]—some say it was Atlantis. Almost nothing survived except those glorious tales of heroes—the tales later made famous by the Greeks, which I researched for years and have now retold.

In all of them the hero has his or her teachers and guides, villains and monsters— all sorts of positive and negative authorities. Some of the heroes make it and some of them don't.

Do you remember when you first discovered the Greek myths? For me, I was a little kid nosing around a big library.

I was used to glossy books of fairy tales, dinosaurs and cute fuzzy animals.

Then I saw on a higher shelf a faded and old-fashioned book. On its spine, embossed in gold, was an image of a Greek hero. He was facing—I don't know what— a monster, I suppose. Maybe he was Hercules searching for the Great White Bull or Theseus about to wrestle the Minotaur or that hero of the intellect, Daedalus, inventing the Labyrinth.

The book was beyond my grasp, quite literally, and when I asked the librarian for help, she shook her head. She didn't think I was ready for that higher level of literature. Instead she handed me a big book of trucks.

It took a couple of years before I could reach that golden book—my first real book —with only a few bookplates and so many tales.

There I found young Icarus flying on man-made wings toward heavenly Olympus, not realizing that the sun was melting the wax that held his feathers. His father realized and was calling up to him, "Don't fly so high!"

And the distressed Princess Europa, who had climbed up on a milk-white bull only to discover it was the god Zeus in disguise and he was galloping off with her over the waves, taking her across the wine-dark sea to begin a new civilization on the island of Crete.

Theseus, the Minotaur, Medea the witch, Phaedra the last queen of Crete, the scheming King Minos, the tragic Bronze Giant, Zeus, Dionysus, Poseidon; it was a whole other world. I feasted with gods and I quested with heroes.

Gradually other heroes joined them from other distant worlds—Moses, David, King Solomon and Joshua at the walls of Jericho; the Norse gods Thor and Loki, Brunhilda and the Valkyries; Roy Rogers and Dale Evans, Zorro and Gene Autry; the Mummy, the Wolfman, Superman, Spiderman and Wonder Woman.

What a glorious pantheon! They were great heroes, every one.

Later, in university, I learned how much they really did have in common. My professor taught me [about] the Heroic Pattern. The hero comes from royal or divine parents but is somehow displaced and ends up being raised by common folk (in my case, those folk were my parents—I always suspected I was adopted and came from finer stuff). There are positive authorities to guide him: a god, an oracle or some Wise One. (I had Mr. Friedman, the butcher at the kosher meat market, and I had Mr. Magoral, the caretaker of our apartment block. He had grown up in the Old Country and he knew the secret ways of gypsies, wonder-working rabbis and Russian revolutionaries. And if both Mr. Magoral and Mr. Friedman were ever stumped, there was usually a school teacher I could call on in a pinch.)

The next stage in the Heroic Pattern begins the Crisis. It summons the hero to a Great Task. I seemed to be constantly on alert, waiting for my task—listening for sirens, screams, a desperate pounding at my door. I did once rescue a bird, which I considered my preparatory task—all heroes have tasks that prepare them for their Great Task.

I knew what I would need: special weapons, magical creatures and, of course, noble companions. I was deciding between Zavy Cohen, who had top marks in school, and Jerome Phomin, who was not only older but had a black leather jacket and his own pocket knife.

The hero then starts upon the Journey, the Quest to fulfill his task. This generally involves defeating a monster, some fearful creature who is threatening not just the hero but others, like the blond and famously freckled Diane Barker, who never paid attention to me but most certainly would have if she ever needed to be rescued. You see, the hero had to serve others, not just himself. That's what made him noble and worthy. If he was selfish and proud, he'd get no help or he'd get the wrong help and he'd fail.

371

Generally the hero had to defeat not just a monster but also a monstrous person, the negative authority figure, a villain with power, malice and a destructive pride that the Greeks called "hubris." I imagined my gym teacher, who'd persecute me with extra push-ups or, worse, a certain teacher—still at large in the school system—who loved to swing a strap.

And even if the hero failed, he could still be a hero if he had stayed true to his beliefs.

But the rewards of success were wonderful. He won the love of a woman, the respect of the community, fame, wealth and power. The old good king or the old bad king conveniently died or stepped aside and the hero, having proven himself, took over and became the new ruler. That's the heroic pattern as I learned it.

Isn't that what we want for our kids? To grow up—to prove themselves and to take over?

Isn't that what someone once wanted for us? To achieve love, wealth, recognition and authority in our world?

That's why those stories are so important.

The hero's journey mirrors our own life journey.

And the heroic pattern is not just in the myths. It's in so many stories that we teach—only the details, the faces and places, change. At its core is the plot structure or narrative arc, which is eternally the same: one can recite it like a mantra: introduction, complication, rising action, climax or anticlimax, falling action, conclusion.

The protagonist faces a conflict where he or she succeeds or fails and at the conclusion, the resolution, there is some sort of understanding: emotional, intellectual or moral. The protagonist has changed, hopefully for the better.

Heroic tales are everywhere. We are overwhelmed with the mass of mass media that mass produces heroes; commercialized, sanitized, vulgarized heroes, antiheroes, celebrities and wannabes.

Why? Because we need heroes so badly that we keep consuming them like fast food. Just the other day I saw a fellow walking down the street with a six-pack of beer and a six-pack of videos. I'm sure they were all action hero movies.

Are we substituting quantity for quality? Substituting appearance for the real thing? Maybe we're not understanding or not teaching what a hero really is. Maybe that's why so many remain so unsatisfied.

The problem is that all the false heroes are obscuring the real ones, confusing the true nature of a hero, especially to our kids. A hero is not someone with the bling, the sex appeal, the fancy cars, the movie or record contract and the paparazzi.

I think we know, at least instinctively, what a hero is. But how do we describe one? How do we teach our youth so they can recognize heroism in its wonderful but often modest forms? Because when our youth do recognize the traits of heroism, they will emulate them.

As a young child I knew exactly what a hero was. My world may have been limited but it was crowded with heroes. Until there came a point when I lost them. I think what I actually lost was that part of myself.

Gene Autry was a Saturday afternoon soap opera cowboy. His movies were all pretty much the same: he had to save the beautiful heroine from losing her father's ranch to the dastardly villain and his gang of thugs. I would sit in the Deluxe Theatre on Main Street with hundreds of other kids, gobbling our popcorn as we waited for Gene. When he appeared on screen we exploded into cheers and then booed the bad guy. I sat mesmerized in that innocent darkness, not yet realizing that the world was far more complicated than the movies.

Now I understand that we weren't all cheering for Gene. He was too perfect, too much of an ideal. Some were secretly cheering for the villain. Some already knew that they could never be a hero but since they still craved attention, power and perhaps some pretty girl, they had found another role to admire—the role of bad guy or one of his thugs.

There were other roles as well: the beautiful but helpless victim; the kindly but impotent father. As for myself, I gradually shifted away from imagining myself as the hero. I began identifying with his harmless sidekick, Smiley Burnette, the fellow who couldn't do anything well except make the hero look good by comparison. Smiley was the foil, the joker, though he was not really a joker; he was more of a joke. He probably had a drinking problem and a string of wrecked marriages. But I just saw him as Smiley, whom the great Gene Autry liked almost as much as his horse. In truth, Smiley was a loser. Smiley was, to put it in Yiddish, a shmo.

Then Mrs. Slawchuk told me what could happen, what had happened to her in Poland when she was a girl. How the Nazis took her from her farm and her family. How they made her a slave labourer in a munitions factory with little food or possessions and no rights. How she was considered a subhuman.

"We were dirt to them," she told me, "and dirt can say nothing and do nothing." Then one day one of her friends accidentally damaged a machine. The Nazi supervisor began beating her terribly. Without thinking, Mary pushed herself between them and glared at the man. What could have happened then was that he would beat her as well or probably something far worse. But the man hesitated, lowered his eyes and turned away. Mary had saved her friend. That had happened sixty years ago but as Mary Slawchuk recalled it, her face glowed as proudly as it must have on that day. In that defining moment she had proven that she was not dirt, that she was a greater human being than that member of the "Master Race." Mrs. Slawchuk did not go on to do anything extraordinary; she did not become a freedom fighter or a great social activist. She led and she still leads a simple life of family and home, but that moment can never be taken away. It changed her and changed her world.

There are real and true heroes among us. Even within us.

We need to think about the people who have been heroes in our own lives.

Who are your heroes? In your family? In your community? Among those you've met in the larger world? Who has inspired you, given you courage, hope, faith, vision? Who has awakened your mind or spirit, your heart or will?

I think of my personal heroes as my private board of directors. They are always with me, in the back of my mind or the bottom of my heart. I sometimes hear their voices, see the expressions on their faces, especially when I'm making some important decision. I think, what would they do? What would they say? Perhaps we each have a private board of directors. And it's up to us if we fill that board with friends or enemies, with heroes or villains or shmos, with harsh judges or caring teachers. It's one of those caring teachers I want to tell you about now.

The teacher who taught me the most was not trained or certified. In fact, I was probably the only student he ever had.

Mr. Friedman was a North End butcher who used to frequent my parents' café on Main Street. He was a short, stout man with a bad lisp and glasses as thick as Coke bottles, yet Mr. Friedman had a remarkable talent. He could walk confidently into a room, face an audience and hold them with a clever and convincing speech.

My mother decided that if Mr. Friedman could overcome all his obvious handicaps, he could teach me how to overcome mine. I was merely awkward, self-conscious and lacking basic social skills; afflictions of a typical thirteen-year-old, especially an isolated child lost in books and daydreams. The two of them made some sort of an arrangement. I doubt any money was involved.

Mr. Friedman stopped by the café one evening when I was working a shift. He studied me as I washed dishes and swept the floor. He eventually called me over and told me what he and my mother had decided. He said he wanted me to write a five-minute speech and to present it to him at his house on Sunday.

I have no idea what I wrote or how I sounded but I do remember that he was tremendously impressed. He then gave me tips on how to speak, how to pause, how to stand and gesture. The next week I returned with a better speech and a better presentation. Again, he was tremendously impressed and offered even more tips.

His praise would have surprised my teachers, who were not at all impressed with me. They would cite my short attention span, poor work habits, lack of respect and, of course, my constant daydreaming, further afflictions of a thirteen-year-old.

So I was left to Mr. Friedman, who managed to inspire me to write and rewrite, to memorize and rehearse week after week, because Mr. Friedman offered me something no other teacher did; something rare and wonderfully nurturing—his sincere and enthusiastic appreciation.

I made about fifteen speeches before he judged me ready for the next level. He took me downtown and had me address his public speaking group, a dozen or so businessmen who formed the local Toastmasters Club. I practised for days and gave them my best speech and all of them were tremendously unimpressed. After all, I was just some kid.

But I wasn't just some kid to Mr. Friedman. He kept me writing and memorizing and trying more techniques. What an odd pair we were as we got off the bus from the North End every Monday night and entered the YMCA, especially odd to that stodgy group of businessmen—me, a gangly, self-conscious young dog and my "teacher," the lisping butcher.

Yet somehow I learned, or somehow Mr. Friedman changed me, because finally one night I earned that group's grudging applause. It was a great moment for a kid like me, a kid who could have turned out to be anything, or nothing at all.

That experience changed me greatly. It woke me up to the world "out there." I was no longer lost in my thoughts and feelings and fantasies. I could connect. I could speak.

Now, of course, I speak before groups all the time—to my own students, to whole schools when I visit as an author, to conferences of teachers and writers and to the general public. I can even watch the people in the audience as they watch me. I'm seldom nervous; I like it up there. But I'd surely like to see my old teacher one more time, see him watching and listening as I present, nodding and smiling the way he always did, following everything I say as if I were speaking the golden truth, and no one could say it better.

Oh, Mr. Friedman, you old alchemist, when I think of how you thought of me, I shine.

/ BREAD & WATER

/ BY DARIA **SALAMON**

I look up at the house on Dorchester Avenue and glance down at the address I've scribbled into my notebook. The numbers match. There's a horse perched on the fence, the plastic kind on springs that children used to ride before the days of Jolly Jumpers and car seats and child safety. I walk up the path and knock on the glass door—despite the horse.

I'm not sure what to expect or what I'm even doing here.

A black dog with a red bandana draped around its neck tears around the corner and pushes its nose into the glass. Behind him I see grey hair, a black beret, a warm smile.

"Hi, I'm Obie." The man tugs the dog back as he pushes the door open. "Come on in. She doesn't bite."

A few minutes later I'm sitting in Obie's office sipping tea and talking about my mentorship. Obie catches me ogling his Governor General's Award. I've spent a considerable amount of time staring at my computer, daydreaming about winning one of these.

"That stuff's nice," Obie says, gesturing at the engraved glass, "but it's not important. We should talk about stories and where they come from and what makes a story. Is there anything that you want to talk about? I could go on and on."

"I don't know what makes a story, well—good. Sometimes I start writing something and then stop because I can't really imagine someone actually reading it."

"That's okay. It's normal. You have to find a story that you want to tell. Start with your experiences," Obie suggests. "That's where I began. Turn them into stories."

Obie and I talk about writers and writing and life experiences and how all of these elements work together to create a story.

"It's important that you have a good space to write in and you allow yourself time. Even if the story doesn't surface right away, you need time."

Speaking of time, it is almost eleven o'clock and three hours have flown by—Obie practically has to heave me out of this house that I was reluctant to enter. My homework is to dig through my experiences and find one that I want to write about.

I walk home, past that creepy horse, and I stay up half the night writing the beginning of a story that I deliver to Obie's mailbox a few days later.

Fall

"It's the wind." I lifted my head, my cheek raw from rubbing against the coarse fabric of the curtain.

"Wind comes off the bay. Makes the trees look like that," the small woman in the next seat continued, not raising her eyes from her cross-stitch as she spoke. Her brown hands pulled the needle and its tail of red thread in and out, in and out of the butter-milk linen on her lap.

Sunlight the colour of mandarin oranges pushed through the curtains and filled the train. Tundra slipped past, bits of brown vegetation and every so often a tree. It looked like someone had scraped a dull axe blade down the left side of every trunk.

The train finally pulled into the station, the end of the line. My back ached from the thirty-six-hour trip, but anticipation pitched me onto the wooden platform. The wind was cold and the town was a haggard bit of land dotted with low, cheap-looking buildings. It was late August and there was no grass, only grey rock sliced up by grav-el roads. The town was pinned by water on three sides. It took only minutes for Churchill to sting me with its bleakness and isolation.

While I settled into my apartment, two boys played on the shore of Hudson Bay. I placed folded sweaters into wooden drawers as the wind flicked one boy's hat into the icy water. He waded into the waves to retrieve his cap and was swept away. The second boy vanished into the waters as he tried to rescue his friend. I slid my empty suitcase under the bed. An undercurrent lurked beneath the surface of Hudson Bay—the boys didn't stand a chance.

In the days that followed I watched the townspeople gather in clumps along the shore and grope the waves with their eyes, desperate for signs of life. The human sil-houettes appeared slight and weak pressed up against the enormous bay, splays of cold water lashing at them. They would not abandon their vigil.

Days passed and the wind and water slapped and bit at the boats, at the shores, and at everything—especially hope. The buzzing helicopters and boat motors lulled the townspeople into reluctantly accepting that the boys would not be found. Rescue turned to recovery. One body was pulled from the bay, but the second boy was never found and would remain in the waters. The boats and helicopters disappeared. The blasts of hollow wind didn't let up and life returned to normal.

People pushed rusted carts through the Northern Store. The woman with the black vest filled steins of beer at the Legion and Friday night meat raffles started up again. School resumed and children returned to the safety of English class and to a new teacher.

Mr. Lahti, the imported superintendent, was a stout man with thick-lensed glasses and a straight moustache; he led me to my classroom at the Duke of Marlborough School.

"This is what you'll teach," he said, handing me a copy of *Sound and Sense*, a poet-ry anthology published in 1956. Mr. Lahti had enlisted me in his crusade to better a community I hardly knew, with a textbook that hardly mattered. Two boys had just died in Hudson Bay, but order would be restored through education, through poetry.

On the first day of class there were twenty-four eighth grade students seated in desks and twenty-five names on my roster. The empty seat in my classroom was more chilling than any January night I would experience in Churchill.

A twenty-one-year-old teacher, I dared not disobey Mr. Lahti's orders, even if I'd known how. I turned to page sixty-eight of *Sound and Sense*. Figurative language. Robert Frost. "The Road Less Traveled." There was no road leading to or from Churchill.

I allowed the students to give me a tour of the town. *Sound and Sense* wasn't working out and I couldn't think of anything else to do with them. Their feet chipped at loose stones on the gravel road as they brought me directly to the Northern Store. This was the most important place in town, they explained, as we wandered through the aisles. The shelves were stocked with milk, snow boots, toasters and tampons—provisions for the winter. When we emerged, the students unloaded licorice, chocolate, gum and chips that they had stuffed into the pockets of their windbreakers. Living in this small northern community didn't impede them from satisfying their thirteen-year-old angst.

As I shuffled them back to the school, a polar bear with two small cubs appeared in the distance. Finally, a bear. The only thing I knew about Churchill, polar bear capital of the world, was that I had a pretty good shot at spotting a bear. The town was situated on the bears' migration route to Hudson Bay, where they hunted seals through the winter. The students were uninterested; bears were more common than junk food around here. These bears looked as if they'd strolled right off a calendar. The mother bear paused and turned her head toward us. I was terrified as I tried to redirect the students. Then, she gently nudged her cubs and they carried on. These bears restored my shaken faith in nature. It could be vicious, but also exquisite.

The bears had broken the only rule they were obliged to obey—they were not permitted in the town. Clearly, they'd ignored the signs posted for their benefit. The "Polar Bear Police" pursued these Arctic renegades, as public safety—especially new-teacher-in-town safety—was at risk. We watched as the Natural Resources officers pierced the mother's white fur with a tranquilizer dart, and, drugged, she stumbled off into the bay. Her two cubs followed and clambered on top of her groggy body, desperate for comfort. They pushed their mother into her grave beneath the water's surface.

Two mothers robbed of their sons, two cubs deprived of their mother—life devoured by Hudson Bay. This was no longer the anonymous puddle of water that I labelled and shaded azure blue in tenth-grade geography class. I viewed the bay with trepidation and awe.

Obie returns the story to its folder and looks up. I'm not breathing—it matters deeply to me what Obie will think.

"Azure blue. I like that," he finally says. I breathe. "It's good. The parallel between the mothers of the boys and the mother bear works." More breathing. "It needs to be structured around the bay. The bay is important in this story. It's a character."

I madly write down everything Obie says.

"What do you think the story is really about?" He looks up.

I try to think of something insightful. "I don't know. Churchill?"

"I mean, what is really going on in this piece? Why does it need to be told?"

"Maybe it will be about how this place, this cold strange place, affects the narrator," I suggest.

"Good. How will she change and how will the reader *see* this?" Great. More questions. We work through them together and I'm beginning to understand what makes a story readable.

Winter

I awoke to my apartment door opening and shutting. The bedroom lights flicked on, my back stiffened. Two men stood at the foot of my bed. I recognized them. They had guided a bear tour I'd taken in the fall. They had a key to my apartment; Churchill is the kind of place where people have the keys to one another's lives.

Hello teacher, one of them said. I'd grown used to being referred to as *that new teacher*. There had been many teachers, but few stayed and I would have to earn my name by committing to Churchill.

I slid deeper under my down quilt.

It's cold up there, my baba had said as she stuffed the feather quilt into a cardboard box. Another thing people who've never been to Churchill know a lot about—the cold.

These goose feathers would become my armour.

The men clawed at my quilt and climbed into my bed. I could smell Friday night Legion—sweat, cologne, smoke and liquor. Friday night Legion was different from Tuesday night Legion. There was less cologne on Tuesday.

My relationship with Churchill was about to be consummated.

Remain calm and quiet. Fighting back or making noise will only aggravate the bear. I had read what to do if I encountered an aggressive bear, but I was ill prepared to deal with predatory people.

They didn't rape me. They pawed at me the way a lazy bear noses around in the garbage at the local dump before it gets bored and strolls away. New teacher initiation, they told me, and left.

I didn't report the incident. To this town I was still a curious novelty the train brought in along with the weekly produce. The lettuce was usually bad before it arrived. The same could apply to the teacher.

I wanted to leave. But I was tethered to Churchill for reasons I could not yet grasp. I stayed, vigilantly crossing the days off my calendar. Two hundred and eighteen until the end of June.

Leo, one of my students, stayed after school one day and told me that he dreaded the school bell at the end of the day. He had no idea how to fill the hours that stretched out after the bell had rung.

His best friend had drowned that fall.

He said that hardly a day would go by when they weren't exploring with their snow-mobiles or four-wheelers. The two boys used to drive their snowmobiles to a secret spot, down the tracks, into a wooded area. Tundra spilled north of the town, but to the south the boys could lose themselves in the last stretch of boreal forest. They would build a warm fire from dried twigs and spruce branches, eat roasted wieners stolen from their mothers' kitchen cupboards and laugh until their stomachs ached. Leo said that most of all, he missed his best friend's laugh. I asked Leo to write a story about Blair. The next morning he handed me ten pages.

I read all about Blair's and Leo's antics—the landscape infused humour and adven-ture into their lives. One afternoon they had miscalculated the depth of the water in a ditch they were crossing with their four-wheelers. They began to float and spent the rest of the day recovering their vehicles. Blair and Leo's friendship grew from their ability to bond in a hostile environment. This environment had also robbed Leo of his best friend.

Upon Leo's advice, I learned to drive a snowmobile. This thirteen-year-old was right, tearing across the frozen bay at 100 kilometres per hour *was* "really, really cool." A local polar bear photographer taught me how to take pictures, taught me how to look at the bleak landscape with fresh eyes. I lay across the snow on my stomach, neck arched, peering through the lens of my camera. The half-bald trees were sirens that rose up out of the tundra, luring my camera, begging to be subjects in my pictures.

On my walk home from the Legion one evening I was bundled up, cursing the cold through my frosted balaclava, when I glanced up at the sky. I was paralyzed, not by the fifty-below temperature, but by the aurora, a magenta-green-lavender-white-violet light show swirling above my head. I was stunned, my toes went raw. The brutal cold and beauty fused together in the sky that night. I understood Churchill.

"I have to undergo cancer treatment, so we may have to schedule some of our sessions around the chemo," Obie tells me matter-of-factly when I arrive, armed with writing.

"We should stop the mentorship," I protest, confused that he even wants to contin-ue. I cherish my meetings with Obie, but I'm certain he has more important people with whom he should be spending his time.

"No, no. I want to keep up our sessions. I need this as much as you, because I can't do much of my own writing." Despite my protests Obie will not waver in his commit-ment to my mentorship.

He reaches for the latest revisions of my story. "I think the story is working. This bit about the aurora is a nice metaphor." I beam and feel guilty all at once.

We continue to meet. Sheldon becomes weaker physically and I'm becoming a stronger writer. More guilt. I don't want to be the last writer Sheldon mentors. He could do better than me.

"Come downstairs. I want to show you something," Obie suggests during one of our last sessions together. He brings me down to his workshop, to his bookmark factory.

He's made dozens and dozens of bookmarks out of purchases from his infamous garage-sale expeditions. "Pick one." After too much deliberation I've narrowed them down to two choices.

"I can't decide." One is an iridescent water pattern, the other loaves of bread.

"Okay, fine, you can have two," Obie smiles. "Bread and water. I like those choices."

Many friends and writers have Obie's bookmarks—mine serve as reminders of my mentorship with Sheldon. But I'm lucky enough also to have a story as a symbol of my mentorship. I wrote many stories under Obie's guidance—the Churchill story is one of which we were both fond. Obie saw the first draft and he worked with me through many rewrites until our mentorship concluded that summer.

Obie lost his battle with cancer the following spring. He never did get to see the final draft of the story and I had to conclude it without his guidance.

Spring

The frozen seams of the bay cracked and burst into massive ice sculptures. The thaw signalled an end to the long winter. Everyone was relieved. Especially me. Seals poked their heads through openings in the ice, tiny fuchsia-coloured flowers sprouted from rock crevices on the shore.

Birdwatchers from around the world descended on Churchill to count birds returning from their winter migration. Churchill is one of two breeding spots on the continent for the endangered Ross's gulls. The bland-looking birds and landscape blend together and both demand close inspection to reveal subtle beauty.

Locals would clear the bakery of British and Japanese birdwatchers by starting a rumour of a Ross's gull sighting. Last year I would have vacated the bakery with the tourists in pursuit of a glimpse of one of these birds, but now I was *in* on the joke—I enjoyed my Saturday morning fritter and coffee with the rest of the bakery regulars.

I boarded a Zodiac boat to see the hundreds of beluga whales that congregate to feed and calve in the mouth of the warmer waters of the Churchill River. The boat wove its way through water pathways amidst a labyrinth of icebergs. I spotted the white creatures, with their curious eyes, gliding beneath the boat.

A year ago I saw Hudson Bay take life, but it also sustained it. The boy who had mysteriously been absorbed by these waters was now accompanied by these gentle whales. I imagined the lost child spinning and sliding, bumping against their silky, tender bodies.

I was leaving the next day. When I told Leo that I wouldn't be back for the following school year he looked at me, puzzled. It had never occurred to him that I would stay.

/ THE LIFE CYCLE OF A FEMALE MOTH

/ BY DEBORAH **FROESE**

Using a Tweety Bird magnet, Mya dutifully secures the postcard from her sister to the fridge where Steve and the kids will be sure to see it at the end of the day. New Zealand this time. Cathedral Cove, Coromandel. It's hard to resist the image: a massive rock arcs over white sand and lures the eye to a pool of crystal blue ocean on the other side. Mya can almost feel hot sand biting into her itchy soles, the foamy lap of waves over her toes. She would like to dive into the picture and escape the tiresome drudgery of her days. This unsettles her in ways she can't quite put her finger on. Guilt? Regret? She has never been outside of Manitoba, unless she counts high school band trips or childhood summers camping in Kenora. She tends to overlook those disasters; travel should be worth remembering. She ignores the sudden gnawing in her belly—maybe it's just hunger—and she flips through the rest of the mail: telephone bill, Visa bill, a letter addressed to "Occupant."

Steve glances at the fridge and takes one last mouthful of coffee. He straightens his tie. "From your sister?'

Mya nods. Her senses are too numb at this time of day to respond verbally; the words remain stuck somewhere in the folds of her grey matter. She'll deal with conversation later.

"Good. I'll read it after work. Can you pick up some golf balls for me today? You know which ones. I've got a game tomorrow afternoon with a client. Love you." Without waiting for a response, he plants a kiss on her cheek and throws a playful punch at their youngest son, David.

"See you later, Dad." With a clatter, David slides his breakfast plate onto the counter by the sink. In this small duty he is well trained. "Mom, don't forget my book."

"Your book?" Mya looks up from her envelopes and blinks. She will be dealing with conversation sooner than she'd like.

"From the library. For my science essay."

"Oh." Mya studies David for a moment while his comment registers and then connects with the memory of his request. She isn't sure whether the reproachful expression on his face springs from simple irritation or preteen contempt. She feels responsible, nevertheless. "How could I forget?" She hopes her attempt at a cheerful but apologetic tone will be perceived as a peace offering. She drops the mail on the counter and, cruising on autopilot, picks up his plate to dump toast crusts into the garbage bin under the sink. Which part of her day will she sacrifice for the library errand? Laundry, housecleaning or dinner preparation? She'll have to avoid the fiction section or her day will be lost. "I'll pick it up this morning," she says.

"Thanks, Mom." David snatches his lunch bag from the counter and with a gleeful whoop, he swings his arms back and thrusts himself forward. He clears the three steps down to the landing and after a split second of airborne silence, he hits the floor with a thud, a screech and a triumphant howl. His rubber-soled runners will surely leave marks. Why can't he ever remember to keep his shoes off inside the house?

Mya reminds herself that it won't always be this way; children constantly transform. She remembers dimpled cheeks and a toothless smile, the scent of downy hair that almost overnight became a patch of bristle with a sweaty, damp-dog smell, and laughter that has changed in depth over thirteen years, but has never lost its joy. How can she complain about such an endearing child?

Rustling and banging extinguish her moment of bliss as quickly as it had erupted. "Where is it? Where's my backpack?" David shouts. He reappears at the top of the stairs and gives Mya an accusing stare. "It's not here. It was here yesterday."

Mya's first instinct is to shout back defensively, but instead, she glances at the clock. He's late. That's why he's angry. Or it could be hormones. He is at that age. Backpack . . . backpack. Ah, yes. "Your backpack is in the front closet," she says with measured calm.

"What's it doing there? I always leave it here."

"Not yesterday. Remember? You came in the front door after the Fosters dropped you off and—"

"I put it here. I know I did. *Some*body moved it."

Mya bites her tongue and closes the dishwasher. An argument will only spoil the day for both of them and his mood is not one to be reasoned with. She fetches the backpack and holds it out to him, forcing her lips into what she hopes is a smile.

"What's for supper?"

"Roast beef."

"Good." David charges out through the back door and it slams closed behind him. Mya winces and tries to not take it personally. Two down, one to go.

Enter Josh. "Mom, I need my soccer jersey washed. For the game tonight." Josh speaks carefully through a Duo-Tang clenched between his teeth while he balances several binders, a textbook and a grass-stained shirt in his arms. His curly hair is dishevelled and the faint stubble of an almost-beard peppers his face. A rush of adoration presses against Mya's rib cage. Flesh of her flesh. How can it be?

The phone rings. Somehow, Josh manages to toss the shirt onto the table, slide the Duo-Tang into one of his binders without setting anything else down, and grab the cordless phone before the second ring. Before Mya can reach it.

"Hello?"

His expression softens into a look that Mya can only describe as lovestruck. It has to be that girl, the one with the dark, persuasive eyes and T-shirts that skim the top of her gold-ringed navel. Instinctively, Mya does not like her. Instinctively, Josh suspects this. He turns his back to Mya and his voice lowers. "Breakfast? Not yet . . . a spare . . ." He leaves the room uttering a series of muted, one-syllable words.

Before Mya can put aside images of belly-button jewellery to remember the girl's name, Josh returns with the phone. He slides the receiver from his shoulder down his arm to the palm of his hand and then turns his wrist to drop it on the counter. "And don't use fabric softener," he says, as if the interruption had never occurred. "Please. That stuff smells gross."

Mya wants to ask how he expects her to keep the cling out of his polyester jersey without fabric softener, and how that girl will feel if she gets static when—*if*—she touches him, but the question would only raise his ire. It alludes to subject matter mothers should not be aware of. She makes a mental note to buy a bottle of unscented product on her way to the library and then changes the subject. "Did you eat breakfast?"

"I'm meeting a friend at McDonald's."

"Which friend?"

"Just a friend, Mom. Geez." Josh rolls his eyes and Mya knows she's treading on thin ice. She'll tackle this again later, when she's had time to consider her approach. "Don't you have something due today?" she asks. "An English essay."

"Right here." Josh taps his binder and grabs a peach from the bowl on the table. He bites into it and juice dribbles down his chin.

"And you have a test."

"Yeah. Math." He wipes the juice away. "Don't worry. I studied."

"Good. Wish you luck."

"Thanks. See ya. I need the car tonight."

The door slams closed before Mya can respond. She'll have to think about the car. His request has many implications.

Sunlight streams through the kitchen window, illuminating the room with a yellow glow. Mya is never sure whether to bask in its warmth or hide from its glare. Perhaps she only feels this way because it is morning and mornings always leave her exhausted. They fly past her in a blur, before the illusory edges of sleep have shifted into consciousness. If she could capture these early events on video tape and then play them back at slow speed, every moment could be absorbed and appreciated. She could pick up subtle clues to mood and circumstance that she missed the first time around. Sound tracks could be edited until points were clearly made and understood. This, she thinks, is what contemporary life lacks; time to effectively communicate.

Her eyes are drawn back to the postcard on the fridge. Claire is efficient in that regard. She will call as soon as she returns from her vacation to share each day of her adventure in exotic detail. The places, the food, the people. Mya will nod and smile at the expected intervals. She is happy for Claire, but she's also rife with envy, not only for the experience, but for Claire's ability to grab life by both horns and enjoy the ride. Claire has always been the outgoing one, a real "social butterfly," as their father would say. She has never found it difficult to strike up conversations with perfect strangers, to ask directions or share quiet pleasantries. This gives her an edge for travel, among other things.

Mya pours coffee into her favourite brown mug and finds her way to the office. She turns on the computer and checks her email. No messages. She leans back in the chair with her hands clasped behind her head and stares at the ceiling. She wonders what her life would have been like if she had finished university. If she were working in an office or in and out of a Toronto newsroom, like Claire. Under those circumstances she might feel she had earned the right to accept one of Claire's travel invitations, to experience a world larger than Winnipeg, beyond the hot, crowded pavilions of Folklorama. But she is a wife and mother, not a successful journalist. She has different obligations and a much smaller budget.

She would not trade her family for Claire's freedom, but lately, she's been feeling restless. Unsettled. On the precipice of change. What happens when her boys no longer need her? Brick by brick, one experience at a time, Josh is erecting a wall between her and an inviting new world of possibilities. David is beginning to pull away, too. What does she have to look forward to? A return to university? Her mind has become more like a sifting device than a steel trap. A job? For what is she qualified? She visualizes herself, a plump, just-past-middle-aged woman in a uniform and cap asking, *you want fries with that?*

No, the die has been cast, her life is on course. Birth, birthing and fading away; the life cycle of a stay-at-home mom.

Mya sighs, and with great effort, hauls herself to her feet. She would prefer to escape her angst by delving into the pages of her new novel—it would be interesting to discover what the main character, Christina, is going to do about her missing passport—but Mya knows she will have trouble enough completing her chores before her family returns. Sleep is a temptation too, but how could she justify her day with unmade beds and dirty laundry? Perhaps a week of pampering at a fancy health spa would revitalize her; lots of sleep, gourmet health foods, a pedicure, a manicure, a facial—and waxing. God knows she has far too much hair. Everywhere. But a spa is out of the question. She adds depilatory wax to the list in her head. She thinks the better of it and reaches for a pen. Now, what is it that she is supposed to buy for Josh?

Milk and unscented fabric softener. Check.
 Telephone and Visa bills. Check.
 Golf balls. Check.
 Library. Check.

With Josh's soccer jersey in the dryer, potatoes peeled and the roast ready to slip into the oven, Mya stands in front of the bathroom mirror, naked. Even in a one-piece designer suit, she would feel out of place on the shore of Coromandel. Or any beach. She has never been slim but the curves of her waist and hips thickened with childbirth and then disappeared altogether. Her breasts droop low with the texture and weight of pendulous cantaloupes, and her thighs and upper arms already display a generous

385

supply of dimpled flesh. Although her face is still relatively smooth—except for that damned hair—the skin on her hands and arms is beginning to scale and flake and lose elasticity. What will she look like at fifty? She is morphing into the likeness of her mother and her mother's mother, complete with a head of hair that refuses to turn white or grey but fades into unmanageable strands of weathered beige.

Is this what Steve sees when he looks at her?

Maybe she should skip potatoes and gravy tonight, and pick up a bottle of hair dye tomorrow. Some anti-wrinkle cream too—something with collagen for firming.

Mya tentatively dips a finger inside the jar of sugar wax next to the sink. It's still warm, but not hot. She takes the small wooden stick provided, stirs the golden liquid and spreads it over the left half of her downy moustache. She presses a strip of paper into the wax and squeezes her eyes closed. She rips it away.

As the eye of round browns, Mya falls onto the sofa, spent and stinging from head to toe, flaming red on her face and legs and certain other areas of her body. She prays the colour fades quickly, before anyone else notices, but she isn't hopeful. There is time for a short nap, she reasons, glancing at her watch. Or she could uncover the mystery of Christina's passport. But before she can make a choice, she remembers the book she brought home for David. *Butterflies and Moths*. He will spend more time asking her questions about his subject than he'll devote to reading, regardless of her insistence. And she needs to be prepared to guide him, to propel him along, or he'll miss his deadline. She picks up the book and skims the table of contents before reading on. Butterflies and moths belong to the same family. The same order. Lepidoptera. Scale-winged insects. Despite similarities in physiology and life cycle, they are opposites in many ways. Butterflies are colourful creatures of the sun, with smooth, slender bodies. The delicate and favoured sister, subject of fairy tales and poems of spring. Moths are muted insects of the night, with plump, fuzzy bodies, known for languishing over porch lights and candle flames, hiding behind curtains and in drawers. While butterflies hoist their colourful wings like sails when they rest, moths blanket themselves with theirs, hiding beneath a canopy of scales.

Poor things.

She dozes, her arm draped over her face, and she dreams of soaring above the coast of Coromandel in a fluttering cloud of monarchs.

"Mom. Mom. What happened to your face?"

Mya opens one eye, then the other. David leans over her with a look of concern in his eyes. She sits up and the fresh sting of depilated flesh resurfaces. She runs her fingers over her cheeks, under her nose. "Oh, honey. Nothing's wrong. I used some hair remover."

David takes a step back, horrified. "You have hair on your face?"

"Not anymore." She wonders how an adolescent mind would cope with visions of the other waxing she had done.

Although it is still bright outside when Mya sets the table for dinner, the sun is on the west side of the house, casting the dining room in soft shadows. She lights candles for ambience. Her boys—her men—devour in ten minutes the food that took two hours to prepare. Conversation is pleasant and light, and to her great surprise, no one else comments on her facial rash. Perhaps it is fading. From time to time she touches her upper lip, delighted at how smooth and soft the skin feels.

"Your book is on the coffee table," she says to David. "Why don't you read it and make an outline for your essay?"

"It's not due for two weeks." David downs the last of his milk.

"You don't want to leave it until the last minute."

"Mom," David groans, wiping his mouth. "I want to go to Josh's game."

"You can't," Josh says. "I'm taking the car and I'm going out after."

Mya gathers up the plates and looks at Steve as she speaks. "It's only Monday. I didn't say you could use the car."

"But I want to—"

"I think we should all go to the game." Steve pushes his chair away from the table. "We'll leave in twenty minutes, in one car. Josh, tonight is a school night. You can go out on the weekend."

Josh looks up from a forkful of mashed potatoes. "But Dad, I—"

"On the weekend. Boys, help your mother clear the table. David, you can read your book in the car." He winks at Mya, and she is eternally grateful for this man who knows what she is thinking with little more to go on than a glance.

She stares into the candlelight for a few moments and, with a sigh, extinguishes the flames.

Lunches have been made, the table is set for breakfast and a loaf of bread sits on the counter to thaw. All the wet bath towels have been neatly hung to dry, the bathtub sparkles and a fresh roll of toilet paper has been placed in the holder. It is eleven o'clock and the boys are sleeping. Mya gently closes her bedroom door, confident that Steve is on the verge of sleep as well; she's taken care of that. The painful task of exfoliation was greatly appreciated, and judging from Steve's reaction, dimpled, dry flesh was not a concern.

With her duties met and no one to interrupt, she pads barefooted down the hall toward the office, dressed in nothing but a brown terry robe, her hair askew. *Maybe Christina's missing passport isn't a bad thing; she'll have to stay in Morocco a bit longer. And she'll have to step outside of her comfort zone to find it . . .*

The blue glow of the computer draws Mya in. Her ears ring with the steady hum of the processor, a sound she likens to the drone of insect wings on summer nights. She positions herself at the desk and begins to type, her fingers flying over the keys.

/ from A POET TICKS

/ BY TANIS **MACDONALD**

In which the Writer looks into the Poem

This poem owns you, lifts you from
sleep, shakes you into your socks and down
in front. A real writer wouldn't take it, wouldn't

sit still for such bad treatment. No one likes
a know-it-all, and don't you know it.

The poem holds its hand over your mouth and
pinches your nostrils shut. You refuse the hood.
The poem's a sadist. It blows smoke in your face.

The poem insists it is worth more than the lines you count.
The poem claims it would be epic, if only.

The poem writes itself on your circadian
rhythms, salts your porridge, rides the humping
rails of peristalsis into your small intestine.

The poem is legion. You would thrust it into
the pigs but for their knowing eyes.

The poem is no angel, but you wrestle. The night is
eight stanzas long. Hip shanked into cadence:
impossible, necessary history.

In which the Writer wonders whether Auden was right

Poetry makes nothing happen over and over. Nothing
slides into your life and heaves itself onto your tall
lap. What a load of old bollocks. Nothing weighs
you down; you squeeze out from under and it lolls

at your feet, never shifts itself, nothing's a lazy bastard.
Its great galumphing absence slows you. You trip
over its long naked tail on your way to the cellar,
where you want to hide from the nothing ripped

from poetry. Spiders spin webs between your fingers.
Arachnids know from nothing. So does damp.
Something shuffles from behind the box of books
you saved from the fire, curling adventures and camp

manuals, something small shambles out. It's
nearsighted and does not love your excuses.
Something's ugly and nothing's got the long
sick suck of shallow good looks. It's got its uses.

It burns the fat of time in heat units of revision.
Your undivided attention. Nothing's your decision.

In which a new year has the Writer resolving

I resolve to write poems only for the common good, poems that don't lecture, poems that evoke and do not confess.

I resolve to write poems that I can hold in my hand, and I resolve further to give up on those poems that fly around the room like trapped pigeons, poems that stun themselves on the window and lie there twitching.

I resolve to resist poems that tangle with the flux of lies, damn lies, and pop culture.

I resolve to give up words like devotion or loss or sparrow, and to write more about oceans and concrete and chickens.

I resolve to never again construct a fort of chairs in the dining room and hide inside it, scribbling and forgetting to talk.

I resolve to give up cheap puns about the body.

I resolve to get into trouble.

In which the Writer Reads

If I hadn't read this line in John Newlove's book, I wouldn't be writing.

If I hadn't read a line of Newlove's in Erin Moure's book, I wouldn't be writing.

If I hadn't hauled out my bike and ridden eight kilometres to the library to get out Newlove's book, I wouldn't be writing.

If I hadn't worked in a branch library for five years, I wouldn't have found this misshelved Newlove where it was living an uncirculated life among all the Ondaatje and I wouldn't be writing.

If all the undergraduates hadn't gone home to their small towns, if they hung around the library all summer, smoking cigarettes and borrowing all the Newlove, I wouldn't be writing.

Energy equals mass times the velocity of light squared. Relativity notwithstanding, this has nothing to do with writing. Newlove says.

If I weren't such a liar, I would write off any horizon.

/ TAKE NO PRISONERS, WRITE NO ADVERBS

/ BY WILLIAM DEXTER **WADE**

October 13:

I hate this professor. Angus MacPherson. If you read, especially CanLit, you'll know the name. Oh, as profs go, he knows his shit. He writes well himself, I guess. One of his novels was shortlisted for one of the prizes—the GG maybe, or was it the Giller? I just don't like talking to him about writing. Since that's what he teaches, well, yes, there's a problem. Talking to him hasn't been much of a problem lately, though. Hemingway is his god and, when I mentioned that I sometimes found Hemingway to be self-serving and all that terse dialogue made his characters seem wooden and dimensionally deficient, he looked at me the way my mum used to look at the life forms that crawled out of my pockets when I was seven. I mean, does anyone even read fucking Hemingway anymore?

Well, since then, he pretends he's never seen me before and my papers have all been returned with the same C, neither plussed nor minused, and completely devoid of the red pencil scrawled lavishly across the papers of the other students, sometimes outdoing them in word-count alone. Not that I care about the mark. I submit a manuscript or a sample chapter, I expect the first thing the editor will look for will be the SASE, not the GPA.

I do resent the lack of direction, however. I mean, this is a required course and May is a long way away and I don't think I'm going to learn anything that I don't get from the textbook. See, MacPherson's magisterial advice is unwaveringly rule-bound and formulaic and I'm a little looser than that, more along the lines of Kerouac, say.

Still, I know I have to learn to do things the MacPherson way. It's hard, though. Here's an example. Today, in that sickening tone of reverent admiration, he informed us of Hemingway's abstemious attitude toward modifiers. Needless to say our assignment for the following week was to write a dialogue between two people in such a way that you knew a great deal about both without narration. "And," glaring straight at me, "without a single adverb."

All eyes in the room followed his to me, some with sycophantic scorn, others with that "you poor bastard" sort of pity, and a few with a smug "better you than me" look. I was recognized now as a marked man, the target of MacPherson's derision. Last week he informed us, again staring all hard-eyed at me, that we shouldn't expect to get rich from writing and that some of us would be better advised to quit immediately and look elsewhere for more likely reward, "something in computing, perhaps, or social work." Oh, fuck you. I'll write the damned Story Without Adverbs.

October 20:

Well, I turned in my Adverbless Story. I lost a lot of sleep and tanked badly on my psych exam, but it was a damned good story. If he gives me a c on this one, I'm going to have it out with the old bastard.

Today's lecture·was more of the same—the pre-eminent importance of nouns and verbs, with long, exemplary passages from Hemingway. God, I hate Hemingway almost as much as I hate MacPherson.

Beginning to wind down at last, he announced, "Your next paper will expunge all adjectives," with a sardonic smile just for me. "Next week, we'll examine Maugham's attitude toward adjectives. Why, did you know that he once wrote . . ."

I didn't hear what Maugham once wrote. My brain froze on the name. Oh, please, not bloody Maugham. Can it get any worse?

October 27:

Well, I got my Paper Without Adverbs back. Surprise! This one got a D and some red pencil:

> When I said NO ADVERBS, I didn't mean JUST A FEW ADVERBS, nor even
> ONLY ONE ADVERB. I meant NO BLOODY ADVERBS. Perhaps you would be
> better advised to withdraw from this course and look for something in TESL.

I was so stunned I didn't even react to MacPherson's infantile sarcasm. I looked at each page of the paper, front and back, but there were no other red marks anywhere, nothing to indicate what he had mistakenly taken to be an adverb.

After the class, I went to the student union for a coffee, then sat and read the paper again from beginning to end. Hah! I've got the old bastard this time. Doesn't seem to know an adverb when he doesn't see one.

October 28:

Damn damn damn goddamn. Okay, the old sod was right. There was an adverb. But, shit, it was so right, so necessary, that I didn't even see it.

Sitting in MacPherson's cluttered office, I argued. I pleaded. I cajoled—I think . . . not quite sure what that means. I remonstrated. I nearly reasoned passionately—until I saw what an adverbial mistake that would have been.

I argued thus: "Damn it, man, when I have the passenger say 'thanks awfully' to the purser, I've told the reader with a single word that he's British, of a certain class, that he's not young, and hinted at so much more about his personality. Depriving him of a harmless adverb makes him sound like . . . like . . . like an American."

To no avail. After frostily warning me never to address him as "man" again, the old dildo offered to read my paper again and revise the mark accordingly—"with no assurance that I'll be as charitable as I was first time round."

393 ▪

Nemesis, your name is MacPherson.

The best I could do was get him to let me try again. He gave me till next class—six days—and the best I could possibly do would be a в, because it would be late. Old prick.

If I didn't get at least a с in the bloody course, I'd have to take it again, so I returned to my dorm room and went to work. I worked on that bloody paper every available minute. The night before it was due, I finally admitted defeat. Life without adverbs just didn't seem possible. I looked at what I had written and knew that even I wouldn't give it more than a d.

As if things weren't bad enough, when I checked the date for voluntary withdrawal from the course, it had passed two days earlier. I could have vw'd instead of trying to write the bloody paper and avoided a lot of grief.

I sat down with a calculator to see what an f would do to my already not very impressive gpa. It wasn't good. It would sink my plans for grad school and wouldn't help my already nebulous career plans. I sat on the edge of my bed in despair and came to the conclusion that maybe old MacPherson was right. Maybe I should think about an mba. Dental hygiene? Welding? Oh God, was I depressed. I toppled over and went to sleep.

November 3:

It was dark when I woke up, cold and disoriented. I crawled under the blankets and tried to remember who I was, where I was, all that. Then I recalled with a rush of despair my decision to drop out of school. As I lay there in the dark, I started to get angry at the injustice of it all. When I couldn't stand it any longer, I got up and put some coffee on. While I waited for it to brew, I paced in rising agitation.

"No, goddamnit. Not with a whimper."

As I poured the first of many cups of coffee, it occurred to me that Hemingway must have developed his style. Surely he didn't just start writing all that boring, virile, noun-verb crap right away. Maybe he got bored with it himself and took excursions. Better still, maybe he started out more or less like other writers, indulging indiscriminately in all parts of speech. Maybe there had been a time, perhaps during an interval of alcohol-induced delirium, when he had availed himself, with uncharacteristic generosity, of adverbs. I'd take the f in the course and withdraw from school, seek a new career, but I could at least do it on my own terms by demonstrating to MacPherson that Hemingway himself hadn't always eschewed modification.

Sure that I was onto something important, I went in search of Hemingway. I only had *The Old Man and the Sea* and *A Moveable Feast*. I paused for a moment, remembering how much I'd enjoyed those two books. Ah, but that was before I'd ever even heard of MacPherson.

A quick scan told me that they wouldn't be enough. They were both pretty adverbless. Odd, I thought in passing, that his style hadn't bothered me much when I read those books. Oh well, I was young.

I charged out of my room and plunged down the hall, pounding on doors, leaving a growing cloud of rancour in my wake, borrowing all the Hemingway I could get. I was a little surprised, really, at how well I did. I managed to collect *A Farewell to Arms*, *The Fifth Column* and the *First Forty-Nine Stories*, *The Sun Also Rises*, *Men Without Women*, *A Farewell to Arms* again, *The Nick Adams Stories*, *Islands in the Stream*, *Across the River and Into the Trees*, *Death in the Afternoon*, *To Have and Have Not* and *In Our Time*.

I piled the books on the desk, poured more coffee and began to scan for adverbs. This proved to be daunting. The sun was well up and my coffee pot empty when I finally threw in the towel. I closed *Death in the Afternoon*, having satisfied myself that not even in his earliest work did Hemingway show the slightest affection for adverbs, adjectives, or even innocent little conjunctions.

No, damn it, I won't admit defeat. It's not my fault that stingy old wretch didn't like half the English language. I'll demonstrate to MacPherson, and to the world, that, much as they admired Hemingway, even his prose could be more appealing with a few—no, goddamnit, a generous sprinkling of modifiers. With special attention to the adverb, of course.

I started my computer and opened the file in which I had stored sixteen kilobytes of flaccid attempts at the required adverbless paper. I block-deleted all of it and centred a new title at the top: Hemingway Unplugged.

I tapped in a brief, plagiarism-avoiding, explanatory introduction, then took up *The Old Man and the Sea* and began to leaf through it, looking for a suitable passage. Then I had second thoughts. No, MacPherson was going to be a hard enough sell without taking on the Pulitzer committee and a few billion critics. Frozen now in indecision, I nearly gave up, until it came to me that those critics mostly hadn't liked *Across the River and Into the Trees*. Perhaps that had been its problem—just an arid desert, unshaded by adjectives, unwatered by adverbs. Yes. Good choice. Seeing that I didn't have a lot of time left, I quickly chose a passage near the end of the book that was about the right length for MacPherson's paper, or would be after I added the salvaging modifiers. I quickly typed the passage and set to work making those wooden words come to life. Then, to dramatize their enhancing effect, I carefully changed the colour of my additions to grey, leaving Hemingway's original words in stark black.

After I'd finished, I read over my—well, our—work, made a few changes and sat back, smiling happily. I'd done it. Not even MacPherson could fail to see the dramatic improvement I'd wrought. Oh, he'd never admit it, of course. Still, he'd know. It would come to him in time that he had lost a writer of huge talent. God, if only Hemingway's time and mine had concurred, what glorious collaborations we could have done. A Pulitzer would have been ours. A Nobel too, no doubt.

I came down to earth when I recalled that, of course, those prizes had come to Hemingway without me. But still, I'm sure recognition would have come to us much sooner.

In the mood now to celebrate, I flipped through my CDs until I ran across Ode to Joy, its appropriateness instantly clear to me, put it on, and cranked the volume.

395

I typed a cover sheet and saw that I had time for a shower, during which I bellowed along with Beethoven's chorus, "*Wir betreten feuertrunken, Himmlische, dein Heiligtum . . .*" Damn, I felt good.

Later that same day:
There was no point really in sitting through another one of MacPherson's lectures, so I just dropped my paper by the lectern and stood aside while the other students were still coming in, making their way to their seats.

After glaring at me for a long moment, MacPherson glanced down at my paper, stared at it a minute or so, then looked away as he flipped the cover page over, like it was an accident. Taking his time, he eventually glanced down at my paper. Then his eyes narrowed as he picked it up, his interest perhaps captured by the unusual pattern of grey text scattered among the carbon-black. As he began to read, his face became red and a tremor began in his hands. The room was suddenly very still. I looked around and saw everyone frozen in place, like one of those photographs taken in the last instant before thermonuclear obliteration, watching the old man. His face grew redder still, mottled with purple. His whole body trembled, and veins stood out on his forehead. At last he crumpled the paper in his fist and said "Shit!" in a terse, guttural voice and kept repeating it in time with the pounding of his fists on the table.

I had the impression that there was a lot more he wanted to say but was so enraged that he was HOPELESSLY inarticulate and could ONLY distill his thoughts into a single wrathful word. Then he hurled himself VIOLENTLY backward, hitting the wall RESOUNDINGLY. He fell HEAVILY to the floor, eyes staring UNSEEINGLY upward, his heels drumming RHYTHMICALLY on the floor. The motion of his body ceased ABRUPTLY and he lay rigid, staring ACCUSINGLY up at me.

November 10:
MacPherson's funeral was today. Class was cancelled, of course, not that it mattered to me.

There was a huge crowd, mostly his university colleagues, since he didn't have much family, just his daughter, who looked pretty old herself. The service was impressive in a depressing sort of way. The dean did the eulogy, which was very moving, I guess, and the organist played Fauré's *Requiem*. A number of people wept. I almost did.

There was a reception afterward in the basement of the church, with lots of food. I didn't eat too much, out of respect, I guess. After I paid my condolences to MacPherson's daughter, I wanted to go. I tried not to leave too soon but, when I finally got away and was walking down the street away from the church, it came to me that there really was no reason to follow through on my plan to drop out of school. Or even to withdraw from the writing course. Wait and see, right?

November 17:
Well, the new professor, Colin Hedgerow, is a young guy, not much older than I am, just three years past his Ph.D. I found myself really enjoying his first lecture. Which,

by the way, contained all kinds of modifiers. At the end of the class, he asked if there were questions. Mine was the first hand in the air. I asked if there was any particular twentieth-century writer he thought was of particular importance.

He insisted that he had no heroes, thought they were inappropriate, but admitted enjoying ". . . the works of Atwood, Findley, Ondaatje, Vanderhaeghe, perhaps Pynchon in the States, and, oh, a pretty long list, really, now I think of it. No reason to be narrow."

Pynchon? Can't get much farther from Hemingway than that.

When I asked how he felt about Hemingway, he thought for a moment, and said, "A very important writer, of course."

Oh God, here we go.

"In his time. He provided a new direction that was badly needed in his day." After a thoughtful pause, he added, "Not a writer we would find it necessary to emulate today."

Yes!

"A-and how do you feel about writing without adverbs?"

Well, I had to be sure.

He looked perplexed, then said, "Hemingway is not the only writer from whom we can learn." Then he added, "Why would anyone want to forego the appropriate use of any instrument of grammar?"

December 1:

My first paper got an A- and some really quite helpful blue pencil. I've always liked blue. It seems so much less judgmental than that garish red MacPherson used.

Did I mention that Colin—Professor Hedgerow, I mean—has been very encouraging about grad school?

Oh, MacPherson? Well, I feel bad about him. I do. Really. But if you're thinking that his stroking out was my fault, forget that. No way. He did it himself. Anyone can see that. And, you know what? He was just completely wrong about adverbs. They can be very useful.

/ SHADOW-BOXING WITH ANNIE DILLARD

/ BY GLOE **CORMIE**

Why should we be raising Cain
Instead of raising tomatoes, Annie?
What's wrong with the lush blooming
Of tomato plants, anyways? say I &
On my side Komunyakaa says,
Pan wasn't raising Cain among the reeds.
He was lying there puffing ganja &
Blowing smoke rings.

I, a poet with ancestors farming prairie &
Steppes, a plethora, certainly, of
Tomato growers among them, say,
The tending of tomatoes nurtures
Eros in one's life surely as spring
Warmth after winter ice.

Growing tomatoes & sunflowers
In my backyard pulls me into
A kind of ganja smoking reverie.
I watch the first leaves open &
Multiply
Watch the first buds form
Burgeoning
Into firm tomatoes,
Flirty petalled sunflowers.

It relaxes me—stretches me into
In-between time, dreamtime
The world morphs into treacle toffee
Concerns soften & melt
In lava lamp wax
Floating up
Sashaying down
In amorphous shapes
When I tend my growing
Garden the hours open too,

Edges melting, my tomatoes ripen,
My sunflowers
Bloom.

/ THE STRONG PRESENCE OF LILAC ROSES

/ BY GLOE **CORMIE**

Far-off kitchen roses. As Prairie voyageur, I have to beeline in the dark, through my bedroom, the bathroom and the guest room, to get to the sterling-petal scent, folded with the grease of cutlery soaking in dishwater.

If only I could impersonate the look of a stranger arriving in moccasins, wheat clinging to feet, hair matted from the long journey against prairie wind.

The room was quiet except for a murmur of rose leaves in my wake, and moist dust clumps that land with aplomb on the hot cook stove.

/ ON ARRIVING

/ BY NADINE **DE LISLE**

A red Liz Claiborne wallet hides the subterfuge within. New photo identification. Under the photograph, my new identity: Artist.

I am ready to begin this new life at the Banff Centre with breakfast in the dining room at Donald Cameron Hall, but I can't find it. I must look as lost as I feel because a tall, elegant man approaches and offers assistance. I comment on the lovely setting. He murmurs appreciatively. I note the expanse. He nods quietly.

"The Centre is undergoing a renovation," he whispers to me, "a revitalization, actually. There is a capital campaign. Over a hundred million dollars. They will decommission Donald Cameron Hall to build something new and sleek and avant garde."

"That's an ambitious project," I say.

"Millions," he repeats, his voice low, as he glances behind and in front of me.

Capital campaigns. Fundraising's highest stakes. Not at all like that humble arts staple: the bingo fundraiser. Grab your comfy shoes and toss on a t-shirt. You'll get an apron and a wad of tickets—break-opens perhaps, or a thick stack of bingo cards. Snake up and down and up and down the room. Ah, your first customer. Put on your best *How may I help you, miss?* smile and approach. "Give me the fourth from the bottom and the second from the top—Stop! That one is creased. I don't want that. Give me the third from the top. Don't touch anything else."

During hour two, your feet and your motivation wear thin. You have already begun little games for amusement. You have assessed the room and picked your favourites: Gene in the cowboy shirt in the back and Martha, up front with her battalion of little trolls. You know where the undertow is, that current of evil combatants along the wall and into the centre. Stay away from them; they will bring you down. Nothing you can do will please them. You reach for a break-open ticket. "No, I said don't touch it; it's no good to me now. Let me have the twenty-seventh from the bottom. No, never mind, I want the first one from the top and the second one from the bottom too." Do not be offended. Just don't knock over the trolls.

The pace will slow. You will become—although you really try to appreciate the human dimension and the social science of it and you know it is for a worthy cause—you will become bored. You will wish it were over. There is only one remedy. It is Diversion. It is Folly.

First, choose a trusted friend. Next, sweep through the defined territory. Give no hint of your mission. Do not change your face. If you have been aloof and distant, remain so. Likewise if you have been charming and friendly. Report back. Do not be concerned if you find no one the first time; you have two more turns. Remember the rules: if you do not choose for yourself, someone will be chosen for you. No friend will choose the absolutely loathsome, that is why you have partnered in trust with your comrade. One more turn. Nothing. Now you have two choices: you can be more inventive with your quest—urgency will spur you on—or, you can lower your standards. Oh, what are a few missing teeth? What is all the rage with a full head of hair? It's only one moment. It may be quite fleeting. You will close your eyes and think of England, or perhaps you will be delightfully surprised. Expand your horizons. Break through the preconceived barriers limiting your choices. Buck up, dear one. Lifelong marriages are still arranged in many cultures. This is only one night; choose your mate. Then return to your compatriot, announce your decision and enjoy a good laugh. At the end of the evening, go home and soak your feet.

A capital campaign is nothing like bingo. You must dress more carefully. (Unless you are bestowing one of the major gifts, in which case, be as haphazard as you like.) A business suit is appropriate. Gentlemen may wear golf shirts (as long as they are expensive) and slacks (so long as they dimple demurely at the shoe). Ladies must have an evening gown for the Top Hat Ball, a frock for the Coming up Roses Garden Party and something smart for luncheons and meetings. And money. You must have money.

Here in Banff my new fundraiser friend raises a long, delicate hand towards a doorway and we say our goodbyes. Inside, the stairs curve in a grand and gracious gesture from the entrance down to the dining floor. Mission-style chairs are set against white linens. The 180 degrees of arts and crafts windows form a proscenium stage facing the mountains: Rundle, Sulphur, Cascade and Norquay. I expect Fred Astaire to dance down the circle, Noel Coward to enter stage right. I envision the perfectly themed black tie dinner party: absolute elegance and sophistication. I am not properly dressed, I realize as I head to the stairs. I walk slowly to savour the moment and to prevent myself from tumbling against swirls of carpet patterns that cleverly mask where one step ends and the other begins. The hostess at the bottom stands poised to greet me as I stammer down the staircase. This takes some time; yet, all the while she smiles, as if she really is happy to see me.

Two or three wait staff glide among the tables. A few patrons have chosen quiet spots at the side or the back. I scan the room and walk to the front. I sit at a round table with a high-flying place card that says ARTISTS. There are nine empty chairs and there is me. Just me, looking out to the mountains: Rundle, Sulphur, Cascade and Norquay. I look at each of them, look them right in their mountain eyes from my place centre stage.

Silently, a full-bodied waiter appears at my side. I order decaffeinated coffee with milk and a vegetable egg-white omelette, and he gracefully waves to the white-skirted stations behind me and bows towards me to mention: "It's buffet-style, madam."

That is quite fine with me; I'm nothing if not adaptable, so I get up, rest my napkin lovingly on my chair and walk thoughtfully to the skirted tables (pleated, not gathered) to choose from the salads and fish and cheeses. Then I top up the pile with three eggs Benedict. I had to request the additional two, but I did so graciously and pleasantly, and the serving staff didn't flinch at all. At the table, I set my back to the room and arrange my abundance around me. I can hear rustlings behind but no one sits down. I am reminded how I love to read the paper at breakfast. I will remember to bring a *Globe* along tomorrow.

The next morning, I tuck a newspaper under my arm and walk right out of Lloyd Hall directly to the dining room. I greet the hostess warmly, and note that a number of people are already at the tables. I survey the buffet stands—seafood eggs Benedict today, I see—and I nod to the mountains. Someone is already at the artists' table. He is a stocky fellow, barrel-chested, hair shorn tight, big hands.

"Can you believe all this food?" he asks me after we've said hello.

"It's fabulous," I agree, minding the tower of fruit I've wedged between French toast and country scrambled eggs.

He's from Australia, Aboriginal, he tells me. "I love it here."

We talk about the mountains.

"Ain't they just amazing," he says; and the air: "I'm tired all the time," and about the beautiful dining room of Donald Cameron Hall. "And it's all included," he laughs and I laugh, too.

Others join us.

"It's hard to believe," I suggest as my new friends turn towards me, "that this building, Donald Cameron Hall, is being" (pause) "this dining room is being" (pause). They lean forward. "Is being decommissioned."

"What?"

"Soon it will be gone," I explain.

"Can't they save it?"

"Apparently not; they're starting a capital campaign for a new one."

"Oh my God, what a pity," we all pine, looking out from our elegance to the mountains and the trees.

The next day, I meet the class; we sit tentatively in a boxed alignment of tables facing one another.

"Why don't we go around the table and introduce ourselves, talk about why we are here and what we expect to get from our time in Banff," says Mark, our leader. It's begun.

By the third day it is *my* writing group and *my* writing group has its own tables democratically mixed with visual artists and poets. At breakfast, lunch and dinner, we talk about our work (writing) and what we do in our other lives (work). My Australian friend joins us, and that's when I realize I am a fraud. He is the real thing. Art is what he does—for a living. Right now, he's working on a large installation. He'll be working on it for months. Months and months. He goes all over the world making art. Instead of following snow, like the ski junkies of Lake Louise, he follows residencies and grants. He gets lots of them, he says without a wisp of conceit. Would I like to come and see it? His studio in the woods. He is in the Leighton Studios.

403 ■

His workspace is tall and open and light. I don't know what it is called, but it is not the boat. (I don't understand the studio in the boat, although everyone tells me it's clever.) I myself long for the Evamy—the glass house with its wraparound desk in the sunlight. The Hemingway would do, although it is a trifle dark.

I go back to my room to write. I click in a row of words and erase them all with the ease of an Etch-a-Sketch. I move my little round table to the balcony and set my laptop on it. I look at my mountains and realize I can't tell them apart. Which is Rundle? Where's Sulphur? It's all a sham, a forgery, a pretense. I thought I was an artist because of the ID card. Oh, I have a room at the Banff Centre, a nice one, and the bed is large and very comfortable and there's this balcony, too. There is tea and coffee outside the elevators each morning. The writers' lounge is here. I know the code so I can get in but there is never anything going on. No writers lounging or discussing their work. Just one or two checking email. No one turns around to say hello. So I usually just go back to my room to write. Click. Click. Click. See. I'm writing.

Then I lift my eyes over the BFI bins and look at my mountains again. I feel the cool air on my face and the warmth of knowing that there is no other place I want to be. So I write. Then I write some more. When I'm finished, I remedy a wayward pronoun and change an article. I remove a comma and put it back again. It's not bad. I reread it. It's not too bad. Take more emotional risks, my writing group has offered, so in a fit of exuberance, I sign up for reading night.

I've chosen my story carefully and I've practised. Stood right in front of the mirror and read out loud. Played around with the words. Rewritten a few sections. I'm ready. I look into faces in the audience as I glance up from the page. And that first face responds and says go on and I do, and soon the next face is nodding too, and then I wait just a second, because now that I'm into it, I really think they are going to like this next part . . . and they do! Then, just as I'm getting used to the experience, it's over. I say thank you and there's applause and I get a hug from Mark and more encouragement from my writing mates and later a few people come up to me and say they liked my reading.

"Good story," says a noted poet who's moved from Winnipeg to BC, so I have another glass of wine.

"Going to the lounge?" someone asks.

"What's going on?" I reply with adolescent nonchalance.

"Oh, a few of us are going over to hang out—have a few drinks, some food."

"I couldn't; I was planning to get to sleep. I stayed up last night finishing the story. It's already midnight and I have another story to finish and our group meets at nine a.m."

There are potato chips and beer and red wine and we sit on the floor and on low-slung couches in the writers' lounge. Someone orders pizza, and I stay up until two in the morning.

My ears crack open as the plane lurches to concrete at the Winnipeg Airport Authority. I'm back home. For now.

/ THE SUITCASE

/ BY SMARO **KAMBOURELI**

An Incomplete Dictionary of Unmitigated Desires

A Aubigny (as in D'Aubigny or d'Aubigné). A name that evokes a measure of splendour, nobility, forfeited grandeur, cross-dressing, Trappist monks who made honey and cheese, alleged debauchery, and, naturally, scandal. The name of villages in France, Scotland, and Manitoba, Canada, its claim to history is best traced to La Maupin. Born Julie d'Aubigny (1670-1707), she was truly a product of the Baroque. An intrepid swordswoman who often donned male attire, professional duellist in the Latin Quarter, volatile diva at the Paris Opera, and the heroine of Théophile Gautier's novel, Mademoiselle de Maupin (1835), she was sentenced to death by fire. Her crime? She had followed her blond female lover to the convent where she had been placed by her outraged parents. To flee the convent unobserved, La Maupin "disinterred the body" of a nun who had died recently, "placed it in the bed of her beloved," and "set the room afire." The two escaped in the havoc that ensued, though La Maupin soon tired of her lover. Her first lover, Compte d'Armagnac, whom she had taken to her bed at the tender age of fourteen, had no trouble persuading the King to annul her sentence. Here were two men who could see reason in what the rest of society saw as aberration. No wonder advances in the lives of women in the fin-de-siècle period were referred to as *Attitudes à La Maupin*. On August 21, 1891, DOMLM (Devotees of Mme. La Maupin) held their bi-annual meeting in Aubigny, Manitoba.

B Beauty is not in the eye of the beholder. Beauty is the loosening of hardness, the touch of [not legible]

C Chance is a man who wants to be undressed.

G Gabriel, the character played by Wesley Hill in the film *The Green Pastures* (circa 1932). Gabriel, according to the *Encyclopedia Acephalica*, is the angel who presides over Monday. Credited for seducing Eve, and later Mary, he is also one of the three archangels, and the chief among angels to experience guilt.

405

Coda

The Dictionary of Unmitigated Desires was found, unbound, inside a pillowcase of Egyptian cotton, in the battered suitcase of a Greek immigrant woman who settled, briefly, it would appear, in Winnipeg, Manitoba, circa 1950. With many of its pages missing and some irreversibly damaged, it is doubtful we will ever know who authored it, what exactly inspired its inception, what audience it was intended for, or, for that matter, how it fell into the hands of the anonymous Greek immigrant. The name on the label, tied to the scuffed brown-leather suitcase with fishing line, is not legible. Only the name of the Greek city of Thessaloniki is decipherable (presumably her place of origin). Perhaps that city's Oriental history—for centuries a hotbed of assorted races cavorting with each other—can account for the mongrel character of this so-called dictionary. Surely it must have been composed by someone whose voracious appetite for dubious pleasures was fed by an active imagination that can only defile civilization.

As to how we can surmise the gender of the suitcase's owner, the contents speak for themselves: the photograph of a couple holding hands with a female toddler, strolling on a promenade (Thessaloniki is a port city in the Mediterranean Basin), kept inside an empty package of Wonder cigarettes, a Greek brand of tobacco long extinct; an unfinished manuscript, albeit written in unorthodox English, about the fictional-ized life of Juan de Fuca (a.k.a. Apostolos Valerianos), the particular brand of lyricism which bears, according to the distinguished Canadian literary critic, Dr. Helen Binks, a distinctly female signature; silk and fine cotton undergarments (including a peeka-boo bra) and other kinds of female apparel such as a frayed satin *robe de chambre* (a gum wrapper with Greek lettering in its left pocket, the wishbone of a chicken in the right); a tattered pocket-size guide, *Women Travellers in Canada*, edited by Freya Becker, sparingly annotated in Greek but with an excess of semi-colons (question marks in the Greek language) in the margins.

This evidence leaves no doubt as to the gender and ethnicity of the suitcase's owner. Notwithstanding the lack of documents that might shed some light on her identity or the circumstances that saw Winnipeg as her temporary destination, we can easily infer that the woman in question, who evidently had writing aspirations and was French-reading, if not French-speaking, found Winnipeg unconducive to pursuing a career as authoress. One need not have an unbridled imagination to deduce what kind of "profession" [sic] she practised. Lest it be seen as an untoward conclusion, it is com-mon knowledge (the kind that can be historically proven) that adverse conditions such as the ones most likely encountered by this female Greek traveller, and a novelist *man-qué* at that, were the most probable reasons that put the second sex, however reluc-tantly or intermittently, on the path to debauchery. (Modern theories have debunked earlier social views according to which women had a natural proclivity toward immorality.)

The suitcase was found in a pile of debris after the waters of the 1950 Winnipeg flood receded. Nobody claimed it. But its forlorn contents, notably the unfinished novel, appealed to my historian's sensibility. An amateur writer myself, I have an abiding interest in all things related to Saskatchewan, the province where my grand-parents settled. For a Juan de Fuca (a.k.a. Ioannis Fokas), a member of the Francisco Eliza expedition (circa 1790), is supposed to have crossed the Rockies and gotten as far as the Cypress Hills. He cannot possibly be the same de Fuca who explored the Anian Strait, but this woman's fiction would seem to suggest so. I have never been known to eschew difficult questions, however implausible they may be. Hence my rescuing the suitcase's contents from perishing forever. As soon as I finish tracing all references to Juan de Fuca and complete my transcription of the dictionary [sic], it is my intention to deliver this woman's suitcase to the local archives. It may serve as valuable testimony to the dangers inherent in immigration (especially in relation to single female immigrants), the imperative to secure means of screening undesirable persons, namely, persons with dubious desires.

As for the dictionary, it is a perverse travesty of the science of language, a wicked distortion of history. Indubitably the figment of a diseased imagination, it is the kind of book that would have been written by a depraved Frenchman. Many a night I have retired to bed at a healthy hour, only to stay awake while pondering the unfathomable turns of history: Juan de Fuca, a Greek islander who ended up serving the Spanish Court, visiting Saskatchewan; a spoof of a dictionary mocking decency; and the mys-tery of the Greek woman. Who was she? What did that innocent girl in the photograph grow up to look like? What decent woman would venture—alone, I presume, for lack of evidence to the contrary—to travel as far and as light as she did? Was her sojourn in Winnipeg just one stop among many in her peregrinations around Canada? What company did she keep? Did I ever encounter her, unbeknownst to me? What became of her? If, on one of these restive nights, I open her suitcase and let my fingers linger over the soft surface of her garments, or take her robe to bed with me, trying to imag-ine her scent, it is only because I pray for insight, some opening into the mystery that surrounds her.

J.B.

Winnipeg, Manitoba, 1972

Coda, my eye. What a self-conceited prig. Joseph Buchan was a high school teacher many years ago who took early retirement when he was still in his mid-forties. Don't ask me why, I've no idea, though these days I have a suspicion or two.

In fact, I never knew him well at all. He was Sarah's uncle. An oddball, she used to call him. A quintessential bachelor, he was never seen without that burgundy bow tie of his, barely visible under the folds of his second chin that shook comically when he got agitated about something—usually "an idea" of some sort. His suspenders were so stretched over his paunch, you'd think they'd burst loose any moment. And his beady eyes were always watery. To complement his meagre pension, he eventually got a part-time position as a secretary at a notary's office. I don't recall him ever mentioning his writing in my presence the few times we met for dinner at Sarah's house. But then I always tried to avoid him and sit as far away from him as possible. I remember him as a quaint old man who never said much, perspired for no apparent reason and gave off a faint smell of mothballs. You couldn't help but have the sense he was merely tolerated—his presence at the Sunday dinner table a duty.

It was common knowledge that he had literary aspirations, but that was not to be discussed over dinner. Sarah's father had put a moratorium on hearing his brother-in-law going on and on with his outlandish speculations about a suitcase that belonged to a missing Greek woman, and the story he was writing about her. These are either the fantasies of a sick mind or those of a guilty conscience, he shouted as he left the dinner table in a huff. All this, of course, according to Sarah—my best friend during my high school years in Winnipeg, the only person from that time I'm still in contact with. Her parents were too proper ever to make a scene in my presence. Apparently, Joseph Buchan complied, for he never mentioned that story again. It would seem that he would either talk about that suitcase's contents endlessly or not talk at all. He ate quietly, now and then shaking his head vigorously to suggest consent or disagreement to what was being said, occasionally muttering something incomprehensible while dabbing his mouth with his napkin. I used to think he was a sad and pitiful figure.

It was when he started skipping family dinners that Sarah's family realized he had found a more willing audience to subject to his obsession. He became a regular at the Canadian Authors Association's events, and eventually those of the recently founded Manitoba Writers' Guild. But it was not about that novel of his, the one he claimed to have found in a stray suitcase, about exploration and discovery (a.k.a. colonialism), that the Guild had called Sarah's mother. They didn't call to tell her that her brother had won a writing contest, that's for sure. They called to invite the family to his reading, a nice ploy to alert them to the spectacle he made of himself. He had become such a nuisance at open mike sessions they'd had it with him. Readings weren't the kind of event Sarah's parents attended, but she and I were persuaded to go instead. In fact, that evening was the last time I saw him. It was the open mike session after the Guild's conference banquet. As his name was announced, he stumbled toward the mike—the same paunch, the same bow tie, the same suspenders. He wasted his five minutes or so by shuffling his loose pages and mumbling some version or other of his Coda. (Why on earth did he call it that?) I can still see the audience members rolling their eyes or lighting up (in those days you could still smoke indoors). But he did have a flare for inventiveness—I give him that—a telltale sign of his wackiness. A box of Greek cigarettes called Wonder, yeah, right. He probably saw an old-timer at Kelekis's drawing a cigarette out of an exotic-looking package, I thought, and that's how he got the idea. But it was the peekaboo bra that, as far as I was concerned, gave him away. The dirty old bugger. Not to mention his concern for single immigrant women. There's another instance of subtle racism for you. Sarah was so embarrassed she made sure we didn't run into him in the crowd. I don't know what she told her mother about that evening, but Uncle Joseph stopped appearing at Guild dos. But not Sarah. Though not a writer herself, she never missed a Guild event until she saw again the young man she had met that first evening. She and Doug got married a year later.

I hadn't thought of Joseph Buchan in ages, though I vaguely remember Sarah telling me that he had passed away. When Sarah and I get together, mostly when I visit Winnipeg to see my mother, we have other things to talk about. Her second husband (Doug was a five-month-long mistake) and two children, our aging and stubborn mothers, whoever my lover happens to be at the time. Beyond birthday and Christmas cards, we never write to each other, so I was surprised to receive a letter from her. "I'm sure you remember Uncle Joseph," her letter began unceremoniously. "The cat is out of the bag at last."

Is it ever? I feel bad for her mother. She must have felt horrified to keep what she had discovered about her brother after his death a secret all these years—she was always protective of him—but not tell even Sarah? Perhaps she kept quiet until now for fear that her brother's stories were not just a sham. How else to explain the evidence she came upon? "Here it is," Sarah's letter concluded hastily. "Don't you think that there must have been something after all to his story about the suitcase? Will call on the weekend."

What her mother had found in Uncle Joseph's closet, hanging between his outdated suits, was an old, stained and smelly satin robe. The peekaboo bra, black lace with red trimming, was carefully folded and hidden away under his underwear. Somehow I wasn't surprised. I had always thought he was at least a harmless fetishist, but Sarah's mother must have felt mortified. It's one thing to know you've got a boring old brother to contend with, and another to discover that he had the kind of secret life that can turn your orderly, well-arranged world upside down. Though she got rid of both the robe and the bra right away, she kept the rest of what she had found. Under his bed, pushed all the way against the wall, was an ancient, musty-smelling suitcase. It was empty, but a homemade label was still attached to it, though she couldn't make out what it said. Inside it she found an empty box of Greek cigarettes, as well as a few old printed pages, most of them so stained with mould that they were completely undecipherable or crumpled as she handled them. Dictionary or not, this was obviously what Joseph Buchan had been alluding to all those years. Stuck in between those pages was a snapshot of a couple strolling with their little daughter on a promenade. There was no evidence of the unfinished novel, nor did she find the travel book he referred to or any other female clothing, new or old. What he called a Coda, with an array of other papers, was neatly placed in a folder by his typewriter. And it was his own text, along with the three, still legible, pages of that bizarre dictionary, the flattened cigarette box, and the family snapshot that Sarah's envelope contained.

I'd never heard of La Maupin before, but I have since discovered that she is—was—real. And Aubigny, well, Aubigny is the little farming community south of Winnipeg where the Manitoba Writers' Guild was founded. As far as I'm concerned, this is its only claim to fame. But what about Uncle Joseph? Where did he find that suitcase? Did he really know a Greek woman? Did he take her in and then somehow things got out of hand? What happened to her, assuming she ever existed? Is she the mother or the little girl in the photograph? Sarah's mother didn't recognize either the man or the woman. Who are these people? Suppose Sarah's uncle bought the suitcase in some junk shop—why did he become so obsessed with its contents? Perhaps he was a real crackpot, the kind that needs to give shape and substance to his fantasies. Sarah may have already figured something out. Until this weekend then.

/ CONTRIBUTORS

ARTHUR ADAMSON, born in Winnipeg in 1926, taught English literature and creative writing at the University of Manitoba. He has published art criticism and three volumes of poetry. He is also a visual artist; *Arthur Adamson—A Celebration, a book of selected paintings*, was published by J. Gordon Shillingford Publications in 2006.

GEORGE AMABILE's work has appeared in numerous periodicals, journals and anthologies in Canada, the USA, the UK, Europe, South America, Australia and New Zealand. He has edited two poetry magazines, published eight books and won half a dozen national and international prizes. His most recent book is *Tasting the Dark: New and Selected Poems* (The Muses' Company 2001).

DAVID ANNANDALE teaches literature and film at the University of Manitoba. His novels are the thrillers *Crown Fire* (2002) and *Kornukopia* (2004), both from Turnstone Press.

DAVID ARNASON is a poet, fiction writer, playwright, editor and professor of English. His most recent book, with Mhari Mackintosh, is *The Imagined City: A Literary History of Winnipeg* (Turnstone 2004).

JONATHAN BALL is a writer and filmmaker. His writing has appeared nationally in Canada and sporadically in the USA, the UK and Australia. He edits the literary journal *dANDelion* and writes a humour column, Haiku Horoscopes, which appears at <www.haikuhoroscopes.com>. Visit Jonathan online at <www.jonathanball.com>.

PAMELA BANTING is the author of *Body Inc.: A Theory of Translation Poetics* (Turnstone 1995) and the editor of *Fresh Tracks: Writing the Western Landscape* (Polestar 1998). She teaches courses such as Writing the Rural, The Literature of Wilderness and Wilder Places, Literature and the Environment, and creative non-fiction for the English Department, University of Calgary.

GERARD BEIRNE, originally from Ireland, has been living in Manitoba for almost ten years. His novel *The Eskimo in the Net* (Marion Boyars 2003) was shortlisted for the Kerry Group Irish Fiction Award and was selected by the literary editor of the *Daily Express* as his Book of the Year for 2004. His collection of poems *Digging My Own*

Grave (Dedalus Press 1996) won second place in the Patrick Kavanagh Poetry Award. His story "Sightings of Bono" was adapted for a film featuring Bono of U2. While living in Norway House, Manitoba, he edited for publication an anthology of interviews he co-conducted with Métis and Cree Elders.

DAVID BERGEN is the author of four award-winning novels, most recently *The Time in Between* (McClelland & Stewart 2005), which won the Scotiabank Giller Prize, the McNally Robinson Book of the Year Award and the Margaret Laurence Award for Fiction. He has also published a collection of short fiction, *Sitting Opposite My Brother* (Turnstone 1993). His new novel, "The Retreat," will be published by McClelland & Stewart in 2008.

DONNA BESEL lives in Lac du Bonnet. Her story "Dead Skunk" won second place in *Prairie Fire*'s 2002 non-fiction competition. In 2004, the Manitoba Arts Council awarded her a grant to expand this story into a novel. Other writing has appeared in several publications.

SANDRA BIRDSELL has published three collections of short fiction, four novels and a novel for young readers. Her bestselling novel *The Russländer* (McClelland & Stewart) was nominated for the 2001 Giller Prize. She was awarded the Marian Engel Award in 1993, and has twice been nominated for the Governor General's Award, for the novel *The Chrome Suite* (M&S 1992) and for the short-story collection *The Two-Headed Calf* (M&S 1997). Her novel *Children of the Day* was published by Random House Canada in 2005. Sandra is a founding member of the Manitoba Writers' Guild.

A writer/storyteller from Brandon, Manitoba, **LAURIE BLOCK** has performed and published across Canada. His story "While the Librarian Sleeps" won the 2003 *Prairie Fire* fiction contest and the 2004 National Magazine Gold Award. His essay "Midnight Train" was shortlisted for the 2006 CBC Literary Competition, in the creative non-fiction category. His latest book of poetry, *Time out of Mind* (Oolichan 2006), won the inaugural Lansdowne Prize for Poetry.

DI BRANDT is delighted to be back in the Manitoba prairie, her beloved home landscape, after a decade away. She holds a Canada Research Chair in Creative Writing at Brandon University. She has published six books of poetry and three books of creative essays, most recently *So this is the world & here I am in it* (NeWest Press, The Writer as Critic Series, ed. Smaro Kamboureli, 2007). She is co-editor (with Barbara Godard of York University) of an anthology of poetry and multimedia works by Canadian women poets, artists, scholars and musicians, *Re:Generations: Canadian Women Poets in Conversation* (Black Moss 2005).

MARTHA BROOKS is a novelist, lyricist and jazz singer. Her young adult title *True Confessions of a Heartless Girl* (Farrar Straus Giroux 2002) won the Governor General's Award and found an international market in Germany, Japan, Italy, Spain and the USA. *Mistik Lake* (Farrar Straus Giroux 2007) is a multi-generational novel about family secrets, love and loss.

ROB BUDDE teaches creative writing, contemporary critical theory and postcolonial literature at the University of Northern BC in Prince George. He has published two poetry collections, *Catch as Catch* (Turnstone 1994) and *traffick* (Turnstone 1999); two novels, *Misshapen* (NeWest 1997) and *The Dying Poem* (Coach House 2002); a collection of interviews, *In Muddy Water* (J. Gordon Shillingford 2003) and a book of short fiction, *Flicker* (Signature 2005). He edited and introduced a collection of poetry by the late Al Purdy called *The More Easily Kept Illusions* (Wilfrid Laurier UP 2006). Due out in 2007 is a third book of poetry, *Finding Ft. George*, from Nightwood Editions.

ALISON CALDER teaches Canadian literature and creative writing at the University of Manitoba. She is the author of one poetry collection, *Wolf Tree* (Coteau 2007) and the editor of three books on aspects of prairie literature and culture. She lives in Winnipeg with her husband, Warren Cariou, and their two cats.

MELANIE CAMERON is the author of two books of poetry: *Holding the Dark* (The Muses' Company 1999), which was shortlisted for the Eileen MacTavish Sykes Award for Best First Book by a Manitoba Writer, and *wake* (The Muses' Company 2003), a finalist for the Carol Shields Winnipeg Book Award. She has been twice nominated for the John Hirsch Award for Most Promising Manitoba Writer and is a former poetry co-editor for *Prairie Fire*.

WARREN CARIOU has published a book of novellas entitled *The Exalted Company of Roadside Martyrs* (Coteau 1999) and a memoir, *Lake of the Prairies* (Random House 2002). He teaches English at the University of Manitoba and is working on a novel.

SHARON CASEBURG is a Winnipeg poet, critical writer and editor. Her work has appeared in several Canadian literary journals, including *Room of One's Own, Contemporary Verse 2, Lichen, The Antigonish Review* and *Prairie Fire*.

LORI CAYER's first collection of poetry, *Stealing Mercury* (The Muses' Company 2004), won the Eileen McTavish Sykes Award for Best First Book. She is a past member of the literary journal *CV2* and the Staccato Chapbooks publishing collective and has served as president of the Guild. Lori is poetry co-editor of *CV2* and is co-founder of the Lansdowne Prize for Poetry. By day Lori works as an editorial assistant for a National Research Council scientific journal.

415

RICK CHAFE's play *The Last Man and Woman on Earth* was first produced by Theatre Projects Manitoba. Other recent plays include *The Odyssey* (Playwrights Canada 2001), *Strike! The Musical* (with Danny Schur), and *Shakespeare's Dog*, adapted from Leon Rooke's novel, scheduled for production at Manitoba Theatre Centre and the National Arts Centre in 2007–08.

MÉIRA COOK lives and writes in Winnipeg. She is the author of the poetry collections *A Fine Grammar of Bones* (Turnstone 1993), *Toward a Catalogue of Falling* (Brick 1996) and *Slovenly Love* (Brick 2003). She is the author of a book of critical essays, *Writing Lovers: Reading Canadian Love Poetry by Women* (McGill-Queen's University Press 2005). She recently edited a selection of poetry by Don McKay, *Field Marks* (Wilfrid Laurier UP 2006), and won the 2007 CBC Literary Award for Poetry.

DENNIS COOLEY lives in Winnipeg, where he teaches at St. John's College, University of Manitoba. His latest titles are *country music* (Kalamalka 2005) and *the bentleys* (University of Alberta 2006). A collection of selected poems is forthcoming from Wilfrid Laurier University Press.

GLOE CORMIE's book *Sea Salt, Red Oven Mitts and the Blues* was a finalist for several awards, including the Eileen McTavish Sykes Award for Best First Book in 2003. Her poetry has been published internationally and in Canada and broadcast nationally on CBC Radio. She is working on a second poetry book, "Under a Different Dark Sky." Gloe has been the Manitoba representative for the League of Canadian Poets and treasurer of the Guild, which she joined in 1986.

Since participating in a workshop at the Banff Centre in 2006, **NADINE DE LISLE** has focused on creative non-fiction while working as a communications and media specialist. Nadine is the mother of a son (Brett) and is writing a book of the same name exploring the true-life adventures of mothering a boy-child.

ELIZABETH DENNY is a Métis writer from Manitoba, based in Winnipeg. She writes in several genres, with a current focus on screenwriting. Her work appears in two APTN children's series: *Wapos Baby* and *Tipi Tales*. Her children's book "The Jigging Contest" is due to be released in 2008. Her historical novel "Where Rivers Meet" is shortlisted for publication by Theytus Books in Penticton, BC.

CHARLENE DIEHL is a writer, editor, performer, and the director of THIN AIR, the Winnipeg International Writers Festival. She has published a collection of poetry, *lamentations* (Trout Lily 1997), two chapbooks and a critical book on Fred Wah. Excerpts in *Prairie Fire* from a yet unpublished memoir, "Out of Grief, Singing," won the 2005 Gold Award for Best Article–Manitoba at the Western Magazine Awards.

MAGGIE DWYER is a former Winnipegger and Guild member who was a participant in the inaugural year of the wonderful mentor program. She has also served on various committees and as president of the Guild. She moved to Vancouver Island ten years ago, where she is a rural writer and island nomad. The excerpt published here is from an as yet unpublished novel titled "Tasting the Dark."

DAVID ELIAS is the author of two collections of short fiction. His stories, novel excerpts and poetry have appeared in such magazines as *The Malahat Review* and *The New Quarterly*. His latest book, *Sunday Afternoon* (Coteau 2004), is a novel, and he has another forthcoming in 2008.

VICTOR ENNS hosted the first meeting of the Guild in 1981 at his brother's property on the Red River near Aubigny. His recent collection, *Lucky Man* (Hagios 2005), was nominated for the McNally Robinson Book of the Year Award. His work has appeared or will appear in *CV2, dANDelion, Grain* and *Prairie Fire*.

CLARISE FOSTER is the author of two collections of poetry, *The Flame Tree* (The Muses' Company 1998) and *The Way Boys Sometimes Are and other poems* (The Muses' Company 2006). She is the managing editor of *Contemporary Verse 2: The Canadian Journal of Poetry and Critical Writing*, which is published out of Winnipeg.

MARVIN FRANCIS (1955–2005), writer, poet, playwright, artist, was originally from Heart Lake First Nation in northern Alberta but he grew to call Winnipeg home. Marvin won the 2003 John Hirsch Award for Most Promising Manitoba Writer for his book *City Treaty* (Turnstone 2002). Marvin's book *Bush Camp* will be published by Turnstone Press in 2007.

Along with a dozen books of poetry and a book of essays, **PATRICK FRIESEN** has released two CDs and written several stage and radio plays. Friesen has also co-translated, with P.K. Brask, four books of Danish poetry. His most recent book is the poetry collection *Earth's Crude Gravities* (Harbour 2007).

DEBORAH FROESE was born in Winnipeg and has spent her life on the prairies wondering, what if? That question eventually led to a writing career that embraces fiction and non-fiction, and includes InkWell, a column for the Guild's magazine *WordWrap*.

DONNA GAMACHE is a writer and retired teacher from MacGregor, Manitoba. Her publications include numerous short stories for both adults and children, as well as short non-fiction and verse. She has published one novel for children, *Spruce Woods Adventure* (Compascore Manitoba) and is working on other children's novels.

ARIEL GORDON is a Winnipeg writer. Her collaboration with composer David Raphael Scott, "Tranquility and Order," had its premiere at the Winnipeg Symphony Orchestra's 2006 New Music Festival. The work was commissioned by CBC Radio to commemorate the 2004 Asian tsunami. Palimpsest Press will publish a chapbook of Ariel's poetry in 2007.

BRENDA HASIUK has spent the last decade working in communications for a variety of non-profit organizations while writing fiction in her spare time. Her award-winning short stories have been published in literary journals and anthologies, and her first novel, *Where the Rocks Say Your Name* (Thistledown 2006), was shortlisted for the McNally Robinson Book of the Year Award, the Margaret Laurence Award for Fiction and the Eileen McTavish Sykes Award for Best First Book. She lives in Winnipeg with her husband, author Duncan Thornton, and their two small children.

HEDY WIKTOROWICZ HEPPENSTALL lives in Winnipeg, where she works as a public health nurse. She has been a writer for Manitoba Artists in Healthcare, and has been published in *The Canadian Nurse, The Manitoban, The Prairie Journal* and *A Cup of Comfort For Women*.

LINDA HOLEMAN writes for both adults and young adults in a variety of genres. She has published contemporary and historical novels as well as short-story collections. Her latest novels are *The Moonlit Cage* (2005) and *The Linnet Bird* (2004), both published widely internationally. Linda has worked as an editor, a teacher of creative writing and a writer-in-residence. She speaks regularly on the craft of writing.

JAN HORNER has lived most of her life in Winnipeg. She has published two books of poetry with Turnstone Press, including *Recent Mistakes*, which won the McNally Robinson Book of the Year Award in 1989.

CATHERINE HUNTER is a poet, critic and novelist, who teaches English and creative writing at the University of Winnipeg. Her books include the poetry collection *Latent Heat* (Nuage 1998) and the crime novel *Queen of Diamonds* (Turnstone 2006). Winnipeg is her home town.

SALLY ITO is a poet and fiction writer living in Winnipeg. Her two books of poetry, both from Harbour Publishing, are *Frogs in the Rain Barrel* (1995) and *A Season of Mercy* (1999).

FAITH JOHNSTON was in the Guild's 1995 mentor program. Since then her work has been published in *Dropped Threads 2, The New Quarterly, Prairie Fire, Other Voices* and *A Room of One's Own*. Her first book, *A Great Restlessness: The Life and Politics of Dorise Nielsen* (University of Manitoba Press 2006), won the McNally Robinson Book of the

Year Award, the Alexander Kennedy Isbister Award for Non-Fiction, the Eileen McTavish Sykes Award for Best First Book and the Mary Scorer Award for Best Book by a Manitoba Publisher.

SMARO KAMBOURELI, raised as a Canadian in Winnipeg, was a founding member of the Guild. She is now Canada Research Chair in Critical Studies in Canadian Literature at the University of Guelph. The editor of the Writer as Critic series (NeWest Press), she has also edited *Pacific Rim Letters* by Roy K. Kiyooka and *Making a Difference: Canadian Multicultural Literatures*.

LIZ KATYNSKI is a Winnipeg-based freelance writer, instructor and communications expert. She leads creative writing workshops, teaches business/professional writing classes and mentors writers. For further information, visit <www.lizwords.com>.

SHIRLEY KITCHEN lives in Winnipeg. Her work has been published in Canadian literary magazines and she has written scripts for film and television. She was a member of the Guild's founding board.

SARAH KLASSEN was born and raised in Manitoba. Her most recent poetry collection is *A Curious Beatitude* (The Muses' Company 2006). Her second short-fiction collection, *A Feast of Longing*, was released by Coteau Books in 2007. She has received a National Magazine Gold Award for poetry (2000), the Gerald Lampert Award (1989) and nominations for the McNally Robinson Book of the Year Award and the Margaret Laurence Award for Fiction. She has taught high school English in Winnipeg, and English language and literature in Lithuania and Ukraine.

ED KLEIMAN has published three books of short stories, *The Immortals* (NeWest 1980), *A New-Found Ecstasy* (NeWest 1988) and *The World Beaters* (Thistledown 1998). His stories have also appeared in twelve anthologies. His essays have been published in scholarly journals in Canada, the United States, the Netherlands and Germany.

LARRY KROTZ is the author of five books, including *Midlifeman* (Capital Books 2002), *Tourists* (FSAndG 1997), *Indian Country* (McClelland & Stewart 1990) and the novel *Shutter Speed* (Turnstone 1988). He is also a journalist and documentary filmmaker, in which context he has made numerous trips to east Africa over the past fifteen years. Krotz lives in Toronto, but he spent twenty-five very happy years (1973–97) in Manitoba, where he was active in the writing community, including one year (1986) as president of the Guild.

SYLVIA LEGRIS's most recent poetry collection, *Nerve Squall* (Coach House 2005), won both the Griffin Poetry Prize and the Pat Lowther Memorial Award. Her other books, both published by Turnstone Press, are *iridium seeds* (1998) and *circuitry of veins* (1996).

419 ■

JAKE MACDONALD has been a member of the Guild since its inception. He has published eight books of fiction and non-fiction, the latest being the book of stories *With the Boys* (Douglas & McIntyre 2005).

TANIS MACDONALD is the author of *Holding Ground* (Seraphim 2000) and *Fortune* (Turnstone 2003). A long-time resident of Winnipeg, she currently lives and writes in southern Ontario.

BRIAN MACKINNON is a retired inner-city English teacher. He taught for years at R.B. Russell Vocational High School, where he edited three award-winning anthologies of creative writing. He is now an anti-poverty activist working as the director of the Knox/R.B. Russell Downtown Y Program. Brian is the author of the poetry chapbook *Fathers and Heroes* and he has had numerous poems published in anthologies and magazines. He is married to writer Margaret Shaw-MacKinnon and together they have three teenage children.

DAVE MARGOSHES is a fiction writer and poet living in Regina. His latest book, *Bix's Trumpet and Other Stories*, will be out in fall 2007 from NeWest Press. He was writer-in-residence in Winnipeg in 1995–96.

CAROL MATAS is an internationally acclaimed author of more than thirty-five novels for children and young adults. Her bestselling work, which includes three award-winning series, has been translated into a dozen languages. Awards for her books include two Sydney Taylor awards, the Geoffrey Bilson award, a Silver Birch award and The Jewish Book Award, and her books have been included on honour lists such as the American Library Association's notable list, *The New York Times* notable list, The New York Public Library list for the Teen Age, and the Voice of Youth Advocates best book list. She has been nominated twice for the Governor General's Award.

CHANDRA MAYOR has written two award-winning books, *August Witch: poems* (Cyclops 2002) and the novel *Cherry* (Conundrum 2004). She has won the John Hirsch Award for Most Promising Manitoba Writer, the Eileen McTavish Sykes Award for Best First Book and the Carol Shields Winnipeg Book Award. She is a poetry co-editor for *Prairie Fire* and was the 2006–07 writer-in-residence for the Winnipeg Public Library.

MELINDA MCCRACKEN (1940–2002) was born in Winnipeg and received her Honours BA in English from the University of Manitoba in 1961. She attended the Bynam Shaw School of Drawing and Painting in Paris (1962–63) and the Hornsey College of Art in London (1963–64), where she took silversmithing. McCracken returned to Canada in 1964 and worked as a journalist in Montreal and Toronto. She was the author of *Memories Are Made of This* (Lorimer 1975), Manitoba's contributing editor to the *NeWest Review*, and Carman's writer-in-residence in 1996.

BRUCE MCMANUS is the author of twenty plays, including "All Restaurant Fires Are Arson," *Ordinary Days, Schedules, The Chinese Man Said Goodbye* (Blizzard 1988), *Selkirk Avenue* (Nuage 1998), which was nominated for a Governor General's Award, and *Calenture* (Scirocco 2000). His adaptations for the stage include *Three Sisters* and *A Doll's House*, produced at Prairie Theatre Exchange in 1998, and *A Christmas Carol*, produced at Manitoba Theatre Centre in 2005.

ALEX MERRILL is delighted to be called a Manitoba writer. She started out in Quebec and criss-crossed Canada before landing in Winnipeg in 2001. She has written short stories, non-fiction, poems, limericks and quiz show questions. Her work has been published in *Prairie Fire, Event* and *Creekstones: Words & Images* (Creekstone 2000), an anthology of northern BC writers.

MAURICE MIERAU's first book of poems, *Ending with Music*, came out with Brick in 2002. His poetry has been published in journals across Canada and the US, most recently in the spring 2007 issues of *The Malahat Review* and *Prairie Fire*. His nonfiction book, *Memoir of a Living Disease* (Great Plains 2005), won a Margaret McWilliams Award. Maurice writes a monthly poetry review column for the *Winnipeg Free Press* and maintains a website at <www.mauricemierau.com>.

MARK MORTON is the author of a book about food, a book about sex, and a book about how things end. His latest book, about Shakespeare, will be published by Greenwood Press in 2007.

SHELDON OBERMAN (1949–2004) was one of Canada's most popular children's authors, winning awards including the McNally Robinson Book for Young People Award for *By the Hanukkah Light* (Boyds Mills 1997) and *The Wisdom Bird* (Boyds Mills 2001). *The Shaman's Nephew* (Stoddart 1999) was nominated for a Governor General's Award and *The Always Prayer Shawl* (McClelland & Stewart 1994) won the Sydney Taylor American Librarians Award and the National Jewish Book Award. In March, 2004, the Guild renamed the Emerging Writers' Mentor Program the Sheldon Oberman Emerging Writers' Mentor Program.

PATRICK O'CONNELL (1944–2005) published many poetry books, including *Hoping for Angels* (Turnstone 1990), *Falling in Place* (Turnstone 1993), and *The Joy That Cracked the Mountain* (The Muses' Company 1999). A Winnipegger, University of Manitoba graduate and winner of the John Hirsch Award for Most Promising Manitoba Writer, Patrick was a talented artist, photographer and musician, but was best known for his beautiful lyric poems.

UMA PARAMESWARAN was born and educated in India. She has been a professor of English, president of the Immigrant Women's Association of Manitoba and a member of the National Council of The Writers' Union of Canada. Her publications include the national-award-winning *What was Always Hers* (Broken Jaw 1999) and two novellas from Larkuma Press in 2006, *The Forever Banyan Tree* and *Fighter Pilots Never Die*.

ALISON PRESTON was born and raised in Winnipeg. She has been twice nominated for the John Hirsch Award for Most Promising Manitoba Writer, following the publications of *A Blue and Golden Year* (Turnstone 1997) and *The Rain Barrel Baby* (Signature 2000). Her novel *Cherry Bites* (Signature 2004) was nominated for the McNally Robinson Book of the Year Award, the Carol Shields Winnipeg Book Award and the Mary Scorer Award for Best Book by a Manitoba Publisher. She is working on a fifth novel.

TALIA PURA has had plays produced locally and in New York City, Toronto and Minneapolis. *Strawberry Monologue* was published in *New Monologues for Women by Women II* (Heinemann 2005), and "Delivery" appears in the Canadian anthology *Instant Applause II* (Blizzard 1996). An excerpt of "Cheap Goods" is being adapted for a screenplay.

VAL REED has become a messy old coot of 64, much to her surprise. She lived through breast cancer in 1990 by incredible good luck and karma, and she believes the challenge in life is always the in/constant changing. She has three brilliant and somewhat tormented sons, who have paid the price for her oddness more than she has. She agrees with Molly Ivins, regarding breast cancer, that first they mutilate you, then they poison you, then they burn you. Val has learned that that path gives you a lot of stuff out of which to write and paint. She still does both.

HARRY RINTOUL (1956–2002) was a playwright, writer, actor and director. The founding artistic director of Theatre Projects Manitoba, Harry was best known for his plays *Between Then and Now*, published in *A Map of the Senses* (Scirocco Drama 2000), *Brave Hearts*, published in *Making Out* (Coach House, 1992), *Jack of Hearts, montana* and *refugees* (Blizzard 1988). *The Convergence of Luke* was included in *Perfectly Normal* (Playwrights Canada 2006) and was produced by the Carol Shields Festival of New Works in May, 2007. In 1997, Harry served as writer-in-residence at the Saskatoon Public Library. The Harry S. Rintoul Memorial Award is given annually to the author of the best new Manitoba play to premiere at the Fringe Festival.

CAROL ROSE is a writer, educator and counsellor. She has taught courses on Women & Spirituality in Canada, the US, Israel and Denmark. Her poetry collection *Behind the Blue Gate* was published by Beach Holme in 1997. She is the co-editor (with Joan Turner) of *Spider Women: A Tapestry of Creativity and Healing* (J. Gordon Shillingford 1999) and the author of the creative colouring book *A Free Hand* (Wood Lake Books 1990). She is working on a new poetry collection, "from the dream."

KERRY RYAN lives and writes in a blue house in Winnipeg. Her poems have appeared in *Carousel, Grain, The New Quarterly, CV2, Prairie Fire* and *The Windsor Review*, as well as in the anthology *Exposed* (The Muses' Company 2002).

DARIA SALAMON's journalism has appeared in the *Globe and Mail* and the *Winnipeg Free Press*. Her first novel, "The Prairie Bridesmaid," will be published in fall 2008. Daria lives in Osborne Village with her husband and son and their cat, Dr. Puddles.

DEBORAH SCHNITZER is happy she has found her way here and appreciates the opportunity this collection makes possible. The selection "a rose" in *A/Cross Sections* has a central character called Gertrude, a complex in Deborah's writing that has led to the long poem *loving gertrudestein Loving Gertrude* (Turnstone 2004) and the novel *gertrude unmanageable* (Arbeiter Ring 2007).

BRENDA SCIBERRAS was raised in rural Manitoba, and now lives and writes in Winnipeg. Her poetry has appeared in *The Collective Consciousness, Room of One's Own* and *Contemporary Verse 2*.

MARGARET SHAW-MACKINNON is a writer, mother of three, and is married to Brian MacKinnon, retired teacher and poverty activist. For many years she has taught story writing and illustrating in the Manitoba Arts Council's Artists-in-the Schools Program. Her children's book *Tiktala*, illustrated by Laszlo Gal, received the McNally Robinson Book for Young People Award in 1997, and has recently been reprinted by Fitzhenry and Whiteside. She is currently working on a book of short stories involving Manitoba's colourful past.

LESLIE SHEFFIELD is a long-time Winnipeg resident. Her work has appeared in *Prairie Fire, PRISM international, Rhubarb, TRANSITION, A Room of One's Own, Adbusters, Reader's Digest* and on CBC Radio.

CAROL SHIELDS (1935–2003) was the author of ten novels and three collections of short stories as well as plays and poetry. *The Stone Diaries* (Random House 1993) won the Governor General's Award and the Pulitzer Prize. *Larry's Party* (Random House 1997) won the Orange Prize. Born and raised in Chicago, Carol lived most of her life in Canada. She was a Companion of the Order of Canada.

JACQUI SMYTH now lives in Waterloo. She teaches creative writing and has recently finished a poetry manuscript, "How the West Was Won," about Transcona in the 1970s.

BIRK SPROXTON (1947–2007) was an award-winning writer and editor who divided his time between the Alberta greenbelt and a house on Lake Winnipeg. In 2006 he published *Headframe:2*, a follow-up to his long poem *Headframe:*, both from Turnstone

423

Press. He edited *The Winnipeg Connection: Writing Lives at Mid-Century* (Prairie Fire 2006), a volume by many hands addressing the writing life of the 1940s and 1950s. For his 2005 memoir, *Phantom Lake: North of 54* (University of Alberta Press), he won the Margaret McWilliams Local History Award and the $25,000 Grant MacEwan Alberta Author Award.

MELISSA STEELE is the author of two-award winning short-story collections, *Donut Shop Lovers* (Turnstone 1999) and *Beautiful Girl Thumb* (Turnstone 2006), which received the Margaret Laurence Award for Fiction. Melissa won the John Hirsch Award for Most Promising Manitoba Writer in 2000. She lives in Winnipeg and teaches creative writing at the University of Manitoba.

MARGARET SWEATMAN is a playwright, lyricist and novelist who lives in Winnipeg and Toronto. She is the author of the novels *Fox* (Turnstone 1991), which won the McNally Robinson Book of the Year Award, *Sam and Angie* (Turnstone 1996) and *When Alice Lay Down with Peter* (Random House 2001), which won the Rogers Fiction Prize, the McNally Robinson Book of the Year Award, the Carol Shields Winnipeg Book Award, the Margaret Laurence Award for Fiction and the Sunburst Award.

JIM TALLOSI's poetry has appeared in *Prairie Fire, NeWest Review, The Antigonish Review, Border Crossings* and *Canadian Literature*. His two collections of poetry are *The Trapper and the Fur-faced Spirits* (Queenston House 1981) and *Talking Water, Talking Fire* (Queenston House 1985). Staccato Chapbooks published his long poem *Stone Snake* in 2001.

Writer, teacher and editor **WAYNE TEFS** has published eight novels, including *Red Rock* (Coteau 1998), which was broadcast on the CBC's Booktime, and *Moon Lake* (Turnstone 2000), which received the inaugural Margaret Laurence Award for Fiction. His short story "Red Rock and After," won a National Magazine Gold Award and appeared in the 1990 *Journey Prize Anthology*. His personal survival narrative, *Rollercoaster: A Cancer Journey* (Turnstone 2002), has taken him to speak all over the US and Canada. His non-fiction novel *Be Wolf* was released by Turnstone Press in 2007. Tefs lives in Winnipeg with his wife and son.

DUNCAN THORNTON's first book, *Kalifax* (Coteau 1999), was shortlisted for both the Governor General's and Mr. Christie's Book Awards. It was followed by two further books using the same New World mythology as background: *Captain Jenny* (Coteau 2001) and *The Star-Glass* (Coteau 2003), which won the McNally Robinson Book for Young People Award (older category). In 2004–05 he was the writer-in-residence for the Winnipeg Public Library. He lives in Winnipeg with his writer-wife Brenda Hasiuk and their two young children.

MIRIAM TOEWS's most recent novel is *A Complicated Kindness* (Knopf 2004), which won the Governor General's Award, the Canadian Booksellers Association Libris Award–Fiction Book of the Year, and the McNally Robinson Book of the Year Award, and was shortlisted for the Scotiabank Giller Prize. She lives in Winnipeg with her family.

MARGARET ULLRICH was born in Malta and raised in Queens, New York. A Pratt Institute graduate, she moved to Winnipeg in 1975. She has edited newsletters and written for various publications. CBC, PTAM and UMFM have produced her work. She is broadcasting on CKUW and adapting her play "Women of Culture."

KATHERENA VERMETTE is a writer of fiction and poetry who lives and works in Winnipeg. Her poetry has appeared in *Prairie Fire* and *Juice* magazines as well as in *Bone Memory*, an anthology of writing by the Aboriginal Writers' Collective. Her fiction can be found in *Tales from Mocassin Avenue* (Totem Pole Books 2006).

WILLIAM DEXTER WADE is the nom de plume of an aged blind Zen archer and former astronaut who lives in a humble shack in the Atacama Desert. He holds a black belt in extreme tai chi flower-arranging and is nearing completion of a multi-volume collection of Esperanto haiku.

MEEKA WALSH is the editor of the art magazine *Border Crossings*. She has contributed essays to a number of Canadian and American art catalogues. She has also published a collection of short stories, *The Garden of Earthly Intimacies* (Porcupine's Quill 1996). She lives in Winnipeg.

JOHN WEIER was born out on the broad prairie but grew up on a tiny peach farm in Niagara-on-the-Lake, Ontario. The author of books in a variety of genres—poetry, fiction, children's literature, as well as non-fiction—he's still pushing out those small farm boundaries. An avid birdwatcher, John works in Winnipeg as a writer and violin restorer.

ARMIN WIEBE was in attendance on the day the Guild was founded in 1981 and he has served on the boards of the Guild, Prairie Fire Press and the Mennonite Literary Society. He has enjoyed writer-in-residencies in Saskatoon and Dauphin and teaches in the Creative Communications program at Red River College. His Gutenthal novels, all from Turnstone Press, include *The Salvation of Yasch Siemens* (1984), *Murder in Gutenthal* (1991) and *The Second Coming of Yeeat Shpanst* (1995). His most recent novel, *Tatsea* (Turnstone), set in Canada's Subarctic in the 1760s, won the 2004 McNally Robinson Book of the Year Award and the Margaret Laurence Award for Fiction.

425 ■

DAVE WILLIAMSON is a past president of the Guild (1986–89) and a past chair of The Writers' Union of Canada (1992–93). He has published four novels, a collection of short stories and a memoir; he also co-edited (with Mark Vinz of Minnesota) the anthology *Beyond Borders* (New Rivers 1992) and co-authored (with Carol Shields) the stage play *Anniversary* (Blizzard 1998). For many years he was Dean of Business and Applied Arts at Red River College, until his retirement in 2006. Dave regularly reviews books for the *Winnipeg Free Press*, the *Globe and Mail* and *Prairie Fire*.

JESSICA WOOLFORD lives and writes in Winnipeg, home of her poetic muse.

ACKNOWLEDGEMENTS

Thanks to the contributors for submitting such a wealth of splendid material. Special thanks to the board of directors of the Manitoba Writers' Guild under then-president Jessica Woolford for initiating this anthology and allowing it to develop into a new configuration. Thanks to Robyn Maharaj and her staff at the Guild office (Jamis Paulson, Jim Chliboyko and Melissa Kent), who have been unstinting in their support and courtesy over the long gestation period. Additional thanks to Perry Grosshans, president of Prairie Fire Press, for making it possible for us to use *Prairie Fire* staff and facilities to bring *A/Cross Sections* to life. Thanks to Janine Tschuncky, who served as project general manager, and to Heidi Harms, who acted as both copy editor and production manager. As well, thanks to Karen McElrea for proofreading the galleys. We also wish to thank the many people who made the Manitoba Writers' Guild possible. Without their efforts, this book would not exist.

"Planting Trees in Ear Falls" by Jan Horner (pp. 136–137) first appeared in the conference proceedings volume *A World of Local Voices* published in Germany in 2003.

The two poems by Alison Calder (pp. 274–276) appear in her first collection, *Wolf Tree*, published by Coteau Books in 2007. They are published here with permission.

"Diary Excerpt" by Melinda McCracken (pp. 16–18) appears courtesy of Molly McCracken, copyright the Estate of Melinda McCracken.

"Travel Diary" by Carol Shields (pp. 54–58) appears courtesy of Don Shields, copyright the Estate of Carol Shields.

"Hanging on Lion's Gate Bridge, a Western" by Birk Sproxton (p. 93) appears courtesy of Lorraine Sproxton, copyright the Estate of Birk Sproxton.

"from The Distance Between Trees" by Harry Rintoul (pp. 103–106) appears courtesy of Dolores Rintoul, copyright the Estate of Harry Rintoul.

The two poems by Marvin Francis (pp. 203–204) appear courtesy of Cindy Singer, copyright the Estate of Marvin Francis.

The poems by Patrick O'Connell (pp. 316–318) appear courtesy of Heather Armstrong and Colleen Clevens, copyright the Estate of Patrick O'Connell.

"The Hero, the Villain and the Shmo" by Sheldon Oberman (pp. 370–375) appears courtesy of Lisa Dveris, copyright the Estate of Sheldon Oberman.

PHOTO CREDITS

Photographs on pages 7, 8, 9, 11 are by Andris Taskans.

Photographs of Katherine Bitney and Andris Taskans are by Mandy Malazdrewich.

WORKS CITED

Quotations from the following books appear in Sandra Birdsell's article, "A Letter to My Friends Who Are There":

bluebottle by Patrick Friesen (Turnstone 1978)

Seed Catalogue by Robert Kroetsch (Turnstone 1977)

When the Dogs Bark at Night by Valerie Reed (Turnstone Press Chapbooks 1979)

"Bones, for John Berger" by Meeka Walsh includes quotations from *And our faces, my heart, brief as photos* by John Berger (Random House, Inc., 1984).

ABOUT THE EDITORS

KATHERINE BITNEY was born in England, grew up in Saskatchewan, and has lived in Winnipeg since 1971. With her sister, Elizabeth Carriere, she founded the Winnipeg Writers Workshop (W3) in 1975. Together they edited *I Want To Meet You There, The Poetry of W3* (Hanaco Press, 1976). In 1978 the sisters joined with Andris Taskans, S.G. Buri and others to launch *Writers News Manitoba*, a 'zine that morphed into the literary quarterly *Prairie Fire* in 1983. During the years 1977 to 1981, she was part of a group of writers working to establish the Manitoba Writers' Guild, of which she became a founding member/director. Katherine is the author of three critically acclaimed books of poetry: *While You Were Out* (Turnstone Press, 1981), *Heart and Stone* (Turnstone Press, 1989) and *Singing Bone* (The Muses' Company, 1997).

ANDRIS TASKANS was born in Winnipeg and has lived here all his life. He first became interested in writing and publishing while in high school, subsequently studying creative writing at university and joining the Winnipeg Writers Workshop in 1977. In 1978 he became a founding editor of *Writers News Manitoba*. He guided the periodical through its transition from 'zine to the literary magazine *Prairie Fire* and has remained its editor to this day. Under his direction, *Prairie Fire* has come to be recognized as one of the best literary quar-

terlies in Canada. Andris is the author of a poetry chapbook, *Jukebox Junkie* (Turnstone Press, 1987). He is a founding member/director of the Manitoba Writers' Guild, a founding member of the Manitoba Magazine Publishers' Association and the founding president/volunteer artistic director of the Winnipeg International Writers Festival, now THIN AIR.